Written by

Joe DeVito & Brad Strickland

Illustrated by

Joe DeVito

King Kong of Skull Island: Exodus © 2025 DeVito ArtWorks, LLC & World Builder Publishing. All Rights Reserved. Reproduction of any part of this work by any means without the written permission of the publisher is expressly forbidden. All names, characters and events in this publication are entirely fictional. Any resemblance to actual persons, living or dead is purely coincidental. World Builder Publishing, 814 S. Westgate Ave. STE 130, Los Angeles CA 90049 USA. King Kong of Skull Island ™ and © DeVito ArtWorks, LLC.

Second Edition, Revised and Expanded

"King Kong Redux: A Kid's Tale" is a revised version of an essay first published in Kong Unbound (2005), ed. Karen Haber.

DeVito ArtWorks, LLC is an artist-driven transmedia studio dedicated to the creation and development of multi-faceted properties including Skull Island, War Eagles, and the Primordials. DeVito ArtWorks is founded and lead by renowned artist, illustrator and author, Joe DeVito. Mr. DeVito has painted and sculpted pop culture's most recognizable icons including Doc Savage, Superman and Batman and has had his work exhibited in museums and galleries throughout the world. DeVito ArtWorks is exclusively represented by World Builder Entertainment (www.worldbuilderent. com)

DeVito ArtWorks, LLC, Chalfont, PA www.kongskullisland.com, www.jdevito.com
On Facebook: Kong of Skull Island DeVito ArtWorks

ISBN: 978-1-966434-02-3

Printed by Lightning Source.

Joe DeVito and his collaborator's stunning KING KONG OF SKULL ISLAND is a heartfelt, deeply imaginative and truly canonical accomplishment that echoes all the awe and thrilling wonder only to be found in Merian C. Cooper's original 1933 production of KING KONG, and this new expanded edition promises to lead us even further into that rich, fog-shrouded and much beloved lost world I've personally dwelt in since the age of three. There is only one King Kong and this is his story!
—David Conover
Author of WAR EAGLES: THE UNMAKING OF AN EPIC

The only books ever to truly expand on the story of King Kong and reveal the secrets of Skull Island and its human inhabitants. This must have brilliantly illustrated achievement is a high adventure to fill your days and enliven your dreams.
—Miron Murcury
Curator and author of WILLIS O'BRIEN: The Oaklander Who Brought King Kong To Life, Director emeritus Oakland Film Society

Joe DeVito's *King Kong of Skull Island* is a dense and delightful prequel and sequel to Merian C. Cooper's classic story. With his co-author Brad Strickland, DeVito presents an epic history that chronicles the origins of Kong and the ancestors of the native people who built the Wall, telling how both came to inhabit that small spot of land "way west of Sumatra," and showing how the giant ape triumphed over the vicious alpha predator that killed his parents and became the king of Skull Island. In their text, DeVito and Strickland tell an exciting tale packed with thrilling action, sweeping drama, an——d enough crypto-historical, biological, and anthropological detail to make their fantastic tale feel utterly believable and utterly real. DeVito then illustrates this sprawling saga with a series of vivid paintings and striking drawings – all of which bring Kong and his mysterious world to brilliant visual life. *King Kong of Skull Island* is a remarkable achievement that Kong fans will relish and that will introduce the uninitiated to the marvels of the Eighth Wonder of the World.
—Ray Morton
Film Historian and Author of *King Kong: The History of a Movie Icon*

Legendary animator Ray Harryhausen frequently visited California from London during the 2000s. I often drove him to various VFX studios where CGI practitioners and fans eagerly awaited the opportunity to meet him. During these drives, I would play an audio recording of "King Kong" that I had made for him to pass the time. His eyes would light up as the familiar soundtrack and dialogue filled the car. As a super fan of "King Kong," Ray could quote every line from the film, including the made-up language of the native islanders, always with childlike enthusiasm. Our discussions about Kong often overshadowed conversations about his own impressive body of work. This deep appreciation is why I believe Ray would have treasured Joe DeVito's "King Kong of Skull Island." This beautifully illustrated book offers another opportunity to experience the most compelling adventure tale of all time. It stands as a worthy tribute to the legacy of storytellers who brought impossible stories to life–a legacy that continues to inspire visual effects artists like myself today. Tabe! Bala kum nono hi. Bala! Bala!
—Craig Barron
Visual Effects Supervisor Los Angeles, California

"Some years ago, Joe DeVito set out on an expedition into the dreamscape of *King Kong*. This book is a full report on their explorations, from the revelations of Carl Denham's diary to a chronicling of the native culture, geology, natural history, and primordial mysteries of Kong's Skull Island home. *KING KONG OF SKULL ISLAND* is not merely inspired by Merian C. Cooper's classic fantasy—it enriches and expands upon it."
—Mark Cotta Vaz
Author of *Living Dangerously: The Adventures of Merian C. Cooper, Creator of King Kong*

"Joe DeVito's *KING KONG OF SKULL ISLAND* peers back through the mists of time to uncover the secret history of Skull Island as no one short of King Kong creator Merian C. Cooper ever could...prepare to be struck with awe."
—Will Murray
Author of *Doc Savage: Skull Island & King Kong vs. Tarzan*

"Whether it's Wonder Woman, Doc Savage, Lobo, or Superman, Joe DeVito is an expert at bringing larger-than-life, mythic characters to life. Now he's focused all of his imagination, skills, and passion to excite a new generation with the secret history of The Eighth Wonder of the World. *KING KONG OF SKULL ISLAND* is a beautifully illustrated, riveting adventure that would have made Ann Darrow swoon and Carl Denham envious!"
—Arnie Fenner
Co-founder of Spectrum: The Best in Contemporary Fantastic Art

"Joe DeVito and I first became friends when he began painting covers for Doc Savage. I quickly realized Doc was not the only thing we had in common. King Kong is one of my favorite movies of all time. Joe's first Kong book is one of my prized possessions. His new book, *KING KONG OF SKULL ISLAND*, is even more epic in scale!"
—Jim Bama
Acclaimed Artist

Dedication

This book is dedicated to all those whose combined efforts have contributed to making this extended journey to Skull Island possible. In particular, I would like to thank: The Cooper family; Dannie Festa; Barry Klugerman; Randy Merritt; Bob Seigel; John Leonhardt; Carol Ginsburg; Joe Viego; Vito DeVito; Vincent DeVito; my wife, Mary Ellen; our daughters, Melissa and Emily; and last but first, Mother Mary and St. Jude.

My cowriter, Brad Strickland, adds his dedication to his wife Barbara, who for many years has been his continuing inspiration.

Acknowledgements

Special Thanks To:

Dannie Festa, for everything; Harry Markos and Ian Sharman, for help and coordination across the board; Rich Greene, for book design input; Will Murray, for his editorial input; Henry Lopez and Glenn Zimmer for their invaluable help, lastly with special gratitude to my dear friend, the late Michal Mims, for his decades long graphic design assistance.

DeVito ArtWorks

MCC

CONTENTS

There are certain stories that never leave us. They live in our imaginations, echoing through time, reinventing themselves for new generations while somehow staying exactly what they've always been: iconic. For me–and for so many fans around the world–*King Kong* is one of those stories.

So, when I was asked to write this introduction for a new edition of *King Kong of Skull Island Part 1: Exodus & Part 2: The Wall*–brought to life by the legendary artist Joe DeVito, it felt like both a privilege and a deeply personal moment. Not only because King Kong has had a lasting impact on film, storytelling, and culture, but because the creator behind this edition is not only one of the finest I've had the pleasure of working with–he's also a dear friend.

Joe has poured an unbelievable amount of energy into these stories. If you know him, you know that he doesn't do anything halfway. Every design, every narrative thread, every historical detail is thought through. He didn't just want to tell a story about a giant ape. He wanted to build a history that feels like history–something that connects the dots in a way that makes you believe this world might actually exist, somewhere just out of reach. I've seen firsthand how much heart, discipline, and obsession went into making this book. Joe has poured decades of knowledge and love into every detail. It's rare to witness someone who cares so deeply about honoring a legacy, while still daring to innovate. That's what makes this work so compelling–it feels both classic and entirely new.

We've been collaborating for more than 15 years now across projects big and small. So to be here now, ushering this book back into the world together, feels like the culmination of something we've both been building toward. It's also the first release under the banner of World Builder's new publishing company–a leap of faith, a new chapter, and one I couldn't be prouder to open with this particular book. We want to create books that have substance, that respect the reader, that bring new life to worlds like this. Leading with *King Kong of Skull Island Parts 1 & 2* sets the tone. It reflects the kind of work–and the kind of authors–we want to support.

There's a kind of magic in this edition. Not just because of the story but because of the art. The visuals in these pages don't just illustrate the tale; they expand it. They honor the spirit of the original while adding something bold, fresh, and unforgettable. They come from someone who has spent a lifetime honing his craft, and whose respect for the source material shines through every line and shadow.

This release is for the fans–the ones who have loved *King Kong* since childhood, who remember the first time they saw him atop the Empire State Building or roaring through Skull Island's jungle. It's also for the new fans, the ones who are just discovering the beauty and tragedy of the great ape and the world that created him. Whether you've come to this book through art, film, or folklore, what you'll find inside is something special. It's a reminder of why *King Kong* still matters, why his story continues to resonate, and how Merian C. Cooper's creation has been made into something timeless.

And now, thanks to the support of many generous hands–and the determination of a small but passionate team–we're finally able to place this book into yours. It's more than a reprint. It's a celebration. It's a thank-you to the fans who kept the flame alive, and an invitation to those just arriving at the gates of this mysterious island. If you're new to this material, I think you're in for something unique. And if you're a longtime fan who's been waiting for these books to come back–welcome back. Either way, I hope you'll take your time with what's inside. There's a lot here–not just in terms of story, but in terms of vision.

On a personal level, this book represents something else: a beginning.

Launching this publishing company has been a dream long in the making. It's something I've wanted to do not just to put beautiful books into the world, but to support the kinds of stories and creators that matter. Ones that take risks. Ones that last. Ones like this.

So yes–this book is the start of something. Not just for the company, not just for the artist or the fans, but for me. It's a chance to honor where I've come from while stepping boldly into what's next.

If you're holding this book in your hands, you're now a part of that journey too.

I hope you lose yourself in these pages. I hope you marvel at the artwork, at the scale, at the heartbreak and heroism that still defines *King Kong*. I hope you see the love that went into bringing it back to life. And most of all, I hope you feel the same sense of awe I do–standing in the shadow of a story that refuses to be forgotten.

Welcome back to Skull Island.

And welcome to the beginning of something new.

Dannie Festa
CEO
World Builder Entertainment
2025

A KID'S TALE REDUX

It was the spring of 1963 in New York City, and the Alligator was waiting for him. That's what the kid called his godfather's Citroen station wagon. It idled hungrily behind a fully-loaded moving truck, and he knew why: it was waiting to take his family away from their home on West 43rd Street.

The mover's meter was ticking, but no one was going anywhere until the reluctant six-year old could be packed into the car with his five siblings. That wasn't going to be easy–he had wrapped himself around the railing of the front stoop like an octopus.

His older brother, Vito, knew the one thing that would work. But it was a drastic measure, so he kept silent and watched as every possible coercive action was taken. From the promise of ice cream to the threat of physical pain, none made a dent. The kid was tough and ferociously held his ground.

Finally, the older brother couldn't stand the thought of hearing screaming in his ear the whole trip. "Hold it!" he yelled. "Listen, you nut, if you let go of the railing and get in the car right now, I'll cut all the King Kong pictures out of my monster magazines and you can have them." A sudden silence fell, followed by an incredulous, "Really?"

"Yeah, but it will cost you twenty-five cents." After all, the magazines were part of his collection and he did not want the deal to be a total loss.

The kid didn't hesitate. "Okay."

The standoff came to an abrupt end, and the family finally moved to the 'country': the town of Berkeley Heights, New Jersey.

I wish I still had those pictures. To this day, over fifty years later, my fascination with King Kong transports me to another world. Perhaps our early fantasies endure because they carry us back to a time when all our memories are good ones. This is true for me. My childhood enchantments have lasted also because they can be so *real*.

King Kong is still real to me. More than any other film I have ever seen, the original 1933 *King Kong* has engendered a perpetual sense of wonder. How I envy those who sat in the audience for its opening. It must have been mind-bending. I can only imagine what it must have been like to see such a spectacle!

The impact of the original *King Kong* is hard to quantify. At a time when audiences were just getting used to people talking on film–the first "talkie", *The Jazz Singer,* was only six years old–the technical wizardry and extraordinarily original story of King Kong gave them an experience they had never even imagined. This could only have been achieved by the allying of some amazing intangibles; things that go beyond the creative desire in and of itself and have their origin in historical serendipity. To begin, there was the partnership of a charismatic dynamo like Merian C. Cooper with another artistic pioneer of extraordinary abilities, Willis O'Brien, not to mention the work of a host of other inimitable personalities. Kong was also the first giant movie monster (aside from dinosaurs); the film introduced some, and perfected many other, novel animation and film techniques. Kong's climactic scene atop the Empire State Building (which had just been built) was a juxtaposition of elements reserved for only the rarest confluence of cultural and archetypal imagery. Max Steiner's monumental film score was the first to employ a full range of leitmotifs to characterize the personalities and actions in the film. The list goes on. Many stars had to align to create a film of such lasting originality and imagination. The lightning struck, the magic happened. King Kong has left an appropriately large footprint on the world's collective imagination.

Over ninety years after its initial release, *King Kong* still has the power to rattle my imagination. CGI be what it may, and other technical advancements in movie effects notwithstanding, the original Kong remains alive in my mind as no other movie monster has ever done. Stop-motion animation simply has a charm that computer generated characters are hard-pressed to equal. In fact, current effects are often so hyper-real that they can actually make it harder to suspend disbelief. It's odd. The more real something looks, the more believable it should be. But that is not always so when you *know* it is not real. The slightly jerky motion of stop-motion can be more dream-like and can engage the imagination more effectively. It enables the viewer to subtly project his own sense of reality and imagination onto what he is seeing.

Tellingly, the great stop-motion movie monsters of Willis O'Brien, and of Ray Harryhausen, were essentially the product of individuals. Because of this there is a clearly definable personality instilled by a single animator's direct contact with the creature that a team of people working together through computer screens could find tough to match. Because of the time-consuming nature of stop-motion animation such films, which were often associated with the fantastic, were relatively rare and therefore something of an event. To paraphrase Harryhausen, the ubiquitous nature of CGI has made the extraordinary seem commonplace.

This is opinion, of course, and can be debated since there are no absolutes. A good many extraordinary new effects movies exemplify that point. The techniques and approaches to visual storytelling are improving all the time and have really pushed the envelope of spectacle.

All that said, for a guy like me who first had his brain blasted by fantastic cinema long before the days of CGI, perhaps the most powerful intoxicant is sheer nostalgia: nothing can top an initial experience and the memories associated with it. To be sure, an infinite number of reasons contribute to an individual intimately bonding with a film, or any work of art.

The stage was set for my enthrallment with King Kong in a very predictable way. Before I ever saw the film, I had fallen in love with dinosaurs, and to me, King Kong was a natural extension of them. As a boy, I was lucky to live within walking distance to the American Museum of Natural History in New York City. Anyone who has ever been there can understand what that adventure must have been like for a kid with an overactive imagination. Walking through the Hall of Dinosaurs was an experience to inspire the wildest daydreams. The paleo-art of the museum and the world had been shaped by the pioneering painting and sculpting of Charles R. Knight. His groundbreaking murals inspired the world, echoing into the turn of the twentieth century and beyond. For my generation, Knight's dinosaurs defined the way the creatures looked.

By the time my small footprints began stalking the paved jungle of the city decades later, a whole new slew of dinosaur images had arisen, spearheaded by Rudolf Zallinger's Mesozoic mural that appeared both on the cover and in LIFE magazine in the early 1950s. The images were all part of a coffee table book, *The World We Live In*, which was published shortly after. That was followed by his fabulous Golden book, *Dinosaurs* in 1960. Other dinosaur-related things that stand out in my mind from that time are *The How and Why Wonder Book of Dinosaurs* and the Marx plastic dinosaur set, all of which I loved dearly (perhaps greatest of all, although I did not see them until a few years later, were the multiple large format volumes of the great Czech artist, Zdenek Burian).

All in all, the fifties and sixties were dinosaur heaven for any kid so inclined. By the age of four, in 1961, I had become a certified dinosaur fanatic. I drew constantly and copied the pictures from the pages of my favorite books. It was a time of pure fascination. Every detail was important. I remember being serenely content in my world of dinosaurs. I actually knew how to spell *Tyrannosaurus rex* before I could spell my own name!

At the same time, I developed a love for anything having to do with nature in general, in particular such spectacular creatures as whales, giant squid, wooly mammoths, along with other kid classics like saber-toothed tigers, great white sharks, and similar giants. I guess I was predisposed towards such things. Was there ever a boy (and a good percentage of girls) who hasn't been at one time or another?

Then one day my older brother sat me down to watch *King Kong* and my self-created prehistoric world was abruptly turned inside out. I do not have a specific memory of the event, only an over-riding feeling of sheer wonder. I remember struggling to grasp what I was seeing–it astounded me. I don't remember specific details other than the impression left by what I saw on our family's small b/w TV. I didn't have enough life context yet to absorb and make sense of what was unfolding before my eyes.

No longer were dinosaurs imprisoned on the page of a book, a drawing, or lurking elusively in my imagination. They now moved and breathed–they were *alive*. Everything was so perfectly realized. The Gustav Dore-ish atmospherics were enhanced by the vagueness of the small B/W screen, contributing to the dreamscape of it all–except it *wasn't* a dream. I immediately accepted Kong's existence as a fact, even though I'm sure I was told it was "only a movie."

Nothing about Kong contradicted my common sense–I knew animals could grow that big, because I'd seen dinosaur bones up close! And he was so convincingly portrayed, his personality was so remarkable, that in spite of what I must have been told, I *wanted* to believe. King Kong was so authentic to me that from then on when I visited the Museum of Natural History, I roamed the halls hoping to see a magnificently mounted exhibit of Kong's bones. Where else would he be?

What added to the magic was that it was all so fleeting. Today re-watching a movie is easy, but back then, it was technically impossible to freeze the picture, let alone replay the movie at will. When it ended, I had to wait . . . and wait . . . until it aired again. This was excruciating, but waiting only heightened the excitement. Nothing is so desirable as that which you want desperately and cannot have. I can't overstate this inability to view *King Kong* at will as a reason for the charm and fascination the film has fostered in the imaginations of generations of people, particularly kids.

From that time on, whenever I heard the beeping RKO radio tower at the beginning of a film it was the source of genuine panic. I would fly towards the TV set–only to be shattered to realize that the beeping sound was most times the prelude to a different movie. But so great was my desire to see the Kong that despite my experience to the contrary, it never quite sank in that the beeping sound could belong to any other film. In time I accepted Kong as a fiction, but the reality of the fantasy remained.

So far as I can remember, there were only two real antidotes to my Kong addiction. The first was *The Million Dollar Movie*. Anyone who lived on the East Coast in the 1960s would remember that *The Million Dollar Movie* showed the same film twice a day for seven straight days at 9:00 AM and 3:00 PM (I didn't know it at the time, but there was a third showing at 9PM that I wasn't told about because of how late it ended). Outside of owning a print of the film, it was the closest one could ever come to getting the maximum of *King Kong*. A distant memory recalls seeing it fourteen times in one week–twice! If I actually pulled it off, unless is was in the summer that was not an easy feat for a kid who is supposed to be in school.

The second way was seeing pictures of Kong in Forry Ackerman's *Famous Monsters of Filmland* magazine. This offered the possibility of viewing various stills at will. But even that presented a problem in the beginning since I was very young and my parents would not let me buy the magazine, which is where my older brother, Vito, came in. Being artistically inclined himself, he could empathize now and again and let me page through his collection. That is, when he wasn't trying to kill me for rifling through his desk drawers, using his art supplies, and looking for his stash of monster magazines when he wasn't at home. I still have a box of his charcoal pencils from that time with an encouraging note to me on the back:

Around 1963, the movie *King Kong vs. Godzilla* came out. While I loved it as a kid, even then I knew it was not in the same universe as the original Kong and the two movies (along with all subsequent men in monkey suit Kong or gorilla movies, though they could have a charm of their own) always remained separate in my mind. By the mid-sixties Aurora released their classic monster model kits, King Kong included, with that classic box art by Jim Bama. The magazine images and model kit were followed by a King Kong trading card set that had the most comprehensive group of Kong images from the original movie that I had ever seen to that date–albeit with comical captions superimposed over them (one of the all-time great memories of being a kid is the intoxicating aroma of bubble gum that suffused every pack of trading cards). These things all combined to stoke my fascination with King Kong for years.

Of course, life moved on in every other area and inevitably, Kong, along with so much else associated with childhood, faded amidst the din of growing up. Still, when word got out that King Kong was being remade in the mid-seventies, I was thrilled–along with countless others, I'm sure. The hype was unremitting; from an actual 40-foot robot being constructed for the film to a mass call for extras that were needed for the final death scene at the foot of the World Trade Towers (for which I was present with a group of my friends). The actual movie was a disappointment to many. The giant robot had minimal screen time, and was terribly stiff and unnatural in the one scene in which it appeared. For most of the film, King Kong was portrayed using the time-honored man in the costume approach. For connoisseurs of the original stop-motion animated film like myself, I think the sight of Kong's broken body embedded in the fractured sidewalk at the end of the often tongue in cheek remake was a perfect metaphor for any hope we may have had for the movie itself.

Thankfully, all was not lost. In 1975, I remember seeing for the first time a book called *The Making of King Kong*, by Orville Goldner and George Turner. Another great compilation released a year later was *The Girl In The Hairy Paw*, edited by Ronald Gotteman. There was also a great tome on the work of Ray Harryhausen called *From the Land Beyond Beyond* by Jeff Rovin (1977), which prominently mentioned *King Kong*, followed by a reissue of Ray Harryhausen's *Film Fantasy Scrapbook* (1972, 1981). Following a few years later was a marvelous homage to the work of Willis O'Brien in *Cinefex* magazine. These were the kinds of books and magazines I had been waiting years to see.

They could not have come at a better time for me since their release generally coincided with my entering art school. I can't remember how early they started, but along the way I would occasionally have dreams of King Kong in scenes that I never saw before. Sometimes they were terrifying, other times they were incredibly evocative as though I was a spectator watching primordial history unfold from the arc of time. Infused with the same sense of Mesozoic wonder inspired by the paleo-art I had grown up with, these dreams melded the fantasy of Kong with saurian reality.

Regardless, they were always fascinating and fun. I loved them and would go to sleep the next night hoping to dream more of the same, vainly searching for a way to make them repeat at will. Unfortunately, that rarely happened. On the other hand, ideas began to form, but over ten more years would pass before I had a clue of what to do with them.

From as far back as I could remember being able to read books on my own, I had developed a fascination for just about everything. Virtually every spare minute growing up that I didn't spend hanging out with my buddies, girlfriends and working, I was either drawing or reading about a never-ending variety of subjects. I did not quite realize at that time, but those Kong dreams formed the shape of things to come...

I entered Parsons School of Design in 1979, where I was first seriously introduced to many forms of art and illustration, anatomical studies, oil painting and tangentially, sculpting (which I later pursued in earnest on my own). After three years of very intense academic work, followed by ten years of non-stop professional work, I showed my paintings for the first time in 1991 at a prominent East Coast science fiction convention called Lunacon, in Stamford, Connecticut. At Lunacon, I first met Barry Klugerman and James Warhola. James is the nephew of Andy Warhol and a spectacular illustrator in his own right. Barry is both an artist and acknowledged historian in the field of Illustration. After knowing Barry for over a quarter century, he remains the most knowledgeable person on the genre (and art critique in general), that I have ever met.

As fate would have it, Barry and James had just started a company called Elfin Light Press. Within weeks, if not days, Barry and I met again in New York City, where he broached the possibility of doing a project together that he thought I would be perfect for: an illustrated coffee table book on King Kong. Little did he know! It was a dream undertaking, but with one common caveat: he had no financing lined up. It did not matter, I quickly realized I did not want to do the project because it had already been done: Nothing could ever surpass the original, 1933 *King Kong* in my mind. I decided that if I was going to work with King Kong, I was going to do something different, which triggered an avalanche of what had formerly seemed to be unrelated plans and interests. King Kong was to be the nexus on which many life-long personal creative roads converged.

Shortly after unrelated circumstances serendipitously began to fall into place and I saw the opportunity to write and visualize my own tale. I would not retell the original King Kong story at all. Instead I would finally bring to life in words and images what I had been subconsciously developing for decades: I would take my lifetime of musings and create the first true detailed prequel/sequel to King Kong.

The adventure was ready to begin!

Joe DeVito
2025

For the rest of the story, read the Introduction to *King Kong of Skull Island Part 2: The Great Wall!*

These observations and notes have largely been culled from the diaries and journals I began in 1957, during and after my first visit to Skull Island. While the more detailed and technical portions of those writings are destined to become the foundation of scientific papers suited to a specialized audience, I have decided to present my diary passages as I wrote them, in everyday language, in order to introduce the general public to the lost world of Skull Island.

My diary is not the only source: much of the information was given to me by Penjaga, the Pendonjira (Storyteller). She is an ancient sage of the Tagatu tribe who lived on that remote island for centuries untold, isolated from the rest of humanity, and by Kosa-Tsu (informally called Kara), her apprentice; and most important to me personally through another, more intimate source. More about that later.

My father, the filmmaker Carl Denham, became notorious in the early 1930s when he brought a primeval creature to New York–a living denizen from a remote and uncharted island. That is the animal he and the press called King Kong, the beast-god of Skull Island. The story of Kong's escape, rampage through Manhattan, and tragic death in a fall from the Empire State Building has become the stuff of legend.

At different points in my youth, I became convinced that my father was a great man, a misunderstood genius, and that Kong was an evolutionary relic, an impossible survivor of a forgotten era; I then came to believe that Father was a nothing more than a showman performing some gigantic hoax, who left a wake of casualties and broken lives, including those of his own family. At the last, I was left to ponder the mysteries and to wonder–was there an island that somehow existed outside of all known time? If so, what was King Kong and what happened to his body? Where had Carl Denham gone? I burned with the desire to find the answers to these mysteries and many more.

I never anticipated that my quest would inevitably become entangled in an ancient life-and-death struggle for the soul of the strangest, most challenging place on Earth: *Skull Island*.

– Vincent Denham

SKULL ISLAND JOURNALS

In January of 1957, I was moving to a new apartment. In packing, I took down from the wall an enlarged framed photo of my father, mother, and me, taken in 1931 when I was just two years old. It means a lot to me because it's the last photograph of us all together, and is possibly the last one in which both my parents are smiling. I dropped the picture, the frame broke, and between the photo and backing, I found two things: the original map to Skull Island and a letter from my father saying that he was returning to the island and might be away for some time.

He never returned at all.

I can only guess that in the uproar that followed Kong's downfall, my mother hid the map and letter there to keep the authorities from finding them. Or is it possible that my father left them there for Fate to decide when we would–if ever–learn his secret? At any rate, my mother passed not long afterward, and if she knew about the map, the letter, or what had become of my vanished father, she never told me. When she died, my father's old sailing partner Jack Driscoll and his wife Ann–the former Ann Darrow whom he had saved from the very grasp of Kong–took me in, raised me, and managed at last to put me through college. I was a good student, and fellowships made it possible for me to continue my education and eventually to earn a doctorate.

At the time when I discovered the map and letter–I was only five years out of University and three into my new profession as a paleontologist with the American Museum of Natural History in New

York City–I knew about as much regarding the island as the average person: It was a rumored Lost World, and my father had visited it with a film crew and had brought back a gigantic animal, King Kong. It was a gorilla, most accounts said, though the few surviving blurry photographs of it did not much resemble any gorilla I, or any other scientist I know, had ever seen.

Whatever he was, the enormous beast escaped, caused millions of dollars of damage, killed at least eleven people, and injured scores of others. In a spectacular showdown between modern civilization and a sheer force of nature, Army Air Corps planes riddled King Kong with machine gun fire after he climbed to the apex of the Empire State Building.

As I write, I cannot help but both pity and admire this magnificent creature. I would wager that few humans would display as much courage as he in defending Ann Darrow to the death. What, I wonder, did he perceive the strange, loudly buzzing mechanical contrivances that reeked of petrol fumes to be? They were unlike any pterodactyl he had ever encountered; none of those had ever stung him, weakening him to the point of death. They stayed so tantalizingly out of reach!

Once a king and a god, all-powerful in the world he knew, even Kong could not withstand repeated machine-gun fire from airplanes. Mortally wounded, he fought defiantly to the very end. I can only imagine his uncomprehending thoughts as he fell, plummeting through the void, his huge bulk crashing like a meteor into the pavement below, the confusion as his last seconds of life ebbed away.

King Kong was dead. His body vanished from the streets, removed by men either hired by my father or by those politicians and others in positions of power and wealth who made his fiasco planned display of Kong possible. Or so the rumors went. If they were true, then no doubt threatened by those same people my father likewise vanished. Leaving behind a mountain of debts, an ill and bewildered wife, and a small son–me. Within two years I was adopted by Jack and Ann Driscoll.

My college education was interrupted when I spent three years in the U.S. Army during World War II, mustering out in the summer of 1945 and returning to college the following September. I graduated in 1947, entered graduate school, and received my Ph.D. in 1952. Within a year, I had found a position with the Museum.

Jack Driscoll had managed to rejoin the U.S. Navy, despite technically being too old; his sea-going experience proved invaluable and he served heroically on the cargo ships during the exceedingly dangerous but all-important Atlantic convoys through the wolfpacks of Nazi U-boats. He had done well for himself after World War II, building up a fleet of trading freighters, beginning first with surplus Liberty Ships, some of the very ones he had skippered.

I consulted with him, and he agreed to take me to Skull Island. He frankly dreaded the trip himself, but the letter obscurely hinted that my father might still be alive and on the island, and Jack agreed with me: we had to find out. Truth be told, I believe Jack had issues of his own to resolve from his first journey to Skull Island and wanted to face down the nightmares he experienced as a result his personal encounters with King Kong, and perhaps he even harbored some guilt as well over Kong's demise.

I will not write of the voyage out, except to say that we located the island. It was quite different from the one so crudely and inaccurately outlined on the map. It proved bigger than I had imagined from the rough outline my father first obtained from "that skipper of the Norwegian barque," as Jack snarled out like curse words all the way into the only "harbor," threading the treacherous reefs and sandbars. I fell overboard and was attacked in the water by a gigantic sea-monster from the dawn of time (a mososaur descendant would be my best guess in hindsight)–my first encounter with a living relic from the Mesozoic.

I lost consciousness and recovered hours, perhaps days later, in a great, silent, dim room illuminated by oil lamps emitting an earthy, pungent scent that was completely unknown to me. I had a serious wound and a fever, and my attendants were a strange old woman who spoke good English–the "Pendonjira" or Storyteller–and her young, beautiful (but ominous) apprentice, Kara.

While I healed over the next weeks, the Storyteller told me of my father's actions. He had caused widespread destruction in Manhattan, true. However, the damage he had done to the people of Skull Island was much graver. The very last vestiges of their former Tagatu civilization had long ago atrophied as a result of living in the shadow of the giant Wall in a state of fearful thralldom. They had fallen into savage, primitive ways–even sacrificing themselves like animals to an animal. For they had made King Kong into their veritable god, believing Kong to be their greatest protection against the gigantic beasts of the island jungle.

As I slowly recuperated, the Storyteller's tale strained my credulity to the point where, physically and emotionally fatigued as I was, I actually doubted my own sanity. But the Storyteller constantly reassured me, showing me relics, bones and hides, of animals, and even allowed me to hold a living Archaeopteryx, or a descendant of that creature. It was as much dinosaur as bird. As a paleontologist, I found myself both excited and bewildered. The creatures from whom these bones and skins had come certainly were dinosaurs or their contemporaries–yet the bones and hides were not from a distant geologic past. Some were clearly from recent times. And yet–

Yet I saw radical differences. I could easily identify dinosaur bones, but there were details that I knew deviated from the norm; proportions, altered areas for muscle origins and blood vessel insertions and, most intriguing of all, some whose skulls contained brain pans of an unheard size for a dinosaur. I slowly came to realize that these were not merely new species of animals from the era of the dinosaurs, but whole new orders of creatures. These were what dinosaurs and their kin had become after 65,000,000 years of continued evolution.

I say I learned. However, my progress was not rapid or continuous. In addition to my wound and loss of blood, some other illness attacked me, one that I did not understand at the time. I lingered weak and feverish for weeks until finally I recovered enough to explore the island and discover the strange truth.

It took some time for Jack Driscoll to find me–he was under the impression that I had been taken prisoner. When he learned to the contrary that the Storyteller had saved my life and was nursing me back to health, he agreed to remain on the island with me as I regained my full health. Even so, he never quite took his suspicious eye off anything or anyone, including the Storyteller, who I noticed was wont to smile to herself after passing by him.

I wanted to get outside the confines of my–well, call it a primitive sort of hospital (though the medicines the Storyteller compounded compared superbly to the best of modern Western health care).

The things she showed me and told me excited my imagination, they were not enough. As a scientist, I wanted to explore the domain that my father had visited twenty-five years earlier, the one that offered an irresistible lure for a paleontologist. Unfortunately, due to my illness I had to wait . . . and wait. Yet I burned now with a purpose that I knew I must fulfill.

I had to learn about, I had to discover, the mysteries of Skull Island.

Over the weary days of my recovery, the Storyteller unfolded a history of her people. One particular account, as far as I can judge, belongs to the 19th Century, probably between 1870 and 1890. But beyond that, she hinted at stories from the very depths of memory, tales going far back into prehistory. The notes that follow are what she told me during my recuperation. Later on, as I came to understand much better, every one of her stories had a purpose. She spoke nothing in vain. Her vision was nuanced and vast, always weaving apparently unrelated skeins into a cloth of common good. She was ever mindful of her calling. It was incumbent upon me to be intelligent and wise enough to follow the trail of her tales and discern the various degrees of illumination that lay hidden in her words….

The people of the island called themselves the Tagatu, a united but not a completely harmonious tribe. Even that name had roots going back beyond the memory of conventional history: "Long ago, lost in the mists of time, two cultures came together: the warlike Atu clan, fighters and inventors of things that could be built with hands, and the Tagu, a reflective, thoughtful people whose expertise was with living things and who wished peace, not war."

After many struggles, eventually the Atu and Tagu made a truce, united against outside enemies, and created a unique civilization far pre-dating those of the Fertile Crescent, Egypt, or China. They were not islanders then. For many thousands of years, somewhere on the southern mainland of Asia, the Tagatu settled a lush, broad valley between mountain ranges. They prospered there, but never lost their caste identifications. Within the one civilization, the Atu still perceived themselves as warriors, and the Tagu as philosophers (or "penjilo"), with both producing brilliant scientists (the common term was "miawan," which depending upon context could mean "scientist or scientists," "science," or even "discovery").

Eventually, the Storyteller said, a terrific geologic upheaval threatened to exterminate them all: "The mountains belched lava and hot gases. The air and water became poisonous. The Tagatu desperately fled their homeland, intending to populate some distant islands their explorers had discovered. In the end, though, the survivors all came to this island."

With them they brought the Kongs, giant anthropoid apes (not merely enormous gorillas, but a distantly related species) with intelligence inferior to that of human beings, but above that of modern apes. Some of the Tagu people, those of the Zantu clan–I almost wrote, "tamed," but that would be highly misleading. Had *partnered*, let us say, with the Kongs. Together in the countless years before the volcanic eruptions they often served as guardians of the Tagatu frontiers. These Kongs, the Storyteller explained, were some eighteen or twenty feet tall when standing erect, very much shorter than King Kong, but he had been born perhaps ten thousand years after the first settlement of the island by humans–I have no way of really knowing, for the islanders did not keep count of the years as we do. Calamitous events and their fallout made that impossible. For that matter, I do not know whether the Storyteller truly cares about that kind of exactness, since her preoccupation is always what moral or spiritual lesson may be gleaned. What matters here is that like the dinosaurs, the Kongs had been changed by Skull Island itself.

When under pressure of the geologic upheavals the Tagatu evacuated their old homeland and sailed to the islands, they brought an unknown number of Kongs with them. On Skull Island, the Kongs became again guardians, fighting the big predators that had survived there since the end of the Age of Dinosaurs they assisted even in building the great Wall that divided the dangerous jungle from the settlement the Tagatu raised on the relatively safe peninsula where their remote descendants still live today. Those details I will relay at a more opportune occasion.

By the time of the events that the Storyteller most urgently wanted to relate, though, the few remaining Kongs had gone completely feral. The caste of their human companions, the Zantu, had ostensibly died out. The Kongs that remained in the vastness of the island jungle were few in number and rarely, almost never, glimpsed. But even though they had reverted to the wild, some sense of connection to humans must have remained. They continued to struggle against the huge predators that could have exterminated the Tagu, who huddled in safety on their side of the Wall.

The Storyteller spoke of a time when a Tagu king, a sickly man called On-Tagu, ruled the island. He faced a dire challenge to his authority in a kind of half-crazed shaman: "Bar-Atu was a Shatain, the evil leader of a cult," the Storyteller said. "An ambitious man, with a lust for power. He, his forebears, and his followers, created cruel, dehumanizing laws. They worshiped a creature of the jungle called Gaw."

Gaw was a saurian horror. Huge, intelligent, and deadly. A bipedal carnivore, more enormous than a tyrannosaur, Gaw possessed much larger arms ending in powerful, dexterous three-fingered hands. Most dangerous of all was its cold, calculating intelligence, born of a sentience that sparked to life over 65 million years of evolution. Gaw was a nightmare creature capable of forethought, calculation, and planning—formidable enough both mentally and physically to take on and defeat a full-grown Kong.

The Tagatu called the creatures to which Gaw was related "Deathrunners." Of them all, only one became a true giant, acquiring the name of Gaw. The rest were human-sized or somewhat larger, occasionally reaching nine feet in height. They were vicious predators that seemed half bird and half saurian. The Storyteller believes that Gaw and its smaller minions shared a spoken language of sorts, ranging from guttural sounds and bird-like twitters, and that they had other means of communication.

"There was always a Gaw," the Storyteller said. According to her, "One female Deathrunner would grow to be Gaw whenever the species needed it, but never more than one at a time. Except for one recorded instance, Gaw was always a female, though we did not know that at first. Conversely, Bar-Atu and his cult, believed there was only one Gaw, an immortal creature, the god of the island. In the time I speak of, the Tagatu were split, with some supporting the sick king, others Bar-Atu, who preached that if we gave Gaw human sacrifice, the god would be appeased and our people would be allowed to live behind the protection of the Wall.

"This was the drivel expounded by Bar-Atu, who positioned himself as Gaw's sole acolyte. He held power by precisely predicting when Gaw would appear, and once even walked in the open right in front of the monster without being killed (a provisional explanation of this ability will be addressed later). In time, when his authority was beyond question, he demanded an enormous, hammered metal disc to be suspended atop the Wall and used as a gong to "announce" Gaw's arrival. It did not take long for the monster to make the gruesome connection of the grotesque dinner bell. The fear of a family member being the victim of such a terrible sacrifice utterly devastated the Tagu population, with the avoidance of such a fate leading to even more subservience on their part."

When she deemed me ready, though I was still unable to sit upright for any length of time, the Storyteller read to me the following records that helped explain how such a bizarre cult gained power. What I did not, could not, know at the time was the underlying reason for her allowing me to, in effect, become part of her story. I was an alien to both her and her apprentice, Kara. As I became all too aware, I was also a potential conduit to the extinction of their race.

All of this the Pendonjira weighed in the balance as she opened a weathered book that contained an unusually nuanced tale – not at all like what I would have anticipated hearing from such a cryptic, ancient island elder. She began by way of her own, personal introduction. This was spoken in a slow but fluid English that contained a completely unplaceable accent.

"The following is the account of two young islanders," I remember her beginning, "a young man named Kublai and the daughter of On-Tagu, the King of the island, who was called Ishara. They were the first to rebel against the darkness of soul imposed by the evil Bar-Atu's cult and to fight back. They refused to be imprisoned by his fears. They determined to break free from both the spiritual and physical bondage of the Wall and strike out into the wilds. To go in search of the mythic Old City, a place their legends said once existed at the heart of Skull Island. A place where the long-forgotten knowledge of their ancestors could still be found, to conquer the monsters that lurked there—if they had the courage to persevere and find it. This they sought to bring back to their dying people, to dispel the darkness and restore their former greatness."

It was here that I received my first glimpse of what was to come when Kara angrily interjected, "Why would you reveal these secrets to this intruder from another world, who we know can only bring more death and destruction to our people?" With this she moved menacingly towards me, her hand reaching for the hilt of a lethal blade on her hip.

"RUKO!" the Storyteller commanded in their tongue, the authority in her voice stopped Kara dead in her tracks. Then, switching back to her strange, lilting English, "You, too, will listen to my story—it is meant for *both* of you!"

I can still feel the hackles rise on the back of my neck as I lay on my cot with barely the strength to defend myself. The last thing I could afford was to appear threatening to Kara, who often saw to my needs, my medicines, my food—who could poison me, or worse, at any time. The Storyteller leaned forward, her face eerily lit by a flickering green-tinged torch. It emitted a botanical scent I had never experienced before and will never forget.

"This is also the story," she continued, "of a young, orphaned giant and his fight for survival. He became the king and god of his world. His life and death will prove to be the center around which the lives of many, past and present, converge. Listen to this story and learn, in the hope that we still have time to alter the destiny that awaits each of us."

With that, the Pendonjira turned the page and began her tale…

Kublai

On a night of storm, when rain slashed the village and savage winds tore at trees and maddened the ocean, Ishara and Kublai sheltered in a hut. Kublai said bitterly, "Bar-Atu spoke of this in his prophecy."

"We always have storms in the rainy season," Ishara said. Both the young people stood straight, slim, and tall. Not quite of an age for betrothal, the two had the usual freedom of islanders to be friends, and they had been almost from birth. Now they wondered if they would have a future.

Kublai rose and paced. "Bar-Atu will make the people believe this storm's an omen! He'll lure more followers to join him."

Ishara closed her hand over a pendant she wore on a thong around her neck: a graceful little figurine, though worn smooth by centuries. It had been given to her by the Storyteller of the island. It came from a time long before the Shatains had risen among the Atu caste.

"Your father is very ill," Kublai said softly. "When he dies, Bar-Atu will make himself ruler. He will have to kill you—and though I am of his own heritage, me as well. You're the chieftain's daughter, and everyone thinks I will be your husband. Bar-Atu won't let us live."

They stared out the open doorway of the hut at the murky night. Lightning split the sky, exploded a wind-whipped palm into fiery splinters and billowing steam, and the thunder slammed into the hut. Even with the rain the tree burned, and in its fitful red glare Ishara could glimpse the great Wall.

Kublai reached for his spear and shield and stood in the doorway. "The Wall was built to protect us. But we've become its slaves."

Kublai and Ishara were almost the only Tagatu who spoke of the ancient days and the builders who had created the enormous Wall—they and the Storyteller. The other islanders had forgotten. To them the Wall was something always there, like the earth under their feet, the clouds in the sky, something taken for granted. Or it had been until Bar-Atu had made a god of Gaw.

Then it became the separating line between the ruler of the island and its subjects, cowering in awe and fear. Ishara said, "It's wrong. Bar-Atu will tell the people that the storm was sent from Gaw! He will demand the sacrifice of a woman to Gaw to satisfy its blood-thirst. The Storyteller speaks of ancient times when our ancestors understood and controlled the animals beyond the Wall, without fear or worship!"

A violent explosion, and the world turned white. Ishara fell back, and Kublai dropped his spear and shield. The roar of thunder made her ears feel as though she had dived too deep into the ocean, and left them ringing. Kublai grabbed his spear back up, pointed with it, and shouted: "The Wall!"

Ishara got to her feet and stumbled out in the rain. Beyond the farthest huts, the Wall smoldered red—no, not the Wall itself, but one of its two gigantic wooden gates.

Kublai grabbed her arm and shouted into her ear: "Get everyone into the strongest longhouses! Send the warriors to me!" He dashed out into the storm.

Ishara grabbed a spear and followed him out. No need for her to spread a warning: voices everywhere yelled, "The Wall! Warriors to the Wall!"

She sped past the houses, joining a troop of spear-armed men and women. Kublai stood at the base of the smoldering gate, motioning urgently in the flickering light of torches. He spotted her and looked furious. "Get back to safety!"

"I have a spear! You need every weapon!"

Now she saw that the lightning had struck the base of one of the massive timbers of the gate. A smoldering red gash was opened, looking strangely like the bleeding wound of a living thing. Wide as her body, the crack ran a jagged path from high above her to the sodden earth. Sentries atop the walls shouted down an urgent warning: "Deathrunners are coming!"

"Bring wood and tools to make a shield barrier!" Kublai shouted. "Get men to close that breach! Hurry!"

Ishara pressed past him, taking a sputtering, hissing torch from another person, and she stared through the gap and into the dark. At first, she saw nothing, but then two red sparks gleamed, moving, and near it others: eyes! "Deathrunners!" she yelled, backing away and dropping the torch. "Get ready!"

From atop the Wall the sentries hurled spears. Ishara saw a nightmare head thrust through the opening, its furious jaws gnawing the still smoking wood, trying to enlarge the breach. Kublai sprang forward and thrust his spear hard, piercing an eye. The monster screeched and jerked back. Ishara heard the others fall on the bloody creature, heard their snarls and the ripping of flesh as they tore the wounded animal to pieces.

Then a human scream—another Deathrunner had forced its head through and had managed to seize a warrior's leg. Ishara watched in horror as the vise-like jaws of the creatures dragged him backward, his arms reaching for help, his hands briefly clinging to the hissing, rain-spattered wood before the things on the other side of the gate ripped into the victim.

A ferocious twittering, and this time the Deathrunners hit the gate with such force that four of them broke through. "Hold them!" Kublai shouted.

The warriors rallied. One of the Deathrunners, the last one through, back out the breach under a concerted attack. The other three leapt, clawed, and bit—in the uncertain light their feathers spiked and glistening, their teeth ghastly white in a flash of thunder and lightning.

A party of builders came running to the wall, hauling a lashed-together grating. At the break in the wall, warriors had thrust long torches through, holding the other Deathrunners off. The creatures feared fire, but in the rain fire was not a sure defense. Kublai and six other warriors had cornered one of the three Deathrunners that had broken through. A dozen spears found its vulnerable points, and it screeched in its death-throes, blood gurgling from its mouth as it lunged, staggered, and collapsed.

Off to the side, another of the creatures had torn open a warrior's abdomen, but more warriors speared it, piercing its scaly underbelly. Now it, too, lay dying, snarling and kicking in its throes. Ishara had lost track of the third, but heard shouts from the village and realized a party of warriors had pursued the monster there.

"Hurry, close the gap!" Kublai yelled.

But as the workers raised the patch, the ground trembled and the gate bulged inward. Wood cracked and splinters flew. Ishara blinked in disbelief. The great bar that locked the gate bowed. Men buttressed either side of the gate with timbers meant for that purpose—

Still, the gate slowly creaked open as enormous, clawed fingers secured a grip. With one echoing crack, a bolt sprang loose and the doors began to give way. Some twenty-five feet off the ground a gargantuan head began to slowly peer through; first the sharp, spike-feathered chin of a massive, protruding lower jaw appeared, lined with rows glinting teeth. A fortress of horns, spikes and scales on the head took shadowy form. The sputtering torchlight glinted in eerie yellow eyes as they peered down at the human confusion below.

"Gaw!" someone shouted.

Ishara hurled her spear, aiming for the creature's eye, but her throw could not reach and it bounced harmlessly off the monster's thickly scaled chest. Gaw heaved–but the buttresses held, for a moment, and the other carnivores could not get past the bulk of their leader's immense three-toed foot that was wedged in the base of the opening.

"Get out of here!" Kublai yelled at Ishara. He pointed upward. "Climb that! Go to the Storyteller! GO!" She blinked, pushing her wet hair out of her eyes. A knotted rope ladder dangled–the one that led to the prayer-hut atop the Wall where the Storyteller meditated. She leapt and caught the lowest rung, calling, "Kublai! Come on, come with me!"

Gaw roared, for a split-second eyeing the fleeing girl, and Ishara hauled herself up, hand over hand. Then she heard a dying scream, a human scream from below. "Kublai!"

"Not him. Come!"

A hand closed on her arm with a vise-like grip, and the old woman, the Pendonjira, pulled her up to whatever safety the top of the Wall offered her just as a massive, claw swept beneath her feet.

In the little hut, Ishara clung to the old woman. "The oil is hot now," the Storyteller said. "It will not be long!"

Just a few feet away, warriors stood at a cauldron right above the gate. Below them, Gaw still struggled to shatter the last remaining beams and buttresses, giving all the Deathrunners a way into the village. Red embers glowed beneath the cauldron, and steam rose from it. "Now!" one of the warriors yelled. Another blew a signal on a horn, a sign for the warriors below to beware.

Grunting, four men leaned on levers, tipping the cauldron–and from it a spattering, hissing stream of boiling oil poured through a drain feeding into three openings in the overhang above the main gates. Superheated fluids gushed straight down onto Gaw's head and back, drenching everything else in the great expanse beneath the overhang of the gateway. Even Gaw's thick, scaled hide could not endure such heat causing the beast to writhe, screeching in fury and pain–many of the smaller Deathrunners died instantly in the searing shower of death.

Ishara heard the people at the Gate cry out in unison, chanting, and she heard the doors slam fully closed again, heard the rattle as the bar slipped back into place, followed by hastily positioned buttresses to secure it, heard hammering as the workers got the latticed patch into position–

Gaw's intense roars of pain and anger receded into the distance, trailed by the snarling and chattering of her underlings–

"The others will follow their leader," the Storyteller said. "They will not return this night."

"Kublai–"

"He is alive and unhurt." The old woman chuckled. "How do I know? I am the Storyteller, child. Storytellers have ways of knowing that others lack. Sleep now. When you wake, I have a story for you."

Though it seemed impossible, Ishara did sleep a little that night. With the morning came sounds of serious building–below, the workers swarmed, repairing the gate. The rain and storm had ended, though the day remained overcast. The dank smell of jungle saturated the densely humid air, mingling with the smoke and sweat produced in a turmoil of human activity. The Storyteller offered Ishara food, and when they had eaten, the old woman spoke of ancient days.

"The time has come," she said, "for me to show you a place that very few know about. I am one who does, and your father another. I will take you there—and if you wish, you may then show Kublai, for his destiny and yours are tied closely together."

To visit this strange place, they had first to climb down from the hut, and then to follow the Wall to the north. A crowd of workers somberly nodded as they passed. Pendonjiras were figures commanding great respect and not even Bar-Atu's henchmen had been able to openly disrespect them—yet. Ishara saw that the people must have worked all through the night, for the gate had been mended, though its charred scars still showed. The workers had cleared away bodies of Deathrunners—and of men and women.

Not far from the gate, the Storyteller paused and gestured at a flat, grassy spot. "Here," she said, "the Kongs and their mysterious Zantu companions camped when the Wall was first being built. It is kept clear for their memory—though few now remember."

'The Kongs helped built the Wall, I know," Ishara said. "You've told me that. But how did humans control the Kongs? They are huge, people say—as large as a saurian and even more fierce."

"They were not always. Much larger than a man, three times as tall, but in later times as a result of living on Skull Island, they grew even larger and stronger still. It has been long since anyone on this island has even seen a Kong."

"They may all be dead."

"No," the Storyteller said quietly. "Some live yet. A few, but some."

"Where?"

The Storyteller gazed out into the jungle, her mind perceiving what her eyes could not see. "That, my child, that is a mystery. As is the place I am taking you."

They followed the Wall to a place where it ended. Beyond lay a steep cliff dropping nearly vertically down to the ocean, and on the island side beyond that, vast waterfalls uncrossable by anything but creatures of flight. "You have never been here," the Storyteller said.

"No. It is forbidden."

"Not to me, nor those I choose. Carefully now—there is no handhold, and the steps are worn." Much to Ishara's wonder, the old woman lithely stepped over the edge of the cliff. Following, Ishara saw steps, hardly more than footholds, carved into the face of the stone. From here she could see the honeycomb cliffs on the island side of the Wall, ancient stone riddled with cavities and caves, some of them pouring waterfalls out into rainbow spills that splashed into the ocean. Ishara noticed that the clouds took on beautiful colors, the moisture in the air reflecting the light in unusual ways.

It was her first sense that the reality beyond the Wall could be different from how the superstitious fears she had grown up with portrayed it.

The descent was not far, not much more than two spear-lengths, but it made Ishara feel dizzy. "Here," the Storyteller said, stepping sideways into a shadowy niche. Ishara followed, and looked around in surprise: the opening led back into a cave. A corroded metal bracket in the wall held a bundle of torches. Carved into it were the faded symbols that the Storyteller interpreted as "TAIGU", which she said meant "Brave" or "Courageous" in an old Tagu dialect. The Storyteller took one, and Ishara used flint and iron to strike a flame. "Bring one more," the old woman said, leading Ishara into the dimness of the cave.

"What is this place?" Ishara asked.

"Part of the memory of Skull Island. Few know that below the surface, caves and tunnels reach far. Once our ancestors could penetrate the jungle all the way to the Old City by traveling underground. Though there were dangers there as well, they were of a different kind."

"The Old City? Then the stories are true?"

"They are true. Look." The Storyteller held the torch over her head. Ishara gasped. In the wavering light, she saw–

Wall paintings, detailed and colorful, though clearly made in eons gone by. Little by little the colors seemed to take life from the torchlight and to glow with their own inner fires. As the Storyteller pointed out scenes, Ishara fell entranced into a tale of the far-off years when Kongs and humans ruled the island.

"These are the seeds that produce plants for medicine and for safety," the Storyteller said, illuminating a whole wall with pictures of plant materials, ranged largest to smallest. "The symbols show what they were used for. These–" she pointed to a row of a half-dozen seeds–"when burned in a censer in special combinations produce a smoke that repels most of the dinosaurs."

"You mean there was a time when we were able to protect ourselves from the beasts of the island, when we did not live in fear of our own shadows?" the girl asked incredulously.

"Yes," the Storyteller assured her, "We were once great, advanced beyond your wildest imaginings, with a noble history that flowed with the force of a mighty river."

"Even Gaw and the Deathrunners could not conquer us?" Ishara pushed, struggling to absorb it all.

"It was a battle at first, but in time, yes, we proved that even they could not conquer us."

"Then how–"

"In time, my young apprentice. Time is short and there is much to learn here first," the Storyteller smiled.

She pointed to other plants and seeds and recited all their uses. "Once the Tagu knew all of these plants. But sadly, since we have lived confined behind the Wall, we have lost them all. Now only Atu hunting parties go into the jungle, and they disdain the use of repellents, saying only cowards shield themselves with smoke and magic."

"But it wasn't magic!"

"No, knowledge gained with difficulty and used with wisdom, but never magic. Our ancestors were beyond such things, the long line of Storytellers guided them truly." The Storyteller led her deeper into the cave. "But look here."

At first Ishara did not know what she saw: A circular valley, perhaps, sprawling and with the oddest plants growing in it. Then she noticed a tiny figure, and more like it. "These are people?"

"They are our ancestors," the Storyteller said. "And they lived there, in what we now call the Old City, though this recalls a time when it was new."

Ishara caught her breath. For most Tagatu, the Old City was only a fairytale, an imaginary place of legend, *It's real*, she thought incredulously.

"It was real. And here is the great secret." She led her deeper into the cave. There a mural larger than the rest occupied one whole smooth wall. At first it seemed dingy and only a smudge, but the Storyteller said, "Patience," and before long the dim colors began to clarify and shine under the torchlight. "Now watch."

Ishara saw a scene unfold: In a great round space men and women stood on a terrace of fitted stone. The single stone in the center had been cut into a circle, and with ropes and levers fifteen or twenty people were lifting it, or lowering it. The scene continued to appear, top to bottom; now beneath the circular terrace Ishara saw people placing what looked like sealed urns into a hollow chamber. Only when she realized the top the others were lifting was a hatchway did she ask, "Are they taking something or hiding it?"

"They are storing urns in the underground excavation for safety. The vessels they use are specially treated. Seeds placed and sealed in them will retain the spark of life for thousands of years. That is our hope. Ishara, that is the storage place of the Old City, beneath the amphitheater. Our ancestors put a cache of all their most precious plant remedies there–spores and seeds. If we could retrieve them, the Tagu could once again create the repellents that kept us safe. Perhaps we could even re-create one that would turn away the Deathrunners and Gaw."

"I will go," Ishara said at once.

"Wait. I want you to see another picture, so you may understand."

This one looked like the oldest and most weathered of all. It took many minutes of the Storyteller's holding her torch close before the pigments caught illumination, and then it came to wavering life: A cavern, like the one she stood in, but opening on a vista that showed it was high above the jungle. Dark figures—she first thought them men in ceremonial robes—appeared. And then she gasped. "Kongs!"

"And their Zantu, the humans who partnered with them," the Storyteller told her. "See, there are two. And these Kongs are big, but not as enormous as the living ones are today. These are the Kongs who helped built the Wall, or their immediate descendants. These are Kongs who went with their human partners to dwell in the wild places when, we thought, we had made the island completely safe from the Deathrunners. We were mistaken. Since that time, it appears the Zantu have died out, and the Kongs have grown in stature but dwindled in numbers."

"But how are these images possible?" asked Ishara, struggling to understand.

"The miawan of our ancestors were great indeed. They had unlocked many of the secrets of nature. These walls were created using specially prepared pigments made from sea creatures found in the deep pools of caves and other waters surrounding the island. I no longer remember with exactness such details, it is not my calling, but these secrets may be discovered again within the Old City by those whose calling it is. These and greater discoveries await all our people if were succeed in our quest," the Storyteller intoned, "Come. One last place."

They had to stoop to go into the farthest chamber of the cave. It was not much larger than a longhouse, with a high domed ceiling that let them stand. No pictures here—but arranged all around, idols or statues: Kongs. "Was this their cave?" she asked.

The Storyteller shook her head. "I believe not. We have no proof, but I think—I feel in my heart—that the Kongs' last stronghold was the mountain with the skull's face that towers above the jungle. If any Kongs at all are left alive—I feel we will find them on Skull Mountain. Let us hope, for I feel strongly that as in the days of old, the Kongs will again have a pivotal role to play in saving our people, this time not only from the dangers of the island, but from the dangers within ourselves."

"How can that be possible?"

"Nothing is impossible to those who never stop hoping and trusting in what is good."

"But how?"

"How? Even I do not know, for our story is not finished yet!" the Storyteller smiled, "Come! We must be brave and continue to go forward. Together, we will see how it ends…."

As they had feared, Bar-Atu, the leader of the cult of human sacrifice, lost no time in proclaiming that the "god," Gaw, was angry, and that the islanders owed the great beast the sacrifice of a living maiden. Ishara's father, On-Tagu, asserted his power as king and sternly forbade the sacrifice, but he was old and sick. To make matters worse, it seemed to Ishara that more and more islanders found themselves swayed by Bar-Atu's ranting orations.

She took Kublai into her confidence, they furtively met the Storyteller, and she provided them with some of the last of the repellents left over from days gone by, a small supply possessed only by the Storytellers whose long line was instrumental in first gaining knowledge of the use of them. They handed them down from generation to generation, to be used secretly and only when necessary. She showed them how to properly apply the oily paste to make it last, even in water, and instructed them on what its limitations were.

"If you proceed carefully, this repellent will make it possible for you to walk unnoticed amongst most of the creatures of the island. If used sparingly and properly, it will save your lives." She made sure that they brought only whatever tools and weapons were necessary. And lastly, she gave them each a uniquely shaped device that looked something like a chambered shell. It was made of an unusual material.

"What are these?" they asked

"You can use these to communicate should you be separated. The sound that they make is unlike any other. I may hear it as well, and if at all possible, I will come to your aid. They are made of a material called ilu, which is nearly indestructible. These were fashioned in a time long forgotten. Bring them back to me, along with yourselves!"

They prepared, and on a foggy morning they set off for the jungle.

The Storyteller accompanied them to the spot where a cave, obscured by brush, opened in the cliffs, not too far from the one that Ishara had visited. This time, however, the cave turned out to be a tunnel, perhaps an ancient lava tube. All three of them bore torches, and in the red flickering light, the Storyteller led them to a place where human hands had made the tunnel impassible except for humans who could squirm through the narrowest of openings. "This keeps the large beasts from finding this way behind the Wall," the old woman told them. "Make sure to leave scratches or marks that you cannot mistake as often as possible to help you retrace your trail in case you get lost."

She gave them final instructions, and they set off, underground. She had warned them that the tunnel offered its own dangers. It might have eroded since the last time she had ventured in many years ago. It certainly felt dank. The rocks sometimes reflected strange and wondrous flecks of color from the light of their torches. At one point, well beyond the Wall, a few shafts of dim daylight barred the darkness—a place where, ages ago, a gigantic sinkhole had opened. It had collapsed about five feet of the right-hand tunnel wall, and Ishara and Kublai had to clamber over it.

At one point, they could not tell which branch ahead was a man-made trail and which was an eroded tunnel and were forced to pause, moving their torches over the uneven walls. Just as shadows began to creep and strange sounds began to echo towards them, Ishara saw an ancient mark with the name 'Taigu' indicating a proper path and they took it.

They followed twistings and turnings as silently as possible, found wider chambers with murals and curious weapons from ancient times, so age-eaten that even the metal crumbled to dust when Kublai picked up what in the dimness looked like a handsome spear. Finally, after hours of travel, they emerged.

The tunnel was similarly shielded at its opening from view by a high growth of jungle vegetation. They had to cut a passage through before it opened on a hillside where it sloped downward. Then the land turned almost sharply and rose to the central plateau of the island, heavily vegetated. The morning fog had burned off, and now the sun shone with a watery luster through breaks in a great many clouds. Beyond the trees, closer than she had ever seen it before, loomed Skull Mountain. Their way led toward it—the Old City lay half a day's travel inland from the mountain. The Storyteller had told them, "You may see from a distance a plateau with strange-looking trees atop it. That will be the Old City. The buildings will not look like ours."

As the Storyteller had advised, the two young people skirted the jungle, finding grassland where they could make better time. "Look," Kublai said once, pointing upward. A flight of the broad-winged soarers passed over, a dozen or more of them, gliding like spirits against a sky of broken clouds. Another time they heard the grunting and bellowing of longhorns, massive frilled herbivores that fed on ground vegetation and were generally dangerous only when provoked.

The route they took forced them to ascend the northern rim of the plateau, and finally they came to a place where the land dropped away sharply to their left, down to an enormous inland sea. This time Ishara was the one who called out, "Look there, in the bay!"

They stood side by side. The turquoise water churned to creamy whiteness in one place. Racing gray-green forms—their heads like those of gigantic lizards, but elongated and lined with re-curved teeth, and instead of legs they had four flippers—leapt shimmering in the sun and dived, attacking something in the water. They could not clearly make out what it was—but a dark thing lay on the water and did not seem to move. "I would not like to be swimming in those waters," Kublai mused.

They came to a spot where the drop to the left grew sheer, and they climbed up to the crown of the plateau again. Now their way led through rubble and boulders, nearly a desert, and the going became slow. After an hour they came to a gorge, not very deep, through which a river rushed.

Ishara said, "I think I know this river from a map the Storyteller showed me. It leads close to Skull Mountain, to the great pool at its base, which spills into the ocean when the river flows outward again. We should follow its path."

"I have a faster way," Kublai said. "Come with me."

He climbed down the rocky slope of the gorge, Ishara close behind him. "There," he said. "That's what I saw from the bank. I think we can ride this."

It was part of a shattered tree trunk as long as a canoe, and it lay snagged in the water: dead vines, tough lianas, had fallen with the log, and they had caught on thick brush. "Will it hold us?" Ishara asked.

"It's big enough. Get on and I will climb on behind you. I'll cut the vines, and the course of the river will bear us along faster than we can walk." He laughed. "I've done this before, when I was a boy," he said.

Though uncertain, Ishara lay on the log, clutching some of the vine that had embraced the growing tree ages ago and still did not let go its hold. She heard Kublai behind her. When he sawed through one of the four lianas, the taut vine made a twang, and then another and another—

"The last one," he warned.

A moment later the log moved, slow for a moment and then with dizzying speed. The river was narrow enough to keep it more or less straight. They then dashed through sprays and boils of white water, gasping as the cold waves sometimes buried them, then breathing deep when they rode along with their heads above the river surface on smoother stretches. From time to time they glimpsed Skull Mountain. Before long it seemed to fill half the horizon, then the log bucketed down a long natural spillway into what looked like a deep, crystal-clear pool. Driven by its own momentum it exploded the water on impact, heading toward to bottom like a missile. Ishara and Kublai managed to abandon it just in time and kicked to the surface.

"We can climb out on that side," Kublai called hacking and panting, pointing to the landward shore, where the bank sloped more gently.

Ishara, a strong swimmer, set out–but found herself pulled backward by a current. "Kublai!" she shouted. "I need help!"

Kublai immediately struck out for her, but just as he grabbed her hand, the water dragged her under. She held her breath, her ears ringing. Just then, from the dark of the depths the water thrust her back into the light as she, Kublai, and the water tumbled down in a waterfall to yet another pool. This one was nearly on the level of the inland sea. Ishara struggled desperately in the furious roil of water, but finally she crawled out, coughing and retching, onto a sandy margin.

She rolled over. Kublai was just staggering ashore himself.

"I didn't expect that," he confessed.

Ishara gave him a quizzical look as if to say, *Are you crazy?*

They gazed upward. High above their heads, the waterfall issued straight from an overhanging rock face, a kind of dam that held the higher pool. As they watched, a dark shape jetted out–their log. It hit with a great splash. "Where are we?" Kublai asked.

"Not far from that sea, I think," Ishara said, pointing to where this lower, smaller pool gave birth to a stream that ran nearly straight toward the sound of surf.

"Let's get to a place where we can see the mountain," suggested Kublai. "Then we can find a way to the city."

They followed the stream and saw that it fed into a small lagoon. Ishara strode over the sandy beach and leapt into the water, its incoming waves gentle after having been broken by an offshore reef, lapped over her feet and ankles. "It's warm," she said. "I'm going in. The river was freezing."

"There may be predators," Kublai warned.

"No, I sense none." She walked into the water, enjoying its soothing embrace, and swam a few strokes before she heard Kublai yell her name in alarm.

She raised her head. Blue-gray forms raced toward her, their sharp dorsal fins homing in on her. She opened her mouth to scream–and laughed instead. "Sleeks!" she called. The swimming reptiles, some ten to fifteen feet long with slender, toothless snouts, were harmless and playful. When the home lagoon was full of sleeks, it was safe even to swim there. She had done it often, and from the time she was a little girl she even felt that she could communicate with the animals in some strange way. Again, she strongly had that same feeling. "It is your special gift," the Storyteller once told her. "It is a sign." The thought flashed through Ishara's mind in an instant. She had always wondered, "A sign of what?"

Ishara's attention sprang back to the present when a sleek swam by so close that she seized its fin. It took her weight without strain, and then she frolicked with the pod, letting them toss her and carry her, even riding one. "They won't hurt you!" she called to Kublai.

"How do you do that?" he shouted, but he finally waded in, too.

The sport of riding sleeks was exhilarating. In their excitement neither of the young people noticed, but the sleeks took them far out from shore–so far that when Kublai next shouted, "What's that?" neither of them could clearly see. The sleeks, though, seemed panicked, and they sped toward the sea, revealing their creamy white underbellies as they leapt over what must have been a break in the reef.

It was something dark, rising above the surface of the water, pushing out from shore. Then it stopped, roared, and dived, rising with some huge form in its grasp, thrashing and snapping. "An eel shark!" shouted Ishara. "But what is fighting it? Not a dinosaur!"

The struggle was furious but brief. Whatever the dark creature was, it had powerful limbs, and it seemed to break the spine of the predator it fought. It turned and waded from the water, dragging the carcass behind it. After beaching the huge shark-like creature, it rose, seemed to glower around the bay, and then, satisfied there was no further danger, drummed its chest.

"A Kong!" Ishara said. "It's a Kong! They do live!"

"We are *not* going after it," Kublai said with determination.

The two regained the high ground that afternoon, and when night found them on the northwestern slopes of the hills that led to Skull Mountain, they made camp inside a shallow cave. They risked a small fire–most of the carnivores avoided man's flames–and the Storyteller's repellents were proving surprisingly effective, but they added a little more just to be sure after their multiple water adventures, and some to the fire as well for good measure. They took turns keeping watch, but nothing menaced them. Then before the sun rose high the next morning, they set out again.

They came across the rubble of a paved roadway. Now it was overgrown and ruined, but at least they could follow the track. "It has to lead to the City," Kublai said. "The legends tell us that once it was to be the center of many settlements. The roads would have made passage easier."

Before noon they came to a shallow, bowl-shaped valley. Ishara put a hand on Kublai's arm. "This is where they stored the seeds!" she said. "This is the amphitheater!"

Perhaps the center of it had once been smooth and level, paving stones laid out in a perfect circle, but centuries of silt had collected there, and now brush and even trees had reclaimed the space. Shrill cackles and shrieks broke from the trees–"Claw-wings!" Ishara said.

Unlike the giant pterodactyls that soared and swooped down upon the sea before gliding off to their more distant haunts, these smaller, bird-like creatures were thankfully rare near the village. Colorfully plumed, with bodies the length of her forearm, they had claw-wings and pointy snouts filled with tiny sharp teeth that could deliver a nasty little bite. Fortunately, they kept to the trees and ate mostly insects. Fast and always hungry, they had longish necks and delicate, brightly feathered tails gradually spread out into an elongated "V" shape. They were curious animals with large eyes and clattered and chattered as they fluttered from limb to limb to keep the humans in sight.

For a long time, Kublai and Ishara explored the depression in the earth without finding anything. All the while, one of the claw-wings chattered *Oji! Oji! Oji!* over and over. As Kublai grew increasingly frustrated and impatient, Ishara urged him to keep his temper. They rested at one point and Ishara imitated the claw-wing's cry so accurately that several of the birds fluttered in–and the young one that had been pacing them came right up to her and perched in a bush not an arm's length away. It tilted its head, turning first one bright eye and then the other, on Ishara. "*Oji!*" she said.

The bird fluttered its wings, bowed, and its throat swelled as it screamed, "*Oji! Oji! Oji!*"

Ishara slowly raised her arm. The claw-wing drew back, but then leaned forward and gave her an inquisitive look. Then, daintily, it stepped from the branch onto her forearm. "*Oji?*" it seemed to ask, cocking its head inquisitively.

"Look, Kublai," Ishara said. "We have a new friend. I think its name is Oji."

"*Oji!*" the bird agreed.

"Tell it to help us find the center stone," Kublai sarcastically complained. "Can you help us?" Ishara asked, smiling. "Don't say just 'Oji'!"

The bird launched itself into the air and flew, giving its call over and over. "Your friend deserted you," Kublai said.

"Maybe not. I added a touch of the herb-oil to its snout and immediately its tongue flicked out to taste it–I thought hard of what we are looking for. I have a kind of link with animals. Let's follow it."

"It'll get us lost!"

"Come on. I'm following it."

Oji–as Ishara thought of it–had landed on a tree branch. As they came close, it called out again and sprang into the air. It made three short flights then it suddenly dived toward the ground and vanished in a clump of waist-high weeds.

"Where'd it go?" Kublai asked.

"Let's find out."

They pushed through tangles of tall grass and briars–and then found themselves at the edge of–

A hole. A round hole that had to be the entrance to the storage chambers. Except for stinking, stagnant water several feet below, the chamber looked empty.

"Nothing!" Kublai said bitterly, "Think harder next time." "Maybe beneath the water–"

Kublai crouched on the edge of the hole and reached into it, thrusting his spear. It grated on stone. "No. The chamber is not deep. Just water and muck and then a few inches below that, stone." He stirred the mud with his spear. "No vats. Nothing. Nothing! A wasted risk!"

"Like your water log idea? Keep looking!

He pulled away from the hole and sat brooding. Behind him, Oji shot out of the hole, its tail dripping wet. "*Oji!*" It perched on a bush and began to preen its tail feathers.

"They must be somewhere," Ishara said. "Perhaps some of our people lingered in the Old City and retrieved them. We could find the City and–"

"Or we could just die out here!" Kublai stood, grasping his spear. "It's time to go back and tell the Storyteller what we didn't find!"

"I think we should–"

"Seeds!" Kublai yelled. "Stupid! Better than seeds would be to have a Kong to protect us!"

"There are no more Zantu to team with them," Ishara said.

"Once there were no Zantu at all–and somehow they learned to control a Kong. We saw one. We could capture it, drag it back to the village, tame it, make it serve us–"

"That would be wrong!" Ishara's face felt hot. "The Kongs are not–not like ordinary animals! We do not tame people and enslave them!" She began to walk away.

Behind her, Kublai said, "The village is the other way!"

"But the Old City must be this way," she said without looking back. "If you're afraid, go home. I'm going to explore–perhaps the vats were taken there when the city was on the verge of falling!" She heard him start out behind her, following her. Then she thought he had grabbed her shoulder, and angrily she twitched it, but the grasp stayed firm, and it had claws. She looked sideways.

"*Oji!*" said the claw-wing that had perched on her shoulder. It seemed she did indeed have a new friend.

IN THE OLD CITY

Like the amphitheater, the Old City had donned a disguise woven by centuries of neglect and the slow encroachment of the jungle. What at first Ishara took to be a gigantic grove of trees proved to be a rampart three times the height of a man, thickly overgrown with brush: the walls of the Old City.

Time and torrential rains had smoothed them and worn them down. Climbing the slope was not difficult, especially with so much growth offering hand and footholds. When Ishara reached the top, she pushed through the brush and saw—

Trees and mounds. Her heart sank. As far as she could see, no works built by human hands survived here. But she found her way down the inner slope. Now she could see two breaks in the ramparts, places where gates must once have stood, gates long since decayed. Kublai came grumbling down behind her. "There's nothing here!"

"I think there is," Ishara said. She had paused beside one of the mounds. It was, she saw now, actually a squat, stumpy tree, its bole at least twenty feet in diameter. It sent out branches with deep green, spiny leaves.

What she thought were knotholes were—windows? She went around the base of the mound and found an oval opening tall enough for her to walk in without stooping. "It's a house," she said.

Though again drifting dirt, growths and fungi clung to every surface overhead, encroaching everywhere, it was clear that the strange tree had once been fashioned—or perhaps had grown?—into a habitat. Windows dotted the walls. There were even traces, a few uprights—roots trained to grow straight, perhaps—that showed where interior walls might once have divided the space into rooms.

Kublai grudgingly said, "Tagu lore says that once we had the knowledge to persuade plants to work for us and with us. I'd imagined the Old City to be a place of stone, but maybe—perhaps—it was always one of living houses and of trees that did the will of their masters."

Oji, still perched on Ishara's shoulder, suddenly stiffened and shrieked. It leapt, spread its wings, and clumsily sailed out through the door opening. Ishara heard strange voices, human voices, and then a boom like short, sharp clap of thunder. She looked at Kublai with wide eyes. Brandishing his spear, he said, "Come on!"

They burst out of the doorway, and then stopped short—and not far from them, a group of the strangest people she had ever seen faced Ishara and Kublai, both groups staring at each other in astonishment.

One, two, three, four, five, six of them, four with pale faces, two with browner skin, outlandishly dressed in cloth that covered their legs and arms. They held sticks, one of them smoking. Oji was in the air, circling, and came to alight on Ishara's shoulder again. One of the men raised his stick, and the tallest of them thrust out an arm and pushed the stick up into the air. It exploded with a flash, a burst of smoke, and a terrible noise that made Ishara flinch, and Oji shrieked again.

The one who seemed to be the leader—the one who had thrust the stick up before the explosion—spoke to the others in an angry jabber. They looked sullen, even the youngest one. Holding both his hands up, empty, the leader stepped forward and said something.

Kublai and Ishara exchanged a glance.

The man tried again. And again. Finally, Ishara caught just one word she knew: bala, "friend." "Friend?" she asked.

The man grinned and nodded. He had a broad, strong face and a muscular body, shrouded though it was in those strange garments. He tapped his chest and said something that sounded like "Magwich." Then he pointed to the youngest among them, hardly more than a boy. "Skeets." He pushed the boy back and pointed at a shy-looking young man, maybe a little older than Kublai, his face sunburned. "Char-lee."

Ishara realized he was naming them. She pointed at herself. "Ishara."

"Ishara," the man, Magwich, repeated.

Ishara nodded and pointed again.

"Kublai." "Coo-blai," Magwich said, coming close.

He then introduced the others: Slirm, Wicksum, and Coo-kee. He tried a few other words, but neither Ishara nor Kublai knew them. Magwich tried to tell them something with gestures. Ishara realized that his hand making a wavy path through the air meant "ocean." But then he tried to indicate something that must have been violent—something tall leaned over, men swimming, dying— and more than that she could not guess.

He led them to a patch of sandy soil and with a stick he sketched something that looked like a canoe, but then he drew in men in the water beside it, and their size meant the canoe would have to be gigantic. He also sketched in fish shapes much larger than the men. "Dead," he kept repeating, pointing to the pictures of men.

Then Magwich made signs with his hands, miming the act of eating. *They are hungry*, Ishara realized. She nodded and opened the leather bag that held her own provisions. She handed out dried fish and fruit, and the men ate them ravenously. Magwich pointed to all his men and then held up his ten fingers, closed his hands, and held them up again, and then pointed toward the sea.

Magwich

"There are . . . twenty more of them," Ishara said slowly. "I think they came over the ocean. Something happened and many were killed. The others are . . . back near the beach. They need food."

Magwich seemed to know the word for "food." He nodded and repeated it: "Food. Food."

"We can take them to the village," Ishara said. "My father may send some men in canoes to find the rest."

"They are strangers," Kublai said in a low voice. "They can't even talk! We can't trust them."

The man Magwich had called Wicksum, a hulking figure, raised his firestick and rumbled something that sounded threatening. Magwich, putting a wide smile on his face, again pushed the weapon, this time so it pointed at the earth. He knelt in the sand, then, and repeated, "Food. Food."

Ishara took his hand and he rose to his feet again. "Magwich," she said, "come. She pointed in the direction of the Wall and the village. "Food."

He rose, smiling, and said something to his men in his own strange language. "We should not do this," Kublai warned.

"We must. They are strangers. They need help," Ishara said simply.

"This way," Ishara said, walking toward the place where the Old City gate had once stood. They moved out in a body. But then, when Ishara started toward the place where the ruined old road ran, Magwich closed his hand on the girl's arm and pointed toward the lagoon.

She shook her head and tried to start again. Magwich said something, and Wicksum raised his weapon, an evil sneer on his face. Magwich tugged her arm, gently enough.

"We'd better go with them," Kublai said.

And so, they started back toward the ocean, with Ishara fearing what might happen, Magwich so happy that he started to sing in a rusty voice, and only Charlie speaking words of comfort to her–they sounded like words of comfort, anyway, from their soft tone. She understood none of them.

The strangers seemed to know their way. They marched straight through the fringe forest of the plateau–not jungle, not open land, but relatively arid and free of undergrowth– toward Skull Mountain.

The attack came without warning.

The party was crossing a sandy clearing between groves of coconut palms when a running form, man-sized, burst from a cluster of brush and flung itself through the air at the one bringing up the rear–Skeets, the boy. He had time for one scream, and the other men reeled and scattered, shouting in loud alarm.

The Deathrunner was not an adult, it still had its stubby wings and was fully feathered, but already too heavy to fly. It must have been ravenous. One slash of its great claws tore open the boy's stomach. As he writhed in agony, jetting blood, the cruel jaws snapped forward, seized his head, and with one shake the creature broke the boy's neck.

The weapons of the men fired, filling the air with acrid smoke and the stench of sulfur. Though Ishara saw the predator's body jerk, saw wounds open on its back, none seemed deep, and it did not hesitate, but turned and menaced the men. Two more of the creature's kind melted from the jungle, heads low, eyes glaring.

Kublai shouted, "Run!" He stood with spear braced as Ishara and the others fled for the nearest grove of trees. Only Magwich lingered behind with Kublai, drawing a great curved sword and crouching to meet the onrush of the monster.

But then–a roar. Ishara stumbled to a stop.

A Kong–much bigger than the one they had glimpsed near the ocean–exploded from jungle cover behind the Deathrunners. They whirled to face the threat, tails twitching, mouths hissing.

"Another Kong!" Kublai yelled, grabbing Magwich's arm and pointed to a safe retreat. Charlie, who was holding Ishara's arm, asked, "Kong?"

Ishara pointed. "Kong! Kong!"

The great anthropoid was far, far larger than any Kong depicted in the cave paintings. It towered over the wounded Deathrunner–but with the blind courage of its kind, the dinosaur did not retreat, instead it leapt over the dead body of the boy, its vicious hind claws slashing–

With an astounding dexterity, the Kong pivoted and swatted the carnosaur out of the air as though it were an insect. Another charged, but its leap carried it past the dodging Kong and hard into a tree. It fell to the ground, rolled, and scrambled back upright, spreading its forelegs, feathers bristling in an intimidation display. Several others screeched piercingly as they emerged from cover, forming a phalanx that moved forward in unison. The Kong paid them no heed; instead it looked around agitatedly, sniffing the air. The men, who had regrouped with Charlie and Ishara as the Kong, distracted by the Deathrunners, stood frozen. Ishara whispered to Kublai in their own language, "Do you notice? This Kong looks to be a female, there's also something about her movements–she's defending something, I can feel it!" With Kongs the difference in genders was not obvious, but Kublai nodded.

Magwich growled something that neither of the islanders understood. He began to back up when a large drop of something viscous slopped on his shoulder. Magwich looked up, and following his gaze, Ishara saw the gaping, toothy maw of Gaw high above him. She was enormous, much larger even than the Kong. To her it was obvious the puny humans were not its focus of attention.

Charlie stammered something, and Magwich nodded and said something to him, something that sounded sarcastic but nervous.

No one seemed to notice the utter silence that had descended on the scene like a pall. When they did it was too late.

The jungle erupted in a cacophony of chaos as the mother Kong let out a terrifying howl that rolled into an indescribable, guttural sound, scattering the Deathrunners in all directions. If it was to intimidate Gaw, it did not work. This was clearly going to be a fight to the death. The female Kong pounded the ground with one enormous fist. In a flash the other hand, holding a stout bone of some kind, swung high as she charged headlong at Gaw to deliver a crushing blow.

Gaw bobbed low and to the outside, then darted quickly upward to clamp her jaws on the Kong's free arm. Razor sharp teeth instantly drew blood as the saurian reached with clawed hand to stop the Kong from striking. Gaw pressed home her attack by securing a vise-like grip on the mother Kong's upper arm and yanking it downward, dislocated the Kong's shoulder.

With strategic purpose, Gaw grabbed the Kong's ankle and swept it out, causing it to stumble backwards. The mother Kong sought to gain balance by pushing the arm away with her other foot, but it was too late. Gravity completed what Gaw's forward thrust had begun and the Kong fell back. In an instant Gaw delivered a death bite to the stunned Kong, ripping out her throat.

Magwich swore, awed at Gaw's methodical attack, her quck destruction of such a fearsome creature as a Kong. Against his nature, a twinge of fear crawled up his spine…

Gaw never saw what hit her as the massive form of a bull Kong collided with the saurian killer's flank with the force of a landslide. Gaw was sent sprawling.

Over five feet taller than the female, heavily scarred and gray-furred, this Kong was much more massive and terrible to behold. One eye was missing, the empty socket raked with three long-healed scars. The size, Ishara noticed, could easily fit the pattern of Gaw's clawed forelimb. His right arm had limited use due to missing muscle mass and teeth marks in a similar gruesome pattern that was also long healed.

"Run!" Kublai yelled. Magwich beckoned, and they all ran after him. They reached the slope that led down to the beach of the lagoon, and half-ran, half-stumbled downward, pausing to look back at the fight.

From their vantage point they could see that from behind the battling giants Deathrunners surged, converging on the Kongs, roaring and hissing as they raced to aid their leader. Several of them swarmed the dying female Kong while the others flew to Gaw's aid as she scrambled to regain balance under the onslaught of the enraged bull Kong.

His blows shook the trees and his roars deafened the ears as several Deathrunners leapt onto his back, making him lose just enough balance to send his strike off-target. Gaw managed to feint a turn to one side then shift with impossible swiftness for a creature its size to the Kong's blind side, knocking him against a group of trees. As Gaw did so she sprang backward and, trapping the Kong against the trees, impaled him on her huge dorsal spikes. The Kong's immediate reaction was to push her body away with a mighty shove of his one good arm, leaving him badly bleeding from four great puncture wounds in his chest. One of them had found its target in the Kong's heart and he staggered forward, coughing blood. Without hesitation Gaw turned to finish the dying female Kong. That was the last Ishara, Kublai and the rest saw as they fled for their lives. From a distance they heard a mournful, high-pitched shriek followed by more roaring. The jungle obscured the rest of the battle, but the bedlam re-echoed in the canopies of the trees, which rattled and rocked spasmodically from the impacts below, sending flying creatures cawing in a frenzy.

Magwich said something that included the word "Kong." It sounded like a question.
Kublai said, "One of the Kongs at least is dead. Dead."
Magwich didn't understand. Kublai mimed falling.
"Dead," Magwich said in English. His grim look showed he understood.

In ancient times the ancestors must have made a pathway down to the beach. Perhaps it was a place where their fishermen went out on the sea. At any rate, thousands of years ago, someone had carved rude steps in the cliff leading down to the shore of the inland body of water, which had one opening to the sea–but the route, treacherous now with the smoothness brought by erosion, was at least a way to descend.

Before they even started, Ishara saw the tents well back on the beach, above the high-water mark, two of them, and men standing there, gazing upward, some of them armed with the thunderspears. And far out a strange sort of canoe, very big and rigged for a sail, had been pulled up onto the sand. Lying stranded on the beach of the largest of three humped islands in the lagoon rested a huge vessel, the biggest one Ishara had ever seen. Waves creamed around it, and its tangle of sails and ropes trailed and dangled.

They came here on that, she thought. They are fishermen from some strange place, and they came through the break that leads to the ocean, ran upon the sands there and lost their vessel.

With a shiver, she remembered what she had glimpsed earlier: something dark on the water and the lizard-headed monsters feeding. Feeding on men, she realized now–these were the survivors.

They reached the foot of the cliff and some of the men from the beach crowded over, asking questions in their strange language. One of them asked something about Skeets, and Magwich said shortly, "Dead," a word that Ishara now recognized. He summoned another man over, not the same kind as he, but a smaller man, crooked of limb and back, and relatively old. Magwich pointed at him. "Lanun," he said. He pointed to her. "Ishara." Then he said something to Lanun. The old man hobbled forward, peering at her and Kublai with red-rimmed eyes.

Ishara winced. His breath came foul even from an arm's length away. Magwich was telling Lanun something, and the codger nodded and asked a question: "Apa yang orang anda dipanggil? Apa suku yang anda?"

Ishara caught only a little of it: orang sounded like oranka, a word not used much, an old, nearly dead word. It meant "people" or "tribe." Apa might be the Tagu word aba, "what." Anda sounded like the old Tagu word "thou," though that was almost never spoken, either. Guessing that the man was asking about her tribe, she said, "We are Tagatu. Tagatu. People of the island."

"Ta-gah-tu," the old inquisitor repeated. He said something to Magwich, who spoke to him. Then the old man asked, "Anda akan membawa kita kepada bangsamu?"

Ishara frowned, trying to decipher the meaning. "Wilt thou something take something?" To Kublai, she said, "I think he wants us to take him to the village."

Kublai nodded and mimed eating. The men grew excited and chattered like Deathrunners closing in on prey. Magwich pointed to the great canoe pulled up onto the beach.

"They want to sail there," Kublai said. "Will that canoe take us all?"

"Let's see." They walked down the beach. There were nearly thirty men, plus Ishara. The boat might just hold twenty if they crowded in, though it would ride low in the water. Magwich pointed at the much larger vessel and said something to his men. He pointed at six of them. Reluctantly, they pushed the canoe, as Ishara thought of it, into the surf and hurriedly scrambled aboard and grabbed oars. Ishara watched them row out.

At the beached ship, they climbed through ropes with the agility of suncreepers, the round-headed lizards the size of a man's forearm that swung in the jungle trees. One dropped down and seemed to saw at something, and three others helped him haul a capsized boat from the wreckage. They tied this to the canoe and rowed back, towing it. Once ashore, they pulled the capsized boat up and dumped the water from it. Another canoe, Ishara thought, but it would easily hold a dozen. Together with the first one, that would suffice.

It took the men some time to break camp and load the boats. They handled four kegs very gingerly and carefully. Ishara wondered what was in them. Not food, for they seemed to have none—fresh water, perhaps. These men and the ones who had—befriended Ishara and Kublai? Or captured them? Anyway, they carried a total of twelve thunderspears among them.

Magwich appointed a dozen men to the smaller boat, and then he gestured for Ishara and Kublai to climb into the larger one. He motioned them toward the stern. He and the other men ran the boat into the sea, and then Magwich easily leapt in and urged Ishara and Kublai all the way back to the stern. He sat on the stern thwart, grasping a steering oar; they sat on either side of him.

The other men, several of them shoeless, shirtless and covered with many strange ink markings, had climbed aboard, seized their oars, and rowed them out from land. Magwich called out something, and from the thwart ahead of Ishara the scraggly-haired Lunun nodded as he turned and asked her, "Arah mana?"

Ishara recognized that: "How do we go?"

She pointed. To Kublai, she said, "The old stories say not all of our ancestors reached the island. I wonder if some found a home elsewhere. Some of the words are like ours. If the descendants—"

"Belay, girl," Magwich said from behind her, and she understood not a word of that. But he tapped her on the shoulder, and when she looked at him, the big man touched a finger to his lips, a clear sign for silence.

Ishara, feeling more like a captive than a rescuer, folded her hands in her lap and spoke no more.

Kublai, who had been on many fishing expeditions in his short life, made his way forward to the prow of the big boat and offered guidance by hand signals and gestures. He helped the sailors thread the treacherous rocks and guided them through the one opening of the lagoon and into the northern expanse of the inland sea. With an ebbing tide, they shot through with a speed that reminded Ishara of their wild ride on the log down a rushing river.

At a command from Magwich, the sailors raised a mast and spread a triangular sail. Eventually, they turned westward through a straight with the rugged cliffs of the island off to the left that opened into the great ocean. Emerging from the strait they turned southwest, hugging the coast, but continually shifting the sail, tacking left and right to stay well beyond the breakers crashing into the rocks. The men in the boat they towed had oars out and now and then rowed hard to take the strain off the towline and keep their own craft on course.

Then they came to a maze of sandbars. The other boat, the smaller one, was light enough to glide over them, but the larger one scraped bottom three or four times. The men shouted in alarm when long necks rose around them–larpenu, the Tagatu called the creatures, "turtle-snakes."

The great honeycomb cliffs appeared, waterfalls and cascades roaring over them with a constant thunder, sending up sheets of fine spray that spread through the air like a fog. "There is a passage through," Kublai said. He tried to make signs, but Magwich looked puzzled. Ishara spoke to Lunun, repeating and varying her words until he grasped them and spoke in Magwich's language: "Crooked passage. Have to furl sail. Oars only."

The men reluctantly followed Magwich's order and veered to the south east, away from the ocean back towards the island. Kublai knelt in the bow. He raised an arm and moved it to indicate which way Magwich should move the tiller. And so, the islander slowly led the two craft through a maelstrom of boiling white water, past the very foot of waterfalls greater than Niagara. The spray alone threatened to swamp them, and Magwich had his men bail furiously.

"There!" Kublai shouted, moving his arm backward and forward. "Ahead! The little hidden beach!" They passed through the troubled water and suddenly glided over what amounted to a still pool. The prow of the boat crunched into the sand, and sailors leapt out to drag it up onto the beach.

"Well done!" Magwich shouted. The second, towed boat, came in nearly swamped, but still barely afloat. The sailors hauled both up as far as they could and lashed them to a few sturdy tree boles. Then Kublai led them on a zigzag path that came out at the seaward foot of the Wall.

Tagatu sentries saw them at once and shouted down a challenge.

Kublai called out, "It's Ishara, daughter of On-Tagu, and Kublai the hunter! We have found strange people, lost and hungry!"

Within minutes the straggling party reached the gates, and the guards cautiously opened them. Magwich stood back and motioned his men through. The islanders crowded around, touching them and murmuring in astonishment. Magwich said something, and his men pushed the islanders away–not violently, but insistently–and Kublai said, "They have left their canoes behind at the secret beach. They don't want you to meddle with them."

"What is this? What are these? Men or devils?" The voice was harsh and hoarse, and the twisted figure of Bar-Atu, his face a devilish mask behind its network of self-inflicted scars, the sign of a high-ranking Atu warrior.

"Fishermen, I think," Kublai said. "Men of–another island?"

"There are no other islands beyond those we can see with our own eyes!" Bar-Atu snarled.

Magwich pointed to himself. "Magwich."

"What does he say?" Bar-Atu demanded.

"His name, we think," Ishara told him. "Magwich." "Magwich," the cult leader repeated.

Kublai pointed to the Shaitan and said, "Bar-Atu."

"Barratu," Magwich said, mispronouncing the name slightly. He extended his hand.

Bar-Atu stared at it. "Is he cursing me?"

"Maybe begging," Ishara said. "They have no food." She could not hold in the news any longer. "We saw a Kong! A living Kong–two of them, a mother and a young one–maybe even a third!"

"Two or three Kongs?" the crowd buzzed. "They challenged Gaw!" Ishara said.

Bar-Atu gestured savagely. "Enough talk!" These words disturbed him and he quickly redirected the focus. He pointed with his ceremonial scepter at the group of strangers, eyeing them cautiously but confidently. "Atu! Take these men to the lodge. Allow them their fill and make them content–for the time being."

"Food," Lunun said, shambling through the crowd to stand beside Magwich. He said pleadingly, "Kami lapar! Kami lapar!"

The crowd murmured, for the words sounded something like their own language. If so, the old man was saying, "We starve!"

"Take them. Feed them," Bar-Atu said.

Ishara mimed eating and gestured for the strangers to follow Bar-Atu. Magwich held Charlie back and took two rifles from the others, giving one to Charlie. He motioned to the others, and they followed three of the Atu to the village and the longhouse where islanders were already bringing food and drink.

Magwich gestured to the doorway into the longhouse then to himself and Charlie. "What does he mean?" Bar-Atu asked Ishara.

"I think he and the one named Charlie will guard the door," she said. "They don't trust us yet. The spears they hold spit thunder and death. They are weapons."

"They may stay," Bar-Atu said. He gestured to four of his warriors. "Remain here with spears. Guard these humans. If they attack, kill them." But he smiled at Magwich, who smiled back. Ishara shivered a little. It was like two great sharks baring their teeth at each other.

The Storyteller sagged in disappointment when Ishara told her the storage vault had been emptied. She agreed that perhaps the people of the Old City had removed the stored materials as a last resort.

She said, shaking her head wearily, "So many centuries have passed. None but the Storytellers recall that this is not the first time that the Atu have caused troubles for the Tagatu people. They were also the reason the Old City fell."

Ishara said in a soft voice, "I often wondered, if we are descended from a great people from the center of the island, how did we come to live behind this Wall?"

The Storyteller seemed to gaze into the past. "Our stories tell that the Tagatu people came to this island to escape a terrible catastrophe. They brought the Kongs with them to ensure their survival. The Wall was built for protection against the island's monsters. In time, the Tagatu overcame the Deathrunners and even Gaw! Our Tagatu ancestors reached heights so great that the Kongs themselves were no longer needed. The Tagatu moved beyond the Wall, to the most fertile and beautiful piece of land near the center of the island between the forked branches of a great river. There they built what we now call the Old City, and it thrived for ages."

"If that is all true, how could we have come to this?" asked Ishara.

"Misplaced pride proved their undoing. The Atu were prone to such temptations and took for granted the strength gained by combining their considerable gifts with those of their Tagu brothers and sisters. Something happened. I cannot see clearly whether it was intentional or accidental, but the monsters of the island breached the protections of the City, and the Tagu were made to blame. They were banished from the City and forced to flee back to the protection of this Wall. Perhaps the greatest of all the Storytellers, Mari, led them through this terrible time, and because of her, we still exist."

"But the Atu, why did they turn on the Tagu?"

The Storyteller explained, "The Atu followed a charismatic leader made insane by his monomania for the Atu culture. In banishing the Tagu, he sowed the seeds of doom for the great City of the Tagatu. Only the Tagu compounded the repellents that kept the monsters at bay. After some generations, the Deathrunner population increased, and Gaw re-emerged to lead them. The end came suddenly, and the last vestiges of the proud Atu people were forced to flee. Those who survived arrived at the Wall and begged for sanctuary. The king of that time naively allowed them through, but they had to swear loyalty for all time. What else would they say?"

Ishara and the Storyteller sat in the hut atop the Wall. From below came shouts and cheers. Grimly, the Storyteller said, "Sometime after that, I know not how many years, the Atu broke their promise. A horrible war broke out that forever altered the unity of our people. Some suggest that the long, unbroken line of Storytellers was interrupted for the first time, perhaps as punishment for our foolishness in trusting the Atu again–who can tell? The special gifts that had always been the hallmark of the Storytellers vanished, until Providence saw fit to restore them sometime later. You, yourself, are the recipient of such gifts, are you not?"

Ishara blinked. "You mean I–"

The Storyteller seemed to gaze into the past.

The question was rhetorical, and the Storyteller did not pause for the startled Ishara to speak. "The result was a blankness in our memory as the Wall grew ever larger in our minds, ever more intimidating and crushing to our souls. We began to lose our sense of self and now, the Atu madness has taken over completely with the rise of the maniac, Bar-Atu. Listen!"

Even from that distance they could hear the Shatain's loud, hoarse voice: "If there are Kongs still alive, let On-Tagu prove his right to rule! Let him capture and break one of these creatures and make it a servant of ours, to protect us! He is a Tagu, and descended from the fabled Zantu! If he is a true king, let him prove it!"

The Storyteller stood abruptly, as though she could take no more. She strode out of the hut, and from atop the wall, she shouted down to the people who had gathered to hear Bar-Atu: "My people, listen! What Bar-Atu proposes cannot be done! No Zantu traditions have survived. No one now knows how they gained the trust and loyalty of the Kongs! Remember, the Kongs are not just fierce, not just powerful, but intelligent! A Kong can never be broken! No Kong has ever been a servant!"

But Bar-Atu's thugs jeered at her. Some even threw stones as high as they could. Though not able to reach her, it was an act of disrespect that would have been unthinkable in earlier times. Shaking her head, she went back into the hut. "Ishara, I fear for your father. On-Tagu is sick and weak in body. Do not allow this plotter Bar-Atu to provoke him to do what would surely kill him."

"I will try," Ishara promised, "but it seems hopeless."

"It is never hopeless, Ishara, never forget that. There is always a way. Even if it is not granted that we find it at the time of our choosing, there is *always* a way. Of this I am certain. *Believe!*"

Days passed with things still balanced between Bar-Atu's challenge and the opinion of many, perhaps most, of the villagers, that what he spoke of was not possible. Their allegiance to the Storyteller and their traditions was deep. The Storyteller's warning that any attempt to capture a Kong could end only in disaster for the Tagatu was not taken lightly. And so, the villagers hesitated, their collective will poised between two fears: fear of Gaw and the monsters of the island, and the fear that following what Bar-Atu proposed, to conquer those monsters, would bring into their midst an even more terrible monster. A general malaise descended over the peninsula, making the heat and whiffs of dank jungle from beyond the Wall seem more oppressive than usual.

During those days Ishara spent much time with Charlie, the youngest member of Magwich's crew, now that Skeets, the cabin boy, was dead. She taught him Tagatu words, and in return, he taught her English. Before a month had flown by–the island was entering its dry season–they could converse tolerably well.

But what Charlie spoke of gave her much uneasiness. "Magwich says that Kublai has told him of great wealth in the Old City," Charlie said in a combination of Tagatu speech, English, and gestures. "Treasures. In the old houses and caverns there. Magwich wants it, whatever it may be."

"The treasures are gifts of knowledge, not of gold," Ishara protested.

"Bar-Atu wants a Kong," Charlie said. "He praises Kublai's courage in going beyond the Wall. He tells Magwich that if he will help capture the Kong, then he can have as much gold and jewels as his men can haul from the Old City in one march. He even sent Atu to help repair our ship. During the high tide they helped pull it farther onto the beach where it ran aground. They secured it there when the tide went out. It is half-full of water, but our pumps can get rid of most of that. If the hole can be properly repaired, we would be able to leave, but it needs more work than our crew can do."

"What Bar-Atu demands of my father, though," Ishara said, "is not possible."

"He tells the people that if On-Tagu–did I say the name right? If On-Tagu is a true king, he can tame the Kong. I think Kublai is swayed. He is a young man, younger than I am, and ambitious. Bar-Atu says that Kublai will have the honor of being the chief of the men sent to capture Kong. Bar-Atu says that Kublai is the only one of our people in these days to dare to go into what he calls the 'Otherway.'"

"But I was with him!" Ishara said. "That is not true!"

"Bar-Atu does not count you. Kublai has Atu ancestors. He says he is a descendant of–Kai? Is that right?"

"The Kai were fierce Atu warriors in the ancient days," Ishara said. "It is true, Kublai has Kai blood in his veins."

"And you are a Tagu woman, Bar-Atu will not admit that you had anything to do with the trip."

After that, Ishara repeatedly tried to speak with Kublai, but her friend from childhood had no time. He was busy supervising the construction of great rafts–for the sailors who had gone inland earlier had no desire to take the Otherway back to the beach where their ship now rested. They would rather risk travelling past the falls and up through the wide channel to the north, on the western coast of the inland sea. It was the only way to effectively transport such a large load. They thought they could avoid attack by sea monsters by hugging the coastline, but brought several harpoon-like spears just in case.

On the morning before the day that the sailors proposed to take the rafts out, Ishara finally found a chance to speak with Kublai privately. "This is wrong!" she told him.

He held her shoulders. "Bar-Atu has many followers," he said. "We have to admit that. When I bring the Kong back–"

"Kublai! The Storyteller warns that you will die! No one today knows the ways of gaining the trust of a Kong! Not my father, not me, not even the Storyteller!"

"I will bring the small Kong back, the one no more than fourteen feet tall," Kublai said with stubborn assurance. "He may still be young enough to break. *Any* animal can be broken by the right master! That is the one we will take. But Magwich's men must go to their vessel for more of his 'rifles' and other, more powerful weapons, for ropes and old sails to hold the Kong and bind him."

"The man Magwich–I have heard that he wants gold and treasure. You promised him this? You know there is no treasure in the Old City!"

For a moment Kublai looked defiant but ashamed. "We need his help, and that of his men. I did not lie. I told him there may be gold in the Old City. And there may be. Who knows?"

"You never used to mislead people," she said miserably.

"Our need is great," he said. "Gaw is strong and leads the Deathrunners against us. For now, the Wall is repaired, but they are merciless! One day they will break through, and scatter death when they do! Besides, what if the Kongs have already killed Gaw? We will find pieces of whatever is left and bring them back as proof that it was no god and the people's confidence in that madman will be shaken. Ishara, we have to do all we can to save the people–lie if we must, bargain with Bar-Atu if we have to–even capture the Kong!"

"No," Ishara pleaded, drawing on the strength of the Storyteller's words for courage. "There is always hope, always another way. Kublai, if you care for me, don't do this!"

"I care for you," he said in a quiet voice. "But I care for our people, too. They are more important than either of us. Ishara, I will do what I must!"

The night came, and day followed the night, and as soon as the sun came up and the tide began to ebb, the sailors and some Atu warriors armed with harpoons fashioned from wood and sharpened bone poled the two rafts away from shore. They retraced their path back across the still water, then through the narrow, treacherous route at the foot of the falls, then turned and made their way around the large island and into the mouth of the strait that opened into the great inland sea. Far to the south was the beach to the west of Skull Mountain where Ishara and Kublai had ridden the sleeks. Ishara insisted she go with them to the very end–but Kublai forbade it, and Bar-Atu had his followers push her away, though they offered no violence to the daughter of the king, On-Tagu.

And so, she was not with Kublai as the men rowed out. Even with the expert seamanship of Magwich's men and that of the islanders, the trip took the better part of three days, with only one successfully repelled sea serpent attack, before they reached their destination. A party of four men from Magwich's crew and two of Bar-Atu's warriors camped aboard the beached ship–its holds now emptied of water–and maintained a guard.

By then afternoon had come, and the rest of that day the sailors spent aboard the ship, finding and cleaning firearms. Some had been hopelessly rusted and fouled, but others had remained dry. These they cleaned and tested. At first the loud explosions frightened Kublai, but he grew used to them–and when one of the sailors shot a smaller glider from the sky, he saw how the weapon dealt death at a distance.

Kublai began to desire one of his own.

An hour after arriving on the beach to the west of Skull Mountain where Kublai and Ishara had ridden the sleeks, the Shatain drew Kublai apart. "My men have climbed up to the hills just below the great skull," he said. "In months past they have witnessed Kongs, at least three of them. One very tall male, an older one, whose shoulders are gray. One a little smaller, female it was assumed because of the juvenile one who accompanied them–the one you first saw. My men say they have heard the calls the Kongs made to one another and can imitate them. We will use this as a lure."

"So, you knew Kongs still lived even before my encounter with them?" questioned Kublai, "Why did you not let anyone know?"

"My decisions are not for you to question!" The shaman said, heatedly, then quickly controlled his emotions to reassure Kublai. "You did not think I would embark on such a mission only to fail, do you? My knowledge is being used to benefit our people! Listen to my plan:

"Before we left, I arranged for ropes and everything we need to be ready at the village, so the Kong can be secured once we return with him. Tomorrow–tomorrow we will travel east and try to drive the Kong towards the Wall." He gazed sternly at the younger man. "You. You, Kublai, will be in charge here. See that the Kong comes along the cliffs until he is close to the Wall. Then…we will do the rest." His ceremonial scars gave him a terrible smile.

"My plan is already in place," the young warrior answered.

"Good, I rely on you then. We will allow On-Tagu to prove himself worthy of being king. Then you and Ishara–it would be good to marry the daughter of a king. That could make it possible for an Atu man to then rule as king himself–I would be in support of such a match," Bar-Atu smiled.

And though Kublai did not trust Bar-Atu, he had no choice but to nod and smile back.

The next morning, Kublai and his force set out toward Skull Mountain. One of Bar-Atu's scouts pointed upward. At the summit of a nearly sheer cliff a tangle of jungle showed. "That is where the young Kong has been seen," the warrior said.

Kublai asked anxiously, "What of the mother and father Kong?"

"We have not seen them at all. We watched the young one move about, here and there, anxious, as though looking for something. Then we lost track of him until he appeared atop the mountain."

Kublai feared the worst. *Gaw must have killed both adult Kongs. But I cannot let them know that or they will not believe in the potential of the young Kong's power.*

"We must try to lure the little one while he is still nearby," the Atu insisted anxiously. "While we have the time." He threw his head back, put his hand beside his mouth, and gave a shrill, wavering call. Atu trackers were superlative mimics. "That is an imitation of the cry his mother gave to summon him in the past. We will see if he comes."

They did not have to wait long. A dark form appeared at the summit of the cliff, uttering calls of his own. From time to time the warrior repeated the call, and always they heard the Kong reply, though they rarely saw him.

An accented voice asked, "Do you see and hear what I do, young master Kublai?"

Kublai turned, startled to see Magwich standing behind him. Magwich chuckled at his expression. "Didn't mean to surprise you," he said wryly. "Guess you islanders ain't the only ones who know how to sneak around, eh? Been waiting to get you alone."

For a moment Kublai only stared at the strange foreign man, who merely grinned. Part of Kublai's mind wondered if Magwich were truly as friendly as he tried to appear. "Anybody can be took off guard, lad," the older man said with a wink. "Don't fret about it."

Kublai ignored the comments, not really understanding what was said, except something about "see." Magwich eyed him intently.

"I can see it in your eyes, king-to-be, you heard and saw it, too," said the grizzled pirate, pointing at the mountain. "It's my bet that young Kong is now an orphan. I know something about the movement of critters, been around 'em in all parts of the world. That beastie ain't right. Agitated you might say. I think that screech we heard on the way back from that jungle scrap was the sound of his momma getting her throat ripped out after the big one was stabbed by that Gaw's spiked back. If that's the case, you've got the young one here chasing a ghost, and when he finds out he's been had, you could be dealin' with something worse than a wounded animal. So be careful, boy, or you may end up with a lot of blood on your hands and find that your plan's goin' all t'hell."

Kublai did not understand everything Magwich said, but the tone filled in many of the blanks. After giving the outsider a hard stare, he nodded in the affirmative. Just then Bar-Atu's men, who had doubled back to get Kublai, arrived and he left with them.

They came to the complex, steep honeycomb cliffs that lined the side of the mountain until they fell in sharply near the skull's gaping maw. Here the clamor of the adjacent waterfalls threatened to drown all other sound—but the two warriors, expert in animal sounds, leapt to the lower stones of the cliff and began to climb, finding handholds that a dinosaur could not possibly use. At the crest of the crag, they resumed their calls.

Theoretically the plan was simple, to lead the young Kong to a pre-determined point by carefully orchestrated calls. Others remained hidden, to be joined by those whose checkpoints had been passed by the Kong to correct detours from the chosen general path with fire and spears.

The sentinels seemed ready. Secretly using the last of the Storyteller's repellent from his previous sojourn with Ishara, Kublai went on alone, until he sighted the Wall to the south. When almost there, he stopped at a place where overhead, the solid rock, eaten from below by the sea, jutted out in a great shelf. There he lit a torch that flared bright yellow to indicate to others he was ready. In turn, they each lit their torches to show others the path to the Wall and to warn them to prepare themselves.

Minutes later, Kublai arrived at the Wall. A rope tossed from the top uncoiled in flight, and Kublai seized the end of it. Men above him hauled him up hand over hand, until he stood on the wall-walk and could look back. So far, he could see no trace of the Kong. And then, distantly, he heard the warrior repeat the luring call.

"Move!"

Kublai retreated as a party of men, both Tagatu and the European intruders, hurried along with nets and ropes, things taken from Magwich's ship. "He comes!" one of these men shouted, pointing. Two human figures burst from the undergrowth and ran full-speed toward the Wall, while others stationed atop the Wall picked up the mimicry of the mother Kong's call. "Ropes!" the running men screamed. Kublai helped throw one of the two ropes down, and the man in the lead seized it and they hauled him up. "Just behind us!" the warrior said as they swung him to safety.

A rumbling voice answered it, now sounding angry—and through the trees surged the Kong, crouching low, but on two legs, not four. All calls instantly stopped, causing the young Kong to pause, with a confused expression, looking both utterly bewildered and crestfallen. He hurried across the clearing in a vain attempt to find the mother Kong.

One of the mimics, still some distance from the Wall, his excitement at a fever pitch, re-sounded the call. Others atop the Wall picked it up, causing the young Kong's head to whirl around and stare at them. The intelligent beast realized the sounds were not from his mother. His look of bewilderment quickly contorted into a mask of terrifying anger. He pounded the ground before rearing up and then barreling headlong towards the mimic, who was already being pulled up. As he saw the enraged Kong rushing towards him, the caller yelled, "Hurry! Pull me up!" Five men frantically hauled hand over hand.

Furiously roaring, the Kong leapt, insofar as a creature its size was capable of doing so, trying to seize the man or the rope. But he fell just short and collided with the Wall. The men above felt the impact through their feet as others nervously spread and threw their nets—

They descended with a *thwump* onto the Kong as he fell back to the ground, entangling him.

Instantly a dozen warriors slid down ropes, landing, seizing the nets, pulling them tight.

The Kong roared in outrage, trying to stand and grapple with the men who were tiny by comparison with him. He only tangled his arms more tightly in the meshes—

Atu warriors on the Wall used blowguns to send darts raining on Kong, darts tipped with an Atu toxin that put most creatures to sleep. Many missed their mark, but some stuck in the Kong's scalp and shoulders. He roared again and lunged against the Wall, striking it so hard that Kublai lost his footing and nearly fell off the inside edge of the wall-walk.

He got to his feet and grabbed a rope to swing down and help in the struggle. The Kong still raged, but the nets and ropes hopelessly entangled him—and his movements grew slower as the toxin took effect. Still he was dangerous—one warrior got too close, and a sudden swipe of the Kong's hand sent him tumbling and screaming from the pain of a broken leg.

Kublai managed to seize the net entangling that hand and put a rope through the mesh, tying it tight around the wrist. "Hold it down!" he yelled.

The Kong's strength ebbed as the toxin flooded his bloodstream. He still struggled, but with weakening force. Finally, the great anthropoid crumpled into unconsciousness.

The men cheered. A harsh voice broke out from atop the Wall: "Well done, Kublai! Now bind him securely so he cannot break free. We will haul him inside the gates and tie him so he cannot escape—and then if On-Tagu cannot charm this animal into submission, hunger and beatings will break his spirit!"

Every single Atu warrior, even the one who had been badly injured, guarded as the people dragged the unconscious and bound Kong onto an enormous litter and then used rollers to haul the heavy body through the gates and into the village. Bar-Atu had a particular place in mind, one where an ancient, thick, gnarled tree grew. There he had the villagers lash the Kong to the tree. By that time, the great animal had begun to growl and move weakly, trying to struggle against the bindings.

Ishara had followed the crowd. Now they stood at a distance staring at the Kong. Then, abruptly, the Kong woke, heaved at the ropes with no success, and bellowed in outrage. Kublai, to Ishara's surprise, approached the creature and spoke harshly to him. The Kong writhed more furiously; his face contorted in rage. Kublai shouted at him to be quiet—and then, with a sudden movement, Kublai raised a knotted rope and struck hard at the young Kong's face, causing him to howl.

"No!" Ishara clenched her hands into fists.

Bar-Atu, though, was laughing. "Only the bite of the whip until you obey!" he shouted, shaking his staff in the face of the Kong. "No food, no water, until you weaken and obey! You will serve us!" He turned. "Where is On-Tagu? Where is your king? He is a Tagu! His ancestors first tamed these beasts and made them our guardians! Where is he now?"

"I am here." The crowd parted. On-Tagu, who had a breathing trouble, came forward, leaning on a tall staff. "I am here, Bar-Atu." He took a deep breath and then in a voice louder than any Ishara had heard him use in many months, he said for all to hear: "And I say this is wrong! The Zantu secrets are lost—but I know they did not include starvation. They did not rely on beatings! I tell you, my people, holding this Kong prisoner will take us to disaster!"

The older man gasped for air for a few seconds and then turned and walked away. Already the crowd murmured, many of them agreeing with their king. All of them marveling at the sight of a living Kong in their midst. Even a young one was a creature to inspire awe. An angry Bar-Atu shouted, "Go to your homes! Stay away from this place. Kublai will show you how to tame a Kong!"

Ishara wept, not in public, but only when alone with the Storyteller in her hut. The old woman was grim: "Your father is right. No good will come of this foolish act. Bar-Atu is making a slave of Kublai as he tries to do with the Kong. Yet the Atu warriors support him. I fear for what time will bring. We must remain strong."

In the next few days the Atu built a palisade around the tree and the Kong, concealing him from the people. Kublai angrily refused to speak of what they were doing—he would not say whether the captive had even been fed, or if he, Kublai, were still beating the bound, helpless creature daily. It was clear from the cracking sounds and howls that men were torturing the Kong, and her imagination conjured terrible scenes.

"This is warrior's work," Kublai told Ishara. "Stay away."

And in his words Ishara seemed to hear the voice of Bar-Atu. Five days after the capture, Ishara spoke to Charlie, Magwich's man. By that time, they could converse, haltingly, sharing English and the Tagatu language in a kind of broken pidgin.

"Have they fed the Kong?" Ishara asked.

Charlie said, "No. Bar-Atu won't allow. No food. No water. He weakens."

"That is wrong!"

It took much talk and much persuading, but at last Charlie reluctantly told Ishara that he would be one of the guards at the barrier that night. It happened to be one of the full moon, and by signs and drawings in the sand, Charlie let Ishara know that if she came when the moon stood at zenith—about the middle of the night—she might bring the Kong some food and drink. Ishara determined she would. She did not even tell the Storyteller of her intent.

With a bag of fruit and a basin of water, she went silently to the rear of the enclosure beneath the light of the moon. The usual sounds of the dry season enlivened the night: insects and night-hunters in the trees, distant bellows of the great jungle animals coming faintly from far beyond the Wall. Though the dry season had not far advanced, already the earth beneath her feet had the hard, compacted feel of weeks without rain.

She came within sight of the palisade and waited until Charlie, holding one of the thunderspears, came walking slowly around the outside perimeter, on guard. She spoke his name, and he beckoned.

"Be quick," he told her, pointing to the gap where she might enter.

Ishara slipped through the narrow opening. A torch burned there every night, and in its ruddy light she saw the Kong, slumped, looking utterly despondent. "I am here," she said softly. The creature tried to move its huge head in her direction, but could not.

She slowly came within Kong's field of vision. The eyes had become sunken and without hope. The lips looked cracked. Ishara approached, paused, and bowed her head. "I am sorry for you," she said in her softest voice.

The Kong's gaze shifted towards Ishara.

"Drink," she said, and came close to offer him water. She had to reach high to let him sip from the basin. He sniffed and then gulped desperately, spilling a little. He drank the basin dry and then, pathetically, licked it to get the last drops. Ishara set it aside and picked up the bag. "Eat," she said, holding up a melon half the size of her head.

The Kong took it in one bite, chewed it and gulped, then moaned. "More," she said, and fed him everything she had brought. Now the Kong locked his gaze on her. She felt as if he were trying to memorize her, to burn her image into his mind so he would know her again.

She placed her hand on his body, scabbed from some lashing with the knotted rope, and though he flinched, he relaxed at her soft touch and groaned in—gratitude? Despair? She could not tell.

And then—voices from outside! One was Kublai's. She heard and hurried away without a parting word to the Kong, slipping out through the opening and hiding in the brush. She could hear Charlie: "Don't. He's bad tonight. Fierce. Don't go in."

"I will offer him drink," Kublai said, and for that moment Ishara's heart melted—but then Kublai added, "If he roars, I will throw it on the ground and beat him!"

For some moments all was silent, and then she heard Kublai's exclamation of anger: "Who has done this?" Then, "Fool! You fed him! You gave him drink!" Ishara winced—in her alarm, she had forgotten the water basin, the bag. The sounds of a scuffle came, and in a voice of insane anger, Kublai yelled, "I will have Magwich beat you!"

"I don't understand you!" Charlie yammered in English. "What's wrong?" Ishara burst out from her hiding place. "Kublai!"

Kublai had backed Charlie against the outside of the palisade and held a knife to his throat. "Why are you here? Go to your father!" Kublai shouted.

She strode to him. "I fed the Kong. I gave him water! This man knew nothing of it."

"You had no right!"

"I am the daughter of the King!" she said fiercely. "And my father and I say you have no right to treat the Kong this way! You are doing wrong!"

More voices approaching. Kublai shoved Charlie so hard that he fell. Then, in his own broken English, Kublai pointed to Ishara and told the fallen man, "Stay away! No talk! Death to talk!"

"What is wrong?" The King himself had come, breathing hard, leaning on his staff.

"Ask your daughter!" Kublai snarled.

Bar-Atu joined them. "Is the Kong weak enough?"

"He has been given water and food," Kublai said. He glared at Ishara, but then he said, "I do not know who dared to do this."

"Find him!" Bar-Atu howled. "He shall be killed!"

"No!" On-Tagu had glanced at his daughter, and even in the moonlight he seemed to be able to read her thoughts and her guilt. "I say no."

He drew a deep breath. "Bar-Atu, you say I may prove my worth by bringing the Kong to obedience. So be it. Yes, I am of Tagu blood. Yes, some of my ancestors were Zantu, the partners of the Kongs. I will try. The Kongs were much more than mere beasts to the Zantu; they were their life-long companions. To honor their memory, I will not use starvation! I will not use beatings!" To the crowd that had gathered, On-Atu proclaimed, "Hear me, my people! I will do my best to–" he paused to draw an uncertain breath– "to bond with the Kong as my Zantu ancestors did in ancient times. If I succeed and a Kong once again aids in our protection, I expect you all, all to obey me! Tagu and Atu alike! And you will listen no more to wild words and evil promises! I say this as your king!"

The people cheered. Only Bar-Atu gave the king a sudden, evil glare.

From the shadows, standing unseen, the Storyteller looked over at Ishara, who shivered despite the heat of the night. Both knew the impossibility of the King's speech, and sensed the limit of the days he had remaining.

On-Tagu's personal guard took over the task of securing the palisade. The king and his daughter came every day with food and water. Stout chains from the ship had been fashioned to keep the Kong bound to the tree, and the thick hempen ropes were loosened to allow some movement of his legs and arms. No longer beaten or starved, over the course of weeks the Kong slowly gained strength. Gradually, the great creature accepted without anxiety the water and food that Ishara held to his lips, but it was clear to her that this creature's immense power could not truly be controlled. She sensed a spirit that would never be broken.

She begged her father, "Set him free. This is a wild Kong, not one who's known the companionship of the Zantu from his birth. And that tree will not hold him much longer."

The king shook his head. "I must try. I promised the people. I promised the people. I have Zantu blood in my veins, and surely the Kong must know that. He will listen to me, you will see–"

Ishara looked with great kindness on her father when he said this. "The people are lucky to have such a king as you. Rest here and let me take care of cleaning and feeding the Kong." In her heart, Ishara was crushed. It was clear to her that her father was losing his senses.

Held off by fear and the stench, others had to be sternly ordered to help Ishara in cleaning the Kong, for he had been forced to crouch in his own waste for many days. The Kong did not attempt to strike at those who assisted in caring for him. Occasionally he tested the length and strength of his tethers, but seemed to accept them. Ishara took great pains to calm and soothe the captive giant. She had the uncanny ability to hold his gaze almost to the point of his ignoring all else, though she knew she had no mystic power over the Kong.

And yet she also felt that between her and the Kong a special connection was growing. She had the conviction that Kong did not react or relate to her as a mere animal might. In his own way, he was aware of his situation and knew that he was being helped. But she could also intuit something more. Something she could not quite understand or put into words yet, and it troubled her.

As Ishara gained Kong's confidence, Bar-Atu fumed. He spoke to Kublai: "The king has lost his mind. He shows no sign of controlling the Kong! But his daughter has a strange gift. It could ruin our plans. You must wrest control of the Kong from her! Only the lash and pain will break the creature to our needs!"

Kublai dropped his gaze to the earth, as he frequently did when Bar-Atu spoke belittlingly of Ishara.

The Shatain's voice took on a crafty, confiding tone: "Break the Kong, and you will be hailed as the new king. King Kublai! You are the one to lead our people to recover our old glory. You will have the Tagu behind you for your leadership, and the Atu because you are of Atu blood. And I–I will rally the Atu! Strike down this sick, mad old king and claim your place!"

Kublai said sharply, "No! I will not touch the chosen king. Nor will I do anything to hurt his daughter!"

Bar-Atu

Bar-Atu's fierce features glowered, but he bowed. "I accept what you say. But the middle of the dry season approaches fast. It comes with the next turning of the moon. If you will not tame the Kong, then do the next best thing: Show the people what you can do while the King attempts to fulfill his promises. Show them that should he fail, they have nothing to fear, that the Kong is not their only hope!"

"How?" Kublai asked.

Bar-Atu leaned closer. "For many lifetimes, we have relied on the great protection of the Wall. We ply treacherous waters for the fish we need, and grow our food in the earth of our peninsula, but we cannot increase as a people for lack of enough land and food. Clearly, we do not rule this island, but exist here only as long as the monsters on the other side of the Wall allow it."

"That was not always true," Kublai countered dejectedly, then talking to himself, he added, "… one day, we will take back–"

Bar-Atu's expression betrayed disdain as he continued solicitously, "Generations ago, the people had a ritual that has fallen into disuse. Capture one of the dinosaurs–a killer, a dangerous one. Lure it through the gate, capture it and bind it. Then, as the full moon of the dry season stands high, we sacrifice the creature! If we succeed, we have meat for a feast, meat to last many days, and the hide to make into armor for your warriors. Such a trophy will show the people that what is on the other side of that Wall can be defeated, controlled! It will restore their pride! Then people will begin to see that the strength of Kublai and his men offers them hope without the need of keeping monsters in their midst!"

Kublai said, "This is a mad plan. But I will say this much, Bar-Atu: If your Atu can draw close any but a Deathrunner, my warriors will capture it. That is all I will do. I will not bring a Deathrunner into the village!"

"I will do my part," Bar-Atu said with an ominous grin. "You make sure you do yours."

Ishara heard of the plan late in the day of the full moon. Charlie had come to her, troubled and speaking the island language hesitantly: "Magwich and others helping Bar-Atu," he said. "They–they trick animal to come in. Bar-Atu sacrifice it." He pulled an imaginary knife over his own throat. "Kill it for sacrifice."

Ishara ran to find Kublai–and when she did, he was with twelve of his age-mates, young men already adept with weapons. They were practicing spear-casts. When she told him of the warning, Kublai pushed her away: "If Bar-Atu brings the creature in, we will capture it," he said.

"My father will forbid this!"

Kublai said, "Your father is Tagu. This is an old Atu ritual practiced by our noble Kai warriors. He cannot forbid a tradition made sacred by history."

"You have turned to evil," Ishara said. "Don't you see this is nothing more than blood sport? You risk havoc, even death!"

"No! I will protect–Ishara!" But she had gone.

Night fell. Bar-Atu ordered torches held ready to kindle, both up on the wall and lining either side of the way through the gates. At his order, the Atu guards swung the great, heavy gates open–not far, just enough for one of the dinosaurs to pass through–and in a wooden cage just beyond their radius, Bar-Atu placed a young brush-lurker, a creature only the size of a yearling pig. It shrieked, for he had slashed its skin to make it bleed.

On the wall, several Atu began to mimic the feeding call of a jagai, a smaller, but powerful carnivorous dinosaur. Gluttonous and cunning, one was easily capable of overpowering a human. The creature walked on four powerful legs, the front two the same length as the hind legs. It had a large head in proportion to its body, from which grew an ornate headdress of feathers. The decorative frill offered a strange counterpoint to the hooded, intense eyes and stout, vicious jaws. With its mottled hide, dappled dark greens and browns, spotted with gray and white, it had near-perfect camouflage for lurking in the shadows of the heavy jungle shrubbery. Such creatures were common in the clearings of the forest on the northwestern side of the island. Bar-Atu hoped to attract one of these: It was a creature to be feared.

On-Tagu had gloomily confirmed what Kublai had told Ishara: He could not forbid an ancient ceremony, especially as matters stood. "The people would think me a coward," he murmured. He did, however, warn his private soldiers to stand ready, for he feared what might happen.

The moon climbed in the dark sky. It seemed an especially noisy night, with riotous insect sounds and distant animal roars. Then the calls of the Atu atop the wall ceased–an echo of them dying in the darkness beyond the Wall. The anticipation made what had seemed so noisy to appear suddenly silent. The wait was not long as one of the sentries called down, "One comes, it is a jagai!"

Ishara climbed the rope ladder to the top of the Wall and to the Storyteller's hut. The old woman hauled the ladder in after her. "Evil prowls the night," she said. Her gaze did not move toward the darkness or the dinosaur that seemed to be coming, but remained fixed on the other side of the wall, on Bar-Atu. The brush-lurker became frantic, bawling and trying to force its way through the bars of the cage.

Ishara knew what was happening: *It smells or senses the killer dinosaur!*

Then a roar, from the far side of the wall, but close, nearly beneath them. Ishara looked into the village. In the moonlight she saw the sinister, bobbing head of the monster as it warily walked through the gate, its attention focused on the bait. Now it came fully inside, oblivious to anything but the wounded creature in front of it–

At a quick order from Bar-Atu, torches flared, and in their light the Atu followers atop the Wall flung their nets. The snarling jagai turned, hesitating to attack the torchbearers, for like all its kind it feared fire. The nets fell over it, and shouting warriors charged in to overthrow it and tie it down, as they had the Kong.

But the dinosaur's stiff tail thrashed wildly, striking the men, threatening to rip the net. Three warriors attacked with poisoned darts, but these rebounded from the scaly hide. The creature spun, writhed, and two men lost their hold on the net. The fearsome head burst through the webbing. The jaws snapped, ripping off one man's arm, then another's head. The gruesome corpses tumbled. Warriors tried for a lethal spear thrust. The beast warded them off and bellowed in fury.

Kublai led six men in a charge, spears raised. The saurian felled three with a lash of its tail. Two men still clung to the net for a moment until the maddened creature jerked away, dragging the net but free to fight. The few warriors left flung their spears, missing the target. Kublai shouted for them to re-form, but already the saurian lunged at them.

The Storyteller suddenly looked off in the distance and hurriedly leaned over the Wall, shouting down, "Close the gates! Close them, now!"

But in the tumult, no one could hear her, and the Atu focused on the struggling, netted predator. A terrible shriek pierced the commotion, much louder, much eerier, than the jagai's roar of challenge.

For a bare instant, a frightened silence fell—and in it someone screamed, "Gaw is here!"

Dwarfing the jagai, the gigantic predator strode forward on her powerful, long legs. Before anyone could react, it had arrived at the still closing gates and reached out its arms to seize them. The Atu, torn between keeping control of the jagai and deterring Gaw, let the smaller creature go. With a roar, it quickly fled toward the opening in the gate, away from an entire group of torch-bearing warriors that rushed to close the gate before Gaw could push through. The hapless creature, half entangled in the net, hobbled through the gate only to be crushed under the enormous clawed foot of Gaw.

It was too late. The nightmare monster of their deepest fears now stood before the massing Tagatu warriors. Seizing the gates in its powerful grip, Gaw irresistibly forced them open with one mighty shove. The great wooden doors creaked loudly and swung inward, sending the puny humans who had pushed in vain against Gaw sprawling. Gaw's enormous head leered down at the tiny, fleeing humans. Its glinting yellow gaze darted toward the Tagatu village, intelligently surveying all that lay below it. The roar of Gaw was an ear-piercing roiling bellow trailing into the sound of scraping of nails on slate: it was summoning the Deathrunners from wherever they were lurking—

A thundering howl jerked Ishara's attention from the carnage below. "Kong!" she shouted. Bursting from the Storyteller's hut, she tossed the rope ladder from the wall-walk and slid down it, blistering her palms.

Just as she touched ground, Kublai ran past her, holding a spear, calling to his men to rally—

Ishara ran through the night, her toes gripping the cool, dry dirt under her feet. Upon reaching the palisade, she slipped through—

The Kong had broken two of the tethers that bound him and struggled to pull the noose over his head. "Don't!" Ishara yelled, not an order but a plea. "Gaw will kill you!"

Kong wrenched the loop free, dropped it and then with muscles bulging in his shoulders, he snapped the heavy ropes on both legs. Almost with contempt he pulled the dangling loops from his wrists and ankles and then stood free—and drummed his chest and bellowed again in challenge. The answering roar of Gaw seemed to enrage him. Ishara tried to block the exit. "Gaw is too strong!"

Kong paid her no heed and bolted forward, forcing Ishara to leap aside as he launched himself toward Gaw. Ishara followed, weeping, pleading—but she did not go far.

Gaw rampaged among the longhouses here, kicking the walls to pieces, attacking the screaming villagers as they scattered. The creature did not feed, but strewed death the way a sower casts seed, ignoring the bleeding bodies as they fell.

It did not spot Kong until the great anthropoid slammed into the larger saurian juggernaut. The impact staggered Gaw, and in falling against a longhouse, the creature obliterated it. Horrified, Ishara saw Kong tread on a fleeing villager who was in his way—and then he struck at Gaw, hard, with both fists.

Something in the longhouse caught fire, and flames licked through the shattered roof. In the flickering light, spears flew out of the darkness, thrown by the desperate guards. Some struck Gaw but bounced off. None hit, or at least seemed to hit, the Kong.

Kublai charged, yelling, and instead of throwing his spear, he drove it into the monstrous leg of Gaw. It plunged in, blood spilled, and the beast howled and thrashed its tail. Kublai rolled out of the way just in time–but he had lost the spear. Angrily, Gaw closed its jaws on the shaft and yanked it free as it struggled to its feet, forcefully knocking the young Kong aside with its greater bulk. Regaining his balance, Kong was forced to swing upward at the taller Gaw's armored, spiked skull. Gaw snapped down, and Kong barely evaded the deadly jaws.

Now the monster's whole focus centered on Kong. The beast was intelligent, or wily, enough to back away, cautious, looking for an opening. In that instant Ishara, looking on from a distance, realized what puzzled her about Kong's earlier expression: he was planning! Gaw's tail lashed furiously at her bipedal foe, stopping Kong dead in his tracks. Gaw then spun and stalked forward menacingly, step by step. Realizing he was about to be trapped by being backed up against a huge boulder, Kong took the only alternative and charged forward, grappling hand to hand with the larger beast. In a flash, Gaw's teeth closed on his shoulder, and Kong bellowed in pain and rage.

Gaw's powerful grip and greater heft gave her the leverage to position Kong's body for a death bite. In a second Gaw would rip out the young Kong's throat–

An explosion shattered the night, a flash of light, a tongue of flame, and Gaw screamed in pain as a slug big enough to kill an elephant crashed into her flank. More gunshots, and in the light of the burning longhouse, Ishara saw that Magwich, holding a huge, heavy thunderspear, and six other of his men, had formed a line and were firing at Gaw.

The monster thrust Kong away, and when Kong tried to grapple again, Gaw side-butted him with a jerk of her spiked head, sending him sprawling. With a ferocious roar she crouched and spun, her head and tail leveling anything within its radius then turned and quickly limped for the Wall. Though wounded, the huge carnosaur covered the distance in a matter of a few short seconds. Magwich shouted an order, and his men trotted after Gaw.

Ishara ran to Kong, who struggled to rise. Blood flowed from wounds on his arm and shoulder, and he breathed hard. "Let me help," Ishara pled.

Kong looked up, focused on her, then on the many warriors and torches converging from all angles. Growling, he shook his great head in an obvious attempt to clear it, then sprang up and ran after Gaw, passing the startled sailors and Magwich. Ishara followed, stumbling, until a hand reached out and steadied her–Kublai–no, Charlie. "He wouldn't let me have a gun," Charlie said, words that Ishara only partly understood.

They arrived at the gate just as Magwich's men fired another volley. Magwich fired, too, aiming at the head, but Gaw writhed and threatened, causing Magwich to flinch, and the shot sent a chunk of one of the support posts flying.

The monster reeled through the gates. Close on her heels, Kong shoved through and vanished in the night. "Bar those gates! Deathrunners are coming!" This time the Storyteller's shout came clear. A hundred men did not have to be told twice, and they hurried to swing the heavy panels shut and to bar them. Within seconds the sound of Deathrunners impacting the thick beams could be felt and their screeches heard.

Ishara looked around, half-dazed. At least a dozen lay dead, with a score of others mutilated, sprawling, still bleeding. She looked up, thinking *Why wasn't any heated water prepared?* She then noticed Bar-Atu smirking down at her.

Kublai reached her. "Did any Deathrunners get through?" he asked.

When she could not respond, he grabbed her arms and shook her. "Answer me!"

"Here, now!" Charlie tried to put a hand on Kublai's shoulder, but the islander struck at him furiously, knocking him to the ground.

Ishara hit Kublai's chest as hard as she could. "Stop it! Stop it! You're to blame for all this! You broke your oath to Father, and you sided with his enemies! Get away from me. Get away!"

She helped Charlie to his feet, and they left Kublai standing there, his hands clenching as though in a spasm.

"He didn't have to hit me. I just tried to help you," Charlie said. His mouth had been bloodied.

"I know."

"What will happen to Kong now?"

Ishara glanced back to the Wall, where men and women were still bracing the gates. "He will go back to his lair in the far mountain behind that of the Skull," she said. "It is probably the safest spot on the island, not accessible by Gaw. He will rest and heal. And now—now he will never help us! We broke trust with him."

"I think I understood that," Charlie said. He suddenly sat down. "Sorry," he said. "I think my ankle may be broken."

Ishara found someone to help him to a house of healing, already filled with weeping, groaning islanders. "You're my only friend now," she told Charlie.

"I—I thought you and Kublai—"

"Not any longer," she said. "Never again."

Amid the wails of the injured, she fiercely repeated the words: "Never again."

Ishara

And then … three years passed uneasily. The islanders, still divided between loyalty to On-Tagu and to Bar-Atu, failed to unite. Some of On-Tagu's followers deserted him, saying it was clear that the old king was losing his wits, that the pressures placed on him by Bar-Atu had taken their toll. And memory ran deep of how he had proved unable to protect the village from Gaw's onslaught.

Yet some of Bar-Atu's followers came to the king's side because Bar-Atu's plan for the ceremony of sacrifice had gone horribly wrong. Always the Storyteller worked to steer the people on the correct path, away from Bar-Atu's lies, but with every passing day the king grew weaker and her task harder. Ishara grew from a teenager to a young woman. Kublai became physically stronger and mentally more independent. Aloof from both the king and from Bar-Atu, he gathered disaffected warriors and trained them. They called themselves the Khaja after a famous sect of ancient Kai fighters, which meant "Daggers."

For his inner guard, Kublai insisted on an initiation: Any man wanting to join his followers must kill a "claw-runner": one of the dinosaurs with a deadly sickle-like claw. They were superficially similar to a Deathrunner, but smaller and more primitive. Still, they were extremely dangerous and able to gut a human being in a heartbeat. The warriors could be armed with nothing but a small shield and a dagger, which they would use to take the creature's claw as trophy, earning the respect of any leader–if they survived. Those that did made the claws into weapons, claw-hooks that could rip the flesh of almost all the creatures they went against.

This elite group of warriors, who branded themselves with the blood of their victims and called themselves the "Red Khaja," were thirsty for glory, ruthless in battle. On their forays into the jungle, they killed many saurians–and were killed by them. "That man was not worthy," Kublai pronounced whenever that happened. Ishara and On-Tagu both felt appalled at this wholesale slaughter.

Meanwhile, Magwich became closer than ever to Bar-Atu. The Shatain promised his Atu workmen would help repair the ship that now stood in dry dock on the beach. In exchange, Magwich and his men would use their firearms as Bar-Atu directed. The scarred-faced shaman insisted that soon, soon, his warriors and Magwich's men would venture into the Otherway–using secret passages to the far jungle, past the foothills of Skull Mountain itself–and Magwich could plunder the Old City.

The work on the ship proceeded slowly, partly because Magwich's men and the captain himself fell victim to island fever and their recovery stretched out, and–possibly, Magwich thought–because Bar-Atu's followers now and again sabotaged the work.

Charlie had drifted away from the other sailors and now lived in a longhouse. He had taught Ishara and the Storyteller English and even the Roman alphabet with which it was written. He had become fluent in the Tagatu language. Indeed, the only times Magwich now sent for him were those occasions when he needed a better translator than Lunun, whom Magwich regarded as a stupid man. On one occasion, Magwich had Charlie interrogate a frightened native.

Charlie said, "This man says that Kublai and his crew will go hunting tomorrow in the Otherway."

Bar-Atu had heard, too, and he scowled. "Only my Atu should hunt! We must stop them," he said, through Charlie, to Magwich.

"Ammunition don't hold out forever," Magwich said. He held up a cartridge. "Our weapons must have these, or they don't work. We're getting short. We have to save them for when we really need 'em."

Bar-Atu responded, "The old king weakens fast! He will die soon. Someone must seize power in the island. I would not have that dog Kublai named king!"

"One bullet would take care of that," Magwich said. "I'll be sure to save one for when the time comes."

"Yes, but if the foolish people of the island turn to him and the Red Khaja killers," Bar-Atu said, "they will think my Atu warriors useless. You need them, Magwich. They bring in food to the islanders. They bring in the bone and hide and teeth from which tools must be made. I do not think proud young Kublai would help you as I do."

"Well," Magwich said with a grin, "just take us on this safari into the Otherway you've talked about for more than three years now! We're as prepared as we'll ever be. Let my men find and take these blessed jewels and gold and what not, and then I might feel more friendly-like about disposing of Kublai and his warriors for you—leastways, his key men. The rest will scatter like flies after seeing their leaders fall, trust me."

The old shaman smoldered in his anger for a few moments and then burst out, "We will go in three days! But your men must bring these things you call rifles. You and all of them must obey my orders! And we must take the king's daughter with us."

"Why take a woman?" Magwich asked. "That's taking trouble."

"She is Tagu royalty, and she has been chosen by the old Pendonjira," Bar-Atu said. "That whelp also has a way with animals. With her, I do not think the smaller animals would attack, for she will warn us. If they do not attack, they do not draw the attention of the big killers. She must go."

"I suppose we can tame a wildcat," Magwich said, and Charlie did not know how to translate that word. Magwich added, "Charlie, you come too. We'll need to talk to old Bar-Atu and his men, and to this damn girl."

"I understand," Charlie said.

"The young prince," Bar-Atu said in a tone of dripping contempt. "Kublai. We must deal with him. I tell you, he and his Khaja warriors anger Gaw! He is a traitor to the Atu and aids the Tagu! The Atu are the warrior clan! Now Kublai boasts he and his men will go into the Otherway and bring in more food than my Atu ever have, *as though they could rival the Kai of old.*"

Charlie translated for Magwich, but added, "Captain, I think he wants our guns. He wants to be the one to bring in the big game, not Kublai. He's kind of crazy, if you ask me."

Magwich smiled and looked thoughtful. He should have been an actor, Charlie thought. His sunburned face shows nothing of that mind of his. Then Magwich said, "Tell Bar-Atu this: we will challenge Kublai and his men to go with us into the Otherway. If they refuse, we'll call them cowards. If they go—well, there will be chances to use our guns to stop his threat to Bar-Atu."

This time the shaman smiled and nodded. "Let preparations begin," he said.

Those would take the next three days. Ishara, at first angry that Bar-Atu commanded her to come on the expedition, begged her father in one of his moments of clarity to override the shaman's wishes. On-Tagu had been confined to his bed for weeks. He said in his faint voice, "I cannot. The leaders of our people must be there to keep an eye on Bar-Atu. You must go. Be careful, my daughter, and take no chances. Watch them all closely. When you return, tell me what you have learned of their minds. Or if you cannot tell me, tell the Storyteller instead."

"Tell the Storyteller," Oji squawked. Since he had come to be Ishara's constant companion, the proto-bird had proved a mimic more gifted than a parrot at imitating human speech.

They set out early one morning, before the sun was even up, though dawn lightened the eastern sky. Neither Ishara nor Kublai spoke of the tunnel they had used, and so the group, some thirty men and Ishara in all, took the overland hunting path that the Atu warriors had made to venture a short way into the main body of the island. Oji came too, keeping to the trees, flying a little distant from the men. He seemed wary of them but always within sight of Ishara.

The surface way was easier than the tunnel, and they made good time. Except for the high-flying dragons, the gigantic pterosaurs that fished in the waters around the island and a few distant longnecks rearing above the trees in the distance, they saw no threat. That night they camped at the top of a rocky rise, with a clear view on all sides for many yards. Both Kublai and Magwich stationed guards, but they passed a peaceful night. Not quiet, for animal sounds hissed and growled and roared all around, but a night undisturbed by attack.

They resumed the march early the next morning, taking a somewhat different route. For a good way, their path lay along the spine of a ridge. Kublai, surrounded by his ever-present Khaja, broke ranks and fell back to speak to Ishara for the first time in months: "Look—here. Paving stones where the roots have pushed them up. A Tagatu road once led along this ridge." She did not reply.

They came to a place where they could see the old amphitheater, and beyond that the remains of the Old City wall. They approached from the west this time, and when they reached the place where once a gate had stood, Ishara said, "The line of builders who made our Wall had a hand in this. See, the supports are the same."

She had a strange feeling as she stepped through the opening where once gates had barred passage: She felt as though she were stepping from the real world into legend, into the Tagatu past. *This is where the Tagatu planned our greatest city. This was protected by loyal Atu guards, assisted by Atu and Tagu miawan, and protected by Tagu repellants. This was once our home.*

"It's all in ruins," Kublai said.

That was true. Other than an enormous stone arch flanked by triangular panels, not a structure stood that made any sense. At most, stone foundations filled with muck and slime might be detected, or random sections of assembled stone partially stood. These were deformed and overgrown by the trees that were once fashioned through and around them into wondrous biological habitations. There were no roofs, windows, or doors—if they had them to begin with. More disturbing, mostly buried in the leaf mold of centuries but here and there showing where rains had washed away the silt, pieces of bones were occasionally revealed—human bones.

"The ones who trusted to their weapons and defective repellents no longer created by Tagu miawan," Ishara murmured. "The ones who refused to leave." *Somewhere we may find what they left behind, something I can bring back to the Storyteller to build on and offer hope for our people.*

One of Magwich's men cried out, "Gold, mates!" He stooped and picked up something from the ground, something that had been next to a human skull. It was a necklace of beads as large as a man's thumb from last joint to tip, ending in a triangular pendant. "It's heavy! Solid gold!"

"Stop him," Ishara told Kublai.

"Gold is nothing," Kublai said. "The one who owned it is centuries dead."

Ishara objected, "It's something ceremonial! It may hold great meaning!"

"Perhaps it did then. It means nothing now. Let them have it."

Already the outsiders were arguing about the gold and the division of the spoils. Some of them had pushed into a strange "grown" structure that still existed, wildly overgrown, but showing a few telltale signs of being worked by human hands.

"A weird lot, these ancestors, Kublai," said Magwich, the first to detect the almost invisible dwellings. "Not sure it even vaguely reminds me of other things I've come across in my wanderings, and that was quite a bit, make no mistake." He spoke out loud but half to himself as he hacked through vines and overgrowth, always searching for signs of glinting gold. "Hafta admit, never seen anything like what these people of yours have done here, though. Almost as if they could control the jungle. Neat trick, wish I could learn it."

He suddenly flinched. He had cut through a resistant vine and had jerked as though frightened. "What's wrong?" Kublai asked.

"Felt like an electric shock," Magwich muttered. Then he shrugged. "Nothing. Just tougher than I thought."

"Why waste time here?" Kublai asked.

Magwich turned to him with a grin. "Because! Nobody can hide gold from me—not even your famous ancestors. When I can't see, it I can smell the stuff!" He reached through straggling vines and retrieved a beautiful statuette made from what looked like silver, gold, and oddly colored jewels. "Never seen stones like these. Look here, mates!" He ripped away the rest of the vines, revealing a stone bin, overflowing with jewels and precious metals. A scattering of cut stones, red, perhaps rubies, lay scattered on the stones about the bin.

The men flocked to snatch them up like chickens frantically pecking at grain.

Not long afterward they came to the city center, a round plaza—a raised platform once, now nearly level with the ground. All around its perimeter, stone statues still stood, so eroded by time that Ishara could not tell whether they represented men or Kongs. None had fallen, and all stood more than six feet tall. "Look," Ishara said, pointing to the center of the plaza. "That is like a king's place."

She indicated a dais with a waist-high altar, just like the one in the village where On-Tagu stood to offer proclamations by day and by night to pray and meditate for wisdom. Ishara pointed to another spot beyond the plaza. "That must have been their Storyteller's dwelling."

Though it was of mortared stone, not wood and thatch, it looked like a larger version of the Storyteller's humble hut atop the Wall. Ishara walked toward it. Kublai grabbed her arm, quickly letting it go to slap a huge insect that landed on his hand. Wincing at the bite, he asked with real concern, "What are you doing?"

"You have your work," she said, pulling away. "I have mine. I go to meditate in that sacred place." "It may be dangerous," Kublai said. "I will go with you." He called an order to his second-in-command to keep the Khaja warriors alert, and then he followed Ishara. She paused on the threshold. Though it lacked a roof, the lodge did have "walls" in between trunks and branches that slanted inward as they rose, offering some protection, and it had not filled with vegetation and muck. The stone floors were damp, but not deep in water. Marks on the walls showed where in the past torrential rains had flooded the structure waist-deep, though.

A sound alarmed her, but it was only Oji, fluttering in through the broken ceiling. He landed on her shoulder. Kublai had walked to the rear barrier and called back: "There is a tunnel, like the ones under the Wall!"

"That will be the prayer chamber," Ishara said. She stepped outside and found a dry length of wood. Wrapping one end of it in tangle moss, she dripped oil on it from a flask she carried in a pouch. She rejoined Kublai. "I have a torch," she said. "Light it for me. I must go into the prayer chamber alone. Men are forbidden."

"I won't let you go," Kublai said.

"You can't stop me." She produced flint and iron and struck sparks into the moss. When it smoldered, she blew on the red sparks and the torch flared to life. She took it and descended the stone steps, with Oji on her shoulder.

Kublai took one step—and stopped, head tilted, every muscle tense. The whole building had vibrated. He had felt such a vibration before. Something stalked nearby. Something huge. Something deadly.

Torn between protecting Ishara and shouting a warning, he hesitated for only a moment. The girl was inside, she was safe—but his men must know of the danger. He rushed outside—

His personal guard of warriors had clustered near the hut. "Where are they?" he asked.

"The strangers have gone insane," his lieutenant said. "They throw down the old statues, looking for treasure. Already they are overburdened with gold and jewels!"

"Where are the Atu? Where is Bar-Atu?"

"They have gone to explore the semi-circle of stones that was some sort of gathering place." "Wait here for Ishara, and make sure nothing happens to her! I will return soon!" With that he was off. A moment later a rabble of the outsiders burst out of the what must have been a king's house, yelling and quarreling. As they staggered on the plaza—every single statue had been cast down, some broken to see if they were made of anything special or contained anything hidden within— Kublai saw Charlie pleading with Magwich: "The Tagatu will turn on us, I tell you, Captain! Taking some gold, that's nothing, but desecrating their sacred grounds—"

"Shut up!" Magwich turned, raised his rifle, and smashed the butt against Charlie's head. The man fell back, bleeding, and landed on the circle where one of the statues had stood.

Kublai who had just arrived, shouted, "Danger!"

To his shock, Magwich grinned and raised his weapon. At that distance, he couldn't possibly miss.

Kublai defiantly drew his knife and stared him down, waiting for death to explode at him from the pirate's thunder weapon.

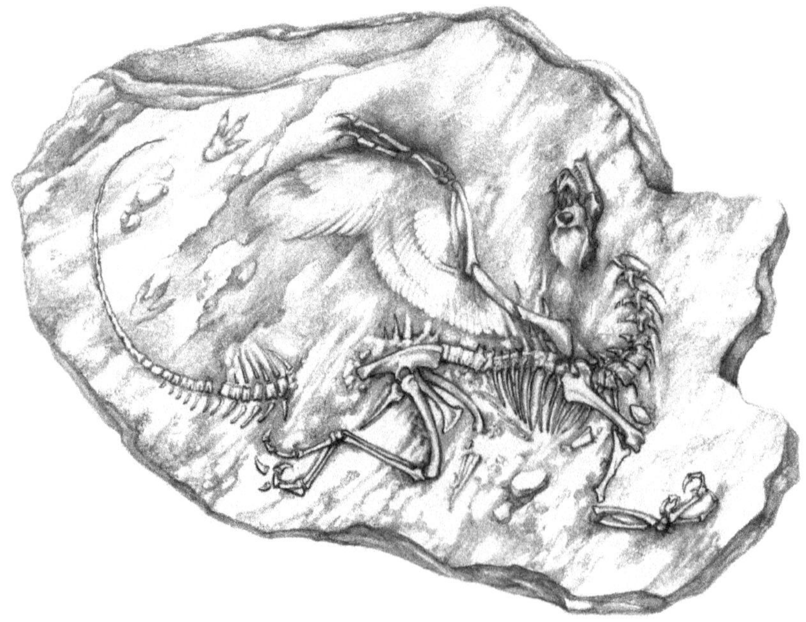

BATTLE OF TITANS

Magwich had left Charlie for dead amidst the jungle wreckage as he shouted for his men to bring as much treasure as they could carry. "We're goin' back, men!" he shouted. "Leave these savages to their friends!"

Charlie heard that as from a great distance. He lay with dim awareness, the smell of dirt and the aroma of green leaves filling his nostrils, but no power to move. Lying on his side, he opened his eyes and saw something–something like a great shadow looming high over the ancient, worn-down wall, a creature out of nightmare, mouth grinning with sickle teeth larger than any shark's he had seen. Its steps set the ground trembling; he felt it through his bones.

Charlie tried to roll and glimpsed Magwich, raising his heavy rifle as though to fire, not at the approaching monster, but at something man-sized. *Stop him, stop him!* But Charlie had no power to try. He lay too dazed to care or to move. Curiously, from where he sprawled directly over a shallow depression from which a tall ancient idol of a saurian had been toppled, what most tugged at his consciousness was a scent, an aroma, spicy and sharp. In his youth, Charlie had been a religious boy, and a strange phrase circled in his mind, inappropriate but insistent: *The odour of sanctity. I am dying in the odour of sanctity…*

And he wept because he knew he did not deserve such grace.

Kublai stared straight into the muzzle of the rifle. Then from behind Magwich, Gaw roared. The burly pirate spun reflexively and fired at the looming creature. The shot had no visible effect–except to provoke the gigantic predator to charge and reach for Magwich.

Instantly Kublai cried to his men, "Attack!"

They burst past Magwich, who was already running, and some leapt over the sprawling body of Charlie. The dinosaur was huge, and when it stood erect, even with their hooked weapons the men could not reach a vital spot. Still they wheeled in, two at a time, one on either side, and struck blows at the hind legs and tendons, trying to cripple the monster.

Atu warriors came sprinting from the gap where the other gate had once stood, some of them already hurling spears that clattered and glanced off Gaw's tough hide, the ricochets threatening Kublai's men. The spears distracted the dinosaur, which took two quick, giant strides from where it stood into the midst of the Atu, crushing one beneath its foot, grabbing one in her giant hands and snapping him in half like a twig, then swallowing another in one quick gulp as he tried to throw a spear down the gaping maw.

"Magwich!" Kublai yelled. "Bring the weapons! Help us! Traitor!" The pirates were nowhere in sight.

Beneath the surface of the earth, Ishara had no awareness of the struggle. She had found a low tunnel that emptied into a circular cavern, whether man-made or natural she could not tell. In the red torchlight, she saw the chamber had been used ceremonially. All around the walls, up to head height, trophies had been fastened or stacked: dinosaur skulls in profusion, reptilian skins, dusty from ages of isolation but suggestive of once-bright colors, spears, ceremonial urns, more.

But above the relics—on the walls themselves, as in the chamber near the Wall that the Storyteller had shown her—she saw ancient pictures, all the way up to the domed ceiling, catching the glow of the torch and illuminating themselves from that, but obscured by overgrowths of mold—

And an awestruck Ishara realized that she saw before her, in sequence, a kind of tragic history.

Turning from mural to mural, she found new impressions and ideas flooding her mind.

Were those Kongs wading in the waters of the bay, hauling behind them what looked to be great vessels, far larger than native canoes—far larger even than Magwich's ship? Other images possibly showed Kongs felling trees and, in the company of men and women, erecting what had to be the great Wall, but it was different from the Wall she knew. Why?

A confusion of warring figures. It looked like the Kongs were fighting alongside them, or were they taking the side of the animals while the humans struck them down? In the background of that, and seeming older, the Wall, still being built, with Kongs laboring on it.

An emblem like the Storyteller's triangular pendant, and beneath it dinosaurs apparently fleeing from the Wall.

Then—yes, the Old City, but surrounded by a fog, and the people and Kongs at work on another—or was it the same?—Wall. Following that, an army not of humans but of Kongs, bearing weapons, clubs and what looked like thongs or chains.

And the next showed why: Deathrunners, emerging from the fog and tearing at humans whose spears looked useless against them. A smaller image of women and a few men with censers, smoke issuing from them—and then a larger one, the city with its ring of fog, with the Deathrunners appearing to mill at its periphery. Bodies of bigger carnivores lay scattered, in different stages of decay. "They had a repellent that worked!" Ishara murmured.

But then the Deathrunners inside the city again, though the fog showed in the background, with piles of Tagatu dead lying on the earth.

And a final image, cruder than the others: Tagatu, bearing great jars from the amphitheater, their passage protected by men and women armed with spears, shields, and hooks.

Ishara put the story together in her mind: The Deathrunners were like no other foe—yes, they were as vicious as the big killers, but unlike them they had a fatal intelligence. The repellents worked against them only temporarily. The picture of the Deathrunners held at bay, but bigger dinosaurs lying dead, suggested that the mixtures that worked on the Deathrunners were toxic to the other species.

"Is it possible they did not want to kill everything else when killing the Deathrunners?" Ishara murmured. "And so, they retreated behind the Wall instead?" She knew of other legends, too: The Storyteller said the shattering of the Tagatu society resulted from a schism between the Atu and the Tagu.

The Atu, believing that the salvation of humans meant the extinction of all the Deathrunners, stayed behind in the Old City and faced the enemies with their weapons, only to be decimated when they tried, until at last the remnants of their force retreated to the Wall and begged the Tagu to shelter them again. Ishara remembered hearing that for the sake of unity, to prevent their warring with each other again, those stories ceased to be told. Even the Storyteller said that a blank spot in history had been created that yet endured.

"But they emptied the storehouse," Ishara said to Oji, who had stayed with her throughout. "They must have tried to recreate the repellents. Where did they hide the jars? They may still exist! There may be hope! Come!"

She bent and hurried down the tunnel, her torch now burning low, guttering in her hands.

The quick tropical darkness was upon the Old City. A swollen full moon had risen as the sun set. Both Kublai's men and the Atu warriors had dodged and retreated from the gigantic saurian. Now they hid in two different stone buildings, almost ruins, as the monstrous Gaw stalked nearby; its sharp ammoniac reek seared their nostrils. "Where is Bar-Atu?" Kublai asked one of the Atu, who shook his head.

"Dead?"

"No. Sent us back. Stayed in the amphitheater," the man said. The dinosaur's guttural growls reverberated in their ears.

Somehow as her torch failed, Ishara had taken a wrong turn, but she emerged in an unfamiliar place, an ancient courtyard that perhaps had been part of a nobleman's house. One wall had collapsed, and she climbed over it—and collided with Magwich, who seized her arm. "Well, Princess," he said, his grin showing in the moonlight. "So glad you ran into me!"

"Where is Kublai?"

"In a dinosaur's belly, I shouldn't wonder," Magwich said. "Me an' my men mean to hide until the thing finishes snacking. Then it's back to the village for us with a mort o' gold to carry us home in style!"

"Bar-Atu?"

"Cut an' run, far's I can see. If he's dead, good riddance. If he's alive, when we get back to your village, I'll use him, until our ship's seaworthy. When he's useless to me, he'll get this." He drew a machete. "What's the matter, Princess?"

"Stay away from me."

Magwich laughed. "You think I'd hurt a girl?" He made as if to sheathe his blade—but then spun and viciously backhanded her. She saw an explosion of yellow light and felt herself fall.

He was on her in a heartbeat, the machete pressed to her throat. "Have to kill you, sweetheart. Hack you up with my blade here, make it look like maybe one of the island monsters did it. Mess myself up a bit, little blood, to show how I tried to help you. When we get back to the village, the story will make me a hero. I may just take over from old Bar-Atu and run the place myself—until we sail off. Then I don't care if I leave every bleedin' Tagatu dead on shore!"

He seized her hair and stood, raising the machete high for the death stroke.

Something flashed down on him, raking his eyes with needle claws. He yelled in pain and anger and stumbled, blood running down his face. The flash again, and he swatted blindly at the fluttering thing. Ishara yelled, "Oji!"

Cursing, Magwich swatted the feathered nuisance aside, raising his machete once more—and screamed, dropping the blade. For a moment Ishara didn't understand—and then she saw that an arrow had transfixed Magwich's right hand.

"Traitor!" Kublai's voice! The young man stepped out of the darkness. "Murderer! Liar! I will kill you like the snake you are!"

Kublai had spoken in Tagatu, but Magwich didn't need an interpreter. With a grimace, he snapped off the head of the arrow and then pulled the bloody shaft from his palm. "No, I don't think so, boy. Look behind you!"

A shadow fell on Kublai, and he spun.

Gaw towered above him, eyes dancing ominously in the wavering torchlight, a rope of saliva glinting to the ground in slow motion! Guttural growls rolled like distant thunder from the behemoth's throat.

"Men!" Magwich yelled. "Quick! Fire!"

Kublai dived aside, barely eluding the enormous snapping jaws. From a ruined building Magwich's crew spilled out, raising their weapons, firing, but wildly in the dark. Magwich cursed, picked up his machete with his left hand, and as Gaw turned on the men with their noisy weapons and waded into them, Magwich charged Kublai.

Kublai stood his ground and drew his pikata, the short sword that in the old days the Kai, fierce Atu warriors from whom he was descended, carried. The blades rang and sparked as they collided– Behind Magwich, Gaw stooped, jaws gaping, and then reared, two sailors caught between her teeth. She champed down, dismembering them, and then sliced into the others, backing them against one of the ruined stone walls. They could not clamber up in time to escape, and between teeth and talons, Gaw ended the fight in seconds, leaving bodies and severed limbs littering the ground around her.

Kublai and Magwich circled each other. Gaw did not seem to notice them, but turned slowly, fangs bared and bloodstained. Her deep-set eyes burned yellow in the macabre, grinning skull. They focused on Ishara.

Gaw took a step–

And a roar louder than that of the thunderspears' thunder burst from all directions. With the quickness of a striking serpent, Gaw turned and ducked low, bracing for a coming attack–

Kong exploded from the shadows like a berserker, hurling a terrifying battle cry. Gaw screeched in response and flung herself forward.

Ishara knew with a dreadful certainty, this time–One of the two giants would die.

TO THE DEATH

Kublai fought, but he stood against an experienced swordsman, even when wielding his blade with his left hand. Backing away, Kublai found his shoulders pressed against a crumbling wall. He raised his sword and struck viciously just as the machete whistled toward him. The blades met, numbing both men's hands, and both machete and pikata went spinning.

Magwich roared, bulled forward, and thrust his right forearm against Kublai's throat, pinning him against the wall. The man's strength amazed Kublai—he could not pry that hold loose. With slow blood running down his arm, breathing hard, Magwich said, "Time to die, boy!" He reached to his belt and drew his last weapon, a skinning knife with a razor edge.

He raised it—

And then jolted, his face in a spasm, as something heavy struck his right shoulder. He looked with unbelieving eyes. Ishara had picked up the fallen machete and with all her strength had hacked at him—the blade had caught in his shoulder and his shirt bloomed with fresh blood. His arm lost its strength and Kublai fought free.

Growling like a cornered tiger, Magwich backed away, reaching with his good left hand to jerk the machete from the wound. Ignoring Kublai, he turned in fury to rush toward Ishara, bloody blade upraised—Slicing through the dust cloud raised by the fighting giants, a well-aimed shovel collided with the side of Magwich's head, felling him like an ox at the slaughter. Charlie quickly strode through the chaos of dust and debris and stepped over the motionless body, shouting, "Get out of here! Go!"

Kublai grabbed Ishara's hand and half-pulled her into a stumbling run.

Behind them, Kong, now in his prime and bigger than even his father was, battled toe to toe with Gaw. He pounded ruthlessly with his fists, controlling his fury just enough to avoid the razor-sharp teeth of Gaw's relentlessly darting head. Gaw shrieked in pain and anger with each of Kong's blows and fought back tenaciously. When even her great size and powerful arms proved incapable of fending off Kong's attack, Gaw sought to eviscerate her opponent with her lethal hind feet, but Kong proved too wily to be caught. Gaw tried to lash with her tail and snapped with dagger-lined jaws at every chance.

The earth beneath them shook. As they parried and dodged for position, ancient walls fell, raising more clouds of choking dust. Magwich's men, the few who survived Gaw's butchery, had scattered. Kong and Gaw both trampled over human bodies, Tagu, Atu, and pirates alike.

The rampage leveled whole sections of the Old City, progressing to the round plaza where once the toppled statues had stood guard. Kong's blows often glanced off Gaw's bobbing, spiked skull and it ripped into even his thick skin, drawing blood.

Gaw continued to snap and probe, trying for a death-grip. Kong keyed on her movements and ducked down, lunging into Gaw's flank. The two behemoths collided with what had been the ancient Pendonjira's dwelling, crushing the stone walls. Ishara, Kublai, and Charlie sprang up—they had run to the central plaza and the half-ruined house for shelter—as now the battle had come to them. Ishara pulled the two men with her, into the courtyard of the King's house. "They are nearly above it!" she gasped, staring at the battle between the two titans in the moonlight.

"What?" Kublai asked.

"A great chamber, the one we were looking for with all that remains of the Tagatu civilization's seed and repellents. It is underground–look!"

Kong had grabbed Gaw around the base of her tail, almost piercing himself on the last of Gaw's massive pelvic spines, the same giant spikes that had killed his father. Trying to impale Kong in the same way, Gaw lurched backward with all her might.

But this Kong had the dynamism of youth, vision in both eyes, and stood even larger than his imposing father had been. He reached around Gaw's flank with one arm for leverage and with a mighty effort ripped one of the spikes out of Gaw's back. Then lifting the great saurian clear off the ground, he hurled the body into a tree. The monster screamed in pain, her agonizing roars transformed into something unearthly.

As she scrambled to her feet, Kong pressed his attack. Try as she might, Gaw could not effectively bring claws or teeth against her foe, and struggled mightily to ward off the prodigious strength of Kong. He had positioned himself safely, parallel to Gaw's remaining dorsal spikes, bringing his whole body weight to bear. With one mighty twist, Gaw frantically reached back trying to dislodge Kong.

But though stronger than any carnosaur limb ever known, her arm strength was no match for that of a bull Kong. The simian juggernaut immediately pinned his opponent's arm back, finally acquiring the leverage to drive Gaw head first into the ground with the force of a crashing mountain.

The earth beneath the giants gave way. They dropped twenty feet, into what had been the great domed room that Ishara had found. The antagonists smashed into the stone floor, the ceiling stones collapsing around them, forming an enormous crater.

Ishara cried out, "No!" and ran toward the giants before Kublai seized her. "Are you insane! Stay here! You'll be crushed like an insect, you fool!"

"Don't you understand?" Ishara cried, collapsing in his arms. "They're destroying everything! It's gone! Our last hope of recovering the knowledge from the past to save our people is vanishing!"

"We have to get away from here while we can! Come!" And with that Kublai dragged a devastated Ishara away from the epic battle for the rule of Skull Island.

Half buried in rubble, the two combatants lay momentarily stunned. Kong's arm had been pinned under Gaw's body. As Gaw began to writhe uncontrollably, three of her huge dorsal spines finally found their mark, ripping gashes into Kong's chest as the great carnosaur scrambled to her feet. Kong, too, rose as Gaw lunged, barely having enough time to catch Gaw's head as the great jaws snapped within inches of his jugular. Kong clamped a vise-like grip around the jaws as they closed, but the impact drove him against one of the curved walls. The sharp spiked cranium of Gaw bloodied his arms and hands as it ripped free of the stunned giant's grip.

The super saurian closed in for the kill, but Kong snatched up a stout, jagged object–the broken thighbone from some long dead creature that had been mounted there–and thrust it like a sword. Some of it shattered against Gaw's armored body, but a thick shard pierced the creature's side–and she flinched away, screeching. Then she leapt, not trying to kill Kong this time–but seeking escape. She made the edge of the opening the two had created and scrambled to haul herself out.

Kong seized a long stake, perhaps once used to brace the roof that no longer stood. With an angry bellow, he rose to his feet–his shoulders and chest now projected above the lip of the opening. A hundred feet from Kong, on the opposite side, Gaw struggled to escape the cavity.

Kong, bleeding, placed his weapon on the rim of the crater and pulled himself out. Rolling to his feet, he snatched up the stake again. Gaw, now also free, immediately turned and rushed around the periphery of the hole they had broken, hoping to shove Kong backward, leap on him, and rip out his throat.

Kong caught Gaw's charge head-on, leaned in and threw the creature to the side, again knocking it completely off its feet. He quickly grabbed the sharpened stake and raised it to make the kill…but instead threw it to the side.

This was a battle as old as nature itself, between combatants who opposed each other down into the very depths of their being. Something in Kong would not kill Gaw with a weapon. This vengeance for the deaths of father and mother had to be dealt with his bare hands.

Kong's fury bordered on insanity.

Only then did the few human witnesses, too terrified or dumbstruck to flee, grasp the true size and might of the creature who would come to be called King Kong. Powerful beyond description, he stood taller than many trees and was bulkier than any Kong who had ever lived. His roar became so deep and booming that human ears could not endure it; all who heard it fell to their knees, their hands pressed against the sides of their heads.

Gaw hissed and snapped at the enraged Kong, but Kong gave no quarter. The great anthropoid went completely berserk and, with bone-cracking blow after rib-shattering blow, literally beat his ancient carnosaur rival to death. Gaw's yellow eyes dulled as the spark of life faded, then rolled up white into the spiked skull. Kong shook the slack jaw to make sure his life-long tormentor was finally dead, then turned to all the jungle and drummed his chest again and again, roaring so deafeningly that the very ground shook.

In the din of Kong's roar, a rifle shot went unheard—and the bullet went wide of its mark. The staggering, gory figure of Magwich, pale with loss of blood, fell to his knees, cursing, trying unsuccessfully to jerk the bolt back for a second shot.

After his roars of triumph, Kong heard movement in the surrounding jungle and took three giant steps towards it. Without even noticing Magwich, Kong stepped squarely on him, crushing him. The pirate captain lay dead at last.

At the perimeter of the jungle, Kong saw that the Deathrunners had finally arrived, far down the central avenue. Summoned by Gaw's repeated calls and screams, they had come—but stopped short at the circular plaza of the toppled statues and stared, as though unable to comprehend the death-scene in front of them.

Aware of their presence, never taking his eyes off Gaw's minions, Kong stepped over his dead foe and grabbed her head with both hands. With an intimidating roar, Kong wrenched the head of their fallen leader, snapping vertebrae within the thickly muscled neck with the sound of a thunderclap.

He left no doubt that Gaw was dead. The Deathrunners fled.

Kong then dragged the body to the far edge of the Old City, to a point where the ancient walls had been perched on the edge of a steep cliff dropping away to a rushing river far below. Heaving and growling, Kong wrestled the huge unwieldy carcass over the edge of the ruined wall. He watched intently as the limp body grotesquely toppled and tumbled, starting a small avalanche as it collided with rocks and boulders for hundreds of feet before finally smashing to the ground below.

The battle had lasted almost half an hour, an eternity for a fight between two such titanic foes.

Kong stood, sniffed the air, and then set off, heading for—

"Skull Mountain," Kublai said. "He's going toward Skull Mountain."

"The Deathrunners did not help Gaw," Ishara said. "Why wouldn't they come to their leader?" She walked from their place of concealment to the plaza. There she stood sniffing the air as Kong had.

"Yeah," Charlie said. "Smells strong of herbs or something. I noticed that."

Ishara knelt in sorrow, utterly drained, "That scent is what was left of the repellents. That's why the Deathrunners wouldn't cross the plaza. That was proof that they did work—and the secrets are lost forever."

"Didn't stop Gaw, though," Charlie said.

"Let's go. Let's get out of this place before some other devil comes."

Maybe not those, but others may have been able to stop Gaw, and now they're all gone. All of them. What now can we do? These thoughts devastated Ishara as they raced back through the jungle.

RECKONINGS

"If we can get to the shore," Charlie said, "one of the boats is still beached there. Best way back to the village."

"We will have to pass the foot of Skull Mountain," Kublai said.

Kublai had left them for a time–Ishara searched to see if any of his warriors were still alive, but it seemed they had all either been killed or had fled. When he rejoined them two hours later, he carried a bloody sack. "What did you get?" Ishara asked.

"I climbed down the cliff to Gaw's body. I have the largest of her teeth–I even managed to cut the patch of reddish hide before my blade shattered. With proof that Gaw is dead, Bar-Atu can never make the people worship the monster again. Come, the night is failing."

So, with the darkness wearing away, they headed for the beach.

The east gleamed pale with dawn, giving them just enough light to race along the trail. Night animals made noises, but not from nearby. "Kong passed this way," Ishara panted. "As long as his scent lingers, other beasts will avoid coming along this path."

They arrived at the very base of Skull Mountain–to their right, rising in terraces, the stone seemed to hold a vast pool, and then above that a ledge, and still above that, the eye sockets and nasal cavity of the stone mountain showed grim. As the rising sun touched first the cranium, then moved steadily down to illuminate the whole skull, Ishara grabbed Kublai's arm. "Look!"

On the ledge before Skull Mountain stood Kong. Bloody, hair matted he glared at the world. The new sun revealed before him, Kong bared his fangs and threw back his head in a proud, defiant attitude. He beat his chest with a sound like distant drums and gave a deep-throated roar, a celebration of his supremacy, a cry of victory over his ancient enemy.

"He is king now," Ishara said with awe. "He is King Kong!"

The dory that had been left upside-down on the beach was heavy, but the three of them hauled it to the edge of the surf and loaded it with the sacks Kublai had filled. "The Storyteller will know best what to do with these," Ishara said, and Kublai let her have her way and made no comment.

Ishara and Kublai climbed into the unfamiliar craft as Charlie leaned into it. With grunts and straining muscles, he shoved the dory off, the water swooshing as it rippled over the hull. He leapt in as soon as it was afloat, and then he showed Kublai how to work the oars, so unlike the native paddles the islander was used to.

They set their backs to it and rowed out, fighting an incoming tide. Then they skirted the cliffs, as far overhead the great flying reptiles took to the air, their wings catching the early rays of the sun.

"We'll never make it as far north as your beached ship," Kublai said as they neared the honeycomb cliffs hours later. "My arms are weary, and the surf will run high."

"Land at the base of the cliffs," Ishara advised, "just past this narrow strait. The rocks there offer a few protected places and we can take that waterway, the one that leads to the glimmering falls, the ones that can easily be seen from the Wall. The sentinels will see us coming and help us."

So, they loaded the sacks and secured them with rope. And like that they made their way until the Wall lay within sight.

The sentries, astonished, heard their cries as they approached and ran to the beach. Ishara insisted they tell no one of the bags' contents until the Storyteller had seen them first. Kublai agreed and said he would easily divert them with news of Magwich's death and the battle between Kong and Gaw.

To Ishara's great relief, the Storyteller arrived almost as soon as they did, and the story of what had happened began to spill from Ishara.

But the Storyteller stopped her instantly, whispering gravely in return, "This proof of Gaw's death may help, but things are not good. You return to a troubled village. Your father has ceded all power to Bar-Atu."

"What?" exclaimed Ishara, stunned. "That can't be—"

"Guards," the Storyteller said, "let these two men eat and rest. I will take Ishara to my hut."

Not another word would the old woman say until they had reached the Storyteller's home. Then, inside, the Storyteller said, "Your father has become weak in mind as well as body. I will tell you what I fear: from the time before you left on your journey to the Otherway, Bar-Atu had bribed your father's servants. They have been putting an ancient Atu mind poison into his food."

"No! We have to help him!"

The Storyteller laid a restraining hand on her arm. "There is worse. I believe Bar-Atu has discovered some of the underground passages to the Old City and has been looting whatever seeds, mixtures, repellents and attractants he could find. That would explain his sudden ability to communicate with Gaw and predict the monster's arrival, and his claiming to be the creature's mediator. But he does not know the danger he has created not only for us, but for himself! The ancient mixtures can be very dangerous when misused, and they are already affecting Bar-Atu himself. He is now clearly going insane."

"Can we stop him?"

The Storyteller sighed. "Perhaps what you have brought may give me a way to shake his power— perhaps not. I will try. The tunnels enabled Bar-Atu and his soldiers to escape the battle and return early yesterday, telling us that Gaw has killed all the rest—you, Kublai, the white strangers. He intended that you would all be killed by Gaw. I'm sure Bar-Atu used his stolen preparations to summon Gaw, and now he calls for a mass sacrifice to his false god. He does not yet know his god is dead! You must confront him when he speaks. Tell him, tell everyone, the truth. Have Kublai show them proof of Gaw's death and I will stand with you both."

Ishara's first reaction at seeing Bar-Atu stride to the King's Place and stand on his podium was rage. He led an excited, fearful rabble who clustered around him as he began to shout, "Gaw is angry! We must appease Gaw! We must give him blood!"

Some of the crowd, probably coached by Bar-Atu, took up the chant: "Blood! Blood! Blood!" Others began to join in.

"Six maidens!" Bar-Atu shrieked. "Six at once! Pure blood! Innocent blood! Blood for Gaw!"

Ishara and the Storyteller pushed through the crowd. Bar-Atu, grinning and sweating, swept his mad eyes around the crowd but they froze, unbelieving, on Ishara and Kublai.

They mounted to the platform and Ishara cried out: "My people! You know me—I am Ishara, the king's daughter—the true king! Not this ranting madman who seeks to control you with lies and fear!"

Beside her, Kublai called out, "And I am Kublai, leader of the Khaja! You see we both live! But we tell you—Gaw is dead!"

"You blaspheme!" Bar-Atu snarled, drawing back to strike Ishara.

"Touch her and you die!" Kublai said, his spear ready.

"Stand away!" It was Charlie, off to the side, leveling a rifle at Bar-Atu—one that held no cartridges, for Magwich had taken the last of theirs on his quest for treasure.

But Bar-Atu did not know that. He backed away, his eyes darting. "She lies!" he insisted. "Gaw lives! The god cannot be killed!"

"Gaw is dead," Kublai said. "I have proof."

The Storyteller came to the foot of the podium but did not step onto it. Instead, she took from her neck the triangular pendant. "Listen!" she cried. "This is the symbol of the Tagu Storytellers from ancient times! You know its lore! Let Ishara, to whom I will pass my authority, press it to her heart and tell you the tale. She cannot lie if she does that!"

Ishara was stunned as this announcement but wisely gave no indication. Bar-Atu's followers began to cluster together, muttering uncertainly. The other villagers shouted, "Let her speak! We will hear her! Let her speak!"

And so Ishara stood tall, the pendant held tight against her breast. "The Kong that Bar-Atu ordered imprisoned, the one that escaped years ago, has grown to adulthood. He killed Gaw!" She told the story of Magwich's treachery, of his betrayal of Kublai and his own men, almost all of whom were wiped out during Gaw's attack. And she told how Kong had come, of the terrific battle, and how Kong had defeated and destroyed the bloodthirsty Gaw, throwing the broken, bloody corpse off a cliff.

Kublai stood beside her and took from the sack he carried the grisly trophies. "Gaw's tooth! Behold! Even a piece of the monster's scaled skin! Look at them! You know them to be real! Bar-Atu's 'god' is dead! Gaw is dead!"

"Those could be the bloody parts of any creature!" cried Bar-Atu. "Who are you two children to meddle in the affairs of a god? Fools! Your insolence will destroy us all!"

At his signal, his men began to shout, so that Kublai and Ishara could not be heard. Atu warriors came forward to menace them. With no protective guard left, there was little Kublai could do without placing the others in danger. The Atu guard took Kublai's sacks and led him away at spear-point to be interrogated by Bar-Atu himself.

Ishara was sent back to her father's house—where she found the old king lying dead, his body neglected. The islanders, obeying their old customs of respect for the king and his family, gave her some protection as she mourned. Afterwards, both Ishara and the Storyteller were sent under armed guard and locked in the Storyteller's quarters atop the Wall.

Even there they heard rumblings from the crowds below.

"Why did Bar-Atu not summon Gaw to prove the god still lived?"

"Why did he seem afraid of Kublai?"

"Why keep the Storyteller under guard, when she had never preached or offered violence?" Still others were heard to murmur:

"If Kong killed Gaw, he must be a god. Only a god can kill another god!"

"Bar-Atu is scheming even now," the old woman told Ishara. "He will find some way to remove opposition to his power."

In the early evening of the second day after Kublai and Ishara's return, the sun was setting slowly and bloodily behind Skull Mountain in the west when a sentinel atop the Wall began to scream hysterically, "It's Kong! Kong is coming!"

The people shrieked and scattered. Bar-Atu quickly appeared atop the Wall with his men. Others ran to the gates to make sure they were secured. Part of the populace ran toward the Wall, not knowing what to expect, while others ran panicked from it, seeking places to hide.

"Come!" the Storyteller said to Ishara, and they both ran breathlessly to the triangular opening in her hut atop the Wall to witness the coming of Kong.

Once atop the Wall, the madman shaman sounded the giant metallic disc, calling the island's new god for the first time. He led the Atu cult leaders in chanting, "Kong! Kong! Kong!"

Before long all could hear the crashing of trees. Bar-Atu gesticulated like a wild man, his eyes bulging as he gestured toward a screaming girl, bound on the ancient altar outside the gates. "The god Kong comes! If he defeated Gaw, he must be a god! He comes to take my sacrifice!" he screeched. "I offer homage to the great god, Kong! All hail the god-king: Kong!" Over and over he insanely screamed these words. Others atop the Wall, men bearing flaming torches, joined in.

With ear-splitting roars Kong rampaged out of the jungle and into the clearing in front of the Wall, glowering in all directions. He stared up at the lights dancing along the top of the barrier against the darkening sky. He sniffed the air and beat his chest, sending out a challenge to anything lurking nearby that might dare threaten him.

When nothing happened, Kong at first seemed confused, as though expecting a battle. As the chanting continued, Kong rose to his full height, now close to thirty feet, taller than any Kong ever known, and again drummed his chest and roared at the tiny humans arrayed in front of him. Again, he sniffed the air and looked down. At last he noticed the human sacrifice below. Having fainted, she sagged in her bindings.

He stretched forth a great hand and nudged the limp figure, then sniffed his fingers. Suddenly he roared again in rage and grabbed the tethered girl like a rag doll, ripping her away from the pedestal. He bit her again and again, as though tasting her flesh, then carried the lifeless body into the night.

Bar-Atu pointed towards the jungle forest with a staff he had taken up, screaming, "He has accepted the sacrifice of blood! The god Kong has heard my call and deigned to listen to my petitions on your behalf! No one can deny that I am his chosen mediator! Now the great Kong will guard us, as his ancestors did of old! Every new moon we will beat the drums and sound his call, and give him another sacrifice! Kong! Kong is our god forever!"

With that Bar-Atu's acolytes took up his praises. Some protested that it was Kublai who should be Kong's mediator, but they were quickly and savagely beaten down. After that none dared oppose Bar- Atu and his thugs.

"It's wrong!" Ishara protested. "He's evil! I cannot understand why Kong would listen to him! Kong is not evil; I have been near him and could feel he is not! Why would Kong take such a sacrifice?

"No, Kong is not evil," Kublai said, suddenly appearing at the opening to the Storyteller's hut. "The man guarding you was a friend of one of my Khaja and allowed me to see you both, but I haven't much time."

Only then did they learn from him what happened preceding Kong's arrival. Bar-Atu himself forcibly took a Tagu girl in front of her distraught family, who were restrained by Atu guards. The girl was drugged and dragged out to the stone altar where Gaw had taken so many victims. It was still covered with the rust-red stains of dried blood. With his own hands, Bar-Atu lashed her to the pillars before quickly fleeing to the side of the stone altar, then through a secret door and down into a tunnel that led back behind the safety of the Wall.

Bar-Atu realized the loud sound of the disc had always been associated with Gaw's presence, and hoped, even though he knew Gaw to be dead, that it would draw the curiosity of Kong. The shaman used scents taken from dead Deathrunners and Gaw's parts brought back by Kublai to trick Kong, adding them to braziers on either side of the gates. He knew that Kong would pick up the scents.

What was truly horrific was that he spread Gaw's blood all over the hapless girl, covering her with the unmistakable scent of Kong's mortal enemy–

Having told them that much, Kublai ended: "I have no time to speak of more. I must go before I am discovered here!"

And with that, he was gone,

"Kublai, wait!" whispered Ishara urgently, but to no avail.

"Let him go," the Storyteller said. "You will have to be strong, Ishara. It is not your fate to become queen of the island. But there are other–some would say, more important–ways to lead than that."

She removed the pendant from her neck and hung it around Ishara's. "You have known for some time now that you have been the recipient of special gifts, awakened by the foundations of this island. As you have grown to womanhood, these things have intensified. They seem mysterious, but you will learn: You were the one who felt most acutely the need to free the people from the thralldom of their fears, who had the courage to act. You inspired Kublai to act, too, to move beyond its shadow into the light of day–and embark on a seemingly impossible quest to save our people. These things tell me that you must become the next Storyteller. You know this to be true in your heart. I have not many years to live. The island must have a Storyteller to guide the people, and it is more important now than ever to counter the madness that Bar-Atu brings, or our race will perish forever."

Ishara wept. "I–I can't. I have no idea how! What can I do? The Old City has been destroyed, there are no seeds left to be found, no repellents to protect us. I feel there is no hope–"

"Yes, you can," the older woman said firmly, "and never forget that so long as you breathe, there is always hope." Then more gently and reassuringly, understanding all too well the weight that such an office would bring, she added, "Did you not know that I have been preparing you for years and will continue to do so until the very end? Already the dreams have started, and you are beginning to remember what you did not know you already knew–do I speak the truth?"

Her seamed face broke into an ironic and bitter smile. "Even Bar-Atu cannot claim otherwise. For you are the one who rescued his god from captivity. You are the one whom Kong will never forget and whom he will never harm because of your kindness to him. You are the one who saw him proclaiming his dominion from the foot of Skull Mountain himself."

She touched Ishara's shoulder and leaned close.

"You," she whispered solemnly, "are the one who named him–*King* Kong."

I have presented the tale of Kong's accession to the death's-head throne of Skull Island. The Storyteller always waited patiently before continuing to read if I dozed off or whenever I needed to take a break. When she closed the last of the several books she had read from, she said simply, "Rest now, Vincent Denham, and contemplate."

A day finally came when I could rise from my bed and totter around. I began to eat more heartily, and encouraged by Jack Driscoll, who rarely ventured out of sight of me, over the next week or so I became stronger and able to walk. I remember very well when the Storyteller approached me and said, "Now you are ready. Come."

Though her assistant, the young and beautiful Kara, had always been wary of me and resentful, she held my arm and steadied me, perhaps taking pity on my weakness. I wondered where we were. It seemed a cathedral almost–on either side slanting walls tapered up to darkness, which the feeble lamps did not penetrate. I estimated the walls would converge some sixty feet above our heads.

The Storyteller led me to a great, heavy door and Jack helped her open it. Beyond lay–another great chamber, the same size and nature (about forty feet long by fifteen wide) as the one in which I had been nursed back to health. Oil lamps flickered and glowed all along the walls.

The first thing I saw upon stepping over a high threshold and into the new room was a long table, stacked with what looked like books, papers, writing implements, and paraphernalia of civilization. A chair, obviously put together by someone not expert in carpentry, had been pulled close to the middle of the table, and draped over it was a jacket–ragged from long wear, but once good-quality tweed.

My heart beat faster. "I know that coat," Jack said. He turned the chair so I could see the breast pocket. It bore a monogram: CD. "It's your dad's," Jack said.

"And," the Storyteller said, "so is this." She handed me one of the books she had read from. "Do you know this, Vincent Denham?"

I recognized it immediately.

The thick, leather-bound notebook had a cover that was embossed CD in tarnished bronze. Those letters are my father's initials: Carl Denham. I opened the weather-stained volume to see that it was written out in my father's longhand! I thought the Storyteller had presented her history to me with her own words.

"The others are the same, my son," she said, reading the expression of shock on my face–or my thoughts, I am still not sure.

I knew those notebooks well. My father ordered them by the gross, filling them with his drawings and story plots. When he was making films, he wrote in them ideas and entire scenarios. I had inherited a dozen of them, none about King Kong, but crammed with the stories and first-draft scripts of his early films. I held this one in my hands, and opening it in the light of one of the lamps, I read the words "King Kong of Skull Island, by Carl Denham. The story as told to me by the Pendonjira, Ishara, Storyteller of the Tagatu people."

That is the story you have just read, told almost completely in Carl Denham's own words. He was a storyteller himself, a filmmaker. The drama and spectacle of the fantastic history of the Tagatu was clear and he wrote what might have been the rough scenario for one of his motion pictures.

But the books offered no screenplay. My father had a different purpose in composing them. I could sense the Storyteller's influence, as though through his writing she was helping him work something out for himself personally. Did they both know that one day his words would come to me?

The rest of the notebooks proved to be a trove of personal information I had yearned for a lifetime to discover. From them I learned my father's complete story–how he left New York City a hunted man, not only by the inevitable lawsuits for damage, but also because in creating the Kong exhibit he had–there is no polite term for it–bribed city officials and departments, and clearly they had collaborated after the debacle to cover up as much of the story as they could.

I suspect they even managed to seize all the clear photographs of Kong, for some must have existed. Surely these officials were behind the unending sensational stories of heartless Denham showmanship at the expense of other people's lives, hoaxes gone horribly wrong, men in gorilla suits with trick photography–even stories that King Kong was a giant robot–that completely camouflaged the true series of events. The real-life horrors of the Depression, World War II, the Korean War and the ongoing Cold War that followed were more than enough to completely push King Kong into the realm of entertainment, myth and legend.

I already knew that my father was an accomplished sketch artist. He was proud of having studied at New York's Art Students League, and he had designed the posters for about half of his movies. Now in book after book I discovered everything from scribbles to elaborate and detailed sketches of the flora and fauna of the island. It became clear from where my own drawing skills and overall love of nature and science stemmed (though my mother, too, was quite an enthusiast).

"He made notes about everything. Your father's curiosity was insatiable," the Storyteller observed.

Opening book after book, marveling at the wealth of information, I said, "He must have worked on these for years."

"Yes. For more than twenty," was her response. "These stories and findings should be–'published,' I believe is your word?– should be made known to the world?"

"Yes, as soon as possible!" I enthusiastically replied. "They will–"

"No!" Interjected Kara, "I told you we should not have brought them here! They–they must not be published, Vincent Denham!"

The Storyteller gazed at Jack, Kara, and me. "The decision must come from within them," she said softly.

Kara protested, "We cannot trust him, we cannot trust either of them!" Her voice was dripped with contempt. And fear.

Of what, or of whom? Me? Jack? I thought. The Storyteller remained silent, and I realized she had not yet completed her advice.

"Is my father–is he still alive?" I asked.

The old Pendonjira bowed her head. "He went to his rest more than a year ago. Kara and I have brought all these here, to preserve them." Then, looking me in the eyes, she said, "Your father sought to atone for the harm he did to us on the island, too. But I know that we were not the only ones harmed by his actions, not the only ones cowering in fear behind a Wall. You have built a Wall inside yourself, is that not true, Vincent?"

For some time, I could not reply. I had not expected to find my father alive, but still, knowing that he had passed on was a blow. Yes, there was a Wall of anger I had built up inside myself over many years for his having deserted my mother. While he had gone on expeditions and found living dinosaurs, I was left on my own to sift through their lifeless bones. It suddenly dawned on me why I had never married, never allowed others to get close: I was living behind a self-imposed Wall, just like the people on Skull Island.

At last I asked, "Is that why he returned? To free you from the Wall?"

Her answer surprised me: "Your father was a complicated man—as your people would describe him—I know that he had a hole in his center as deep as that left in the Old City after the battle between Kong and Gaw, which left Ishara's hopes of finding the precious herbs shattered. But that does not mean he was a bad man. Carl Denham was not a bad man; he was a good man. I know of the stories that were told about him, the same stories you must have heard, stories that were embellished until they were mostly empty of truth. Do not believe them."

She then added, "In my native tongue, I am what is called a 'Pendonjira.' Do you know what that means?" she asked.

I said I was not sure.

"That means 'Storyteller'—which you have been calling me all along. That word has a very different meaning to us than it does in your language. To a Pendonjira it is what you might call a sacrilege to tell stories that lead away from the truth."

She turned her gaze from me to Jack again, her eyes like those of a wise, ages-old owl. "And you, Jack Driscoll, who misses nothing that goes about him, were you, too, not truly afraid—for the first time in your life, perhaps—in coming face to face with King Kong? Maybe you also must silence that raging beast within you before you could move on in peace?"

"It could be," Jack agreed softly.

The Storyteller nodded. "You may both wonder why I reveal so much of our people's secrets to outsiders. The reason is this, Vincent Denham and Jack Driscoll: to tell the truth of Carl Denham's story. The truth will always redound to the good if we can overcome the fears that prevent us from choosing to follow its path."

She then turned her magnetic gaze towards Kara. "Because Carl Denham's truth has been woven into our truth, his story is now inextricably woven into the still unfolding story of the ancient Tagatu civilization. Where that greater reality will ultimately lead, you will determine—when you have cleared your mind of the smoke of your resentment."

Kara fell silent, her face thoughtful. When I touched her arm, she did not pull away.

To me the Storyteller said, "Do not feel too sad that you did not know your father better, Vincent, for his words and actions, you will find, are alive and well as I bring my tale to a conclusion. Listen.

"Before Kong ran wild through New York, he attacked our village. You were there, Mr. Driscoll. Many died. The Wall was damaged and our entire existence was thrown into chaos. The Wall has been partially repaired, though the great gates still do not work properly. But all was not lost: Kong ended the reign of Bar-Atu, biting him in half during his rampage, and wiped out most of that evil usurper's henchmen along with their leader.

"But the Tagatu people remained full of fears, continued to huddle in their village. They remained confused about who they were and became demoralized to the point of despair. Your father knew this, Vincent. He returned here to study the island, as you wish to do. To help find what had been lost and to assist in returning it to us, as I hope you want to do.

"And he did that, in a way that neither he nor I could possibly have imagined!"

The old woman reached out to stroke the hair of her young apprentice. "Now, Kara, you must see to it that that knowledge, gained at such extreme pain to so many, bears fruit that far outstrips the cost. If you succeed, the Tagatu will learn again the old ways of taming the island and you will lead the people when they reclaim their lost heritage. To do this, you will need the help of these outsiders, something they could not properly understand how to do unless they understood your—*our*—story. I also knew you would not accept them unless you came to know their story and the personal price they paid."

The Storyteller stood brooding for a few moments, and then said thoughtfully, "Come with me. One last thing to see." Oil lamp in hand, she then led them through a short maze at the end of which we took a flight of stairs that led up towards a warm, soft glow.

We emerged into an open chamber some forty or more feet high. On either side of the stairs stood flaming braziers, their light illuminating the wonder that loomed before them.

"Behold," the Storyteller proclaimed. "King Kong!"

All my life I had imagined a spectacular museum display of King Kong's bones locked in battle with those of what I imagined was his greatest foe, Tyrannosaurus rex. The display the Storyteller revealed was jarringly different–Kong's bones had been articulated and mounted not frozen in eternal conflict, but in a position of noble repose inside an enormous sarcophagus. An ornately sculpted cover depicted a symbolic image of King Kong breaking the back of Gaw and had not yet been placed over Kong's scarred remains, sealing them forever.

Now, standing before the remains, I saw Kong in my mind's eye as I had never done. I began to understand what my father had accomplished, both for bad and for good. Kong was titanic, beyond imagining, incredible. As my father reportedly advertised, he was the "Eighth Wonder."

"A creature so great as Kong deserved to be buried here, on Skull Island where he was born and revered. Your father and I returned the body here for that reason," the Storyteller said. "And to show the islanders. To prove what we said was true."

"You–you were in New York with him?" She nodded.

I turned to Driscoll, my oldest friend, my foster father. "Jack, you must have known that! You were on the *Wanderer* when it brought Kong to New York. Why didn't you tell me?"

Driscoll shook his head. "Because it's been twenty-five years, kid, and I barely saw her even then. There were a couple of other male islanders who also wanted to come out of respect for Kong–to bring him food and to go to the undying lands or some such superstition. After what Ann'd been through, the less we had to do with them the better! She had nightmares for years; still has 'em."

"Perhaps now you–how do you say it–'see the other side of that coin' and can let go of those feelings?" the Storyteller said hopefully.

Jack took a long breath. "I guess I wouldn't be much of a stand-up guy if I didn't, would I?"

"Good. Because your help will be needed to secretly transport whatever may be necessary from your world to help rebuild the Wall and to maintain contact with Vincent, who will stay with us when you leave." With that she turned to me, waiting for my assent. Jack also shot me a glance of concern, but I already knew, before the Storyteller even said it, that I would not be leaving just yet. The answer must have been written on my face.

"I am pleased that you welcome what your fate holds, Vincent Denham," the Storyteller said. Jack shrugged, grinned, and stuck out his hand. I shook it. We had no need for words.

The Storyteller's eyes smiled. "Then it is settled. Yes. Of all the Tagatu, only I knew the secrets of keeping Kong calm. While he was imprisoned in a cage below the decks of the ship, I was the one who sat with him and spoke to him, fed him, gave him the island's herbs to sooth him. My greatest regret is that I did not go to the theater with your father when the 'exhibit'–she was unsure of the pronunciation and I had difficulty understanding at first–"began, because I could not bear to see Kong again shackled in a cage, made a show and a mockery. If I had been there, I might have–"

She sighed and shook her head. "But to mourn the past is useless. The island must have a future. Kong could not have known it, neither could I, nor your father, but in the wake of his destruction he had left a trail that will lead to the salvation of our people, perhaps even Skull Island itself.

"It is no exaggeration to say that the life and death of King Kong is the center around which all of our combined fates revolve. You will help us follow Kong's trail to its conclusion, Vincent, you will help ensure that he did not die in vain."

I had to sink down to the floor and kneel there. I lacked the strength to stand, and the avalanche of information had made me literally dizzy.

Jack supported my shoulders, and the Storyteller said, "Rest. Drink. This will make you stronger." She offered me a leather flask. Its contents were bland, but strangely warming.

CARL DENHAM WING
KING KONG of SKULL ISLAND

"When you are recovered, I will take you to Skull Mountain itself. And to the Old City. I will show you where your father lived for so many years, a hermit except for my visits, for if he had been discovered by others he might have been killed by those acting out of ignorance. I will tell you how he and I found ways to protect humans from the great dinosaurs and other dangers of Skull Island. I will show you his grave."

Jack helped me to my feet. "Better, kid?"

I nodded. "I think I can handle it."

The Storyteller beckoned, but before we started back, she said, "Understand all that awaits you on this island is not painful or dangerous, even though it may at first seem so." She immediately looked knowingly at Kara and said as if to both of us, "The future is a wondrous thing, and you must never give up hope in its possibilities."

Kara suddenly blushed an incredibly beautiful shade I had never seen before on a human face. She quickly bowed her head to hide it, and said, "I believe you were leading us somewhere?"

"Yes."

"But won't the trip be dangerous?" I asked the Storyteller. Jack Driscoll had already told me something about the horrors of the jungle passage.

"Not as much as you think. Look." The Storyteller leaned down, grasped an iron ring, and swiveled a trap door up. Cool air came out of the opening. I saw steps leading down, to what looked like an opening in solid stone. "Tunnels, long known to my ancestors, forgotten since, even by the line of Storytellers after the fall of the Old City. But I have learned their ways again. This will take us safely to where we will need to go."

"Where are we now?" I asked. "Where is this place? I didn't expect the islanders would have built structures this large."

"They did build one," she said. She smiled. "They had help. Can you not guess where we stand? What is the one great construction that is this large?"

"The Wall?" I asked.

"Until your father came, our people had forgotten that the first Wall was then built into a double Wall after the great Storyteller, Mari, led them back behind it. This was not only for strength, but also to provide a hidden space for preserving their secrets so that they would never be lost. When the last of those who survived the fall of the Old City also begged to be allowed back behind the Wall, the Storyteller of that time, seeing far ahead, had the Wall sealed off before their arrival to hide those precious secrets from those who might be threatened by them or misuse them. Over the eons, the contents of the Wall were totally forgotten.

"Then your father came to our island and caused Kong to attack our village.

"When Kong broke through the great doors, he broke the age-old mortar from sections of the Wall. Your father and I made the connection between ancient symbols on the Wall that were revealed by the mortar damage with those he had uncovered in the Old City."

Jack, who had been uncharacteristically quiet, spoke up: "So the destruction Kong caused may actually be what saves you people?"

"In a manner of speaking, yes, Jack Driscoll," was the Storyteller's answer. "Has this thought, of the gravity of your actions, weighed on your mind the same as it did on Carl Denham's? Does it make you happy to hear that good has come out your past deeds?"

Jack nodded. "I'd–I'd be lying if I said that it didn't. But I always knew one good that came from it–without Denham and his plans, I never would have met Ann! But this is good news, too. How can we help?"

The Storyteller looked at me as if to say, "I know how hard it was for a man like him to admit that." I saw true compassion in her face.

"You see, Kara, I told you that if they were made to understand, they would react as they have. We are all human in the end, and must contend with the same emotions. You will need their help if you are to succeed as the next Storyteller. Instead of the fear of living in the shadow of the Wall, be sure to lead them to a healthy pride in realizing that they could build such things as the Wall, that they could once again master this island and its beasts and explore its incalculable wonders."

Kara said, "But if they reveal us to others who won't understand or wish to help us, what then?"

Then I understood the full scope of the Storyteller's story and the truth it sought to illuminate as they understood it: The purpose of her story was to weave our incredibly different, seemingly antagonistic paths together, to reveal a branching journey in which we all shared a common fate. For my part, in exchange for being freed from my lifetime of fear and doubt about who and what my father was, and why he did what he did – for finding peace–I knew what I had to do, what I wanted to do.

I told her, "I will never reveal your secrets the outside world, Kara, unless you say it's necessary. The decision will be yours alone. I give you my word. Jack?"

"Ditto." There was no flippancy in his statement. He had given his bond.

With that the Storyteller smiled. "Then my quest has finally reached its goal. My story is coming to its end. Yours are just beginning."

Before Kara left to begin preparations for whatever she had planned, she stopped to turn and look at me. My eyes had never left her. Again, she flushed that exquisite shade before quickly departing. Jack went to signal the ship and send it back for supplies. But there was one thing the Storyteller said that did not make sense to me. When she had led me back to the place where I'd healed, I said, "I believe I understand the reason for your story. Then you said your quest was over, but you never said what it was."

Her seamed face broke into a smile and her eyes danced in a way that I cannot adequately describe– perhaps "timeless" would be close to the mark.

She opened one of the books and found a sketch of a beautiful young woman. "This is how I looked years ago. Your father imagined me and drew an accurate portrait." Looking back at me, her eyes glistening in the lamplight, she said softly, "My name then was Ishara."

"But that's impossible," I said incredulously, "you would have to be over–"

"Your mother said to me once that a lady never tells her age," she coyly interjected, and with a sly smile added, "Rest now and be ready. There are untold years of secrets to reveal, and fantastic mysteries to explore!"

THE END

New York City, Autumn 1961
The Origin of
The Following Narrative
By Vincent Denham

Millennia before the Golden Ages of Egypt and Greece, a uniquely marvelous race of humans existed on the shores of what today is a portion of the northern rim of the Indian Ocean,   southeast of the Bay of Bengal on the northeast side of the Andaman Sea. They called themselves the Tagatu. They lived in a world of giants, some approaching the size of the largest dinosaurs, and none were more dangerous or powerful than those to whom the Tagatu gave the name of "Kongs."

Unparalleled masters of the organic sciences, the Tagatu developed many effective formulas to tame, control, and then spectacularly harness the flora and fauna of their environment. Their communion with nature was so complete that some were even able to intuit the essence and rhythm of plant and animal behavior to a degree that still defies our understanding. Fearless, introspective, and observant, they felt an insatiable need to explore. They investigated their corner of the earth on land, sea, and to some degree, even the air.

And then they vanished.

They could have–perhaps would have–ruled the world. Their former greatness, and even more mysterious, their relationship to the giant species of anthropoids known as the Kongs, are only hinted at in a colossal Wall that still spans the peninsula of Skull Island, a barrier as old as the prehistoric denizens that yet thrive beyond it. Its immense height and length, crowned with saurian ridges that rip through the sky as far as the eye can gaze, defy the ravages of time. How did the Tagatu come to live on Skull Island, and how could they have built such a Wall in the midst of so many terrifyingly powerful creatures?

The only remnant of the super-race is a dwindling, atrophied tribe that over untold centuries has diminished. When encountered by my father, they had been reduced to bowing in fearful homage before their legendary beast-god, King Kong. Kong has now been taken from them, but their fear still enthralls them in the shadow of the ever-present Wall. They are no longer willing to confront the dangers–some real and others imaginary–that dwelled, and perhaps still dwell, beyond it.

I am Dr. Vincent Denham. My father, the famed entrepreneur Carl Denham, was the first modern man ever to set foot on Skull Island and view the Great Wall up close with his own eyes. He was responsible for King Kong's demise, among many other deaths, and for the loss of my own family. Eventually I came to understand that my father gave his own life to make amends to the inhabitants of Skull Island, to me, my mother, and to himself, but not before my discovering–and having to come to terms with–a tangle of mysteries and events impossible to have anticipated. As a man of reason, I would come face to face with the undeniable synergy between the knowable and the unknowable.

In 1957, I found my father's original map hidden, of all places, behind the only family photo that still remained from our happy times together. Already a paleontologist, I set out to locate Jack Driscoll, the first mate who had assisted in Kong's capture and who subsequently married Ann Darrow. He had literally saved Ann from the very grasp of Kong himself. Following my father's death, Jack and Ann had become a foster father and mother to me (the least he could do, Jack told me wryly, since Carl had brought them together in the first place).

Captain Engelhorn having disappeared along with my father, Jack had parlayed surplus Liberty ships after WWII into a successful merchant fleet of his own. When I revealed the long-lost map to Jack, we sailed to Skull Island together. In Jack's case, he went to face down the greatest fears he had ever known, but for me the journey meant much more than that. In fact, not until our voyage ended did my own passage truly begin. While Jack has effectively come to terms with himself and his experiences, I continue gradually to understand and acknowledge the connection between what I was looking for and (more important) what I have found.

Four years have passed since my first voyage to Skull Island, and while these notes will deal as closely as possible with my research, they would not be complete without my additional notes and observations, that is to say without a personal memoir, as it were. This strange experience has unalterably blurred the line between empirical science and the unquantifiable things that define me as a human being, things that will forever bind me with the natives on Skull Island and their fate. I feel compelled to provide this context in the event that these notes, for reasons that I hope will become clear in the writing, are discovered only years after I am gone.

Both the unexpected inner discoveries and the scientific revelations drive the writing of these notes, which not only describe and catalogue the world's most mysterious location, a unique spot on the earth, but continue probing into the very depths of those qualities that make me–us–human. It is abundantly clear that the civilization on Skull Island shares the same complex needs, hopes, and fears of all humankind.

At the time, it was impossible for me to see either the true nature of my quest or to acknowledge the emotional barrier I had built around myself. As a scientist, I had convinced myself that empiricism revealed the only reality, the only "truth," that made sense. This attitude had become a metaphorical Wall of my own making, enthralling me every bit as much as the Wall on Skull Island had enslaved the inhabitants there. All that began to change through the life-and-death experiences I encountered on Skull Island. Eventually, I even came to identify personally with the remnants of the Tagatu civilization that formerly I had blamed for stealing my parents from me.

Here are the highlights of what I discovered:

Human inhabitants built a Wall to shield them from the very real monsters on the other side of it. In relying on it, they came to feel that Wall as superior to their own resourcefulness and inner strength. Eventually, their fears degraded them to the point of sacrificing themselves like animals to animals, diminution in self-worth that threatened to extinguish completely this last vestige of a once-proud civilization.

But not all hope was lost. A last defiant light kindled in the hearts of three human beings. Undaunted by dangers both imaginary and real, two young islanders, Ishara and Kublai, with their culture's Pendonjira (the human embodiment and repository of the Tagatu past history), refused to surrender to fear. Against impossible odds, they resolved to break through that Wall and all that it represented, to strike out into the very heart of their island to rediscover the greatness of the former civilization from which they had descended; to find and bring back secrets that would save their dying race.

They apparently failed. However, again some hope remained. Inadvertently, these three became conduits for the rise of a creature of indomitable spirit who would one day overthrow the island's tyrannical ruler, a forward-evolved super-saurian of unimagined size, strength, ferocity, and intelligence called "Gaw." The creature that freed them from Gaw would come to be known as King Kong, the beast-god of Skull Island, the origin of legends. Around the story of King Kong's life and death, the fate of all others—the Tagatu civilization, my life, and that of many others—even Skull Island itself—all continue to revolve and intertwine.

Ironically, as fate would have it, my father's capture of King Kong and the destructive chain of events that resulted completed Ishara and Kublai's failed quest in a way no one expected. The aftermath of Kong's rampage revealed something extraordinary: As my father, and later I, discovered, buried deep within the ruptured Wall, the heart of that ancient civilization has continued to throb for an untold span of years. All the records and mysteries of their lost knowledge, along with secret accounts of their botanical and biologic discoveries remained hidden, placed there centuries earlier to protect them from those who would destroy them. This revelation gives the last vestige of that mysterious people, a remnant literally on the brink of extinction, a final chance to survive, perhaps even to flourish once again—and me as well.

These books convey what I have learned so far from three main sources: The stories of the islanders' ancient elder, the Pendonjira (which aptly translates to "Storyteller" in our tongue), who is the living memory of their culture's history and the direct descendant of her forebears, purportedly in an unbroken line. The second is part of the collection of over a quarter-century of voluminous notes, records, drawings and discoveries based on my late father's personal experiences, many in direct conversation with and under the tutelage of the Pendonjira, on Skull Island. The third are my own first-hand observations, theories and, where possible, initial conclusions as a Doctor of Paleontology with the American Museum of Natural History in New York City.

Collectively, these discoveries will shake the scientific foundation of the civilized world in such fields as anthropology, archeology, biology, botany, geology, oceanography, paleontology, the applied sciences and so much more. The impact of the release of such knowledge even in this early context, and its effect on the remaining population of Skull Island or the terms on which, if ever, that can be done, is not the purpose of these notes. Recording them as thoroughly as possible while there is still time.

I must note that Ishara (the present Pendonjira) says that all Pendonjiras, past and present, do not "pass on" stories like some gossip (her exact meaning is highly nuanced: it contains both humor and dismissiveness, combined with a genuine humility that flows from knowing her gift of storytelling is just that, a gift from God as she understands God to be). I've also been told that Pendonjiras do not receive their stories from spiritual intervention such as dictation or inspiration akin to the biblical accounts of the Ten Commandments or the Gospels, for example. Instead, she says that the stories are a 'part' of her. The closest I can interpret her meaning is that she is a biological repository–in modern terms, it would be akin to the stories being contained in her DNA–and that they are less conventional memories than inherent knowledge.

Even so, she took pains to point out that not every Pendonjira has the same gifts (again, there is great nuance in her language and this could mean many things: Stories remembered, natural talents, proclivities and more). When I asked her if the stories are 100% factual in their details–it is stunning how many there are–she indicated that the answer was 'yes' insofar as the intrinsic meaning needed to be conveyed by the story, but that to my amusing way of looking at things (by this she meant my professional needs as an empirical scientist as opposed to her philosophical/ spiritual needs), she slyly smiled and said, "pretty much." My personal experiences–and those of my father–as conveyed in the accompanying sketchbooks back up much of what she says, but we have discovered some curious and extremely interesting differences.

There is no doubt that Skull Island is more than Winston Churchill's Russia ever was "a riddle wrapped in a mystery inside an enigma." But this one, I might add, is populated by monsters and dangers of every size and form imaginable. The following stories will prove my point.

My first inclination was to present a word-for-word translation, with doubtful readings highly annotated. Yet the intrinsic drama of the narratives all but demands a livelier treatment, an effort at least to breathe life into the people and the creatures who walked our earth as we do. And so, I have written the accounts, as one might say, as a novelist or scenario writer would, yet without introducing fictional elements of my own. I have therefore rendered the English narrative as best as I know how from the Storyteller's translations of the scrolls and texts found within the Wall–presumably recorded by the Pendonjiras of Old. They will contain running commentary from Ishara and Kara, who is her younger, exotically beautiful yet potentially lethal, heir apparent. May I choose my words well.

KING KONG
of
SKULL ISLAND
EXODUS

It was a world now forgotten. No calendars such as we know existed. The earth teemed with creatures of every kind, from exquisite flyers to lumbering behemoths whose fossilized bones have been resurrected in our museums. The land lay lush and fertile, the water clear and life giving, but a change slowly came on and a nascent human civilization was even slower to acknowledge it. The altering world threatened their existence, though most ignored the signs–but some among them did not close their eyes. These read the portents clearly and prepared to grapple with their fate like the Titans they were.

The sky turned the color of a dead man's face, gray-green, mottled darkly as though by blood congealing beneath the surface. Away to the north, twin peaks continued to erupt in unison, long thunderous explosions sounding and echoing, black clouds clotted and roiling, billowing upward until the winds far above the highest fight of birds seized the blackness and spread it out into a streaked dark fan from which ash sifted down.

Beneath Aton's sandal-shod feet the earth shook as if in agony. Beside the man on the narrow, rough-hewn mountain trail loomed Krom, three times as tall as a human, scarred from a hundred battles, his fur now silvery-gray with age. He grumbled low in his throat, shook his head–hot ash had been settling on the fur of his crest–and nudged Aton's body. Time to go.

"Wait," Aton growled. "Something's happening up there. I want to see."

Man and Kong paused, both wary, the Kong so much so that he began to exude a natural, fear-inducing odor that affected enemies and prey alike, though it had no effect on his human counterpart. "Calm," Aton murmured, as much to himself as to the Kong. "Calm. Calm."

Five days before, he had warned the villagers of Kathat-Ran to flee. The mountains had already begun to tremble and belch, and he had seen a jagged crack spread along the shoulder of one, growing red-hot from the surging lava within. "This is going to be bad," he had warned them. Three hundred families' lives hung in the balance, he knew. Some of them, the youngest children, had the good sense to be frightened.

The older ones smiled at him.

"We don't need a Zan to tell us of the eruption," they explained as though speaking to an ignorant boy. "This has all happened before." They told him that in the months past they had sent back messengers from the Pendonjira, far to the south. A great exodus was supposed to commence there on the seacoast, but these inland villagers had never so much as seen the ocean, and they did not trust what they did not know. As they told Aton, they felt certain that what had always happened after a period of volcanic unrest would happen again: the mountains would send steam and ash into the air for a day, a week, maybe even a month, and then slumber again.

"You're wrong," Aton insisted. "This will be bigger than any eruption in memory."

The elders had calmly assured him that abandoning the village was not possible. "Without us to irrigate them, our crops will wilt in the heat season," an old man said with a shrug.

Another had complained, "Say we abandon our homes and treasure-houses and nothing bad happens. Who knows what bandits might creep in from the passes? They swarm like locusts outside the mountain barrier. Bands of the Nagatl have broken through before. You Zantu and your Kongs are supposed to keep us safe."

Nagatl–the name for the uncivilized near-human brutes who ravaged like animals. "If the Nagatl come," Aton had warned, "they will die, and so will you, as surely as we stand here."

But one old woman had chuckled at that. "I've lived with these mountains for all my life. They always rumble and belch. This will pass. It always passes."

"Fools," Aton had growled, turning away in anger. He had grown too old to have patience, and without word from the Pendonjira, he hesitated to use force–truth to tell, Aton worried that perhaps Krom was past his prime and could no longer stand against so many armed men as the village might muster.

So, he and Krom had left the village that same morning, taking to the mountain trails along the western side of Takel-Atu Valley, the fertile triangle wedged between two ranges of mountains, and had hurried southward, away from the eruption. Now, many leagues distant, he paused to gaze back. From here he could see as far as the plain where two rivers joined, where the villagers of Kathat-Ran– the words meant "Place of Plenty"–had constructed their longhouses and their stone granaries, where their burgeoning fields stretched out along the shores of both rivers–stretched northward, toward the smoking mountains. The eruption continued, seeming no worse than it had been, though now the ash had overcast the northern sky. He signed in frustration, anger–and sheer weariness.

With Krom, Aton had traveled hard and long for five whole days and nights, snatching only brief intervals of rest. They drank from mountain springs–though the water now had begun to taste of sulfur and stank like rotten eggs–and when their empty stomachs rumbled, they ignored them. Five days had taken them far. From this height, he could just see where the distant village stood, though he couldn't make out individual buildings, just a faint smudge of brown against the lush green background of forest, dimly reflected in the water that guarded two sides of the settlement.

He felt the earth surge, lift and drop as though solid rock had become ocean. The Negani river, leading south from the mountains, sent waves washing over the banks as the quake rolled down the valley. Another tremor hit.

Aton staggered, and Krom dropped briefly to all fours. Hearing a clatter, Aton glanced up. Rocks leapt and bounded down the steep slope above. He jerked his head, and Krom pressed close against the mountainside. The overhang above them offered some protection. Rocks the size of Krom's head rattled over and down, smashed somewhere below.

Aton growled when he gazed again northward. The twin volcanoes had blown up–the very ground had vanished in an insane, rolling, glowing cloud of gas and lava heated beyond the liquid phase. Jets of material flew into the sky. The burning cloud rushed down the slopes, impossibly fast, faster than any bird could fly or any beast could run. When it reached the forest, everything it touched vanished in surges of steam and smoke, trees and crops and flesh instantly incinerated. The earth shook again, and the water in the river leapt. The searing cloud thundered down the broadening valley. It reached the site of the village–

Kathat-Ran flared to fire and steam, and both rivers died in a pale explosion. Water vaporized instantly. Red streamers of gas flowed in the now-empty stream beds.

"Come!" Aton shouted to Krom. No hope remained that anyone or anything had survived. He could picture the thousand people of Kathat-Ran barricaded in their longhouses, or perhaps seeking the greater protection they imagined they'd find in the stone granaries. The smug elders believed themselves safe there–until the incandescent cloud whisked the wooden buildings to billowing ash in less time than a heartbeat, turned the stone structures into superheated liquid in the same instant.

The roar grew and filled the world. Now enormous white-hot magma bombs flew arcing into the sky from the craters, streaking red trails against the darkening sky, screaming down to explode in the heavy forest, setting trees ablaze. Aton led Krom around the shoulder of the mountain, finding some protection from its bulk, heading for their one path to possible safety–

Until he saw ahead that the High Bridge had vanished. A wonder of woven rope and stout planks, it had stood here for as long as memory stretched, giving the Zantu Watchers a route between Daram Pass and the Karim Pass to the south. An earthquake must have sent the broad ledge on the far side down, down two thousand feet, to the jumbled scree of stone falls long past.

Now only tangles of rope dangled on this side, still tethered to the two great mortared pylons that the ancients had erected. The crevasse wasn't broad–too far for Krom to leap, surely, but not much broader than that–but now their only way to reach the opposite side would be to spend a day climbing down the dangerously steep side of this mountain and longer than that climbing up the far cliff. They had no time. Waves of ash and superheated gas and poisoned air swept toward them.

If they tried to climb down, they'd be dead long before sunset.

Out of sight around the cliff behind them, in the north the eruption continued. If Aton and Krom could not reach the other side of the mountains, the western slopes of the western barrier– impossible here in Daram Pass, where the stone ramparts rose vertically, and they couldn't head back northward in the face of the deadly rain of magma–if they couldn't somehow put the mountain crests between them and the valley, they would die. Karim offered them a bare chance–if they could reach it.

Krom walked to the edge of the drop and began to haul in the tangled ropes that once had been the bridge.

"It's hopeless," Aton told him in the flat tone of a man resigned to death.

The great gray anthropoid looked over his shoulder and glared at Aton. Pausing for a moment, he lifted a shaggy arm and pointed across the ravine.

A gnarled, ancient *pipatl* tree grew on the far side of the ravine, one that probably no longer produced the small, bitter figs of its kind. Aton had passed this way a thousand times and had never paid attention to the *pipatl*, though it must have grown here for centuries and surely had sent fiercely strong, knotted and clinging roots to find stubborn purchase in every crevice and crack. Such trees were tough and sturdy–but this one stood unreachably distant. "Too far to jump," Aton yelled against the roar of the eruption.

Krom grunted as though in disagreement, turned away, and continued to haul up the wreckage of the bridge, his shoulder muscles hunching. And then Aton realized what Krom intended.

"All right," Aton said. "We'll try. We have only our lives to lose."

Above the deafening, universal thunder of the eruption rose sudden, startling shrieks, terrified screeches. An immense flock of brilliantly-colored birds, predominately bright green and yellow, flew past, wings frantically beating as they veered to put the sheltering mountains between them and the annihilation up the valley. A house-sized magma bomb screamed downward–and in its billowing, burning wake Aton saw the laggard birds turn to flame in mid-flight, their charred, blackened bodies tumbling. He caught the scorching wave of heat and turned away from it, gasping as his beard and hair sizzled to ash and blisters rose on his exposed arms–if he'd been a little closer to the fiery trail, he would have been as dead as the birds. He ran to Krom's side. "Let me do that."

He used his knife, then hurriedly tied and spliced while Krom sorted through the wood beams that once had floored the bridge. He found one that he seemed to like. He held it, turned, and battered it hard against the mountain. With a sharp crack the wood broke in half–a beam that had been tough enough to stand the turn of a thousand seasons could not withstand the strength of a

Kong. "Here, I see what you're doing," Aton said. He lashed the rope to the cubit-long piece of heavy wood. "I hope this is long enough."

Krom coiled the rope, studied the distance, and then took two, three, five steps out. His prehensile feet clung to the edge of the precipice.

"You're going to fall!" Aton warned.

Krom glowered at him. They had been a working team for nearly as long as they both had lived. Although they had always depended on each other, they seldom agreed. But somehow, so far they had survived.

"All right!" shouted Aton. Another earthquake made him stagger. The bright day had dimmed to deep twilight, though somewhere far above the impenetrable black clouds the sun stood at noon. With a grunt, Krom swung the bound weight of wood around his head, faster and faster, until the whirling rope whistled. Then, evidently judging his moment, he flung it toward the tree–

If the wood anchor could catch in the contorted, tough branches, if it could only hold–If they could secure this end of the rope to one of the enduring pylons–

If the rope and the tree could both bear their weight–"Odds are we'll die," Aton muttered.

He grimaced as Krom's improvised grappling hook swung down into the crevasse just a handsbreath short of the tree.

Many days' journey to the south of the tormented mountains, the Khaliged River, now grown broad, yellow-brown, and sluggish, had always quietly emptied into the sea. There at its mouth the Tagatu had built their chief port, Temuan, a city of hundreds of great longhouses and broad stone-paved streets, a settlement built hugging both banks of the river and the shore of the ocean. In the broad bay to the south a maze of offshore islets and rugged towers of sea-sculpted rock offered protection from the stormy southern sea–but now destruction threatened from the north. The people of Temuan sensed the ponderous weight of it, the deadly threat of it– and all understood that time was running short. A month earlier, in the midst of their preparations to embark and flee the cataclysm their natural philosophers expected, the people of Temuan had felt the first great earthquake and had seen the first blurred black smoke plume of a distant eruption.

The quake had cracked some of the stone storehouses and had loosened the square-cut stones of the streets, though it had done no great damage, not even as much as past quakes had wrought. Still, the tremor was only the advance warning.

Now the whole northern horizon lay dim beneath a heavy dark smudge, and even from this far away everyone could hear a constant, deep rumble and feel it coming up through their feet and legs. Their worried eyes turned nervously northward, peering, trying to envision the havoc breaking beneath that dark canopy. They could only imagine the terror those further up the valley must feel–if any yet lived to feel it.

For days, rumors had flowed in from the upper valley. The fertile lands to the north, east, and west comprised vast expanses. The forests and plains sustained herds of mammoths and indricotheres, rhino-like giants, among the largest land animals ever to exist. All had been driven to stampede. Word of entire communities trampled in a single day had drifted southward along the river.

Dread of what might be coming added to the turmoil and unrest of an over-crowded city. Packed with throngs of people ready to embark, the port was strained almost beyond its limits. Most of the inhabitants of the lower valley had fled here, with everything they hoped to keep loaded in wagons or even carried on their backs. Dozens of tent cities had sprung up outside the boundaries of Temuan to accommodate them–and now three-fourths of the population of Takel-Atu Valley clustered here, crushed into the open spaces fronting the sea.

The rest, those who obstinately remained behind, were mostly farm folk from the far northern reaches–as were the Zantu, the first line of defense, always patrolling the mountainous ramparts with their Kongs. Yet lately even they and their powerful companions had also begun to hasten down the valley and into the city. Some came with small groups of farmers they had persuaded to flee. Others arrived with grim stories of towns that had collectively decided to risk remaining in the path of danger, who had clung to their fields and homes.

But if the farmers would not travel to the port, the Zantu would. For generations untold, the Pendonjira and Zantu castes had allied in knowledge and power for the betterment of the burgeoning Tagatu civilization. At times their alliance had grown contentious, yet it never broke. The Pendonjiras, the people's philosophical and spiritual leaders, shaped the laws and traditions that wove the Tagatu into a culture. The Zantu, in contrast, had remained aloof, detached, though their ascetic caste powerfully defended the frontiers of Tagatu land. To the time of the eruptions, the Zantu and the Pendonjiras had been partners, but at a distance. Now the upheavals forced them together to work hand in hand.

Each arrival of a Zan with his Kong stirred new awe, and not just from the dire news the Zan bore: In civilized areas, the appearance of a Kong inspired terror. The Pendonjira listened, especially to the accounts of those who had determined to remain behind. She might have sent the Zantu back with orders to force the reluctant ones south–but that would mean packing more bodies into the already seething port. The farmers were free, after all. If they refused to escape, they could remain where they were.

And who knew if the stubborn ones would survive? Would they hold out and remain, or would they finally, when it was too late and all the ships had gone, surrender to the eruptions and the quakes and flee to the south and to the questionable safety of the sea?

As far as that went, who could tell if all of the Zantu, always an aloof clan, would heed the Pendonjira's call to come in, to join the exodus? Rumors ran through the anxious tent cities like fire driven by wind–the Zantu had revolted against the Pendonjira and were actively preventing any stragglers from coming downriver. No, the Zantu were traveling slowly because they and their mighty Kongs were driving the reluctant farmers before them, like flocks of clamoring geese. No, the Zantu were not coming because they and the farmers were already dead.

One tale contradicted the next. No one knew anything for certain, but from all the people of the port could tell, the Zantu and the farmers might indeed all have perished. Eleven days earlier, shoals of decomposing fish washed down the river–bellies burst, cooked alive, all rotting.

The water itself turned poisonously yellow-green, streaked with rainbow stains of putrid fish oil and stinking of rotten eggs and decay. Day by day, the river level dropped so that the reduced flow ran through an expanse of slimy mud reeking of uncleanness. Giant water reptiles and other voracious scavengers surged downriver to feed on the carrion. People slow to leave the riverbanks began disappearing, with stories of cruel monsters invading populated villages to feast on human flesh.

No wind blew strong or constant enough to dispel the miasma. It grew worse over the next three days. Finally, the whole eastern quarter of the port–the smaller side, once an enclave of powerful families who owned huge trading ships and whose dwellings were elaborate and richly decorated– had emptied as the well-off fled from the unbearable stench and any contagion it no doubt carried. The three long bridges swung in the wind or shuddered with the rolling tremors of quakes, but their wild swaying threatened no one, for now no one used them. Below them the wide river had dwindled to stagnant rivulets. The mud dried, caked, and cracked day by day. Someone–possibly a looter, going through the eastern houses for anything they might steal–was careless or malicious with an open flame, and one deep night the eastern quarter went up in a raging fire that lasted for three days. Two of the bridges collapsed from that end.

Thirst became an epidemic. The healers warned everyone not to drink the polluted water that still crept in the constricted rivulets of the old riverbed, and they cautioned the unwary to stay away from the mud, for the tainted air from it would spread disease. Off to the west, the deep wells were still unpolluted, though the water from them smelled of sulfur. However, too many people were hauling water from them, and the underground springs could not keep up with the demand. The ground water levels began to dwindle, like the river.

Steadily the western part of Temuan had become crushingly crowded, and the people murmured and wondered why the river water had vanished, for the great wide stream had always been a source of life to the city. The Zantu knew the reason: The mountain creeks and brooks feeding the watercourse had dried up.

The river now brought death, not life. The harbor bore an ugly broad and expanding stain of polluted, stinking water. The earthquakes grew in intensity and frequency. On the morning that the last wealthy refugees had passed into the western section of Temuan, another plume of dark ash had jetted into the sky to the north and east, very far away to be sure, but still much nearer than the first eruptions. The Pendonjira had sent scouts upstream to investigate. None had returned by the morning of the twelfth day.

"We must leave this place," the Pendonjira said quietly. Her hands rested flat on a stone parapet as she gazed out toward the harbor. Now she clenched them into fists. "We cannot delay more. We must leave. Now."

Malana, the teenage girl standing next to her, did not reply, but looked fearfully down from their high perch and doubted they would be able to leave anytime soon–not for weeks, perhaps months, not until the confusion and the anger rolling through the streets had come under control, not before the creeping rafts had loaded all the ships–and such an undertaking, she thought, was all but impossible. In the harbor, the lee of Lagano Reef–once a thickly-forested island that towered a thousand feet into the sky and stretched twenty times that long from tip to tip–now stood desolate, a crescent of harsh rock completely denuded of trees. But this destruction was no natural catastrophe; it was the work of humans.

The vanished trees remained, transformed by carpenters into the greatest fleet of vessels ever constructed. They rode at anchor, and from this height they seemed uncountable to Malana, so many, she thought, that they could never be filled with supplies–or with the people crowded into the port. Below her, a hundred strong ships and more strained at their moorings, shepherded by the five huge flagships, giants among pygmies, bigger than any other vessels ever made. From the nearly derelict wharves–for the seaport had suffered tremendously in the past decades from tsunamis and earthquakes, and repairs had become makeshift and temporary, since everyone knew the next great wave or quake would undo the work again–convoys of the heavily laden rafts pushed off, taking supplies and passengers out to the ships, a constant convoy. To Malana, though, the crowds on the wharves never seemed to diminish. Impossible.

Then something on the shore caught her attention, down where surging crowds clustered around the wharves. She heard distant voices raised loud in argument and contention. It looked like a riot in the making.

"We can't possibly leave today," Malana murmured. "It's–it's too soon." Up here the wind was fresher, but she suffered all the same. She had never liked heights, and here they stood on the platform of the lighthouse, the tallest structure in the city.

"Too soon?" asked the Pendonjira in a flat, grim voice. "We Pendonjiras told the Tagatu what must be done long ago. A hundred years ago, very nearly. The eruptions were coming more often and were more violent each time. The Tagu scholars read the signs even then. They knew this dark day would come."

Malana, who was a young woman of eighteen–very nearly the Pendonjira's youngest assistant–started to speak again, thought better of it, and closed her mouth instead. The two of them shared the high platform of the fire-beacon tower, where at night a great bronze brazier filled with oil-soaked wood constantly burned to give ships guidance, the leaping tongue of flame visible far out to sea.

Whether the tower would stand much longer was, Malana thought, doubtful. Though strongly constructed of the nearly indestructible ilu mortar and stone, even the lighthouse had suffered from the tsunamis and the quakes and now great slanting timbers shored it up on three sides. Malana had the irrational feeling that at any moment a quake would roll down the valley and the tower would collapse into rubble–or simply topple forward, like a felled tree, into the harbor.

When would I die? In the fall, or when the tower struck earth and sea? When? How much would it hurt?

Nausea wrenched her stomach, and she desperately tried to change the course of her thoughts. All too often, such doubts had threatened to overwhelm her, but she stubbornly refused to speak of them. Again, a gabble of harsh voices came to, thinned by distance. "The Kai are having trouble with the Atu dissenters," Malana said, pointing to the Long Wharf, where a crowd flowed and ebbed before the mounted riders.

"*Ai,*" groaned the Pendonjira. "Let's go, child, and do what we can. We must stand together, we *must*–or the Tagatu people will perish."

They descended the hundred-odd spiral stone steps, the Pendonjira striding firmly ahead, Malana clinging to the rope-rail and following more slowly, carefully placing her feet. The Pendonjira reached the bottom of the steps and gestured impatiently. She reached firm ground and ran to catch up.

"Child, step out. Do not run. Running suggests a lack of control."

Panting, Malana said, "Pendonjira, I am a woman now. Must you name me 'Child'?"

"You are a woman in years. When you are one in behavior, you may leave that name behind you. Hurry now, but don't run."

The Pendonjira's simple garments flowed elegantly as her modest jewelry–each necklace or earring held meaning–jangled in melody with her movements. In appearance and demeanor, she could blend with both kings and peasants–but people recognized her and reacted. As she encountered the jostling crowds at the foot of the long piers, she did not demand passage, but took it, and as the people in the streets realized who walked among them, they either willingly or grudgingly made space. The Pendonjira and Malana crossed the broad street, threaded their way to the wharves, and pushed toward the sounds of argument and the grunts of the draks, the hulking, snorting, half- tamed mounts that the Kai rode. Curses and bellows jagged the air.

Now they walked through throngs mainly of Tagu descent, those who venerated the Pendonjira. Here the crowds murmured as they saw the woman approaching, striding with her tall staff clacking the cobblestones at each step, her robes concealing her long legs and her body, a woman not yet old–though Pendonjiras were always treated as august elders–but mature, high-breasted, and graceful. The crowds parted, the people nodding their respect–though Malana noticed some few with resentment in their eyes. The scowlers were Atu, no doubt, the clan of hunters and warriors that agitated to retreat to a new home on land, not trusting the path over the sea.

A phalanx of Kai, their long spears held leveled and ready, had thrust a mob of shouting people away from the stone storehouses at the base of the Long Wharf. "What is this?" the Pendonjira called in her clear voice, the sound penetrating the mutterings and murmurings.

One of the Atu, a man in middle life with broad shoulders and wearing the ritual facial and shoulder scars of his clan, stepped forward, his face contorted in anger. His thick voice held barely-contained fury: "These pig-riders won't let us take our share of the supplies!"

"The supplies are for all of us," the Pendonjira stated firmly. "We'll need them when we land on the island."

The Atu muttered and cursed at the word. "Island!" one of them said in the same tone he might have used to complain of having stepped in dung.

The Atu leader thrust a fist up in the air, silencing his followers. "We were not made to travel across the sea on those things," he said, gesturing at the harbor and the ships in it.

"We fashioned them to carry us. And we know the ships are safe," the Pendonjira began. "We've had hundreds of years of practice–"

"Not the Atu! Only those weaklings who gain their food through trade! The Atu never traded–we took what we wanted!"

"That changed when our peoples united to become the Tagatu," the Pendonjira retorted. "Your leaders agreed. Will you dishonor your ancestors and their leaders now? Atu value honor, I thought!"

"Atu value life!" the man shot back. With a snarl, he gestured toward the west. "We know of a country far to the west we could take! Our Atu legends tell of it. Our scouts have beheld it! Those who live in this land are weak, mere farmers who cluster in huts between two rivers! We can easily destroy them or enslave them, take their lands, and live there!"

At the mention of killing and enslaving, the Pendonjira's expression hardened. She asked, "It is a good land, then? A safe land? Have they mountains to guard them against the Nagatl?"

"Mountains! We don't need to hide behind mountains. The Nagatl are only animals! *We* can guard against them!" The man brandished his *pikata*, the short weapon halfway between a dagger and a short sword that marked his rank as a sub-leader of his clan.

The Pendonjira stared at him. "You are Tau-Atu," she said in her soft voice. "I know you well. Your whole family have fought against this plan from the first. Your grandfather did not even want to send the first ships out to find a new homeland, threatened to burn them before they could depart. Others of your clan stopped him from doing that. In a later time, your father said the mountains would never erupt. Until a few years ago you agreed with him, if I remember correctly. Yet today they fill the sky with their poison and their fire—just as the Tagu scholars warned you all they would!"

Tau-Atu scowled as people around began to murmur. "We've seen volcanoes before! These eruptions may yet come to nothing!"

Malana broke in: "Nothing! They've killed the river, haven't they?" A glare from the Pendonjira made her fall silent.

Tau-Atu said with a sneer, "Yes, silence your she-cub. I don't know what tainted the river. It may yet run clear again, and what happened may not have been the fault of the volcanoes. But even if they are destined to wipe out all life in the valley, why should we risk our lives on ships? I tell you, there are lands waiting to be taken. And we have the force to take them! We Atu once roamed the wide world and feared nothing and no one! Before we joined with the farmers, the thinkers, the—" he paused for a moment and then spat out a word that he made to sound like a curse—"*civilized* Tagu!"

The Pendonjira raised her voice: "Yes! Your people and ours merged generations ago and became one. And did not the Tagatu civilization then build the greatest and strongest clan the world has known?"

Tau-Atu struck himself in the chest. "At the cost of our way of life!"

The other Atu were looking around at the crowd. Malana noticed them and thought: *They know the mob is half on their side already. A little more and it will be an open fight. Will the crowd join in? On whose side?*

The Pendonjira looked past Tau-Atu and spoke directly to the others: "Listen to me: We have known malcontents before, and one fanatic will corrupt a hundred well-balanced people. Do not follow this man. That will be the ruin of you all. We are out of time. We cannot cling to a past that only divides us! We are the Tagatu! We must be one strong people together!"

Malana heard but did not heed her, wondering, *Where can we retreat?* Her primary duty was to protect the Pendonjira, no matter what. And the older woman was just stubborn enough to stand her ground and try to use reason against pikes and swords.

How many drak riders? She could count only eleven Kai—normally more than enough against thirty or more armed men on foot, but now the nervous animals shuffled uneasily, hemmed in by the fearful crowds. If the Atu started something, the Kai would probably strike out even at harmless bystanders, for they were used to fighting in the open, not in the midst of crowds. Their terrifying drak mounts stood six feet tall at the shoulder, their ragged-toothed snouts over three feet long— effective living weapons in a battle, but overkill in a melee packed with unarmed spectators.

Malana groaned. If the Pendonjira had not picked her out at age twelve to become apprenticed as one of her helpers, Malana might have been among the mounted warriors, for she was of their clan, and the strongest women sometimes became riders, or so legends said. She shivered, recalling how one of the draks had killed her uncle, a trainer—killed him and then partly eaten him—

Tau-Atu roared, "Enough!" Again, he brandished his weapon. "Pendonjira, I would not hurt you unless you force me. I tell you, stand aside. What the Atu need the Atu will take!"

The other foot warriors cheered and drew their weapons.

Struggling to control his grunting mount, which must have sensed how close blood was, one of the Kai shouted, "Remain still or be made to do so!"

Malana tensed, reaching for the Pendonjira's arm. "We need to back away," she told her teacher in her most urgent voice.

But the Pendonjira jerked away from her grasp and ignored her words. "Tau-Atu, don't lead your people into death!"

Tau-Atu leveled his *pikata* and shouted, "Woman, stand back!"

She planted her staff on the cobblestones before her. "Here I stand, and here I stay. You will have to kill me!"

I'll have to drag her!

The thought went against all of Malana's training–she revered the Pendonjira, no matter how exasperating she might be, and to touch her against her will was forbidden–but it was a question of survival–

Malana stepped forward, hand outstretched– Tau-Atu whirled his blade above his head–

And a roar shook the very stones of the street. The crowd yelped, shrieked in alarm, spun around, scrambled back from the looming dark form that had stolen up so quietly.

"I think there will be no fight today," a deep voice rumbled. The crowd melted away as a tall man, not young but strongly made and grim of face, stepped forward.

Malana found she had been holding her breath. She gasped now and yelled, "Aton!"

A cord whipped out with lightning speed, its weighted end wrapping around Tau-Atu's *pikata*, yanking it from his clutch. All eyes froze on the gray-haired Zan who now gripped the weapon. Without a backward glance, he handed the *pikata* to the Kong who loomed behind him. "Break it, Krom."

Krom snapped the blade like a dry twig, then reared up. Fiercely glaring down at the rabble, he drummed his chest, sounding a thunderous challenge old as time itself.

And to Malana for that single instant the world hung on a perilous balance between peace and bloodshed.

The old Kong waded in. Bristling with anger, lifting one drak over his head …

The stench of sulfur cloaked the countryside. A league inland from the port, two hulking Kongs walked slowly–for them–advancing in their distinctive manner. Ponderously bipedal, their gait was more hunched than that of a human, their arms slowly swinging with each stride to maintain balance. Though the Kongs moved leisurely, it was difficult for their two human Zantu to keep the southward pace.

Overhead, the morning sun already rode high and hot. The younger human, the sixteen-year-old boy called Taigu, occasionally stumbled, though he always managed to strategically plant his staff to keep his balance before falling. His father, Vekan, growled, "Do you want me to carry you?"

"No," the teenager replied sullenly, using surliness to conceal his exhaustion. He thought: *Now I know at least one reason why the Zantu value their staffs so much!*

The Zantu staff resembled a simple walking stick, but it was far more. Developed over generations of experience gleaned from battle and survival in the wild, each one was both a walking aid and a weapon. They also contained touches unique to each Zan. Often segmented, the traditional Zantu staff contained ointments, medicines, and poisons in hidden receptacles. It was even used for making musical sounds specifically pitched between a Zan and his Kong. It was an effective and, if necessary, deadly weapon.

Father and son had covered a great distance already, walking each day from before dawn to past sundown. On that particular day, they had risen even earlier than usual and had set out on the last leg of the journey, following a well-beaten trade route that traced the sinuous course of the dwindling river. Normally a lushly vegetated span of lands, now the arid gray soil looked drought-stricken, brittle dry weeds and dead trees offering no sustenance to beasts, and no shade for humans. The ground trembled again, the third aftershock they had felt. A fresh whiff of sulfur tainted the air.

The four plodded onward, the Kongs differing in appearance as much as the son did from his father: the gray-shouldered Chang (unlike their modern, smaller African cousins, mature Kongs silvered on the back of their heads, shoulders and upper arms as they matured), a bull about twenty feet in height, stood two feet taller than his adolescent son Khaan, who was a touch leaner, but still heavily muscled with a rich coat of mixed black and dark umber tones. Both Kongs glanced all around as if seeking a threat, growling and grumbling in their chests.

"They sense danger, but don't understand it. And they don't like what they can't fight," Vekan explained. He glanced at his son. "If you want, we can rest, but see–the Kongs' camp is there ahead, just at the horizon. You can make it out there. It's not too far away now."

"Another sixth of a day," Taigu muttered.

"Not that long, not if we make more speed." Vekan gave his son a smile, something rare in these last few weeks. "What do you want to do, take a rest now or walk faster and then rest longer when we get to camp?"

"Let's get to camp," Taigu said in a grudging tone. His father had taught him that Zantu had to be strong and enduring. Despite his aching legs and blistered feet, he refused to show weakness, not in front of Vekan. His father did not respond in words, but deftly twisted his staff to reveal a waxy salve and quickly massaged it into his knee and ankle. He nodded at his son to do the same. The boy did so and felt instant relief. His father gave a knowing glance and passed him the water-skin. Taigu drank deeply.

"How many Zan do you suppose will be there?" he asked. "No one really knows."

Taigu had learned how isolated Zantu generally were. Pairs of them rarely traveled together. They gathered in a group no more often than once every ten years–and then only at the request of their sister, the Pendonjira. Taigu could barely remember the meeting he and his father had attended years before. The Zantu had spoken of the changing face of the valley and of the movements of its creatures, particularly the Nagatl, traditionally the greatest threat to the Tagatu—but now they had sunk nearly into unimportance. It would be strange to walk into a whole camp of Zantu, of Kongs.

"Come," his father said, and the humans set out again. Both spoke to their Kongs in the secret language that only Zantu trainers knew. The huge, untiring anthropoids immediately quickened their pace. Taigu had to trot to keep up, and even his father walked with extraordinarily long strides. They cut Taigu's estimated time to the camp nearly in half and, as they approached, Taigu could observe at least twenty-odd Zantu and their Kongs. "Twice as many as I have ever seen in one place," Vekan muttered in a serious tone.

Upon their arrival, Chang stood tall and looked anxiously around until he spotted Sakie, his mate. He pushed his way toward her with a determination that made men and even Kongs scatter. "Let them have their reunion," Sakie's Zan, a sturdy, red-faced, middle-aged man named Ranth, told them. He gestured to the newcomers with his staff. Taigu noticed its distinctive features and markings. "Vekan, Taigu, welcome. Here, we have a meal ready. You two must be starving."

After they had settled around the campfire and had taken the edge off their hunger with a meal of roasted dried fish and steaming-hot lentils, Taigu looked curiously at the others. Each Zantu had his own look, developed as a consequence of his close companionship with a particular Kong and of the environment they frequented. Here was one whose clothing in color and texture seemed made to blend in with red sandstone rock. Another man wore dark gray, and even when sitting his limbs had the twisted look of gnarled shrub branches.

Ranth broke in on his thoughts when he asked, "Did you come from the east passes?"

Vekan nodded. "Six days ago." His tone was short, as though he had small desire to speak of what he had left behind.

Ranth's eyebrows rose high on his red forehead. "You made good speed! How is it there?"

Vekan stared into the flickering embers of the campfire. Quietly, reluctantly, he spoke: "The ash falls are terrible—we saw hundreds of animals dead from having breathed in the dust. We were fortunate. We just caught the southern edge of the ash, though I think now the passes must be choked with it, for the wind shifted."

Taigu added in a confident tone, "At least the Nagatl won't be able to invade the valley. Not from that direction, anyway."

The men who had gathered around to hear the news laughed at that, but Vekan scowled. "A good son doesn't speak before being asked to speak until he's of age," he said flatly. "And though I agree that nothing, not even Nagatl, could come through the passes now, that might not be true in a month. Better for us all to board the ships and be away."

A Zantu whom Vekan didn't know remarked, "We've just been debating that. Some of us want to move far to the east, where the eruptions won't threaten us. We know of lands there that offer good hunting, and the people would be weaklings compared to us."

"How many of you think this way?" Vekan demanded.

"Not many." The stranger smiled apologetically. "My name is Athis. I'm not one of that group, Vekan. And it's no more than five or six in all, and they're not certain."

Still, Vekan's voice rang harshly: "That's five or six too many. Since when does a Zan consider meat his only source of nourishment? What Zan would not rather starve than become a marauding usurper? It would have befitted them better to have joined with the Thakus rather than our noble Kong! Besides, we'll need every Zan and every Kong when we reach the islands."

Once again Taigu, who had risen to his feet, spoke up: "Here comes a runner from the town!"

They all looked in the direction Taigu pointed. A skinny young man was indeed on the run, his arms pumping. "Messenger from the Pendonjira," Ranth decided. He called out an order, and the Kongs, who had reared when they noticed the runner, dropped down again, quiet but alert.

The man–hardly a man, barely of age, sinewy and lean and long–pounded to a stop, bent over with his hands on his knees, and panted for a moment, the breath rattling harsh in his throat. Then, gasping, he said, "Pendonjira needs the Kongs to arrive now. Take them to the Great Wharf. Boarding the ships today, before sunset."

"Why did she send you, boy, instead of her birds?" Athis asked.

"Something in the air and a change in the inner workings of the earth," he panted. "They became disoriented–even refuse to fly."

"All right," Ranth told him. "Here, drink this. You can return with us."

"No, more messages." But he took time to drink from a tortoise-shell cup and to catch his breath before running back down the half-ruined road.

It took some little time to break camp, and then the Zantu and their Kongs headed southward, to the outskirts of the town itself. "Is this all of us?" Taigu asked Ranth.

"No. Many more have already left in staggered intervals to board the five *Leader* ships."

"Ships–you mean boats?" queried Taigu.

"No, son, ships: They are much larger than boats, capable of carrying many people and Kongs if designed properly."

"I've heard of this from afar," Ranth chimed in, but your domain is much closer to the Tagatu cities and towns and I presume you have better knowledge than I on the matter. Are the stories of years of preparations true?"

"We shall see," said Vekan. "Our sister Pendonjira is responsible for all the people. She and her Tagatu leaders have had to think far ahead." Thoughtfully, he added, "Unlike the Zantu, who live in the moment."

"Thinking far ahead is always a difficult thing to do for anyone," mused Ranth.

"From what I understand," Vekan said, "the traders and explorers have used their knowledge of the sea and ships to build vessels greater than any others. These ships will bear us to the islands."

Taigu's eyes widened with suspense. "Have they finished these 'ships' and if so, why do they need us? How *big* are they? If they are going to hold Kongs they must be–"

"Patience, we shall see. One thing is certain: We can no longer afford to live apart; the time has come that we must band together as one or cease to exist. Come!"

And so they proceeded. Vekan's face was a picture of seriousness, that of Ranth a study in determination, while the countenance of Taigu was that of an open book written with wonder.

They reached the city gates, which stood open. Taigu and Khaan dropped to the rear of the group

Taigu had never seen a town this size before, and he gawked at the people and the buildings. Many of them had been longhouses built of immense and sturdy logs, with arched roofs that had been caulked with the same strong mortar that waterproofed the ships. Then a layer of earth had been spread on the roofs, covered with living moss. Now the moss had browned and blackened with the changed weather of the last few years. Some houses, especially those on the fringes of the town, lay in complete ruins, collapsed and half-buried in silt.

"Floods?" Taigu wondered aloud.

"No," a crackling, aged voice answered him. "A great mountain-wave from the sea." He turned and saw an old woman, leaning on a staff, slowly hobbling behind him. "Along with dozens of others, my son and daughter-in-law were drowned when that house fell on them. They and their two sons and one daughter," she added in her quavering voice. "That is why I visit here every day. That is why when the others leave, I will stay, to die close to them."

"I–I'm sorry," Taigu said. He had not called Khaan to a halt, and the Kong had pulled far ahead. "I have to go."

She didn't respond, and the last he saw of her was a glimpse as she slowly and painfully knelt beside the ruined house, gripping her staff.

Taigu had not thought of the old before. How many would refuse to go? How many would stay here, where the Pendonjira and the Tagu assured them everyone would die? What was it like to be so old that death must seem almost welcome?

He shuddered and realized he had lost his way. He called to Khaan. "Over here, I think." The Kong hesitated, but obediently accompanied him.

People milled in the broad street. They pointed and talked in low voices as they hurried past, and some parents held children up to see a Kong–not a common sight in the lowlands, Taigu gathered. Then it occurred to him that he must have truly lost his way, for if he hadn't, the onlookers would have seen plenty of Kongs preceding him.

He had almost made up his mind to ask someone for directions to the wharves when Khaan halted and stood as tall as he could, head cocked, snarling. "What is it?" Taigu asked.

Then he heard it too, a distant, hollow drumming–a Kong in threat stance. "Go!" Taigu said in the Zan language. "I'll follow. Go!"

For he had to obey the prime Zantu oath: *When one of our kind needs help, I will give it, even at peril of my lives.* Lives. Each Zan had two–his own and his Kong's.

Khaan cleared the way–not with threats, just with his rumbles and his huge size. Taigu, staff held high like a spear about to be thrown, ran in his wake. The street ahead widened, and now he could hear the squealed shrieks of draks, the bellow of a Kong. "Kai scum!" Taigu growled. "Hurry!"

Then again Khaan halted. This time he reared and drummed his chest–and ahead, across a crowd of people who were pressing back toward him, Taigu saw three Kai riders on their monstrous mounts, emerging like nightmares through a cloud of yellow dust. They had turned against the crowd and now leveled their pikes. "Keep away!" one of them shouted, his voice hot with anger as another twirled a stout hempen-corded weapon with weighted, hooked ends above his head.

Taigu knew that properly handled, such a device might be able to trip Khaan up and immediately reacted by taking an aggressive stance with his staff. "Let us through!" he yelled back. "A Kong is in trouble!"

"Fool of a boy, keep away! If you don't want that monster felled and pierced, keep away!"

From behind the Kai riders, a milling crowd screamed, and for an instant Taigu saw a Kong raise both arms and smash them down on something that squealed horribly. "Forward, Khaan!" Taigu ordered. The receding crowd flooded back on either side, and suddenly nothing stood between the Kong and the draks.

Khaan was a young, aggressive bull who had experienced many battles alongside his father, but who had not yet hunted alone. Although not full-grown, he was still terrible to behold when angered, and he was angry now. Nothing, and no one, dared oppose the path of a Kong.

The drak riders tried to mount a charge, but they were too close together and jostled each other. The middle drak stumbled and lost control. Its enormous neck muscles reflexively swung the huge head, mouth bristling with tusks and teeth, to maintain balance and it inadvertently gored the flank of the drak next to it. The wounded drak whirled and lurched back through to the rear of the crowd, tossing people left and right with bloody sweeps of its terrible head.

Khaan's backhanded blow unseated one of the other two riders. As the third thrust his lance, Taigu shifted his staff like lighting, deflecting it just long enough for Khaan to seize the shaft. The Kong yanked the lance from the Kai's grasp and snapped it as easily as a man might break a dried reed. The Kai that Khaan had knocked to the ground screamed in agony as his drak dragged him back through the crowd, over the broken pavement–his foot caught in a mangled stirrup.

Taigu hurried on. Ahead, the dragged man broke free when the leather strap snapped. Though bloody, he was moving and moaning as Taigu passed him. Khaan roared, and the other Kong, an old grey-neck, Taigu now saw, answered.

The old Kong waded in. Bristling with anger, lifting one drak over his head even as a second beast had clamped its formidable jaws onto his left arm. The draks were fierce, but their Kai riders knew they were overmatched in brute force and fury by the Kongs. With one of their own already wounded, his drak bellowing its death-throes, they sought to retreat. Charging away to the right, their draks knocked townspeople aside with vicious sweeps of their heads, their tusks leaving bloody gashes, their hoofs leaving broken limbs.

Taigu heard a Zan command, shouted above the tumult: "Stop, no more! Let them go!"

Khaan looked back at Taigu, hearing the command of another Zan, but in no doubt as to his allegiance. Taigu did not hesitate, "Do it. Help the hurt Kong."

The crowd had evaporated from the broad open plaza that opened behind a row of gulf-side warehouses. A drak lay dead in a pool of its own blood, its Kai rider nowhere in sight. Khaan gave it a glare and then approached the wounded Kong.

The two eyed each other warily, and then Khaan held out his hand, palm-up, a gesture of submission of a younger male to an older and stronger one. The other Kong grunted, touched Khaan's fingers briefly, and then reached up to pluck out two lances, flinging them blood-tipped to the ground. His left arm dangled, looking useless. Bright blood dripped from his fingertips, making pear-shaped splatters on the stones of the plaza.

He turned to his Zan and sat down, extending his arm, a grim look of determination on his enormous, scarred face. The Zan laid down his staff and immediately began to clean the wound and apply salves and bandages to his companion's arm. As he did, he spoke in tones that were both calming and matter-of-fact. It was clear that this was nothing new to them.

"You seem young to be joined with such a powerful Kong," stated the grizzled, battered-looking man.

"He is Khaan. I am Taigu."

"This is Krom."

Taigu's eyes widened. "You are Aton?" "Yes."

"My father spoke of you! He's Vekan!"

"I know him," Aton said gruffly. "A good man, your father." He did not look around as he examined the wounded arm. "Bones sound. Torn muscles. Curse the Kai." He nodded toward a dust-shrouded shape on the ground some distance away—and only then did Taigu recognize it as a badly mauled body. He felt his stomach heave. The flattened bundle of rags had been a man—a man the draks had trampled into shapelessness. "That's one of the raiders who was stealing food. The Kai claimed they intended to prevent a fight, but really they started it."

"Taigu!"

His father's voice! Taigu spun around, shrinking in guilt. "Father."

Vekan strode toward him. "Did you cause this?"

"No, Vekan, he did not," snapped Aton. Vekan stopped dead. "Aton! You're still alive!"

"Obviously, and so is Krom, thanks to Taigu and Khaan, and no thanks to the Kai—it would be better if we just left those pig-riders to die—"

"That decision is not yours!" A woman's voice. Taigu spun around. A tall, handsome woman in simple, flowing robes that glittered like colorful butterfly's wings stepped forward, an anxious-looking young woman at her elbow, also beautifully adorned. Both wore the headpieces that bespoke their state in life. "Will the Kong heal?"

"Yes, Pendonjira," Aton said. "With treatment and rest. He'll never be young again, but he'll be whole, healthy—and useful."

"Then finish treating his wounds and move him onto your ship. It is waiting in the harbor. *White Leader* is the name of it–it has been specially built for us, who will lead the Tagatu migration to land on Skull Island. There will be room for him and two other Kongs aboard it."

"He gets along with all of his own kind," Aton said. He glanced at Vekan. "How about your Chang coming on the same ship? He is Krom's nephew."

"Only if my son's Khaan can be the third. He is the son of Chang."

The Pendonjira looked impatient. "Yes, yes, that is acceptable. Treat the Kong's wounds. Then before you embark, come and see me–and you, Vekan, and your son Taigu. We can't fight among ourselves if we hope to survive the trip to the island." She paused and then said, "I give you notice, Aton. Three Kai leaders will be there, too. I know how your clans despise each other. You will lay aside your rivalries and your old hatreds for this one day. We will have a peaceful talk, do you understand?"

"If they are peaceful, so we will be," Aton asserted. "Leave us, let me treat these wounds."

"I am not to be ordered away," the Pendonjira said firmly. "Yet I have my duties to perform, as you have yours. In the hour after the sun stands at its highest, Aton. In the Planning Hall, at the base of the Long Wharf."

Aton grunted, and Taigu sensed that the Zan, a lifelong nomad, resented being hemmed in. He hesitated to take orders from anyone–and he did not relish what Vekan had called "diplomacy."

The Pendonjira turned and swept away, her assistant at her elbow. Even in the stench of carnage and sulfur, Taigu caught a fresh, intoxicating aroma as they passed by. It was not something he had ever encountered before.

"Who–who is that girl?" Taigu asked, as though dazed. No one seemed to hear him, and no reply was offered.

As soon as the Pendonjira and her aide were out of earshot, Aton said, "Vekan, do me a favor. Help me with this arm." Taigu thought he meant the Kong's arm until Aton turned and Taigu stared at the odd way his own right arm dangled from his shoulder.

"It came out of the socket again?" Vekan asked. "That will take time to heal."

"I know. It's been like this since I nearly had it ripped out as child. But in time it will be well again, and it will take time to sail to the islands. Have your Kong steady me. You've done this before. Pay no attention if I shout. This will hurt, I know."

"This is my son's Kong. Taigu–"

"I'll tell him what to do, Father." Taigu spoke to Khaan, and the huge anthropoid closed his hands on Aton, holding him firmly by his good shoulder and his opposite hip. He made an uneasy rumbling noise–not threat, but concern. Kongs knew very well how easily they could break bones and sinew.

"Now," Aton said between clenched teeth.

Vekan grasped his useless arm, wrenched it and then jerked. It popped back into the socket with an audible crunch. Aton threw his head back and grunted through his teeth, tendons standing out like taut cords in his neck, great beads of sweat popping out on his forehead. He took some deep breaths, clenched and unclenched his right hand, and grunted, "That will do. Now let's see to Krom."

It would have been bad manners for him to thank Taigu or Vekan. Zantu did not thank each other for such services, but did what they had to do. He knew that, when the time came, the ones they helped would perform a similar service for them–would shelter them, feed them, heal them or bury them, whichever was appropriate.

As Taigu watched, Aton and Vekan attended to Krom's wounds, cleaning them and sewing up the gashes. The Kong twitched now and then, but showed no more sign of pain than his Zan had, Taigu noticed. Then, they found the other Zantu, who had clustered outside one of the warehouses at the base of a long dock. Krom joined the other Kongs–they shuffled around him, sniffing, but did not seem to dare to approach too closely–and Khaan found his mother, Sakie, who began to groom him as though he were a little one again.

"The mob pretty well cleaned this place out," Ranth said, gesturing at a smashed door in the warehouse. "The keepers say they took mostly grains meant for seed. We'll miss them on the island, but if we can be careful with our rations for the next year, they can be replaced after a good crop."

For some time Khaan and Chang helped the other uninjured Kongs move the few remaining crates and urns from the raided warehouse. Then Aton, Vekan, and Taigu set off to find the Pendonjira. "Don't say anything about my arm," Aton muttered to Taigu as he led the way along the waterfront. "It'll be strong enough in a week."

A worker directed them to a longhouse near the wharves. They went in and saw the Pendonjira already seated, her assistant standing beside her. Taigu smiled at the girl. *Again, that scent. She must be of a rich clan,* he thought. *She is beautiful!*

But her gaze swept right past Taigu, instead focusing on the elder Zantu.

Three Kai riders stood in angry attitudes on her right. When they saw the Zantu, they broke into insulting words: "Zantu murderers!" one of them snarled.

"We demand justice," a second spat. "A death for a death!"

"Quiet," the Pendonjira said firmly. "Zantu have been their own masters, roaming the badlands beyond our borders at will, beyond even the perimeter of the Kai patrols. Yet they still keep an eye on any dangers that may be forming and let the Pendonjira know."

"That has always been true," agreed Aton.

"This tells me you still recognize and value the greater purpose and worth of human life." She turned to the Kai and said, "You Kai are tasked with defending us, with both drak bands roaming our borders and drak troops patrolling within them."

"And we have done it both well and proudly!" their leader interjected.

The Pendonjira did not acknowledge him, but continued, "So far, there has been no need for you to share the same lands except on the rarest occasions. Your two castes have separately made it possible for our civilization to flourish. Those times are now gone."

"But tradition–" Vekan began.

The Pendonjira cut him off by raising her graceful hand. With incongruous steely resolve, she said "It is I who am tasked with the wellbeing of the entire people. You will both work with me. The danger that comes to us is more powerful even than all the Kongs combined; it is swifter and more ferocious than ten thousand Kai and their draks. If you do not bury the ancient hatreds between you, none of us will survive! You three Zantu, come stand here. You Kai form on this side."

The Zantu rose reluctantly, but did not object as they formed up in a loose triangle to the Pendonjira's left and the Kai did likewise on the right. None of them spoke. The Pendonjira then went on in a firm, no- nonsense tone: "You Kai know the seriousness of our condition. You have seen what death gathers for us in the far north. We race against time now–when the heavy quakes come, when the sea withdraws and then roars back like a furious beast, it will be too late. Not a single ship will survive, not one hope will live!"

"We guarded the warehouses, as you asked," the eldest Kai responded.

The Pendonjira stared at him. "Guarded them? People saw and heard you, Yarg! They tell me you Kai taunted and goaded the crowd to break into the warehouse."

Yarg denied this: "No! The crowd grew larger and unrulier. We didn't goad–but, yes, we threatened them! We warned them we would kill any robbers!"

"You mean you dared them," the Pendonjira said softly. Her quiet reply seemed to shame Yarg, who stubbornly stared at the floor, his face flushing. "You knew you would provoke them into doing something for which you could punish them! You dared them because you wanted the chance to attack! Why do you thirst for their blood?"

A second Kai snarled, "It is to set an example! Fear is the only thing a mob understands. Useless town-squatters–they have no courage, except in numbers! They deserve to die! They're lower than–"

The Pendonjira's glare stopped him. "You have been spoiled by having so much territory where there are no laws and where ferocity is needed to survive. You spend months without glimpsing anyone from a town. That changes now! It won't be that way where we are going! There is no avoiding others on an island. You must change your ways, too. A warrior's spirit is something you admired and valued where you were, that is good, and those qualities will still be needed where we are going. But an arrogant, haughty spirit is something you cannot afford to have on the island if we are to last as a race. We need you and your mounts, our scouts have brought back stories of large and dangerous animals. You will have more than enough fighting on your hands before long. Believe me when I tell you, every ounce of your courage will be put to the test!"

Taigu, who had been listening with rapt attention–and apprehension–blurted out, "The Kongs will fight them! Nothing can withstand their power!"

The Pendonjira pierced him with a fierce look.

Taigu felt his father's hand on his shoulder. "My son is eager and that makes him foolish sometimes. He will not interrupt again," he said, emphasizing his words with a squeeze that made Taigu's bones creak.

The Pendonjira took a deep breath. "When the Tagu and the Atu became one people, it was to find a way of surviving in a hostile world," she said. "That is what enabled us to tame the Great Valley and keep it secure. That security freed us to learn farming and how to harvest the sea. For many years our way of life prospered and gave us freedom and progress. The Kongs kept the great beasts of the plains, the mammoths and the far greater danger of the colossal Thakus at bay. Even hordes of the wild Nagatl could not pierce the layered defenses of the Kai.

"But now the earth itself has turned against us–do you understand the terror of that? The earth! Something no Kai or Zan can tame or fight! Something so huge that it could kill us all and leave no survivors, not one, to sire future generations. What does a volcano care who you are or if you live or die? It can burn down a forest or set fire to a newborn baby with equal disregard! We seem to live in a vast indifference, but we must not give in to those desolate thoughts!"

She leaned forward her eyes almost burning with urgency. "We believe in a greater power than the earth, the Power that created it. That Power lives in us–*loves* us. That is what makes us different from volcanoes and the mountainous waves they send forth. It is what our traditions call 'Spirit'–it not only makes us human, it makes us noble!

"Our common humanity demands that we rise above the ancient unholy joy of acting out old hatreds and rivalries. Perhaps that is the reason this calamity has been allowed: to keep us united."

She stood up. "Until you can properly convey these thoughts to your respective brethren, the Kai and the Zantu will take different ships on the voyage. We will establish separate camps on the island. But I warn you now, without threat, but as a statement of simple truth: If your clans do not learn to care for each other as fully as you care for your own, *none* of us will survive!"

And as though to underscore her dire warning, at that moment the ground quaked.

As they rounded a low hill overlooking the shoreline, Taigu gasped. Beside him, even the adult Zantu paused to stare in wonder. Some of the Kai who been stationed in the area to keep order had seen the evolution of events, exhibited a certain air of pride in the achievement: As far as the eye could see, an unending bustle of humanity, looking no bigger than ants, swarmed on the wharves and on the mountainous forms of the ships that dominated the harbor.

Taigu had never imagined anything so gigantic could be built by human hands. The provisioning and loading of the ships took on the feeling of a pulsing organism. Endless lines of people progressed steadily up ramps and onto the moored vessels, carrying whatever they could in their arms and on their backs. Winches and pulleys strained and groaned as they raised huge bundles and lowered them into openings in the decks. Rafts loaded with everything imaginable seemed to fill every square foot of water, ferrying their cargoes to the larger, heavier ships riding at anchor. Kai warriors and their drak mounts patrolled ceaselessly up and down the entire waterfront to keep order.

Breaking the pause, the Pendonjira prodded them all to imitate what they saw: "Time is short, and we must hurry as well!"

Behind them, and high in the northern sky, a strange, glowing cloud extended from horizon to horizon, like a burial shroud about to be pulled over the dying Tagatu homeland. A wide path cleared before them as they approached their intended ship, The *White Leader*. It was a magnificent multiple-masted vessel with simple, yet graceful lines. But it was not the largest of the ships.

The largest were the *Exodus* transport ships that would carry most of the Kongs, along with thousands of people and provisions for the entire Tagatu culture. The *Leader* and the *Exodus* ships were of different designs. Whereas the Leaders were 300 feet in length and carried three or four Kongs, the *Exodus* ships were over twice as long, and broader in the beam, able to carry a dozen or more Kongs. Because of their size and configuration, they appeared to ride low in the water. In actuality, due to the enormous beam, the ships had a relatively shallow draft with the sides rising over 30 feet above the waterline on the *Exodus*.

In the center of each *Exodus* hull, starting over a hundred feet behind the bow and extending well over three hundred feet further, were dozens of tents to provide shelter from inclement weather. The stern of the ship, separated from the populace by a tall bulkhead, was reserved for the Kongs. Giant tents connected to the partition shielded them when necessary and they were left the expanse of the stern in which to move. Studded along the centerline of the ship were three enormous masts.

In a tone suggesting pride, the Pendonjira said, "The *White Leader* will lead one-fifth of our fleet, with *Blue Leader, Red, Yellow,* and *Green Leaders* responsible for similar flotillas. Each of the Leaders will be followed by one of the three *Exodus* transport ships–the largest of the ships you see. Each of those will be surrounded by and trail the innumerable smaller vessels that crowd the entire span of the harbor."

Her pride was not self-centered, but thankful. She was fully conscious of the enormity of the achievement and reason for it. She concluded, "Do you see what is possible if we work as one? Only in this way may we save our people from annihilation."

Though *White Leader* looked from the loading-rafts as solid as the land itself, Malana quickly discovered a disconcerting fact when she had hesitantly climbed a rope ladder up the side of the vessel and onto the deck.

She was even more bothered by being on the water than by heights.

Beneath her feet, the deck slowly rose and fell, responding to the movement of the bay as waves broke around the crescent isle and then met again. They were not high, the sailors called them "swells" and they came as regular as calm breaths, but the sensation of being lifted and dropped, lifted and dropped, began to make her stomach feel strange.

The Pendonjira seemed unbothered, though. She spoke to several of the crew, including the crew leader, Corbant, a square-built man with gray hair that had flowed down his cheeks and chin into an extravagantly bushy beard. He himself had taken the two newcomers down a hatchway and to a small compartment forward and on the left side. It was barely three paces wide and four deep, but it held two beds, one above the other, "You will take the top," the Pendonjira told Malana, along with two chairs, a small table and chests and hidden drawers and compartments.

"Your gear has been stowed," Corbant rumbled, touching the chests. "If you want to arrange your clothing and doodads and such–"

"Doodads?" the Pendonjira asked coldly.

Corbant shrugged and scratched his beard. "Um. Such things as ladies have, you know, other than clothes. Pretty things and things that smell sweet, and–and things."

"We have no doodads," the Pendonjira said dryly.

"Um. Through here; pardon me, Miss–"

"Malana," she told him, stepping aside.

Corbant opened a narrow door that she had not even seen; its joinery fitted the boards smoothly into the bulkhead opposite the two bunks. "Through here is the place of ease."

Curious, Malana stepped inside. It was a mere cupboard of a room, with a wooden bench against the curve of the hull–and a hole cut into the bench. Through it she saw, more than the height of two below, the gleam of the harbor water. Oh! Blushing, she stepped back hurriedly. The Pendonjira was smiling at her.

Corbant didn't seem to notice her embarrassment. "Orders, Pendonjira?" he asked, closing the door again.

Now, Malana saw the little recess that served as a handle. "As soon as the Kongs and their Zantu are aboard, we will leave," she said.

"Um." Corbant cleared his throat. "It isn't that easy with a ship, Ma'am. We have to wait at least until almost sundown. The tide will begin to ebb then, and it's safest to go out on a full but ebbing tide, especially with so many ships to follow us. At that, much work still remains, and we may not be ready until near dawn tomorrow, when the ebb begins again. I hope that will serve."

"We will leave as soon as we can, then," the Pendonjira said. "I trust the first *Exodus* and its flotilla will be ready?"

With a nod, Corbant said, "Yes. From the deck you will see it is already moving farther out into the harbor, as are those smaller ships and boats that are loaded and ready. They are awaiting only the tide and their *Leader*."

The Pendonjira politely indicated her approval. "Please signal the other captains. Our course remains the same."

"Yes. To the island with the–rounded mountain."

"You can find it by the stars? It will require exceedingly skilled seamanship," the Pendonjira said, adding encouragingly, "I hear that you are the best at such things."

"Thank you, Ma'am, I will certainly do my best." It was nearly impossible to notice a blush on Corbant's sun-reddened face, but it was there.

"I am counting on it," the Pendonjira said. "What we do will determine the success of the entire migration. Once we have established ourselves on the peninsula of that strange island, we will be able to populate the others."

Hesitantly, Corbant told her, "You know, Pendonjira, Ma'am, the islands don't huddle together. There are many in that sea, but the big one, with the sku–I mean the round mountain, well, that one is apart from the others."

"But it *is* a place big enough for us all," the Pendonjira said. "You sailed on the expedition that located the island, but no one except the Tagu sages know everything the explorers found on shore. Monsters dwell in the interior. We must build a barrier across a narrow part of the peninsula that will give our people safety, and to do that, we need every last person to help build. We could never do that if the Tagatu were spread among many islands."

Corbant looked surprised. "I thought the people and supplies we were transporting were for scientific research and the outpost needed for that."

"They were, but also for much more. Now may I rest? I had little sleep these past nights. Wake me when the Kongs come on board."

"Yes," Corbant said. He left them alone with the Pendonjira's words weighing on his mind.

Malana mentioned that, and the Pendonjira nodded. "Yes, I noticed," she said. She bent and carefully positioned her staff beside her bed. Not as nuanced as a Zantu staff, but still more than a walking aid, its small compartments containing ointments and herbs. The older woman sat on the edge of the bed and removed her sandals, and then pulled her outer robe over her head. She handed it to Malana. "Fold it carefully. Or better, hang it in the small closet, next to the room of ease."

Malana had to search to find the cut-out that let her open the second tiny room. It was indeed a narrow closet, with pegs close together on the three walls and the back of the door itself. She hung the robe there. When she closed the door again, the Pendonjira had stretched out on the bunk. "You may go upstairs," she told Malana. "Don't get in the crew's way."

"Thank you," Malana said. "But first—"

She hastily opened the first narrow door and stepped inside, closing it behind her. But instead of sitting on the bench, she knelt, just in time. Her last meal came up and spurted out into the water of the bay. When her stomach was empty, she wiped her mouth and pushed herself up, feeling as weak as a new-hatched bird. She opened the door and closed it again as quietly as she could. The Pendonjira looked asleep, but Malana could never tell with her. Even in sleep her mind roved, seemingly, and sometimes she had the uncanny knack of knowing just what others had been doing while she dozed.

Malana slipped out into the corridor and climbed up to the deck, hoping that the sea air might make her feel better. A crewman showed her where a barrel of fresh water had been lashed, and she used a strange-looking ladle on a long wooden handle—"carved whale tooth" noted the smiling crewman who noticed her reaction before he walked away—to dip some out. She rinsed her mouth and spat over the rail—and the wind blew the water back onto her. "Ugh!"

A young man's voice from close behind her intruded, "Pardon me. I've never been on a ship before, but it's no different than standing on a mountain: you have to spit with the wind, not against it." Then pointing, "The other side—"

She glared at the wiry youth. "Thank you." But her words carried no warmth and were not intended to. "Who are you?"

"I'm a Zan." he said, standing tall. "My name is Taigu. My Kong is about to come to the ship. You can see them over there on the wharf."

When Malana looked, the wharf seemed disconcertingly to rise and fall—but that was the ship. She did glimpse the dark shape of three Kongs on the long wharf ready to board immense rafts, other boats rowing away from the huge animals as though terrified by them.

"What's your name?" the youth asked.

"Malana. I'm the Pendonjira's apprentice."

"Oh." A sound of disappointment. "Not—not her servant?"

Malana snorted. "Her student! I may be the Pendonjira one day myself!"

"That's, that's, uh. Good. That's good," he said. "I'm going to be a leader of the Zantu one day. That's my destination."

"Destiny," she corrected.

"Yes. I meant that. Uh—how, how old are you?"

"Eighteen."

"Oh."

She gave him an annoyed glance. "What is your age, fifteen?"

"Sixteen!"

"Oh." She still carried some water in the dipper. She took a drink, and felt it gurgle in her uneasy stomach. "I feel sick," she confessed.

"You didn't drink from the river, did you?" he asked in an anxious voice.

Despite herself, Malana felt her throat tighten, and one tear slipped down her cheek. "No."

"What's wrong?" he asked.

"I loved that river."

"My father and I saw it boil away," Taigu said. "Lava and hot ash, you know. And I think upstream the earthquakes and the ashfalls must have stopped its course."

As if she had not heard him, Malana said, "Once its banks were the greenest and coolest place in the city. The Tagu grew pleasant herbs all along it. Even when the summer sun beat straight down, it was a calm place where you could sit until your spirit felt refreshed. Now—mud and stinking death." Her voice caught, and she rubbed another tear from her face with the heel of her hand. "It is gone forever."

"The herbs," blurted Taigu, "are they what you use to make you smell so—"

She gave him a withering look. "What? You think I *smell?*"

"No! No! Just the opposite! I mean every time you come near I, I …Look! That's Krom!" Taigu said. "He's going to be first. And there, I think Aton is coming with him. He's a legend among my people, you know."

"Yes," Malana said, letting him off the hook with a sly sideways glance, though in truth she had never heard the name before that day.

"Easy, easy," Aton said as Krom settled onto the shifting raft, his bulk sending waves spreading out in all directions as the craft settled. "Rest easy, Krom."

White Leader

Krom grumbled and rumbled in his chest. Now the pain of the spears throbbed in his arm, Aton knew, because his own shoulder felt as though a hot ember of pain burned in the center of the joint. The raftsmen clearly were apprehensive about the gigantic Kong who crouched in the center. They began to row, twelve to a side, and the raft slowly moved from the wharf. Ships did not have to be moved to clear lanes to the vessels that were to transport the Kongs. From where he stood near Krom, Aton could see six more rafts spread over the harbor, vanishing behind smaller ships as they and their Kongs moved out.

Behind him another raft was already pulling into place for Chang, and next would be the younger and smaller Khaan. Ordinarily Khaan would be under control of the Zan who had bonded with him, but Taigu's father, Vekan, had questioned Taigu's self-control recently and did not want to take the chance that the new experiences would upset Khaan beyond his son's ability to calm him.

Instead, Vekan would make two trips, escorting first Chang and then Khaan out to the ships. *Not the way I would do it,* Aton thought. *Let the young correct their mistakes by making them first and learning from them!* But such matters were not part of the code of the Zantu, and so he had said nothing to Vekan. A man's son was his concern, not another man's, and Vekan had already sent Taigu out to the ship, "There your wagging tongue won't get you in trouble!"

Almost all the ships would follow *White Leader* when it had been loaded, including the first *Exodus* that carried over a dozen Kongs. People clustered at the rails to watch as they passed. A few bolder souls recognized Aton–or Krom–and shouted greetings. Aton waved back. He tilted his head and gazed up into a blue sky dotted with white clouds. *It has been long since I saw a clean sky. The mountains have fouled the air with smoke and ash. Have turned the upper valley into a place shadowed by death. And now something new begins. Just when I thought we were too old for it, something new comes.*

Aton deeply inhaled the salt air and thought, *I have seen the sea now for maybe two, three times in all. And now I am upon it for the first time in my life. A Kong, three Kongs on a ship! Who would have believed such a tale when I was a young man?*

Yet he knew that, five or ten years before, at least three of the Kongs had gone out on one of the advance explorations. They were still out there, somewhere, on one of the islands, perhaps the one that the fleet was headed for. It would be good to see them, and their Zantu, old friends of his, as old as he was, again.

The gigantic *Exodus* now lay behind them, and the *White Leader* loomed ahead. The stern rose high above the surface, and a hatchway much taller than a man had opened beneath it. Up at the rail two youths looked down on them. Aton recognized one, Vekan's son Taigu. Despite his aches and the burning pain in his injured shoulder, Aton's lips twitched up in a smile. He knew what the boy did not: when Taigu's father was his age, Vekan was always in trouble for blurting out his thoughts without permission. But that was a thing he could not yet tell the son, of course.

"How do we do this?" he asked the man at the tiller of the raft.

"They will use great ropes to lower a ramp. All your Kong need do is walk up it and on through the two doors leading into the center longhouse. The other two Kongs will do likewise and the ramp will be raised and sealed. There is enough room, food and light in there for them to comfortably make the journey–or so we hope! The open deck between the doors of the Kong longhouse and the ramp should provide enough room for at least one Kong at a time to come into the fresh air and sunlight during the trip. Of course, you Zantu will be required to manage things."

"That will be our quarters, too?" asked the Zan.

"Yes. It is amidships. And runs over half the length of the vessel. The larger Exodus will be able to accommodate several more Kongs still, but they will only be sheltered by tents. Your Kongs' quarters are sumptuous by comparison. There are special quarters for you Zantu there, too. You will move forward past food storage, and there is more food forward of the Kong compartment. You will have to take care of cleanliness yourselves, though the Kongs' 'place of ease,' after a fashion, should make things a bit easier in that regard–if you can cajole them to use it."

"We're used to it, thank you for your consideration," Aton said. The designers were aware of the dignity the Zantu demanded for their Kong companions.

Aton reflected, *With my injured shoulder, I'll have every right to ask Taigu to help with that. And his father will probably order him to take care of Chang's and Khaan's waste, too. That will please Vekan! But I'll have to praise the youth and find some reward for him at the end, when we reach the island.*

The oarsmen at the forward end of the raft seized lines tossed down by sailors up in the open hatchway and made them fast to wooden cleats. Then the sailors threw down a netting of wide-woven, heavy ropes. "Wait!" one of them called down while the others fastened the upper corners. Then the man said, "Just in case anything goes wrong, swim to this rigging and we'll haul you to safety."

"If anything goes wrong getting the Kongs on board, there may not be a ship left!" replied Aton. "Careful now, lowering that ramp!" A windlass like those used in raising an anchor steadily lowered a large, reinforced door, like a drawbridge. When it drew level with the raft, the raftsmen hurried to secure it to the ramp with heavy chains and drove stout wooden pegs to hold in place a folding wood platform at the fore of the raft that overlay the ramp. Crouching to keep his balance, Aton carefully walked up the ramp to a platform fifteen feet above the water and then urged the Kong forward.

Krom seemed unsure, so Aton kept calling him, encouraging the Kong to look up at him and not down at the water. Krom used his good arm to steady himself, but, Aton noted, he let his injured one hang loose. The one arm and his bowed legs were enough, and he mounted to the platform where his Zan stood. The entire ship rocked and the stern dipped down when his full weight came aboard. They moved forward until Krom stopped and looked about, obviously wondering about this strange longhouse that bobbed. Behind him, Aton heard a commotion. He turned just in time to see Vekan and Chang clamber aboard. Chang had the stoic look of all Kongs, displaying neither fear nor anticipation, but Vekan did not look happy. He spoke to Chang, and the Kong shuffled forward.

Aton said, "I'll lead Chang, Vekan. You still have your son's Kong to see to." "Yes, that's true," Vekan said.

Taigu had come down. He stood uncertainly a little way forward. "Father, may I approach? Khaan might be easier to manage if you let me help."

Vekan sighed. "I suppose you can come. There will be no opportunity for you to speak out of turn and bring trouble on us. Go on, then, down to the raft. I'll join you soon."

Taigu smiled to himself as he walked down the ramp to the now-empty raft.

Aton said, "Go with your son. I'll get Chang acquainted with our new surroundings. He knows me, he will trust me. You should be with your son."

Vekan seemed to struggle for words for a moment. Then he said, "Yes, you're right. That's a kind offer, Aton."

Aton laughed. "Since when do we thank each other, my friend?"

"That's always been so, but I have a feeling that everything is about to change."

The *Leader* ships had been designed like the larger *Exodus* transports in that they also had a very wide beam to enhance stability, while at the same time decreasing the draft, which would enable them to get as close to the island's shore as possible. The hull had been constructed with a high freeboard to protect in rough seas. Both the transports and the lead ships were essentially enormous rafts, designed to maximize deck and storage space, though the lines of the Leader ships were much more graceful. As far as possible, each was designed to be easily disassembled on arrival to supply much-needed building materials. Nothing was wasted, and everything was meant to give the arriving Tagatu people the best chance to survive in what was already known to be a hostile environment.

The Kongs' quarters, perhaps 150-plus feet long and 60 feet wide, ran through the middle of the ship to help center the ship's gravity. Three Kongs had room to move, but would be encouraged to remain still, to prevent unnecessarily rocking the ship. A series of openings ran along the high side walls, admitting light and ventilation when the giant doors to the rear could not be opened.

Their compartment was large enough for the Kongs to sleep comfortably and had been filled with layers of fresh, sweet-smelling straw. Aton saw that the Zantu were to sleep in a kind of recess at the forward end, big enough for them to sling hammocks. The compartment had six small ports, the height of a man's head, three to a side, but even on this bright day they admitted only a little light. So far, the air smelled fresh and felt cool, with the great rear hatch agape. Aton looked up and hoped that when it was sealed, enough air would circulate through the openings above to keep things from becoming too unpleasant.

Later, with all three Kongs safely aboard, Aton, Vekan and Taigu sat quietly together, discussing their plans. Countless years of interaction with the Kongs had produced a great wealth of knowledge. Zantu knew their companions well, and they themselves were known in return. Every Zan worthy of the name was a master of the plants, herbs and workings of their entire environment, especially as these affected the Kongs. Aton and Vekan brought with them many stores of such botanicals as would be necessary to calm a Kong, and if necessary, even render one of the great beasts unconscious. Most of these could be administered through scent, ingestion or topical application. Taigu, who was still learning, observed every detail.

"Were you able to gather enough kava root should any of the Kongs need to be pacified, Aton?" asked Vekan.

"I had some stores already gathered, and more distilled into oil, Vekan, but could gather no more than that. Most natural growths near us were destroyed by volcanic ash and toxic fumes. Did any survive near you?"

"Some, but time was short. I hope the small amount I have will suffice. The same goes for ginger, and also valerian and other leaves, roots and bulbs should we need them for seasickness or to calm the Kongs in an emergency."

"These I have as well, but again, in limited quantities for the same reasons. Let us hope our stores are sufficient to—"

"You will all have what you need."

The three Zantu started at the woman's unexpected voice. Everyone knew it was difficult, nearly impossible, to sneak up on a Zan. The Pendonjira's face revealed the slightest trace of a wry smile.

She stood over the men, who rose respectfully. She said quietly, "Your handling of the Kongs for a safe entry onto the ship is to be congratulated. I came to see if you needed anything else."

"What you said is welcome news. But how is it you have stores for us?" asked Vekan.

The Pendonjira shrugged. "We humans are not too far different from your Kongs in most physical respects. You spend so much time alone, you forget that you will be travelling with thousands of us. We have need of many of the same remedies for the same reasons as your Kongs. The Tagu sages have been harvesting and preparing for years, my friends." She added with a genuine smile, "You did not think any of these ships would depart with simian giants aboard and not also carry a vast store of kava and other potent herbs to calm them if needed, did you?"

All three Zan, as life-long loners and men of the land, gave a short bow in deference to the Pendonjira's forethought and marveled that such a ship was even possible.

Despite the Pendonjira's urging, they were not able to raise their anchors at the late-afternoon tide. The ships were not all loaded, and too many of the people were not yet aboard. Inevitably, confusion and arguments slowed progress—the sheer volume of activity was staggering—yet preparations proceeded without interruption at a frantic pace. *Considering what might have happened, it's a miracle we have got this far*, she mused, while surveying the activity below her position atop the stern. The spectacular panorama continued to unfold across the entire shoreline and shone gloriously in the red light of a setting sun.

As night fell, she paced the main deck of the ship, gazing back at the city. "How many would not come?" she asked Kentagu, a man of nearly sixty years who had been one of the wealthy backers of the exploration ships.

"Far too many," he said in his hoarse voice. He had once been a fine singer, but a year of shouting orders to crewmen had given him a permanent croak. "A third at least of those who had planned to go lost their courage at the last minute. There are Atu warriors, too, who are swearing they'll take everyone to the place of two rivers far to the west, where they say they will be conquerors and rulers. They even tried to halt the last boatloads, but the Kongs who stayed until the end kept them away." He nodded toward the shore. "Now they are feasting on some of the food they stole. If they become bold enough, they may even try to come out into the harbor to pillage the ships."

"Not tonight," the Pendonjira said. "We left them no boats, no rafts."

"More can be improvised, though."

Ashore the red flickers of torches moved, vanishing and reappearing as those who had remained behind ransacked houses and storage rooms. "Look," the Pendonjira said. "The lighthouse."

The customary fire burned there, its blaze billowing high in the night sky, but it moved oddly, then tilted and cascaded down in a shower of flame and streaking red embers.

"Fools," Kentagu rasped. "They'll set the buildings afire!"

"We don't need the beacon any longer," the Pendonjira said. "Before dawn our next good tide will come, and by sunup we will be heading out to sea. We won't return here."

"Don't the fools realize these houses, these provisions, are their own and that they may need them? Why do they loot and destroy?"

"If they want to burn the town, let it burn. If they bring disaster on themselves, they have only themselves to blame." She thought, but did not say, *A mob always fosters mindless destruction, and this will never change as long as humans are humans.*

Though here they rode at anchor distant from the land, they could hear random shouts from time to time, and now and again hysterical, high-pitched laughter. "What's the matter with them?" Kentagu pondered out loud.

"Some are chewing the herbs," she said. "Properly used, they ease pain and bring rest. Abused, they make people drunk and foolish."

"I wish we could have harvested more."

"We have enough to keep any wild animals under control," the Pendonjira said.

"And the Kongs during our journey?" asked Kentagu

"I believe so. Let us hope. Still, I wish–" But there she broke off, biting her lip. "Wish what?"

With a sigh, she said, "That the exploring team had sent back a ship to report on how ready they are to receive us. But we knew that might not be possible. There's so much to do on the island, and at the best of times the sea is an uncertain pathway."

Kentagu said, "What is that?"

"The trembling? I have been feeling it, too, and seeing it disturb the water."

"Perhaps another earthquake?"

"It could be. I hope not. Too often an earthquake fathers a monstrous wave. If one should strike tonight, that would be the end for the Tagatu. With the crowds of ships in the bay, with no means of escape should the sea drain away and then rush back suddenly–wreckage and death."

"Yet this doesn't feel like a quake," Kentagu mused. "It's gone on for too long and is too steady."

"Perhaps it is a distant eruption, continuing and growing stronger," she said. "I see no stars over the Valley."

"Nor do I," Kentagu said. "Yet that could be clouds."

"Or ash, coming more to the south than it has ever done. We cannot tell, so we shouldn't fret about it. Look, you were right–the wharf near the lighthouse is burning."

They watched, helpless to do anything, as the flames, caught by the strengthening land breeze, flared out, reaching toward the harbor. Crosswinds spread the fire to the longhouses. The Place of Planning appeared, fire flaring from its door and windows, and from there was extending to the western, less damaged, part of the port. Screams came to their ears now, though the insane laughter still broke out from time to time.

"They'll be too busy fighting that to think of attacking the ships tonight," Kentagu said.

"If they even choose to fight it. The Atu may be preparing to strike out for their imagined kingdom even now."

"You don't think they will reach it."

"I don't. The world has changed since their times of nomadic wandering and conquest. And they have changed, too. They are no longer as hardened and resourceful as their Atu ancestors were, and they have grown accustomed to our more civilized ways, though they will not admit it. At least many of the Atu, mostly their Kai riders and other traditional leaders, have come aboard the ships. We'll need them—and they'll need us, despite the wild boasts of the hot-headed ones. The blood still burns red in their veins."

Kentagu suddenly stood up straighter. "What is that, far off? Has the fire spread?"

The Pendonjira looked into the night. Past the dark silhouettes of the port city, higher than the horizon, she could see a glimmering line, orange but muted by haze and distance. Then she understood the shuddering that she felt underfoot, had felt for hours. "No," she said, her mouth suddenly feeling dry. "That is the line of the mountains. All of them. All erupting at once."

"Is there time?" Kentagu asked.

"I don't know." The Pendonjira took a deep breath. "I don't know."

Neither Malana nor her teacher could sleep. When she judged that dawn had to be near, Malana slipped down from the top bunk, dressed, and groped her way out of the dark cabin. She made a wrong turn in the corridor, found herself baffled when she came against a blank wall, at last understood, and with her right hand on a bulkhead stumbled back toward the stern until she found the steep stairway to the deck. The hatch was open above her, and she saw a dim square of red-tinted gloom.

All around her men were running and clambering. She saw the Pendonjira far back, at the rail, and she made her way to the older woman. "Are we leaving now?"

"Yes."

"Oh!" Malana said. "The city!"

At the edge of the harbor, the whole city flamed. Smoke roiled, borne out to sea in coiling billows underlit by the ruddy glow of flames. The very harbor seemed to shake. "The city is no more," the Pendonjira said sadly.

"Are they all dead, the ones who remained?"

"Probably not yet."

Something cracked overhead, and the sound repeated again and again. Malana felt as if the deck were gliding from underfoot. "What's happening?"

"Look up. The sails are set. The wind is taking us out into the open sea."

Malana tilted her head back. The enormous sails, spread between five extended supporting vanes radiating like fingers on a hand, had bellied out, and the masts creaked as they took the strain. Now she could tell that the ship was turning away from the town. The Pendonjira walked back along the rail, as if she were reluctant to take her last sight of the burning buildings.

Malana followed her. "I wish—"

"Don't wish for things that are lost," the Pendonjira said gently. "Save your wishes and hopes for those of us who must now try to live and to endure."

In what seemed like only minutes, the sky lightened in the direction of the sea. But over the land clouds towered, purple-black and ragged. "The smoke from the city?"

"No," the Pendonjira said. "From the mountains."

The sun appeared. Now the rugged seaward curve of the barrier island lay behind them, and all around them the ships sailed on. Through the gap into the harbor Malana could see the shore, the distant, haze-blurred outlines of the ruined city, the tower of the lighthouse stark against the desolation. Then–

Malana screamed.

Her mentor grabbed her arm, perhaps not so much to support Malana as to steady herself.

From inland rolled a half-mile tall incandescent cloud. Before it everything burst into fire and blasted into ash and smoke. The oncoming cloud was too huge, it was too deadly–surely it would reach the sea and would speed toward them and would burn the ships and the Kongs and the people–

I'm going to die!

Ashore, the pyroclastic cloud filled the lower Valley from side to side. Nothing survived it. It burned with an intensity that incinerated wood, that in less than a heartbeat seared the flesh of animals or people to steam and calcified the bones, that instantly exploded standing water into rolling billows of dirty steam. When the flow swept against mountains, the heat caused some rocks to melt and flow.

When it struck the remains of Temuan, it simply vaporized everything that remained standing.

Even the lighthouse vanished, not toppled but exploded into glowing dust.

And then the harbor, vacated just hours before–

The sound reached beyond pain. On the ship, Malana dropped to her knees, her hands clamped over her ears. Her mouth gaped, and she felt the impact of a pressure wave that blasted air from her lungs in a scream she couldn't even perceive over the end-of-the-world roar as the harbor simply vaporized, changed instantaneously into explosive steam.

A wave broke completely over the offshore island, and behind it, boiling up white, a cloud shot up and up and up into the air, spreading as it rose, like a mushroom growing in an instant. But–

But the fiery cloud had stopped, torn apart by the steam explosion it had caused. And then–All around them things fell, ashes, bits of shattered stone, perhaps even the remains of… Malana blocked the thought.

At the tail end of the fleet, one ship lay aflame. Perhaps lava or burning debris had landed on it.

They were too far from it to see whether the crew would be able to save it.

The following waves came, enormous, raising the creaking, wallowing ships up high and then dropping them down into the troughs. The largest ships, and evidently all the main *Leader* and *Exodus* vessels, were far enough out to survive. With the smaller ones it was not clear. The fleet headed due south, leaving the land behind, now an uneven horizon, but dark, all dark, beneath that terrible sun-devouring black cloud. Malana could see streaks falling from it as dust or ash settled out. Ahead of them, though, southward, the horizon was bare, a line where shining water met distant sky, no land at all. Thankfully the horizon stretched, unblackened, as far as her eyes could see.

A man's hand closed on her arm and helped her stand up. She looked, fearfully, into the seamed, grim face of Aton. He said something that she heard only faintly. He repeated it.

"My ears are ringing," she told him.

He bent and spoke more loudly: "That will pass. I asked if you are hurt."

"N-no. No, I don't think so. But…but it's all gone!"

The Pendonjira leaned down. "You will need to rest."

"Let me stay. Let me stay here, in the air."

The Pendonjira tilted her head and nodded.

Now the ringing was subsiding. She heard the Pendonjira ask, "Are your charges safe, Aton?"

"They didn't like it when the ship pitched, but they're unhurt. So long as they could observe their Zantu were safe and calm close by, they behaved well. We are One. We live and we die as One."

For a few moments they stood silently looking back. From the point where the city had been all the way to the east, over the whole land, that black cloud ruled the sky, like death come to claim its own.

"You were right, Pendonjira," Aton said fearlessly, his indomitable, inner strength palpable in his voice. "You were right all along."

Without emotion, the woman said, "I take no joy in that."

Editor's Note: The Naga Event
By Vincent Denham

*T*he great volcanic and seismic upheaval that uprooted the Tagatu civilization from its home on the mainland must have been one of the most spectacular–and deadly–eruptions humans ever witnessed. It literally remade geography over an area at least as large as the state of Texas, and perhaps much larger. Though changing landforms make identification of precise locations impossible, I have tentatively located the volcanic area as somewhere north of the present-day border of India and Burma and have provisionally called the cataclysm the Naga Event from the modern name given to that area.

True, the catastrophe was not of a magnitude to compare with the Deccan Traps eruptions and lava flows, which occurred at the end of the Cretaceous Period, ca. 66,000,000 years ago and are believed to have continued for 30,000 years. However, in human terms at least, nothing, not even the cataclysmic explosion of Krakatoa, can rival the Naga Event for the widespread death, destruction, and havoc it wrought.

Many thousands of square miles vanished beneath lava flows and immense falls of ash, which converted low-lying valleys into plateaus and buried mountains up to their shoulders, so to speak. The courses of mighty rivers changed instantly and forever. The skies darkened over half of what is today East Asia, and extinction of land animals spiked in those ash-shrouded areas over a period of centuries–perhaps the eruptions and earthquakes went on continuously or intermittently for many generations of humans.

However, it proceeded, whether as a sudden spasm or as a centuries-long-drawn-out agony of the earth, the event changed the land so drastically that, had a resident of the Great Valley somehow been able to revisit it a thousand years later, absolutely nothing would have been recognizable. A good portion of the coastal part of the great valley that had been home to the Tagatu subsided beneath sea level and today lies buried under millennia of silt and sand. At the same time, the northern reaches of the valley tended to level out, buried under thousands of feet of ash (soon hardened into porous volcanic rock) and lava.

Volcanic mountains actually shrank as the explosive eruptions blew the cones apart. What was once a nine-thousand-foot-tall mountain might emerge as a much larger open crater, the circular rim only five or six hundred feet above the plain, the lowest center of the great bowl perhaps a thousand feet below the rim. At the bottom would seethe hellish lakes of bubbling molten rock, and hissing from cracks and fissures all about would be poisonous gases.

At Cumae in Italy lies a dormant volcanic caldera that the Romans called "Avernus," or "the birdless place." There for thousands of years–indeed, well into the last century– accumulations of carbon dioxide–not toxic, but heavier than air and incapable of supporting respiration–killed any living creatures that ventured into the suffocating atmosphere. Imagine that on a scale a thousand times greater, and you may have some inkling of what *happened along the volcanic chain that once had formed the northern and eastern boundary of the Tagatu's Great Valley.*

It is perhaps worth mentioning that, to the ancient Romans, Cumae was thought to be the gateway to hell. Biologically, the Naga Event scoured all life from a widespread area of destruction, effectively sterilizing the landscape for at least a hundred years if not more. When the pyroclastic cloud rolled into the harbor, it killed not only land animals and humans (along with all plant life), but sea life for scores of miles out from shore, both through the accumulation of gaseous poisons dissolved into the water and of suspended microscopic-sized volcanic ash particles (they are sharp as glass shards and will fatally lacerate the lungs of porpoises and whales or the gills of fish). The paleontological record shows a great extinction event (though geographically speaking, relatively localized–in the sense that it was not a global die-off, as had happened with the dinosaurs). For a large part of the area there are virtually no significant land fossils of any species between about 100,000 BC and 80,000 BC, and very few for many thousands of years after that.

What happened to the Tagatu who at the last minute lost their nerve and refused to sail aboard the escape fleet does not bear thinking about. Even if they managed to scale the mountains to the west of their valley, their lives were probably brief.

Bands of wild Nagatl would have coalesced into larger, panicked groups, perhaps even hordes, fleeing the catastrophe in the company of stampeding herds of giant mammoths, great rhinos and other species of four- legged giants. The primitive Nagatl would have found the humans easy prey.

And what of the mysterious primitive species of Kong the Tagatu referred to as a Thakus? They, too, posed a constant threat to human life. In short, any Atu who might have escaped the valley's destruction were doomed. Even the great Atu warrior armies of old would not have stood a chance, especially when dealing with such a natural calamity. The best we can hope for them is merely that their deaths were so instantaneous as to be without excruciating pain. As for those outside the immediate area of the eruptions, death came for them, too, premature death through starvation or asphyxiation, and probably it was agonizing.

The ash that had been jetted high into the atmosphere would have choked off sunlight and tainted rainfall for years. Forests beneath the murk would have died, perhaps all the way to the east coast of Asia. The hunter- gatherers that depended upon the forests for the necessities of life would have starved or died from inhaling the particles of ash.

On a lesser and less-organized scale than the Tagatu exodus, humans in the shadow of the event must have fled from their homelands. This, perhaps, was the impetus for the spread of humanity to the islands of Indonesia, and possibly even as far as Australia. They would have traveled in small, wandering bands–families or clans–desperately seeking some land where they might merely survive.

If any of the Atu who resisted the notion of relocation to the islands had by the time of the great eruption moved far enough west of the mountains that formed the western border of the Great Valley, they might– just conceivably–have survived. With the barrier of the non-volcanic mountain range to shield them from the immediate shock waves and heat of the eruptions, and the prevailing winds to sweep away the bulk of the ashes, they stood a small chance of living.

But they cannot have lasted as a coherent culture or in large numbers. Their strength would not have been enough to conquer a primitive civilization such as might–and I emphasize might– have already been growing up at the confluence of the Tigris and Euphrates, far to their west, or even further, the very primitive famers who had begun to cultivate the fertile soil along the banks of the Nile after each year's flooding. Even if they numbered only into the hundreds, however, they might have become mercenaries, tough people who could gain a place as guards and as soldiers. I have the ghost of a theory about that.

In the Mesopotamian myths and legends, we find scores of stories about demigods–beings who are part human and part deity. The very ancient Sumerian character Bilgamesh (more familiar under his Akkadian name Gilgamesh) was one such being–"one-third man and two-thirds god." I wonder–did some few Zan or Atu warriors undertake the unimaginable trek westward as far as the Fertile Crescent? Did their superior bodily strength, their courage, and their prowess with weapons of all types impress the local population as being traits of people somehow superhuman, more powerful, more cunning, in ways of war and hunting more expert, than the common run of humanity? Could they have assumed that such people–particularly if there were miawan among them–must have descended from higher beings, indeed, from gods?

If so, then very dimly, and at a great distance, we possibly might glimpse a handful of tough survivors of the Naga Event.

But if so, they were a vanishingly small minority. By far the greatest part of the survivors (still only a fragment of the pre-cataclysm population of the Great Valley) escaped to seaward.

And the story of their own exodus, their very own epic quest, vanished from the knowledge of history. Until now...

The primitive Nagatl would have found the humans easy prey.

After a horrible sick week of thinking she would surely die, Malana began to wish that she actually would. Everything about the ship, its closed-in stuffiness, the eternal pitch and roll and rise and fall of the deck, the lingering horror of what she had witnessed as the terrible fiery cloud wiped the harbor city from existence, everything made her heave with nausea.

She, unfortunately, was one of the few on whom the herbs and tinctures of the Pendonjira had a lesser effect than on others. This individual variation was compounded to an unknown degree by the fact that Malana herself was to be a Pendonjira, a gift that manifested itself physically and emotionally at a very early age and was still developing. This, of course, the Pendonjira not only understood, but had experienced at its deepest levels herself. For that reason, she indulged Melana far more than she would have any other Tagu, allowing her rest and special considerations.

Malana ate barely anything, because if she swallowed more than a few mouthfuls, it came right back up, leaving her miserable and shivering. She lived on water, mostly, and on nourishing teas infused with herbs brewed by the Pendonjira. When she was able, she nibbled some twice-baked bread (it lasted long and kept well, though it was bland in flavor) or a small piece of dried fruit. Her experienced teacher constantly soothed her, reassuring her, telling her that her body would become used to the motions of the ship in time.

Malana doubted it. So far, she grew dizzy every time she tried to walk on the treacherously unsteady deck, and that led to nausea, and that led to more misery.

However, it was true that for the last day or so the ship had calmed its unpredictable motions. For the whole previous week, the seas had been very rough, the result, the captain told them, of the earthquakes now far to sternward. Curiously, at sea a tsunami is not much to fear—one great surge of the ocean, a hill of rolling water that would lift a ship smoothly and let it down again and pass on, nothing violent occurring until the depths beneath the great moving wave shallowed and the peak of the wave built and broke into crashing white water and overwhelmed any land it encountered.

The ships sailed in open sea now, with the bottom uncountable feet below the keels, and the tsunamis merely passed by without much alarm and without causing harm. Three of these great earthquake-born waves in all had passed beneath the ship, but they troubled Malana far less than the constant smaller ones, the choppy waves that made the *White Leader* wallow from side to side despite its relatively wide beam, or caused it to duck its prow into the water and then raise it high. Those tossings, which made walking all but impossible and which made her stomach rebel at the very thought of food, those were much worse and for the first several days were always assaulting the ship. By sunset on the first day of their voyage, the land itself had dropped completely out of sight beneath the horizon. However, the stark evidence of the continuing eruptions, the towering black ash clouds, they stayed in sight for many, many days afterward, long after all sign of the land had vanished. And, the captain assured them, the ash clouds and perhaps the eruptions themselves had changed the weather.

Unpredictable winds came howling down upon them with little warning and lashed the sea and raised wind-spumed whitecaps on its face, even when no clouds hung in a clear blue sky. In contrast, on some other days a wall of clouds would rush toward them, and far off they could see an unearthly, nearly glowing haze of white hurrying across the face of the ocean, stirring it to fury, a white squall, and then with sudden violence it would burst on them with roaring wind and lashing rain, lightning and thunder all around, and the ship would writhe and jerk like a great animal in agony. Only after one full week of sailing—and often struggling—under full or, in times of storm, reefed sails did they at last reach calmer waters.

Then, after their first day and night of smooth sailing, Corbant came to the Pendonjira's cabin early in the morning. "How is your apprentice?" he asked her, standing sure-footed on the deck and speaking to the Pendonjira, seated in one of the chairs.

"A little better. Yesterday she had two small meals and kept them down. She is quite weak, but not as sick."

So you say, Malana thought resentfully, but she did not speak the thought.

Corbant nodded. "Good. This may help her, too. I mean to order the fleet to furl the sails later this morning. We will try the propellant. If it functions as it should, we ought to have smoother going."

The Pendonjira sounded pleased at the news: "That will make the trip much faster."

Corbant sighed. "Yes, if we can use it long enough. Not all the captains are without concern. It has proven effective in smaller vessels, but never for one approaching this size, let alone the *Exodus.* Using a propellant is far different than conventional sailing. Steering can be difficult. It can also be truly dangerous whenever the seas are rough, because once the propellant reaction is induced it is difficult to regulate. If the bow plows into a large enough wave, the propellant could force the ship downwards, into the water. Just as bad, if the propellant does not dissolve properly, pressure can build and explode the exhaust tubes, which would most likely rupture the hull and sink us fast. We won't use the propellants at night when we can't see weather coming, not at first, anyway, but we will try them after the morning meal."

Malana was almost too petrified to speak after listening to Corbant. "Is it worth such risks?" she asked.

Corbant shrugged. "It is the only possibility of insuring a constant speed. With our cargo of Kongs and land walkers, we can't risk meandering at sea. Men and animals must eat, and we can't risk consuming more than a bare minimum of our food. When I sailed to the island merely on wind power, the passage from roughly this area of the sea took fifteen days. We wish to do it in no more than nine, and preferably in seven, from today."

"I thought you could make good time with the wind."

Smiling, Corbant said, "If conditions are absolutely right, and they never are. You may have noticed the wind does not always blow, and when it does, it is not always in the direction we must take."

"No," Malana muttered. *It changes around, and that makes the ship unsteady, and that keeps me sick!*

Corbant misinterpreted her. "We never know how to predict where the wind may come from or in what direction it may blow. Think about it. If the wind comes from directly ahead of the ship, for example, under sail we can't go straight ahead, because if we spread the sails, the wind would push us backward. We would have to turn from the wind, not completely away from it, but at an angle to it, and then the sails can make us move, but we're not longer going straight toward our goal. Now, if the wind is coming from the very place we want to be, we would have to zig to the left for a long way, then zag back to the right, and so gradually we come closer and closer until we can reach the place we want. That's called tacking. But a crooked course like that means that in the end we may travel twice the actual distance to reach our destination."

"Is it the same even for the small ships?" Malana asked.

"Not exactly, but in general. Everything about a ship affects its sailing abilities: the breadth of beam, the length of keel, the draught of water it needs, the shape of her hull, the arrangement of sails, all these details affect how a ship moves. Understand?"

"Yes," she said, though truthfully, she didn't, at least not fully. In fact, she felt not only weak but also contrary and vaguely angry at the whole world, and at that point, she simply didn't care.

"Good!" the captain said, smiling. "Pendonjira, if she were not your apprentice, I might recruit her as a sailor!"

The Pendonjira said, "Before you do, Corbant, I noticed the ships all appear to be falling into line behind us, can you tell me why?"

"Surely. The larger ships received the limited amount of propellant that the sages were able to make. The smaller ships must be towed behind them if they are to keep up."

The Pendonjira looked troubled. "Is there not a danger of collisions?"

Corbant shook his head. "We must take the risk, Ma'am. One moderate-sized ship from each group will remain in the rear, untethered and relying on wind power. That ship will necessarily fall behind, but if any vessel does have to disconnect, the following ship will be able to offer aid. And as another measure, we leave a trail behind."

"In the water?" Malana asked.

"The Tagu sages call it phosphorous– that means glowing–"

"I *know* that," Malana retorted.

Corbant smiled. "Yes, of course you would. Anyhow, it is mixed with the propellant so that it is always part of our wake. Whatever it is made of, it floats and is charged by the sunlight. For most of the night, it will give off a glow that looks like a path of stars upon the water for others to follow. It will persist for three days and nights or so as a visible mark. Believe it or not, they were even able to make it glow in color–each to the color of its own *Leader* ship! If a ship is separated from the fleet and can sight the glowing trail, it will have at least a direction to take."

"Very ingenious," the Pendonjira said.

Corbant remained for a little longer, stroking his beard as he thought. Then he reported to the Pendonjira the condition of the fleet–all but one ship completely sound, the last one so fire damaged that four others had taken the people and the food stores it bore aboard so the hulk could be abandoned. However, no lives had been lost, and most of the provisions had been saved.

At the clang of a bell up on decks, he seemed almost to wake up. "There's the signal for the propellant. I'd better get below to help with the activation," he said.

The Pendonjira thanked Corbant. With that he bowed and was off in a rush.

Uncertain of what to make of the captain, Malana asked, "Is he confident, or as scared as I am, or just plain crazy?"

The Pendonjira touched her hand gently. "Do not be afraid, little one. What will be will be and you must have faith that it is not by chance."

Malana thought, *On this great empty ocean all seems to happen by chance.*

As though reading her mind, the Pendonjira said, "Things happen by designs great or small. The Pendonjiras over generations have discovered and passed on secrets of the plants and elements of the earth. The Tagu sages have harnessed their qualities for the good of all. The propellant formula is one of their great achievements. I myself contributed a little to its formulation through my study of plant resins that help congeal the mixture so it may linger visibly for three days and three nights."

"How does it work?"

"It is made of a special combination of chemicals. When seawater is added, it results in an incredibly powerful effervescence. As I understand it, this is then channeled through a series of tubes that gradually reduce in size, which concentrates the energy. It is finally expelled with tremendous force through the smallest, single outlet behind the ship, driving it forward."

"Where did they ever get an idea like that?" asked Malana, intrigued.

"As with many great 'discoveries,' it was first observed in nature and then imitated. Haven't you ever seen how an octopus swims by expelling jets of water? But that's enough for now," the Pendonjira said. "It's time to get up. Bathe with only a small basin of water, we have only so much fresh water on the ship, and it must last us. Eat a few morsels of food, perhaps some dried fruit and some of the cheese. You'll feel better."

Malana wasn't certain of that, but she did rise, sponge herself, and dress. Before trying to eat, she swallowed some water and then some herbal tea.

The Pendonjira made her rest until they were sure she would not vomit again. Malana's head throbbed–one effect of not eating enough food was to give her annoying headaches–but gradually the healing herbs calmed the ache and soothed her uncertain stomach.

"Are you going to be all right?" the Pendonjira asked gently. "Is your stomach upset now?" Grudgingly, Malana admitted, "I think I can keep some food and the tea down. I feel a little better."

"Good," the Pendonjira said "Eat a little, and then let us go up onto the deck and into the sunshine. That and the fresh air may make you feel better."

It *might*, Malana thought grimly, *if I can jump over the rail and drown myself.*

Three decks below them, and at the stern of the ship, Taigu grunted as he hefted a heavy wooden vessel full of Kong excrement and vomit. The giant creatures were intelligent and soon learned to deposit their waste more or less neatly into an opening that led to the sea below it, not too dissimilar to a human accommodation made for the same purpose. But the Kongs were not seafarers and, like Malana, felt the effects of the ship's motion. To Taigu's consternation, they did not always make it there in time. Whenever they did not, he had to struggle down the narrow passage between stacked crates of provisions to the stern, where a small hatch set into the great one opened outward at deck level. There he had to carefully tilt the waste tubs and dump their stinking contents into the wake of the ship.

And that wasn't the end of it, because then he had to lower a smaller bucket on a very long rope, haul up seawater, and rinse the waste vessels until they were reasonably clean and no longer stank. The work made his arms and shoulders ache, and yet it had to be done. That morning he had almost finished.

The three Zantu took turns staying with the Kongs, rotating each day. The cavernous hold was possibly more comfortable than most places aboard. The thick cushion of straw made a good place to sleep, though close to the sides of the ship some of it had been wet when rain or spume had blown in through the portholes. It was fermenting and smelled, and despite the care that Taigu took with the waste, that added its own odor to the mix. In the heat and the foul smell, the great anthropoids were restless and cramped, and someone had to be there all the time to comfort them by speaking to them or even by singing, which had a calming effect on the Kongs. They also seemed to like slow, soft tunes played on the flute-like *natha*, an instrument that almost all Zantu had built into a segment of their staffs, which the tough and rugged Aton played with a surprisingly gentle feeling of calm melancholy, a combination of melodies that mimicked the sound of wind through trees and other soothing natural phenomena, Taigu noted, though that he made a point of not imitating running water.

Krom in particular would sit with his back against the wall and stare at the shafts of light slanting in from the row of windows high above. Taigu was learning to play the instrument, too, though sometimes his tunes came out unrecognizable.

And the Zan who stayed with the Kongs also had to feed them twice a day, and see that they had clean water, of course. The Tagu had added herbs to their usual food that helped to calm them, and thankfully they could stand to their full height in the centerline of their enclosure. Regardless, they were very aware of their unnatural surroundings and occasionally became nervous and agitated. Taigu could tell they were getting restless. He, too, yearned for the island, knowing that Khaan and the other Kongs would be their old selves once they stood on solid ground again.

But today–ah, today was not his day to stay here with them, but his father's. After a long day and night of confinement with the Kongs, Taigu himself wanted to see the sun, to stretch his legs on the deck. He could do that the moment his chores were finished. He let down his water pail on its rope again, thinking *This will be the last one. The tubs are clean enough for the Kongs, even clean enough for father's inspection. This last rinse, and then I can go up onto the deck.*

He was tempted just to drop the bucket down, but there was a right way to do it, and letting it simply fall was not the way. He had to lower it, hand over hand, watching it dwindle as it passed, swinging like a pendulum, down to the surface. Grunting, he started to do that, standing crouched and leaning so he could watch the pail as it descended.

Something sputtered and growled down below. He had never heard the sound before and did not recognize it–it sounded a little like water beginning to knock and boil in a big pot–

The water directly behind the ship suddenly turned white with a jetting froth of bubbles, and a moment later the ship lurched forward–

And impelled by his own inertia, Taigu tumbled out, yelping as the motion of the ship simply tossed him out of the hatch.

But he had a grip on the rope. It nearly pulled his arms from their sockets, but he kept his hold, despite the pain. He slipped several feet down, but he held on, and felt dizzy as he spun around and around, the ship and the sea flashing past, then the sky, then the ship and sea again. Desperately he started to climb up to the small hatch, now three times a man's height away. As he climbed closer, his weight pulled the rope straighter, and he swung forward and banged into the hull, nearly losing his grip. He had tied the end of the rope to a beam, but had he tied it well enough to hold his weight?

The ship now was moving faster than it had under sail. It sent a wake creaming out behind it. The rope alternately tautened and then flapped loose in his grip. *The pail must be skimming,* he thought, catching the surface and then bucking free and spilling its load of water. Every time the line slackened, he crashed against the ship. He couldn't hold on for much longer, each lash of the rope threatened to shake him loose–

He felt himself rising and in one dizzy sweep he saw a dark shape hulking up in the hatchway, steadily hauling on the rope.

"Khaan! Pull me in!"

The Kong, head down, did not give any sign of hearing him, but its shoulders bunched and its arms moved steadily as it hauled hand over hand. It reached out at last, seized his arm, and dragged him aboard, letting go of the rope as Taigu crawled past him on hands and knees. The rope made a whizzing sound as the pail's weight pulled it–and then as the bucket hit the water and dragged, the line tautened with a twang, just missing the prone Taigu and slapping hard against Khaan's leg. The Kong roared and jerked back. Behind him, Vekan reached for Taigu. "Are you hurt?"

"No," Taigu gasped, but then he realized he had left a red track of handprints along the deck. His palms were bleeding. The rope had stripped off the skin. But he willed himself to ignore the sudden burning pain and said, "I think Khaan got hit."

Vekan looked at Khaan's leg. The left thigh had lost some hair, but it showed no bleeding wound. "Just a bruise. Send him back. I'll bring in the pail."

Taigu spoke to Khaan in the secret language of the Zantu, and the Kong limped forward, pausing now and then to rub his thigh resentfully. *He's like that,* Taigu thought, struggling to his feet. *When he gets a small injury, he always exaggerates it so I'll pity him and give him special food. He'll grow out of it.*

Vekan grunted as he pulled in the frayed end of the rope. No pail was tied to it. "Broke free," he said. "Well, I'll rig another. We have to remember we can't haul in water when the Captain uses propellants, though."

"What are they?" Aton asked.

Vekan said, "I learned about them because unlike you and your Krom, I have spent much time in the past with the Pendonjira." He briefly explained what he knew about the propellants.

"We should have known about them earlier," Aton said.

"Someone forgot to warn us," Vekan said. "From now on, when we see the smaller ships lining up behind ours, we'll know to be careful. Come into the light, Taigu, and let's see your hands."

Blood dripped from Taigu's fingers. His father and Aton washed the palms clean and applied ointment and wrapped his hands with bandages. "Three days of pain, a week of aches, and you'll be all right again," Aton said gruffly. "The young heal fast." The older Zan was still favoring his injured shoulder, though he exercised it every day.

Taigu stripped bare to the waist. He had bruises coming out on his arms and back, places where he'd thumped hard against the hull, but no cuts, and he wasn't bleeding anywhere else except his hands. The ointment, which contained soothing herbs, helped ease that pain. Taigu asked, "May I go on deck now?"

"If you won't do something foolish and fall off the ship," his father said with a grunt. "If you do, you're dead. The ship would leave you far behind before you knew it, and then–drowning, or the terrible fish would eat you alive."

"I'll be careful."

Once on deck, he felt better immediately. The sun, shining from a clear sky, fell warm on his arms and face, and the deck under his bare feet was nearly too hot to bear. He found a shaded spot near the left rail and that was more comfortable. As Taigu stood in the warm air, even the pain of his bruises and his lacerations eased. He gazed around. Ships were no longer spread out across the whole face of the sea, but had fallen in line, a string of them behind each one of the five Leaders. Connected by great lengths of thick-corded cable, the leading ships trailed white V-shaped wakes on water nearly as flat and calm as on a sheltered lake back in the Valley.

Looking at the endless line of cable and ships, Taigu thought *No wonder they needed to chop down every tree in sight for miles. But at least at the speed we're travelling, our journey won't last long now.* He felt the clean wind in his face–caused by the ship's forward motion, not so much an actual breeze–and took deep, grateful breaths. He marveled at an endless pod of dolphins that very nearly kept pace with the ship as though they, too, were fleeing the eruptions and were happy to have the company of the human vessels. "They're good luck," he heard sailors remark, and hoped it was true.

Far ahead of him, on the same side of the deck, he saw the Pendonjira and her apprentice, Malana. The sailors on deck looked almost embarrassed. Instead of their usual scrambling up and down the shroud lines to the masts to mind the sails, they had very little to do, and above them the sails had all been collapsed against the mainmasts.

A good many of the men had climbed up anyway and stood on man-ropes, leaning against the yards and gazing into the forward distance, joking and laughing at their sudden freedom from labor. As he made his way forward, Taigu passed groups of sailors sitting on the deck.

He heard scraps of their conversation. "Just burned the whole earth clean," and "I say we tell our children nothing about the horrors, just let them think the islands are the whole world," and "I'll never board another ship again, once we come to land." They ignored Taigu as he passed–many of them were Atu, no longer land warriors, perhaps, but now men who fought the sea itself. Briefly, Taigu wondered which ships carried the Kai and their half-wild mounts. He hoped the island would be large enough for both them and the Zantu to have territories of their own.

The Pendonjira glanced back as he came near, but Malana kept her face forward, into the wind. "Here is the young Zan," the Pendonjira said. "How are your charges?"

"Thank you, Lady, they are well enough," Taigu said stiffly. The Pendonjira intimidated him even more than Aton had, and he searched for his best behavior, as far as he could remember it. Again catching the fresh, naturally sweet scent of the Pendonjira and Malana even as it mixed with the salt air, he tried to stand downwind from her. His own aroma could not be so pleasant. He said, "I think they are eager to be on land again, though."

"So are we all. What happened to your hands? An accident?"

Fighting an impulse to hide his hands behind his back, Taigu briefly explained: "A kind of accident. When the propellant started, I wasn't prepared and fell from a hatch. I grabbed a rope and that tore my skin a little, but I'm all right, really."

Malana looked around then, her face shockingly thin and drawn. She grimaced as she glimpsed the bloodstained bandages.

"I'll send you some poultices that will speed healing, perhaps even quicker than those of your Zantu," the Pendonjira said with a warm smile. "It's lucky for you that you could climb back aboard."

"Well, Lady, I didn't really. My Kong pulled me to safety."

Then Malana spoke, sounding surprised: "You have a Kong of your own, and you so young?"

Taigu felt tongue-tied in her presence. "Yes. No. Um, I mean we don't own them, you know. Zantu, I mean, we don't *own* the Kongs. They–I don't know how to put it exactly. They're like partners to us. A young Kong bonds with a Zan. We learn from each other. A Zan bonds with a Kong for life. We even speak with them."

A young Kong bonds with a Zan…for life.

"I know that," Malana said scornfully. "You have a secret language that no one else can hear." "Um, no, people can hear it," Taigu corrected. "But unless you're a Zan, it won't mean anything. And no Kong would listen to you even if you learned the language, because there has to be the bond, you know, between a Zan and a Kong."

"Say something in the language, then," Malana said.

"Malana," the Pendonjira warned, "that is bad manners. What would you do if a Zan or a Kai asked you to repeat the list of sleeping herbs?"

Malana looked irked, but she said nothing.

"I don't mind," Taigu said. He thought a moment and then spoke the peculiar language he used with Khaan, with clicks, whistles, hums, and grunts. "That would be a way of telling Khaan that he is a good Kong and deserves a reward," he explained.

Malana's eyebrows rose. "That's a language? It sounds almost like music."

"It *is* a kind of music," Taigu agreed. "But if I said exactly the same thing to my father's Kong, it wouldn't mean much to him. He'd understand that I meant to be kind and that I was praising him, maybe, but that's all. Every Zan's Kong gets the full meaning only from his own Zan. The reverse is also true: there are sounds and gestures that every Kong's Zan understands when others can't. I can't explain it any more than that."

"The Zantu ways are ancient indeed, and have their origins in the old Tagu culture, the same as ours," the Pendonjira said. "Long before the joining of the great Tagu and Atu tribes, the Zantu joined with the Kongs–almost as far back as the first Pendonjira, though Aton may argue that they go back farther. In truth, it is so long ago that neither of us knows for sure."

"Father says that the Zantu and the sages do the same thing, but in different ways," Taigu said. "That is true enough. From the Kongs the Zantu sought to rediscover the secret truths and workings of nature that had been forgotten after people banded together and lived in protected groups. They had isolated themselves from the dangers of nature, but, unfortunately, also from its truths. Through the Kongs, the Zantu draw closer to nature. The Pendonjiras sought to do the same for everyone, without separating themselves, for they believed that all people needed be in touch with these inner truths if they were ultimately going to survive. Our traditions teach us that the Zantu and the Pendonjira were once very close, that we had, and still have, much to learn from each other. It is why we maintain contact, infrequent as it may be, to this very day. It is something both of you will come to understand and appreciate more as you grow."

Taigu didn't fully comprehend that, but he murmured, "I hope so, Lady."

With a glance at her apprentice, the Pendonjira added, "Perhaps on the island Malana can learn from you and from Khaan."

For an instant Malana looked at Taigu in a most quizzical way that made him self-conscious without really understanding why.

"I…I'd like that," Taigu said shyly.

"If we ever get to the island," Malana muttered. She asked Taigu, "Doesn't the ship make you sick?"

"Sick? No. Are you sick?"

When Malana didn't reply, the Pendonjira said, "She has been ill ever since we left. The motion of the ship, I think. It affects some people more than others."

"Oh," Taigu said. "Well, I like it. It's not like anything on land at all. Except that during the storms it wasn't very good with the Kongs sometimes rolling on the floor as the ship tilted. One could crush you accidentally. But even that didn't really make me feel sick."

"It's not just that," Malana said in a small voice, fighting to hold back a sob. "Back there behind us–they're all dead. It's all gone. The people and the buildings and my beautiful river, gone forever. Their passing has left a hollow place in my heart."

"Life is made of greetings and farewells," the Pendonjira said softly. "That was a great and terrible farewell indeed, Malana. And I too regret the loss of the river and our gardens and the town, but most of all, of the lives. So many died that could have been saved. But here we are, and we live, and in us lives the spirit of the Tagatu people. We cannot swim against the stream of Time, my apprentice. We must let it bear us forward, and we must look ahead to the new greetings, not just behind to the bitter farewells." She touched her apprentice's hair gently. "There will be other rivers and other gardens. True, there have been too many deaths, but there will be births and babies and a future ahead of us."

Taigu had a feeling that he was intruding. He bowed and said, "Lady, I will go back and see–to–I will leave you now."

They watched him walk away, sure-footed on the deck in a way that Malana doubted she would ever be.

Malana murmured, "There's someone who looks ahead. I wish I could learn, Pendonjira. I'm afraid my heart will always be caught in our beautiful lost Valley. I'm afraid that the air of the island will be bitter in my nostrils and will taste of ashes on my tongue."

"Never forget," the Pendonjira murmured. "But never close your mind and your soul to what will come. Patience, Malana. You will be a Pendonjira. You do not yet fully understand that your senses are heightened beyond those of most others. They will become more heightened still. Eventually, you will learn how to not only control them, but to direct them to a greater purpose. Speak to me, when we are alone and the time is peaceful, of your worries. That will help more than you know. How is your stomach now?"

"Better," Malana said, surprised herself. "I–I think I could eat a real meal."

"It's early yet, but let us go have some food," the Pendonjira said. "I want you to be healthy and strong when we arrive at the Island. You will be needed. As will Taigu and his Kong, and Corbant, and all the rest of us. Farewells are hard, young Malana–but sometimes greetings are even more difficult." Then suddenly with a broad smile, "And there are always the unexpected joys–look there!"

As if on cue, another pod of dolphins appeared, gracefully arcing through the waves, the light glinted off their sleek backs and trailed sparkling diamonds in their wake.

Even Malana managed a weak smile at the beauty of the scene as they made their way to their quarters. And, trying hard, Malana ate perhaps half a meal.

But at least she kept it down.

And all the time the ship, the fleet, moved swiftly over the surface of a newly calm sea.

He marveled at an endless pod of dolphins . . .

Most of the next week passed with the ships speeding along under power during the daylight hours and raising sail at night. The constant rolling of water past the hull, the whipping sails, creaking wood, and the muffled hissing of the propellant's exhaust combined to create a soothing background noise that almost faded from perception. The fresh scent of salt air invigorated even the seasick ones, and the knowledge that everyone on board their ship, and those on the multitude of ships behind them, were united in a common purpose heartened everyone.

More than that, the specter of unknown, possibly dangerous times ahead made them all feel as one in spirit. Most went about their chores with great camaraderie. If the calm continued, the Pendonjira believed they should gain sight of their new home well before the next week ended.

But Hope, they say, does not travel on ships. A morning broke dull and gray under a heavy overcast, the air feeling saturated and thick, and Corbant ordered a delay in using the propellant until they saw whether the clouds would give birth to a storm. "It looks touchy," the captain said to Vekan and Taigu, who had come up to get some exercise and a breath of untainted air at the bow. "The sky this morning was red and fiery. That's a sign of tempest. And now the clouds build up and up–you can tell by the darkening of the day–and yet we lie becalmed."

Time crawled by, but before noon, Corbant's fears materialized as the clouds overhead stirred and began to stream across the sky, ripped by unfelt winds aloft into ragged ribbons. Taigu saw strange lanes of white water open on the gray face of the sea, snaking and undulating from the east. Then, with no warning, a downpour burst on them, painfully large raindrops smacking hard onto the wood of the decks, the fabric of the sails, the exposed skin of the sailors. The water felt warm, nearly body-heat, and the rush of rain blinded Taigu. Even shielding his face with his hand and peering under it, he couldn't even see the nearer ships.

The rain began vertically, but then a terrific wind from the east struck, making the masts groan and the ship heel dangerously as the wind caught and filled the limp sails and spun the ship like a bird caught in a whirlwind. On the base of the masts, the sailors struggled in the rain to fold down the sail–wind this powerful might break the masts off short, or blast the sails to flapping ribbons. Corbant ran to the front mast, shouting orders up; sailors lower in the rigging heard him and rushed up to spread the orders, for against the world-shattering wind, no one up on the yards could hear anything from the deck.

When they had reduced sail to one half-furled foresail, they scudded before the wind, helpless to attempt any course. Behind them rolled great seas, as tall as the tsunamis that had passed harmlessly under their keel, but closer together and raging with white water. Vekan dragged Taigu below–but he stopped on the second deck and stared out a small porthole at the maddened sea. The ship groaned and creaked and cracked under the pressures of wind and water, and the deck above warped enough to let streams squirt through. Vekan yelled into his ear, "This is rain water, fresh water. I hope they're catching some in barrels. We may need it if the wind blows us off course."

It was a strange day. The seas grew higher, and when a following wave lifted them high up, the blast screamed like a tormented soul. Then when the prow of the ship tilted down, down, down, and the ship hurtled into the trough of the wave, the water behind them cut off the roar of the wind and an eerie silence lasted until the ship actually nosed into the water. Each time it seemed to labor to raise itself level again, and waves broke across the deck as far back as amidships.

Here, the sailors knew, was the most dangerous time: if the ship didn't have enough speed, then when the next wave rolled in and raised her, the wind might catch her broadside and roll her over.

If that happened–if they broached–they would all die, for water would pour in and the ship would surely sink.

Taigu had heard them talk of such things. Vekan said, "I'm going to the Kongs. They'll be disoriented, confused. You stay here and don't go out again!"

"Yes,"Taigu said.

He held on and caught his breath as the ship plunged down into another trough. Through the port he saw the steep wave boiling as white water, blown from its crest, tumbled down alongside the ship. He heard a scream from somewhere behind him and when the ship leveled out momentarily, he let go his hold on the port and turned. A door had flapped open, and he made his way to it. "Is someone hurt?"

To his surprise, the voice of the Pendonjira answered him, sounding firm and calm: "No. A little frightened. Water is coming in."

A dim lantern gave just enough light for Taigu to see the timbers of the hull visibly twist. Water did squirt in, running down the wall, wetting the bunks and everything else. Malana crouched on the lower bunk, desperately holding onto the posts. "Are we sinking?"

"No,"Taigu said, hoping he sounded more assured than he felt. "Bad storm, but the ship is riding it out. The sailors adjusted the sails, whatever that means. Corbant knows what to do."

Water on the deck sloshed ankle-deep as the ship moved up again, tilting back and forth, and then everything groaned as the wind caught the vessel again.

"This will put us off course," the Pendonjira said. "I hope it does not scatter the fleet. We will need everyone on the island."

"What makes you think we'll even get to the island?" Malana screamed, her face scarlet with emotion. "We'll die here!"

"I think not," the Pendonjira said calmly. "The sailors know their business, and we have had generations to learn how to build good weatherly ships. But whatever happens, let us meet it like Tagatu, not like frightened birds. Malana, recite the names of the twelve plants that help heal infections."

"What!"

"It will give you something to think about other than your own fear. And I don't believe you know them all. Show that I am wrong."

Glaring at the older woman, and through clenched teeth, Malana began: "Fever root. Yellow tangler vine. Sweet blackroot. Swamp lily root. Hacknut shells, green, pounded and boiled to a poultice. Rockbrush root. Mountain fletch, but only if picked before the longest day in the year and dried. Ice vine, best for boiling in a tea. Fever root–"

"You've already mentioned that one."

"Yes, yes, well, autumn flywort, collect the seeds, dry them, crush them into powder. The bark of the river willow, boiled into a tea. Sand thistle root, but the leaves are poisonous. And … the tuber of the strangler vine. Is that all?"

"Don't you know?"

"That's twelve! That's all!" the girl yelled over the noise of the storm.

"Well done, apprentice," the Pendonjira said.

A sweet music began, and both of them, girl and woman, looked at Taigu in surprise. He had taken his *natha* from the small compartment in his staff and was improvising a random tune, note to note.

"What are you doing?"Malana demanded.

Taigu shrugged. "When the Kongs are disturbed, this helps them be calm," he said. "And it is something to do."

"Well done to you, too, young Zan," the Pendonjira said. "Malana, there is always something before you to do. Doing it keeps fear at bay. You were angry at me just now, but for those moments when you thought of the names of the plants, you felt no fear. Isn't it better that way?"

"I don't know," Malana wailed. "When will this end?"

"Soon," the Pendonjira said. "Very soon, measured by the life of a great tortoise that lives for hundreds of years. Or it will end in a long time–very long, measured by the life of a dayfly, that lives for only the hours of sunlight on one single summer's day. It will end when it ends, and if we are lucky, we will be here to see that ending and to see what begins next."

As it happened, they were still there to see the storm's ending, though they had a false hope once, when the winds stilled and overhead they could see a patch of clear sky. Then, too soon, the winds came again, from the opposite direction, and the ship suffered more buffeting and plunging and soaking. That ceased sometime before the middle of the night. The next day dawned with a cloud-barred sky, a ship that had been wrenched and battered but still had most of her sails, and a broad and empty sea.

Corbant came down from the rigging, he was really too old and too heavy for such exercise, but he wanted to see for himself, and when he regained the deck, he panted for breath and then said to the Pendonjira, "It was one of the tempests that come in this part of the world now and again, usually in late summer and autumn. From up there I could see six and possibly seven of our ships, all at a great distance. I don't know if any vessels didn't manage to cut their towlines. I hope not. Tied together, they would smash together and sink. But, by the looks of it the storm has scattered us all, so I believe everyone was left to navigate freely. I imagine the fleet lies over miles of sea now, but the captains know the courses they must steer, and surely as we approach the island we will meet them again."

"Some may have perished."

"Some," he granted. "But my experience tells me more survived than you might at first believe. I'm sure any phosphorous has disappeared completely. At any rate, tonight I should have a clear enough view of the stars to know approximately where we are. I wish I knew how far the storm drove us to the west, though. Oh, and another thing: I don't dare start the propellant again, not until some of the other ships join us. Our men will have to examine the tubes closely to make sure the storm hasn't damaged them, and that the intakes will still function. As things dry out and the sea grows calm, we may try again, but if we can't use them, it could be many days, weeks, before we can reach the island."

"We have enough food and water?"

"Enough food, certainly, but that will mean less to sustain us once we reach the island. As for that, though, I'd be just as happy to take my chances there! And we caught as much fresh water as we could. Most of it is brackish, because in a storm like that the sea spray mixes freely with the rain, you know. But we can drink it. I don't know how long the journey will last now. Two weeks. Two months. We'll be all right, though–unless we run into another storm like that one. If that should happen–" Corbant broke off, frowning and stroking his gray beard.

"I understand," the Pendonjira said.

Decks below them, in the great compartment where the Kongs lodged, Aton offered Krom a basket of dried fruits and grains. The Kong stubbornly turned his head.

"None of them will eat," Vekan told him. "They haven't since the storm began." "Are they sick?" Taigu asked.

"I think not. "Aton reached out and touched Krom's great hand. The Kong stared at him impassively, but did not grasp his hand or respond with a grunt of inquiry. "We should open the rear hatch and let them see the world still exists. We'll let them, one at a time, go back to see the sky and breathe fresh air."

Vekan looked doubtful. "If one goes, all will want to go. Their weight is very great for the ship to bear. They might throw it out of balance."

"I can control Krom," Aton said. "If the young one goes first, and then your Kong, Krom will wait his turn."

"Is it safe?" Taigu asked. "I fell out, remember."

"I don't think the propellant will run today," Aton told him. "But I will go and ask."

"Zantu don't–" Taigu began, but a severe glance from his father silenced him.

Aton said gently, "Zantu don't ask, not when they and the Kongs are roaming free. Nor do they take what is others', nor do they intrude where they are not needed. But we aren't roaming free now, Taigu. This ship is like another country, and we have to consider the knowledge and intentions of those who know it better than we do." He had been crouching next to Krom. Now he rose, stretched his arm, and rubbed his shoulder. "I will go and find Corbant and ask whether he means to use the propellant today."

He did, and the captain told him that he didn't intend so, and that moving the Kongs so they could have a little light and air would be fine. Taigu went first with Khaan, the Kong walking unsteadily, no longer trusting the motion of the ship beneath his feet. When Taigu arrived at the back of the longhouse, he tried to open the doors but they were stuck. The boy heard sailors on the other side yell, "Hold up in there, debris is blocking the hatch and we have to clear it!"

But Khaan was in no mood to wait. The great muscles in his back bulged as he forced the doors open, crushing and cracking whatever was obstructing them–and almost dislodging the sailors who dangled on ropes outside. The men began to curse furiously.

Just then the Kong's huge head appeared from behind the doors. It was well over fifteen feet above the men and the deep-set eyes glared down at them as the rest of his enormous bulk emerged into the daylight. Disheveled, angry, and in no mood to suffer the sailor's insults, Khaan roared deafeningly. Like spiders shocked at finding a deadly wasp in their web, they scrambled back up to the deck on their ropes, and from the sound of their shouts they spread panic throughout the ship.

Then Taigu heard his father's voice from above, reassuring the men, telling them the Kong merely needed air, while craftily pointing out that the hanging debris that had blocked the hatch was no longer a problem. This latter caused Taigu to smile to himself, *I wonder if the men actually agreed or were too scared to protest.*

As though none of it had happened, Khaan took in a great lungful of air. The limitless ocean, silver beneath the morning sun, shone unbroken in the sky. Only two ships, both so distant they were only specks, were visible of all the great fleet.

Relieved that Khaan had calmed down and did not pound the ground in anger as was his usual reaction– the deck in this case–which would have shattered into splinters. *He must have sensed that,* he thought.

"Sit," Taigu said.

Khaan did, folding his legs and straightening his back. He breathed deeply again.

"Here," Taigu said, offering a basket of greens and fruit. He did it carelessly, as something that he did only casually, not much caring what happened. "Are you hungry?"

Without moving his gaze from the ocean, Khaan reached down and took some food and began to eat it. *It's working!*

Taigu began to talk. Not really making much sense, just keeping up a running flow of words to calm the Kong and reassure him: "This is nothing. This is just ocean. Wait until we get to island. Good food all around there. And trees to climb for me–maybe even for you, if there are some giant ones. You haven't climbed a tree since you were only two years old! Grass to roll in. Warm, too, and smelling fresh, not like this cave you've been in for too long now. Take some more. We have plenty. Hungry after so many days, are you? Eat. This is not the best food, is it? Dry and tasteless. On the island we'll find fruit. Sweet fruit like none you've ever tasted before, and a good kill for meat."

And on and on, until Khaan had eaten all that was in the basket. Taigu touched his hand, and the big anthropoid briefly clasped the human's hand, a gesture of mutual understanding. When Taigu went back along the passage, Khaan followed without protest.

"He ate everything," Taigu said.

"I thought he would," Aton replied, "Now you, Vekan."

"Just wait a little," Vekan said.

Chang was sniffing his adolescent son's fur and then his breath. He made an inquiring noise in his throat, and the younger Kong grunted. Chang turned his great head and stared down the passageway toward the light.

"Now," Vekan said. "He wanted to make sure his son was well and had eaten first. Come, Chang."

As light streamed in, the two went toward the open hatch, Vekan carrying a heavier basket of food than Taigu had taken.

"I think they'll be all right now," Taigu told Aton.

"I agree. But how long will they be satisfied with a glimpse of water and sky? The captain doesn't know just where we are. We won't be using the propellant until he can gather up all the ships that he can."

"How will he do that?"

"He signals to all the others within sight. Some of them are halfway to the horizon. They may be able to see and signal to more distant ships that are beyond our sight. And when we have a suitable wind at night, the sailors on the deck will fly kites with burning lanterns. In the dark they can be seen from a great distance. Any ship crew that spots them will head toward us. It will take time–days–but the fleet will re-form."

"But are we lost?"

"I would be," Aton said. "But these experienced mariners have a way of looking at the moon and the stars and having some idea of where they are. Or at least what direction they should take." He stretched. "We have aboard six men who were on the first exploring ship to touch on the islands. As soon as we find some land, they'll have a good idea of where we are, and that will set us right."

"I hope it's soon," Taigu said.

"I hope Chang eats soon," Aton replied. "Krom must be feeling hungry."

And as though in reply the great Kong beside him gave a deep grunt and his gut started to rumble loudly.

And that same day, but far away from the ship, on the island the Tagatu had discovered and called Kai-Kahli, "Island of the Skull":

A hot sun beat down on the cluster of huts that stood in a clearing a little way in the jungle, a man-made one, the trees felled by Tagatu explorers. Amidst a chaos of insect rattles and chirps and the occasional screech of animals, Atl-Atu, the chief of the hunters, stood outside one hut frowning, his head tilted, not listening, but sniffing the air. Something felt wrong. The insects stopped for a moment, but then started again, then stopped once more. He walked to the perimeter of the advance camp and found the Tagu expert, old Hanu, making his rounds. Without even a greeting, Atl-Atu asked the older man, "Have you heard or seen anything?"

Hanu glanced over his shoulder at the warrior. "Nothing unusual, Atl-Atu. Some of the big heavy herbivores passed on the far side of the stream some time ago. And the soarers flew over at dawn." He glanced up at the sky. Here the flying creatures, their enormous membraned wings spread wide to catch the updrafts, rarely came low enough to pose any danger. So far, at least, they seemed no threat to people. Most times they were so high it was difficult to make out their exact shapes. They roosted somewhere in the mountains, and they flew out every day, all day, to fish in the bay.

Atl-Atu looked at the ceramic pot that the older man had taken from its post. "Your preparations are all burning?"

"Yes, of course," Hanu said. "All the smoke urns are smoldering." He raised the one he held. "Even this one, which I'm refilling now. I never let them burn out."

"And there are plenty of them?"

Hanu tilted his head. He was very old for this expedition, his hair white, his eyes deep-set in nests of wrinkles, his throat saggy. But he was sound of body, and he seemed puzzled at the questions. "You know there are. I hoped that we could harvest more on the island, but I can't recognize any of the vegetation, and even the rocks seem different! We've planted some of the most needed ones on the islets, but they won't be ready for harvest for months. Still, we have more than enough coverage." He turned to face the Atu warrior. "Is something wrong, something that I should know about?"

"I don't know," Atl-Atu confessed. "I can't say that, but there is a scent on the air that I don't recognize. It's faint, but sharp in the nose, like a flash of alarm when you see some predator in the brush. I can't tell where it comes from, but it's all around today–drifts on the air."

Hanu sniffed. "I can't smell it."

"No wonder," Atl-Atu said, grinning. "Your herbs fill your nose, of course. And you don't have the scenting abilities of a true hunter. I can smell it, though, and it makes me...uneasy."

Hanu had turned away and was measuring the green-and-brown mixture of seeds. Without looking up from his work, he asked, "Have any of the scouts reported anything strange?"

Atl-Atu made the sideways gesture with his chin that meant *no*, but then realized Hanu hadn't seen it. "None have said anything. Everything is quiet, and yet–I don't know. Something disturbs me. Have you noticed that the insects are constantly starting and stopping their chatter? Listen. Now they're silent again."

"Perhaps," Hanu suggested, "you're feeling that the time is near for the people to come."

"It *is* near," Atl-Atu agreed, "and yet, no, I don't think that's it. It's more than mere worry and anticipation. Something real, something–something I cannot name."

Hanu blew into the ceramic pot and carefully began to scoop out some of the blackened ash, leaving live red embers. "How is the work on the barrier going?"

"More slowly than I'd like. Did you hear about the accident we had in digging the holes for the supports?"

"I heard that you broke into a cave or something. I haven't gone to the peninsula to look yet." "Not a cave," Atl-Atu said slowly, as if carefully choosing his words. "But the rock beneath the soil there is different. Porous. And there are voids that we did not expect. One stretch is involved, two different set-holes, two spears' lengths apart. We had cut one to the depth of my leg when we broke through, and the rock crumbled and dropped far down into water. We heard the splashes only after a long time had gone by. Now that set-hole is this wide." He held up his arms, outstretched. "We'll have to make a framework and fill in with ilu before we can hope to raise a support there."

Hanu gave a grunt of understanding and concern. "The second one is as bad?"

"No, we dug down the height of a man, but then the bottom broke into the same opening, or a similar one. But the stone held without collapsing inward. We'll have to mortar the support in still, but at least there wasn't a cave-in that ruined our work."

"When my Tagu have finished collecting plants and can take care of the smoke urns, I'll travel back to the peninsula and look at the stone there. You didn't draw any water from the opening, did you? No one drank of it?"

"No, of course not."

They didn't speak about the strange sickness that had fallen on many Atu warriors after they had ventured far into the jungle and had drunk water from streams there. They had come back ill and disoriented, feverish and weak, and even after nearly a year had passed, some of them were still struggling to recover their full strength.

It was odd: the sickness did not seem to dwell in fresh-fallen rainwater, such as collected in hollows or in prepared troughs. They'd gathered plenty of it the week before, when the fringes of a great storm had brought drenching, flooding rain to the island.

Instead, the peril seemed to arise only when they drank water from springs that bubbled and flowed straight from bedrock. Strange, because back in the Great Valley the purest water came from such springs. It was a mystery that demanded further study. For now, though, they knew that avoiding groundwater would prevent the disease from spreading, and for the time that knowledge seemed enough.

"We haven't done badly, though, "old Hanu said, carefully adding dried herbs to the embers remaining in the bottom of the smoke urn. He had left enough slow-burning herbs in it to light the new fuel, and within a few breaths the blue smoke began to stream up into the breeze, spiraling and dispersing.

It spread wide through the jungle, downwind of course, but to some extent even on the windward side–and even when diluted by air, it served to calm the strange, huge, sometimes ferocious animals they had encountered. The herbivores became docile when they breathed even traces of the fumes, ignoring the small humans who sometimes preyed on them. The big killers avoided the areas where the smoke billowed. If they caught scent of it, they turned and made their way to other parts of the jungle or to the uplands.

"No," Atl-Atu said after a few moments, when the smoke urn was well alight. "We haven't done badly. We came with twice thirty warriors, scouts, and workers."

"And scholars," Hanu said with a smile. "I respect the warriors and hunters, but we scholars do our part. These repellents, for example. My friends and I discovered these after months of trial and error."

"I number scholars among the workers," Atl-Atu said, but not harshly. He was old enough himself to speak to an elder like Hanu with some degree of impudence, and the two genuinely liked each other. Close friendships among the elder Atu and Tagu were not rare, but generally they gravitated to the familiarity of their own individual traditions as they aged. These two men got along well, often arguing in a good-natured way, but never bearing each other ill-will.

"Very well," Hanu said. "My dozen scholars are workers. Then your thirty warriors and scouts must be workers, too." His smile faded. "But I have lost five of my dozen to illness. How many of your–workers–have died?"

Atl-Atu sighed. "Thirteen. Some stupidly, pursuing game that they did not yet understand how to stalk and kill. A few by accident, falling from the cliffs, trampled when a herd of the big horned beasts stampeded without warning. Two have vanished without a trace. I've lost too many. We have food enough and shelter, and we have clean water. We can hold out. But I wish the people would come."

"Let's make sure the barrier is up soon, then. I think we've gathered enough specimens from the jungle, and your hunters have laid in a fine supply of meat."

"Yes. We should plan to pull back to the peninsula and make sure all is ready–" Atl-Atu jerked his head at a distant, booming sound. "Did you hear that? The grass-eaters are alarmed."

"Probably a predator wondering near." Hanu shrugged as he hung the smoke urn back on its support. "That bellow came from far away. I'm sure it was beyond the reach of our smoke. I do not think it is a nearby threat."

"Still, I had better make the rounds of the sentinels," Atl-Atu said. "I'm sure they're alert, but…" He let his words trail off. "Get at least one of your scholars to help you, Hanu. You're old and slow and these smoke urns must be kept going."

"I'll show you *slow*," Hanu said, chuckling. He picked up his bag of herbs and waved a farewell as he turned and headed down a narrow path through head-high grass toward the next smoke urn station.

Atl-Atu moved in a different direction. At spaced intervals, lookouts crouched on platforms high in the trees. They were well above the reach of even the tallest predators, though admittedly other dangers–the flying spear-beaked creatures, the immense sea serpents–could have reached them. But they were all within the protective shadow of the calming smoke; none of them had suffered from one of the island animals attacking so long as they were in range of the repellent's aromatic fumes. The worst had been an occasional broken bone from a fall, but they had learned caution and now falls rarely happened.

Atl-Atu came within sight of one of the outposts, a tree that soared up a hundred feet or more. Halfway up, Pakal, the youngest of his warriors, would be crouching on his platform, surveying the landscape all around. Atl-Atu gave the shrill whistle of recognition.

No return sound came. Atl-Atu impatiently called, "Pakal! You'd better not be sleeping!"

Of course, he wouldn't be–no Atu warrior would be so weak, would subject himself to the humiliation of a public scolding. Atl-Atu leaned his spear against the trunk, found the vines that allowed a man to climb rapidly, and scaled the tree, scrambling up with greater dexterity than most men of fifty could show.

He reached the platform and pulled himself level with it.

He stared silently at the wood, at the great smear of already-drying blood. Fat black creeping flies buzzed as they landed on the sticky surface, battening on it.

There had been no sound, no outcry, not even a scream.

Atl-Atu almost dropped to the earth, so fast did he descend. He grabbed his spear and ran in a hunter's crouch back to the grassland. He reached the spot where he had last seen Hanu.

The wooden post had been thrown down. The ceramic smoke urn lay shattered, though the herbs still winked red and smoldered. Something had passed through the tall grasses, flattening them.

With all his senses straining, Atl-Atu ran, thinking *It has not been more than a hundred breaths! Hanu cannot have gone far!*

He thought he heard the old man just ahead. He pushed through the grass. Something lunged at him with lightning speed.

Like young Pakal up on the platform, like old Hanu with his bag of herbs, Atl-Atu was eviscerated and dying before he could scream.

7

The Great Valley lay under many feet of steaming hot ash-fall, and still more shattered pumice showered down, and through the darkness flew great arcing streaks of red that were magma bombs, red-hot fragments of molten rock, liquid when the distant volcano spat them out, gaining a black, thin outer crust with zigzag cracks of glowing red fracturing it, as the mass of molten rock screamed through the air. Upon impact, they burst into sprays of liquid rock, but they set no fires, because everything inflammable had already been consumed.

Lava flows inland contributed to the burial of the valley, and new volcanoes steadily appeared, creeping southward toward the sea, one emerging almost every day, growing fast as it gushed out thick black smoke and hot, curdling blasts of powdered rock. The new eruptions added their loads of ash to the great burden that choked the valley. The harbor, too, had been filled, and the ash had embraced and almost hidden the crescent-shaped barrier island. The fallen material there was loose and light, pumice-like, and whole miles-long rafts of it floated off on the surface of the sea.

The eruptions had changed the look of everything. No one who had known the valley in former days would have recognized anything about it.

However, that mattered not at all, because within many hundreds of leagues in all directions, none who had known it were still alive. Even far out of sight of the northern volcanoes the ash had fallen, and for enormous distances downwind, beneath the still-spreading dark canopy of smoke and fine ash, night reigned through every hour of every day. No sunlight could penetrate the gloom—at the end of summer, snow fell in places where it had never fallen, snow dyed a dark gray by the ash it had picked up.

Animals died rapidly from inhaling the volcanic particles—even a big population of feral Kongs, strong enough to confront any earthly foe, but not strong enough to fight the earth itself. For a huge swath of the mainland, the shadow of the eruption stretched long, erasing all life from the surface, bird, mammal, reptile, insect, down to microscopic bacteria.

Even now, after so much devastation, the earth was not through destroying the valley. Violent earthquakes sheared through the bedrock below it all. The centers of the quakes had advanced steadily toward the sea, it seemed, from the time when they had been clustered on the chain of volcanoes to the north—and now they had the insistent, increasing intensity that a caged wild animal might have felt, ferociously testing its bars, searching for a way to break free.

Roughly where the lighthouse had stood, a deep fissure opened during one of these quakes. Searing steam rushed out, blasting the loose ash out and piling it in banks alongside the rift. For the first few hours the split in the ash was narrow enough for a man to leap across—if any man could have lived to make the effort.

Then another quake, and the fissure widened and spread. The standing cliffs of ash crumbled and fell into it. If humans had been able to stand at the brink and look down, they would have seen a hellish, brilliant white-hot glare, magma, rising, coming faster each day, pressure driving it to seek the surface.

However, no one could have seen, for the broiling heat gurgling up from the depths and spreading at the edge of the widening chasm would have killed any breathing creature venturing close, charring its flesh and instantly exploding its lungs.

Four or five days after first the fissure opened—under the midnight-deep shadow of ash, there could have been no reckoning of time, even had someone been there to try to count days—a greater quake than had hit before split the ash layers open from leagues inland to the shore of the buried offshore island. Water that had seeped and soaked into the harbor ash first gushed into the void, and then the sea found the weak spots and drove a violent stream through, and an infernal, clotted waterfall leapt into existence and plunged toward the searing hot magma with an unimaginable roar. It was a titanic elemental battle, a war of fire and water, fought as ferociously as any two creatures that ever confronted each other in a life and death struggle– but on an unimaginable scale. The ocean-fall at first blasted into steam before it even neared the rising super-heated magma. The steam exploded, widening the gulf, deepening the channel, and even more water poured in. More explosions ripped away eons-old layers of rock, and again the earth heaved with quakes.

The magma ate away from below. From mountains to the sea, the entire eastern side of the valley caved in, the magma melting the rock as it struck. The explosions of steam demolished even the rugged offshore island that had endured for millions of years–it had been a volcanic cone when the first dinosaurs emerged, and monsters stalked. Now the island vanished, torn to bits and churned to dust by the agony of the earth.

A week, two weeks more passed, more land sank as the magma devoured it from below, and fully half the whole Great Valley had subsided, the sea claiming victory, the magma sinking gradually back below the hardening surface of the earth.

The valley became a long, narrowing inlet of the sea. Boiling water seethed over the sunken remnants of the land, and nothing made by human hands remained, not one house, not one monument, not anything. In the turbid and near-boiling depths no fish, no mollusk, no microorganism survived. The valley had been sterilized, wrecked, and consumed. Over the coming ages the sea would claim more and more of the land, reshaping the valley until it vanished utterly and salt water rolled many feet above places where once humans had built towns, no trace of which survived.

For thousands of years, now and again a new volcano formed in the expanding inlet, emerging with jets of lava and building cones of ash, and the patient sea, relentlessly pounding in with no offshore island to break its waves, began at once to erode the new cone. Not until over three thousand years had passed would the landscape grow somewhat stable.

By then, no living thing anywhere in the world could remember the Great Valley or the proud people who had lived there. Except in one place.

Just one.

After days and nights of signaling and summoning, Corbant had gathered thirty of the scattered ships in all, thirty-six, counting *White Leader, Blue Leader, Yellow Leader* and *Green Leader* plus *White Exodus* and *Blue Exodus*. Two of them had badly-damaged propellant systems and their captains didn't dare try them. Much had been lost or destroyed in the storm and all were running low on food, though they still had reserves to fall back on, seeds and stored, long-lasting food meant to sustain them on the island. No one, however, wanted to break into the reserves at that point.

The previous day they had come within sight of an island–not their destination island–that seemed large enough to have fresh water and did have a sheltered cove. An exploring party in a longboat had sounded the approach to the sheltered bay and had found plenty of depth and a relatively calm way in. That morning, at Corbant's direction, all the ships sailed in–some of them practically limped in–and moored there. Exploring parties were sent ashore and inland not long after sunrise.

Now it was nearly noon. Corbant called all the captains ashore. On every ship passengers and crew clustered on the decks, staring longingly at solid land. Corbant said, "When we know this island is safe, they can all come ashore for a few days. Let them know that. But first we have to look for dangers– and we have to find fresh food."

The Kongs, especially, needed green provender, and the ones that had been aboard the ships in this part of the fleet went into the wild with their Zantu to seek it. Corbant had ordered them, as far as he could order men who had never known a master, to return before the sun was three hours above the horizon.

Though they were past the turn of the seasons, that tropical sun shone down fierce and hot, and an uncomfortable Malana fidgeted at the Pendonjira's side. The captains seated themselves on a shelving, grassy slope above a wide, curving black-sand beach, while the Pendonjira, Corbant, and Malana stood within the horns of the semicircle that the sitting captains had formed. Corbant, sweat running down his sun-burned face and trickling into his heavy beard, began by asking for each to give an account of how their supplies, stood, first, and then to tell of what repairs were needed to the ships.

The tale from each was much the same: "We'll have barely food enough, though we may yet need to break into some of the stored provisions that we meant to use when we arrived at the island. Our Kongs have only five more days"–or seven, or three, because that varied–"before we'll have to find another way of feeding them."

The damage report was no more cheerful. All the ships had suffered to some extent, and from some of the captains, Corbant learned that at least five ships had been lost, capsized or broached-to and sunk in the insane winds beyond any help of rescue for the crew. Indeed, of the thirty ships that had responded to Corbant's signals, only eleven were from the vanguard fleet. Nine came from the *Blue Leader* contingent, six from *Green Leader's* ships, and four from *Yellow Leader's* set of mostly cargo vessels. No one had seen any of the other flagships go down, and perhaps they were now gathering their own contingent of stragglers, perhaps some were even now near their goal.

But all the surviving ships, wherever they were, would have to deal with the ravages left by the storm: torn sails and rigging at the lightest level, broken masts and stove hulls at the worst. Corbant's contingent of Atu experts from three of the ships agreed to attend to the repairs needed. All seemed practicable, although as Manat, the oldest of the propulsion system designers, said, "We will have to use all of our spare parts, and we'll need to beach the three ships with the worst damage to repair the tubing and seal the hulls. It will take perhaps until the second turning of the moon to repair them all."

"The turning of the moon," Corbant muttered unhappily. That meant a little more than a full month–nearly five full weeks.

"We can do it," Darag, the captain of one of the crippled Exodus ships that carried enormous amounts of cargo and more importantly, over two thousand passengers, said urgently. "We'll have to. You can't abandon seven ships. There's no room for the people aboard the other craft in the fleet, and to transfer all the supplies from the Big Blue"–that was the nick-name given his ship–"would take even more time than a month of repairs."

Corbant looked to the Pendonjira. She said, "It all depends on what the hunters find. This is not a large island. It may have little in the way of food. If they can bring in enough food to carry us through the repairs without having to break into our stored supplies, then let us remain and repair the ships. If there's not enough for that, we will have to take our chances, eat less–yes, even the Kongs–and hope to arrive at our island in good time. How many days' sail is it, Corbant?"

"Difficult to say," Corbant said. "I've spoken with the best navigators we have, and they can't agree on exactly where the storm left us, or how far we may be eastward from the island. Under sail alone, I would say we would have to travel for another six weeks at least before we could hope to sight the skull mountain of the island. And then it will take some few days to thread our way in to the harbor through the smaller islands and sandbars."

The Pendonjira's expression did not change. "If we can repair the propellant?"

"That's different. Only two weeks then, if we have enough left, we did not plan on the possibility of this long of a delay."

"Then that is our best hope," The Pendonjira said. "Which ships are the worst-damaged?"

The captains looked sullen at that, suspecting what might come next. But Corbant said, "Three have to have masts replaced. Two others must have parts of the hulls cut away and rebuilt. The seams opened during the storm and have to be re-sealed. The whole fleet is taking on water. We have a good supply of *ilu*, though, and we can repair them with that."

The Pendonjira nodded. "And the scouts have said that we may find the elements to make more *ilu* mortar in abundance on the island. That will not be as critical as food. Can the ships without masts be repaired?"

"Yes, given time. The sailors can manage that while the scientists work on the propellant. We have spare masts. Unfortunately, two of the ships had mainmasts that were either sprung or broken outright, and for that size mast we have only one replacement. But we have two spare foremasts aboard *White Leader*, and we can cut one of those to size. It will still be taller than the ship's regular mainmast, with greater area, but it will serve—maybe even make it the fastest ship we've got."

"Begin the repairs at once, then," she said. "You captains, I know you were hoping that I would not order one of your ships to be emptied and abandoned. I have decided not to do that—yet. But know that you must work hard, harder, even, than when your ships were first building, and you must finish the task as quickly as you can, or else you may have to abandon your command here. We need to get to our island. The advance party camped there has few people, and they expected us by the season's turning. That came during the great storm, it passed, and now nearly two more weeks have gone by as we collected this part of the fleet. Time has become our enemy. Use it well. Make it your ally and your friend."

Corbant cleared his throat. "There is—another concern, Lady."

One of the captains stood as if not able to wait for Corbant to speak. "I have four draks on my ship!" he said urgently. "Their riders are so angry they're threatening my crew. If we don't put them and their mounts ashore, they say, they won't promise that my sailors will be safe."

Another one stood. "I have ten," he said. "They all claim it's unfair that the Zantu have taken their Kongs ashore and the Kai can't take their beasts. They say the draks are sickening from confinement. They need a run ashore and a chance to graze and rest in the sunlight."

"How many others have draks and Kai aboard?" the Pendonjira asked.

Four more captains stood. "And we have over twelve Kongs in all," the Pendonjira mused so quietly that only Malana could hear. "And this island we're on is not a big one."

The captains were muttering, and she held up her hand for silence. "We will not mistreat the Kai or their mounts," she said. "Yet the Kongs are finding food for all, for the draks and for their riders alike. We will give the Kongs this day and tomorrow to find and bring in food and to report on what game the island may hold. Then the Kongs will remain encamped and the Kai may ride their draks out to forage and to hunt for the next two days. They will alternate, so the Kongs and draks will not be roaming together at any one time. That is my decision."

"They won't be happy," Malana said quietly.

"No," the Pendonjira agreed. "But for me, for this time, it will be enough if they do not kill each other." The sluggish, warm breeze blew from a plateau thickly forested with enormous dark-green trees, and it brought with it a scent reminiscent of spices, faintly sweet—and also brought the echoing call of a distant Kong. Malana turned and looked in that direction at the rising land, at the line of deep green forest up on the plateau, and wondered silently what the explorers were finding.

And if Taigu and his Kong were safe.

"Is it good to eat?" Taigu asked as he leaned on his staff.

As though in answer, Khaan extended his hand, offering Taigu one of the thick, furred vines that he had been stripping of leaves and chewing.

The big Kong seemed to relish it, and it had caused him no apparent harm or distress. Taigu took a small bite of the fleshy vine pith, pale green and dripping with moisture. It was stringy and tough, but the sap tasted sweet.

"All right," he said, after holding the juice in his mouth for a time and then swallowing it. He spat the chewed pith out, as Khaan had been doing. "But don't eat too much."

He stood in the shady fringe of a rainforest. Their job had been to scout for food, and they had found some, both vegetable and animal: coconut trees heavy with the big gray-brown husks that contained the nuts; some low-growing red fruit in clusters of knife-blade-shaped, succulent leaves, no bigger than his fist and shaped like hard little pears, but with a tangy taste; and these heavy vines, some strange-looking spiky-leaved fruits that, when the Kongs bit one open, were surprisingly juicy and refreshing. Taigu had no names for any of these, or for the other fruits that Khaan had collected, so far, but he thought everything was edible at worst, tasty at best.

As to the prey, though, the animals that might be hunted, well, there were birds. There were the rodents. Thousands of them of various sizes, with no fear of humans. They could be rounded up, butchered, and their flesh salted or smoked, Vekan said. He had already used his staff as a spear and impaled one of them from fifteen feet away. "I believe my aim has been improved from practicing on a constantly moving ship," he said. Among all the Zantu, his reputation with the staff was possibly the best.

Taigu had never tasted such a rodent and asked what it was like. "Terrible," Vekan had told him cheerfully as he held up the limp carcass for closer inspection. "This is a fat one. This island must be a paradise for these creatures."

"How is the taste terrible?" Taigu asked.

His father shrugged. "Gamey and foul and stringy, but it will keep a man alive." He removed the dead rat from his spear and dropped it into his shoulder sack. Quick as a flash, he whirled and skewered an even fatter one twenty paces off, right behind the forelegs and through the heart. He walked off to collect it. *I had better practice my staff-work on the ship as well if I am ever going to make my father proud of me,* Taigu thought.

And there were the monster crabs—huge creeping things, the size of a two-year-old child, with heavily armored reddish-brown bodies and pincers that had made even Krom shout in surprise and pain. "They seem to be land crabs," Vekan had said after Aton had killed the one that Krom had curiously picked up.

"These can be cooked and eaten. The flesh from the claws is generally the best part. We can take some for each ship," Aton told him. "If we can take enough of them alive and keep them living aboard the ships, we may have enough for many days. We can feed everyone for two or three days on the sweet meat of these creatures."

I'll take a diet of crab over rodent any day, Taigu thought.

Fortunately, the Kong had discovered a range of different edible plants. Normally not a dietary staple, fresh food of any kind was appreciated. They had also gorged themselves while they had the chance, and now with bellies sated, they moved luxuriously slowly, seeming to enjoy the sunlight and the breeze. When they returned to the beach, each Kong would have on its back a great net stuffed with fruits and vines. Later they would come back to gather as many of the crabs as they needed and, well, rodents, too.

While Khaan sat in the shade of a tall tree, idly eating more of the sweet vine, Taigu decided to climb up for a better view. The rainforest inland grew dense, but here on the fringe a grove of scattered trees like this one waved in the breezes, looking something like palm trees and growing branchless, straight up for about three times the height of a big adult Kong to a brushy crown of long, dark-green leaves. This one had fruit hanging from the crown, too, round green-and-brown balls nearly the size of Taigu's head.

Taigu took his staff and unraveled a good deal of the thin, tough leather cord wrapped around its midsection that served as a grip when not needed as a tether. It was connected at the base of the staff.

It should be just long enough, he thought, and took aim. With all his might, he launched the javelin at the overhanging fruit, but missed. Reeling the staff back in, he tried again, this time just grazing the bottom of one of them, sending fleshy fragments cascading down.

Khaan, who was intently watching behind him, gave Taigu a nudge. "Don't worry, I'll get it this time!" the boy said and with a determined throw did, scoring a solid hit in the center of the husk. The staff quivered with the impact and Taigu cheered, tugging on the line to pull the fruit down. But it wouldn't budge. He yanked again, but neither the spear nor the fruit were going anywhere.

He took hold of the trunk and went up, walking the trunk with his bare feet, moving hand over hand to hold himself in place. *These old cuts sting a bit,* he thought, *but not too bad.* When he got close to the fruit, he held on tight and removed his staff with some difficulty and let it drop. "Look out!" he yelled. Khaan glanced up, stepped aside, then reached over to retrieve it and sniff it curiously, then licked the sweet juice off the tip with his huge tongue. Just then the large piece of fruit unexpectedly fell as well, hitting Khaan in the head, causing him to wince and scowl up as though Taigu had done it on purpose.

"Oops!" said Taigu from the great height, I'm glad *I'm out of Khaan's reach,* he thought. As he clung tight, he gazed down on the bay. No more ships had come in, and beyond the bay he could see no more out on the open sea. However, he did notice that the bay was crawling with many small boats, and at first he wondered what they were doing. Then he realized the fishermen from some of the ships were out with nets, trying their luck. "Well, I think we'll have fresh food, anyway," Taigu called down to Khaan.

Khaan called, a satisfied and peaceful sound like a rising hoot, and he held up the fruit toward Taigu and gestured with it. Taigu saw that it had been bitten in half and that the inside looked both yellow and orange. "If it's good to eat, you can climb up and pick some," Taigu called down. "It's hard for me to hold on." He made his way down the trunk, arms aching and feet beginning to feel sore. "Go ahead," he said as he stepped back on solid ground and pointed upward. "It'll hold you."

With a dubious look, Khaan seized the trunk and grunted, pulling and pushing. The tree didn't even sway. "It's solid, it's strong. I did it," Taigu said. "You're a brave Kong. You can do it, too!" He gathered his staff and rewound the leather cord.

Rumbling, Khaan slowly clambered up the trunk and clung with both feet and his left hand. A Kong did not often have the opportunity to climb a tree of such size, and most were not eager to climb when they did. But Khaan was still relatively young and willing to try it.

Once he came within range, he reached to pick and drop three more of the fruits. They didn't look promising at first, each globe bristled with what looked like green-and-brown fleshy pyramids, but Taigu picked up the bitten one and sniffed it. Khaan had pulled loose a good many of the pyramid-like growths. Each one shaded through orange to yellow, and they surrounded a whitish round heart. Taigu tried to bite into the yellow flesh, and found it tough. But it did seem juicy, and he sucked at the flowing liquid, which tasted wholesome.

"That's enough!" he called up the tree. The fruits were heavy, and though he meant to take some back to the ship, Taigu didn't think they were rich enough in food quality to justify taking more than they already had. Maybe the Pendonjira would know what they were. Possibly they could be cooked in some fashion to make them more edible.

From somewhere off in the forest the hoot of a second Kong came, and at the sound Khaan scrambled down the tree, dropping the last few feet with a heavy *thud.* "That was Krom," Taigu told Khaan—who probably knew very well which Kong had given the signal. "Time to put the food into the pack."

Khaan helped scoop everything in and arrange it so the net wouldn't spill any, Taigu tied the mouth of the net closed, and then the Kong shouldered the load, almost as large as himself, and bent under the weight. "Is it too much for you?" Taigu asked in the special language of the Zantu. The Kong gave him a reproachful look and a pitiful kind of grunt, but it was all in play. Taigu laughed. "Of course, it isn't! Let's go."

They had found a fairly easy way up onto the island's plateau, a place where the bluffs had given in at some ancient time to a flood pouring and rushing from the heights. The sunken, dry watercourse now formed a grassy ramp leading down to the plain where the captains had met. Taigu and Khaan made their way there, along the fringe of trees at the edge of the plateau.

Sauntering along in the warm early-afternoon sun, Taigu let himself be distracted. The island teemed with birds of many species, from broad-winged brilliantly white soarers to fat, dull-witted pigeon-like land birds and one fast-moving kind of hawk. Taigu had seen one of these swoop down and then up again, clutching in its talons a desperately thrashing, squealing island rat. At the moment, a flight of dozens of long-winged sea birds was passing over, and Taigu shaded his eyes to see them more clearly.

And as he did, he heard the first distinctive, deep grunt, a sound that jerked his gaze back to the beach. *Kai!* Three of them, on their draks, were crossing the beach, menacing a crowd that had clustered around them, men and women who were obviously objecting to their being on land. *The Pendonjira told us they wouldn't land today! Taigu thought. What happened?*

Standing tall, Khaan roared and drummed his chest, and although they were still far away, the Kai's mounts heard the sound and began to surge and paw at the sand. One Kai seemed to be arguing with the others. One of the other riders suddenly struck viciously at two men who were trying to seize the bridle, and the crowd fell back from the group.

The drak rider swept in before another word was spoken...

Behind and above him, back toward the plateau, someone yelled, but Taigu was too far away to understand the words. He saw Krom, though, bent under a burden even larger than the one Khaan carried. As Taigu watched, Krom dropped it, pounded his chest with both hands– his old injury evidently mending well–and gave out a deafening roar before striding down the old watercourse. In his wake ran Aton, staff at the ready, shouting in the Zantu language, though all Taigu could tell for certain was that the weathered old Zan was trying to hold Krom back.

He heard more snorts from the beach and saw that the three Kai riders had pushed through those trying to restrain them. They had sighted the younger Khaan, and they were riding for him at an angle to the advancing Krom, driving the draks up the rough path, brandishing their spears and bolas.

"Pull back!" Taigu said urgently to Khaan. "Wait, don't attack! Help is coming!"

Khaan blew air through his nose and drummed again. He roared in defiance. Now the Kai were toiling through loose sand up the slope, and one of them, Taigu realized, was Yarg, the angry and defiant one who had spoken rebelliously to the Pendonjira back on the island. It was hard to tell if he was encouraging the other two drak-riders or trying to hold them back.

"Pull back!" Taigu ordered, almost pleaded, again. Khaan had thrown his net of foodstuff down and stood with teeth bared and fur on his neck and shoulders bristling. "Don't fight them!"

The Kai were almost on them. Yarg had dropped to the rear, the other two coming on side by side. They held leveled spears and they bore down on Khaan. Taigu leapt in front of him, taking dead aim with his staff. "We've done nothing to you!"

"Stand back, boy!" one of the riders yelled. "We want to punish the Kong, not you!"

Taigu raised his staff defiantly. "*No one* punishes Khaan!"

Khaan tensed immediately for battle. With muscles knotting and powerful shoulders bristling, he seemed to grow right before the Kai warrior's eyes. Fighting a creeping fear induced by a strange odor that began to permeate the air, the drak rider swept in before another word was spoken. His drak charged and viciously jerked its head, trying to gore Taigu. The tusks missed him, but the impact hit hard and knocked him down, and he rolled. Krom was almost there, howling in rage. Farther up the slope Chang and Vekan were running toward the fight.

Hurt and dizzy, Taigu staggered to his feet. Roaring, Khaan had knocked aside the first spear-thrust. He struck the second spear so hard that it broke off short in the rider's grasp, but now the other one had circled behind him.

"Stop it!" Yarg shouted. "Fools! You should have waited!"

Khaan shrieked as the spear bit into the flesh of his thigh. With a furious blow he struck the rider squarely in the chest, sending him sprawling off his mount, and the man hit the ground in such a loose, inert way that Taigu realized he had died instantly.

The young Kong yanked the bloody spear from his leg and threw it spinning away. The drak struggled to its feet and tried to gore him, but Khaan avoided the charge, giving its flank a thunderous clubbing. The cracking ribs were sickeningly audible and the drak squealed loudly, unable to keep its balance as it stumbled painfully down the hill on three legs.

Now Krom waded into the fight, snarling. Yarg shouted, "Look out!"

Too late. Krom struck a heavy blow, crushing the skull of the second rider. His drak wheeled and charged just as Taigu's staff found its mark in its thick shoulder muscles, but to little effect–

An enraged Aton leapt atop it, brandishing his pikata. In one powerful thrust, his long blade bit straight down through sinew and flesh. It plunged into the side of the drak's neck with surgical precision, severing its spinal cord. Bright blood leapt in the sun, and the stunned brute stumbled, staggered, and collapsed, bawling in pain and fury, twitching but unable to regain its footing. In a moment, it lay dead. Aton leapt free and turned to face Yarg.

Breathing hard, Yarg shook with suppressed anger. "You have killed two of my men!"

"Yes, and their draks, too! They attacked a boy and a young Kong–two against one, Yarg! Is this the courage of the Kai?"

"I tried to hold them back! The Kong and their keepers had a chance at sun and fresh air and food–these are men of spirit! They demanded no less, forced the crew to ferry them to shore. They wanted to frighten you all, but they would not have killed the boy or the Kong!"

"How were a boy and a young Kong to know that?" Aton shot back. "Taigu, how badly are you hurt?"

Only then did the boy realize that he bled freely from a gash across his side, that his whole chest hurt.

"A cut," he said. "And I think broken ribs. See to Khaan's wound first–they lanced him in the leg."

Yarg's expression flickered between fury and concern. He looked up the slope, where Chang and Vekan were near. A well-aimed staff, already flying through air, found its mark less than one inch in front of the nose of Yarg's drak, making it shy away.

Yarg struggled to control it. "Vekan!" he called. "I came to shore only because two headstrong Kai forced their way onto a boat. I was trying to restrain them! I meant no insult to you and no threat to your boy!"

"If my son is badly hurt," Vekan said, striding past the dead Kai and the dying drak, fearlessly pulling his staff from directly in front of the one living, snarling drak, "then there will be a reckoning this day, and none of the Kai who forced their way onto this island will leave alive!"

"Go, while you can." Aton told the Kai leader, glancing warily at Vekan. "We will tend our wounded. Later you may claim your dead. Go!"

Without another word, Yarg immediately wheeled his drak and quickly rode down the hill.

A sound like the sea seemed to fill Taigu's ears, and beneath his feet the island seemed to bob up and down like a ship at sea. Reaching to steady himself against–something that was not there, he felt the hot flow running down his side.

"M- my staff–"

He realized then that the bleeding was worse than he'd thought at first- blood streamed down his side and over his leg and made crooked red rivulets on the sandy soil. He felt the world revolving, and his sight turned dim and gray, and he felt himself beginning to collapse.

And then he knew no more.

The ship was in trouble.

Ran-Atu and Beront, too late, realized that the advance crew should have withdrawn offshore a week earlier, before–

Before the carnage.

"Are we the only two left?" Beront asked, leaning on the rail and scanning the shoreline. "All I've seen are the…creatures," Ran-Atu said shortly.

Beront pushed himself upright and nervously asked, "Can just the two of us sail the ship?"

"After a fashion. Not well." Ran-Atu clenched his hands. From his left wrist to his left elbow a jagged cut traced itself in a thick line of clotted blood. The wound was not deep, but it felt hot, and that probably meant infection. Which probably meant death. "If I could have one more spear-cast at the big one–"

"We've seen what even the smaller ones can do," Beront said. Of the two, Beront was the taller and broader-built, one would say, to be a fighter. By contrast, Ran-Atu was shorter, wirier, and he had the intense look of a thinker. But Beront was, had been, an expert on plants and growing things, and Ran-Atu had been one of the advance guard of warriors that came early to the island to explore it, map it out, make sure that everything was safe for the settlers.

Safe.

The word rang as hollow as a bitter joke. The killers had come suddenly, stealthily. With a good number of the exploration party ill, with the others spread too thin, the attack–so silent, so fast, and coordinated–had been not a fight but a brutal slaughter. Beront had been safe, for he had that day ferried out to the anchored ship bags of seeds gathered from the plants native to the island when he heard the shrieks, the roars … and the death-screams. He had watched from the deck, but at some distance from the beach, he saw nothing.

That evening, pursued and desperate, Ran-Atu had plunged into the bay, heedless of the sea creatures that usually teemed in the blood-warm water. He dived beneath the surface and swam for as far as breath held out, rolled and came up to gulp more lungfuls of air and then dived again. In this way he arrived within only a few arm-lengths of the ship, and Beront had thrown him a line, pulled him aboard, and treated his wound as best he could. The three healers that had come on the voyage were, almost certainly, among the dead on shore.

The next day passed with no more terrible screams. And the night. Now, in mid-morning on the third day since the attack, the two men wondered if they were the only remnant of the advance party. "We have plenty of food aboard," Beront had said. "Enough water for the two of us for a month or perhaps more. We could cut the anchor rope when the tide is going out, and possibly we could raise at least one or two sails. But I don't know anything about steering a ship."

"Nor I," Ran-Atu said. "I was an Atu warrior on the eastern frontier with no ocean in sight. I never thought I'd even set foot on a ship."

"The settlers should arrive soon."

"Should have arrived already," Ran-Atu said sourly. His arm throbbed, and his anger at the–the beasts, the unexpected and terrible killers–had turned inward.

"Maybe the best thing to do is to wait here on the ship," Beront said. "Keep a watch to seaward. When the fleet appears–"

"*If* it does."

"If the fleet appears, we must signal them not to land. They have no way of knowing what waits for them on the island."

"And what if they don't land?"Ran-Atu asked."Where will we tell them to go? The Tagu wise ones–" he snarled the last words, making them sound like an obscenity–"chose this place of all others. Here we would be protected by the vast sea from our biggest threat, the advancing, ever-growing bands of the Nagatl primitives. Here we could tame the creatures of the island with magical herbs."

"They're not magical,"Beront objected mildly."They're natural combinations of plant substances that–"

"No, what we must do is warn all the other settlers to stay aboard their ships. Every Atu warrior must come ashore, armed and ready for the beasts, along with their drak-riding Kai. And–"he took a breath and said, unwillingly,"and the Zantu and their Kongs must join us if we are to have any chance.

Only when we have butchered the last of those toothed monsters can the others come ashore."

"Can even the Atu defeat the killers that we have seen?"

Furiously, Ran-Atu said, "The Atu can defeat anything! Teamed with the Kai, they are the strongest of warriors!" His pulse raced, and he groaned when pain lanced into his arm.

"Let me poultice that," Beront said. "I'm no healer, but you can see how streaks of red have spread out from the wound. I'm sure you're feverish."

"It's nothing. It will heal. I wash it with salt water four times a day."

Beront frowned. "The island water is tainted,"he said. "It sickened many of our people. Perhaps the same poison is in the water of the bay."

Ran-Atu snorted. "Then why do so many of the creatures swim in it, with no harm to them? How is it you miawan did not discover the poisons?"

Beront had no answer for that. And, since neither of them knew how to sail the ship, and since landing seemed sure death, they waited on board for days, for one week, two. Ran-Atu's wound did not kill him, but he grew listless, lying all day below decks, barely eating or drinking, and the strength ebbed from his arm.

The creatures of the bay, some of them long-necked fishers, others with bodies like great sharks, but with four broad flippers rather than two and serpentine tails. Worse, their elongated heads and toothed jaws gaped larger than those of any shark they had ever seen. The creatures sensed the men aboard and circled endlessly. Beront kept a tally of the passing days and knew despair as the count grew long.

Then, deep into a moonless night, something woke him. He opened his eyes in darkness. Had it been a sound? Something unfamiliar. Not Ran-Atu, for Beront could hear his breathing. Then he realized the ship was moving, bobbing too freely to be riding at anchor. He rose and hurried to the deck. Anchors had secured the ship both fore and aft–and both ropes had been severed. The tide was taking the ship away from the island. "Ran-Atu!"Beront yelled. "Come–"

With a shuddering, grating noise, the drifting ship ran onto one of the sandbars, and the outgoingtide heeled it over. The deck tilted sharply, Beront grabbed for a support that was not there, and he fell, striking the rail, now nearly horizontal, and flipped into the warm bay water. He could not swim. But he felt sand beneath his feet and frantically tried to scramble back aboard. The sand gave way.

Beront yelled for help, and salt water filled his mouth. He heard Ran-Atu call out–

And a swimming sea-beast seized him, clamping its jaws around both his legs. He tried to scream, but the sound died in bubbles as the creature dragged him under and away. Ran-Atu had heard the beginning of the scream, and he launched himself off the deck in a flat dive.

More of the creatures tore into him at once. He had no chance. For some minutes, the water boiled as the monstrous sea-beasts fought for morsels of flesh, even attacking each other in their frenzy. Then a calm descended. The tide, still building, lifted the ship off the sandbar, but it lay on its side, water pouring into its holds. It struck another obstruction, hard, that ripped a quarter of its hull away, and more water flooded in.

By the time the sun rose, only a foot or two of the prow showed above the surface. In a few more minutes, even that vanished as the ship slipped beneath the water, waves breaking over the wooden frame grew calm, and the ocean stretched empty and wide, as though the vessel had never existed at all. Growing dim on the horizon, already low, the huge island lay in shades of distance-muted green.

The writhing jungle near the bottom slowly metamorphosed into craggy cliff faces the higher it went. These glinted strange shades of sienna, teal and rust-red intermixed with slate gray, umber and a purplish black in the dying light. Eventually, the only discernable features were the vast empty recesses that formed eye and nose sockets. Couched in a strange haze, the earth skull leered down at the waves below, seemingly conscious of the secrets hidden beneath them.

———✦———

"Drink some more of this," Malana scolded, sloshing the foul liquid in its cup. "You haven't had half enough!"

"I don't want any more!" Taigu insisted with a shiver. The concoction tasted bitter and faintly salty and it made him feel sick instead of better.

"The Pendonjira says you have to drink it! You need it. You lost much blood," Malana told him. "Finish this much and you won't have to have any more until the evening meal."

With a grunt, Taigu asked, "Will you go away if I do?"

"Yes!"

"Then give it to me." Grimacing, Taigu took the cup and drained it in three long gulps, fighting back a rising urge to vomit. Finally, he turned the empty cup upside down with a gasp. "There. All gone. Now will you let me go on deck?"

Malana took the empty cup, frowning. "Yes, if you want to. But not ashore!"

For many days Taigu had been forced to remain in a small cabin, resting on a cot or pacing unsteadily as he gained some strength back. He had been clamoring to be allowed on deck for two days past. He asked, "Are the others ashore, then? Is today a Kong day?"

"Your father took your Kong and his both. They're making a last harvest of the island food."

Taigu grunted in disappointment. He had lost track of time while he healed, but the fleet had been anchored in the bay for over three weeks now, and he felt mostly whole again. True, the scars on his side still rose above his flesh, pink welts with traces of dried blood still streaking them, as though they might tear open again, and he felt less strong than he should have, but he was growing restless aboard the ship.

Malana had already told him that an uneasy truce had been established. So far the Kai were keeping their own days on the island, alternating with the Zantu. For the moment, uneasy peace held, but if Taigu did not recover, Vekan swore he would kill Yarg. The Kai remained a disgruntled lot regardless, because the island had no large game to offer them, just the rodents in great numbers but insignificant in size, and the lumbering giant land-crabs, which any fool could capture. They offered no challenge for a fierce, mounted Kai warrior.

But the drak-riders had completely circled the island, at any rate. On the far side, the west side, they had slaughtered a few seals, though most of these creatures remained inaccessible, covering a long expanse of low rocks a good way off shore of the island, sunning themselves and barking so loud they could be heard on the beach. Draks did not swim well, and the sea-washed rocks gave the aggressive beasts no foothold, so all the seals that kept to the offshore resting places remained safe. The Kai brought in little in the way of meat.

And because the Kongs brought in a steadily growing supply of vegetable foods, the Kai resented them. Why, Taigu wondered, did everything have to be a competition? If the Tagatu survived, then everyone won. If not—well, if not, then nothing mattered anyway.

When Taigu stepped onto the sun-heated deck, he stepped into an excited crowd of sailors.

"How many?" one called up to the maintop.

A lookout perched there called down, "I count twenty-four sail. One of them is surely *Red Leader* and *Red Exodus* is with her! And they've sighted us."

Taigu saw the Pendonjira, standing at the far rail and gazing out to sea. He made his way to her. "Lady, is it true?"

She glanced at him and smiled. "It is true, young Taigu. More of the fleet, and they should be in the bay within an hour. The lookout thinks a good many of the ships are damaged, but they are all afloat, and that is a good thing."

"There are three more Kong on *Red Leader*," Taigu said. "And many more on the *Red Exodus*."

Corbant had been up in the rigging. Over the weeks he had lost fat, and he slid down with the energy of a much younger man, his white smile flashing through his shaggy beard. "I'd say the *Red Exodus* is sound, perhaps even less damaged than our *White Exodus*–and the signals say no Kongs were lost on either of our ships," he said. "That would mean at least thirty Kongs. Ma'am, do you wish to know my mind now?"

"I think I know somewhat of it," the Pendonjira replied with a rare smile. "But yes, what is your plan?"

"Almost all our ships now can sail under power," Corbant said. "Only one has a propellant system that still needs repair. I suspect that the ships now coming in are in the same shape ours were when we made landfall. Many will need repairs before they make their way to the island. Therefore, what I propose is this: We will take all our ships capable of using their propellant and as many of this coming division as are sound, except we will leave *Red Leader* and three others of the larger ships to escort those that are still provisioning. It's possible more remnants of the flotilla will come to this island, too. Anyway, these incoming ships will do as ours have done–anchor, store food, and make repairs–and then they will follow our course to the island."

"When will we leave?"

"I'd like to haul anchor today, but we need to speak to those who are now coming in and see what their plight is. They may well be short of food and water, or have injuries and illness to deal with. We'll consider what help each may give the other, and then, perhaps tomorrow, perhaps the day after, we will take our division of ships and set sail for Skull Island."

"We have not named the island yet," the Pendonjira objected. "That sounds like a fatalistic name."

Corbant shrugged. "It's what the explorers call it, because of the landmark. Perhaps once we land there we can re-name it. Ran-Tagatun, perhaps, 'Isle of the Tagatu.'"

"I like 'Skull Island' better," Taigu said.

With a laugh, Corbant said, "Then we shall certainly take your preference into consideration." "Is the boy bothering you, Pendonjira?" Malana had come up behind them, scowling.

"I'm barely younger than you–" Taigu blurted.

"He didn't want to take his medicine!"

"I did, though!"

The Pendonjira said, "Lift your tunic. Let me see your wounds."

Taigu pulled the garment hem up to his shoulder. The Pendonjira traced the scars with the tips of her fingers. "You're healing well. Lucky for you the drak missed when he tried to kill you. Their tusks are sharp and merciless." She tugged the tunic down again and said, "The fact that you are growing into a tall, very strong young man did not hurt either," she added, giving Taigu an excuse to cast a proud glance at Malana.

The girl flushed red and tossed her hair, refusing to meet Taigu's eye.

The Pendonjira continued, "Malana, I think Taigu need take no more of the medicine. He is healing now, and should be whole by the time we reach . . ." her thin lips quirked into a wry smile– "Skull Island."

The next two days passed in a fever of greetings and meetings. The newcomers reported that they had seen two more vessels sink during the great storm. A couple of their ships had been terribly battered, and aboard one of them, five settlers had been hurt so badly that they all died from their injuries. *Red Leader's* propellant tubes were wrenched and cracked and needed much repair–a hard job for the flagship, because it was huge. But the *White Leader* had some tubes to spare to remedy that.

Half of the other ships were unable to use their power, but repairs to all of them seemed possible, and if worst came to worst, there were always the sails. The most damaged ships would have to be abandoned, but room could be made aboard the others for her passengers. All the ships were in dire need of supplies and fresh water, and fortunately this island offered both.

Taigu and his father visited the other Zantu, who had tales of how their charges had suffered during the storm. No Kong had panicked, as had some of the draks, and they had neither injured themselves nor damaged the ships. Vekan gave the Zantu advice on where to seek food, and Chang had a day to visit his mate, Sakie. The ships with the mended propellant systems raised their anchors and tried the repaired propulsion systems out, at low intensity. Problems, thankfully, did not appear.

In all, fifty-five Tagatu ships now anchored in the bay. Corbant decided to take thirty-four of them on the next–and, everyone hoped, last–leg of the voyage. The remainder would need six weeks or two months of repairs before they followed. Who knew where all the other ships might be? Perhaps they had already landed at Skull Island, or maybe were well on their way there.

And so, on the third day after the other ships arrived, the greater part of the detachment raised anchor and under sail, slipped out of the bay, into the open sea. It took hours, from before dawn to nearly noon, and they got out just before the tide turned against them. That day they dropped the island off the stern horizon.

Then, the following morning, at Corbant's signal, the ships tethered themselves together and after building up some speed under sail, the *Leaders* and *Exodus'* fired up their propellant. Though one medium-sized cargo vessel that did not have time reinforce its bow before departure almost lost it by leaving too much slack in the line before it tightened, they made better time than they ever could have done under sail alone. Corbant told the Pendonjira that he had decided to run under power for all day and all night. "We'll make up some lost time," he said. "The advance party must be wondering what became of us. They'll be glad to see us whole and safe again."

"And I them," the Pendonjira said. Malana was there, but she said nothing.

Once more she had fallen desperately seasick.

Twice each day, once at dawn, once at sundown, Ganti lowered a small container into the sea and drew it back up, dripping and full of salt water. She then took the container into her workroom aboard *White Leader*. It could scarcely be called a workroom, more of a cupboard or closet. There was room only for a table; a cabinet built into the wall with recessed shelves filled with dozens of earthenware bottles, secured so they would not tip over or fall out when the ship rolled; and a seat for her.

Each time, Ganti would take from the shelf a clean ceramic bowl, very small, and tip into it no more seawater than she could have held in a cupped palm. Into this she carefully blended six drops from one bottle, three from a second, and one from a third. In the light of a lantern, she watched anxiously.

Time after time, nothing happened, and she would sigh, record her findings–or her lack of them– in the symbols the Tagu had developed to take down language as writing. Then she would clean the bowl, empty the seawater container, and wait for the next time.

Then, thirteen days out from the island where they had stopped to replenish the ship's food and water, in the early evening something changed. At first Ganti held her breath, believing that her intense wish was cheating her eyes–but no, the mixture in the white bowl had taken on a peculiar, light-purple tinge– "Yes!"

She picked up the ceramic bowl and hurried down the corridor, from amidships to the forward area, where the Pendonjira's cabin was. She tapped on the door and heard a muffled "Come in."

"Pendonjira!"

"I have been below decks most of the time doing my tests," said Ganti.

"I've been above deck most of the time and have noticed nothing," said Corbant, what're you getting at, Ma'am?"

"When did you last see a dolphin, or any of the usual creatures you might see on such a trip, Corbant?"

"Dolphins come and go, but now that you mention it, the last time I saw them I thought it funny how they seemed to suddenly veer away from riding our bow wave and then sharply turn away. It's unlike them to behave like that."

"While I do not know their regular habits," said the Pendonjira, "I can understand the inward movements of higher creatures reflected in their outward behavior, such as nervousness and fear. I believe that for some reason, where we are going is a place they will not, or cannot, go."

"This is interesting," said Ganti. "I recall in the reports of the explorers mentions of incredibly thick fog far out to sea and surrounding the island. But we scientists were so involved with testing samples and devising repellents the didn't thing about fog!"

"I would advise you," the Pendonjira said thoughtfully, "to turn toward the place where the fog is thickest. There, I think, we'll find the island."

Corbant replied, "As you say, Ma'am."

"And I will continue to test," responded Ganti as she quickly went back to peruse her records, thinking to herself *How could we have* missed *that?*

Corbant signaled the fleet, the ships turned more southerly, and after two hours had passed, she repeated the experiment. "Stronger now!" she reported exultantly.

At dawn the fog had deepened and the color of the tested water had intensified even more. "We're near, and the island must lie due west," Ganti said to both Corbant and the Pendonjira.

As all three turned to look in that direction, Ganti was startled to see a strange creature perched on the rail of the ship. It was the size and coloring of a gull, except for its blood-red head. Its eyes were much larger and instead of a beak it had a long, ragged-toothed snout. It cocked its head oddly, as if observing these new strangers in its domain before quickly spreading its wings and letting the wind carry it away, revealing a long tail with a diamond-shaped tip.

"Have you ever seen a bird like that?" asked Corbant.

"Yes," said Ganti. "A preserved specimen was brought back from an earlier expedition. And now you know why we didn't pay much attention to the fog."

They continued to sail, and one ship, the cargo vessel that had always had some trouble with a steady leak in its bow, had to disengage and lagged far behind. The phosphorous trail left by the propellant would be difficult to see in the foggy darkness to come, but visible enough for a sharp eye to follow throughout the night. Corbant dispatched a medium-sized ship to drop back and pace the cargo carrier just in case.

As the sun touched the western rim of the world, the lookout in the maintop shouted down, "Land!" Taigu stood on deck by then, and without asking permission, he scrambled up into the rigging.

He hung there just below the lookout and asked, "Where? Where is it?"

"Almost against the sun," the man told him. "Boy, you shouldn't be here. The Captain will toss you over the rail."

Taigu ignored the warning, trying to shade his eyes with his hand from the coppery blaze of the sun setting in a clear sky. The horizon stretched wide and flat, but– "I see it!"

It took a sharp eye, or a desperate one, to make out the small nick that the distant island made against the sky. Against the sunset sky, it had no color, just a gray, tiny unmoving spot appearing and disappearing through a thick fog floating on all the flowing water of the world.

"When will we get there?" he asked the lookout.

"Oh, not before sunrise," the man said. "Maybe not before noon. The water around Skull Island is supposed to be dangerous, and he may want to come in slowly."

And so, he did. To Taigu's disappointment, the fleet slowed to half speed. The boy didn't sleep at all that night. He couldn't. He was down with Khaan, he was on deck, he was clambering up in the rigging beneath a sky spangled with brilliant stars, but he wasn't asleep.

At sunrise, the shrouded island could be unmistakably discerned. The most obvious feature was the dome of a round mountain, the top seeming almost white in the level rays of the rising sun, most likely the result of untold years of guano accumulation. Skull Mountain, the explorers called it, though at this distance Taigu could see no extraordinary features.

The sun climbed in a flat calm. The winds seemed to be holding their breath. A leadsman kept heaving a weighted line from the prow of the ship, finding no bottom, no bottom, no bottom.

And then, urgently, he called, "Shelving sharply!"

The sea floor rose and Corbant had *White Leader's* propellant feed closed. The momentum of the ship kept it moving a bit more, but gradually it slowed to a crawl. He sent out three crews in rowboats to seek a passage through the sandbars surrounding the island. The main one seemed to run in an enormous arc, possibly even circling the entire land mass, though they knew from explorers' reports that navigable channels did cut through several smaller islets surrounding Skull Island.

Taigu didn't leave the deck. He ate a little, dried fruit held in his hand, while he stood anxiously as far forward in the prow as he could get. White Leader crept along at its slowest possible speed, twisting and turning as it followed the pathfinders, dropping marker buoys over the rail at every turn. A flock of truly gigantic flying creatures with wings p a n s beyond anything Taigu would have imagined soared out, parting the mists as though emerging from the doorway of a dream. They circled the ship in wide, lazy arcs before catching the rising thermals and spiraling ever upward until they vanished from sight.

Malana, looking better now that the seas were calm, but obviously not free of worry, came to the deck and stood near him. "Why didn't the advance party mark the channel?" she asked.

Taigu made a who-knows gesture. "Maybe they're all busy on the island. I wonder why they don't answer the captain's signals." He looked up over his shoulder. At the tip of the bow hung two smoking beacons, white smoke billowing from both and rising into twin columns trailing behind the ship. The shore party should have responded with fires of their own, but he could see no trace of smoke from the island.

They came into the lee of a long peninsula curving out from the main bulk of the island. It protected the anchorage. Taigu had heard all about that from the sailors, who had told him, "Once we're past the sandbars, there's a good deep harbor and good holding ground."

Nearby, Ganti approached the Pendonjira. "You were right about the mists, Pendonjira, and yet as we came closer to the island they seemed to part miraculously. Do you have any idea why?"

"Perhaps there is something on the island that acts to dissipate them, perhaps its the nature of the island itself. We still have much to learn about our new home," she answered.

Pacing the deck, Corbant said, "Now we know why this island was so difficult to find. I hope we don't find our own wrecked ships here. One should be at anchor: the Vanguard. I wonder where they've gone with her."

"Is there another anchorage?" asked Ganti.

"No. Rough coasts all around, with one, long beach exposed to the open sea and then rugged crags and cliffs. Possibly a narrow inlet close to the base of Skull Mountain, but no one's explored it. This is the only possible landing area."

"Are those things great birds?" Taigu called as a pair suddenly and silently swooped in. One of them, its bright orange eye mimicking the bright orange veins atop the otherwise jet-black head, shot them an intense glance.

"Don't know," Corbant said. "The early reports spoke of giant flying creatures, some with wing spans of over 30 feet. Those may be some of them."

"They're not birds," Ganti said to Taigu. "They have a totally different wing structure, more like bats." "But they are different from bats as well, there are no 'fingers'," observed the Pendonjira. "That is true," affirmed Ganti. "I was referring to their wings being covered with a membrane."

Just then the sun caught the flying creatures, and they wheeled, revealing their beautifully streamlined underside, their gracefully bowed wings coming to long, sharp-tips.

Ganti pointed. "See? There are no feather patterns. The small one I dissected was closer to a lizard than anything else."

Corbant pointed off to starboard. "I see more strange animals over there." They were close enough to see palm trees bending over the nearly-still water of the bay, and Taigu glimpsed what he supposed to be a few dozen seals, he remembered what they looked like from the island where they had stopped for repairs and food, sunning on a beach far down the curve of the harbor.

"Enough sightseeing!" said a suddenly serious Corbant and he ordered the anchors dropped. The deep water offered sufficient anchorage for even the largest ships, and the flukes bit and held well in the bottom of the bay.

"I want an Atu party to go ashore and find the advance group," Corbant said. "Let them be well-armed."

"The Kongs could go!" Taigu said, his voice excited and breaking.

"Not at first," Corbant told him kindly. "First we need to find what's happened here on the island. There may be sickness, or perhaps they've established an inland base. Or–" he stroked his beard, his face darkening with worry–"or perhaps for some reason they abandoned their task and sailed away on the *Vanguard*. They should have been keeping watch. They should have answered our signals. I don't like this…stillness."

In mid-afternoon, a dozen Atu warriors climbed down a rope and dropped into one of the longboats. At that moment, on the far side of the boat, someone yelled out, "Look at that monster!"

Everyone rushed over to the rails, staring down at something splashing and swimming near the ship.

Taigu didn't hesitate, but leapt over the rail, holding onto the rope with one hand, his staff reduced to two sections and strapped across his back. "One more!" he called down, and the surprised sailors at the oars of the longboat held their position. He dropped deftly into the stern.

"What are you doing, boy?" one of the oarsmen asked.

"I'm a Zan," he said in what he hoped was a man's decisive voice. "I'm to look ashore and make certain that the Kongs can leave the ship."

The sailors shrugged and rowed. Taigu looked back. Past *White Leader*, a long string of ships stretched, making their slow way in, following the buoys, threading the difficult channel. No one seemed to have noticed his leaving the ship.

In a few moments, the longboat grated into the shore with a *schluss*! and the lead oarsmen leapt onto the beach, hauling ropes and holding the craft steady. The Atu rose and filed off, alert warriors, nine men and three strong-looking women, heads lifted, eyes keen, nostrils twitching as if they tried to catch a scent on the air.

The sailors stayed by the longboat, hauling it well up onto the sand. Taigu trotted along behind the Atu as they made their way up onto a grassy stretch broken by scattered palm trees and a few wind- twisted hardwoods. Everything seemed to hang in suspension. No animal calls. No birds overhead. Utter silence.

Then the Atu stopped, all of them at once. Taigu, his full assembled staff in hand, nearly blundered into the rear guard. He craned his neck.

Three longhouses, built of island timber, thatched with dried palm leaves, stood in the center of an obvious man-made clearing. He grinned. They were so exactly like the houses in the Great Valley that he knew at once the advance party had built them.

Yet—

The doors all gaped open into darkness. No one appeared at the windows to stare at the newcomers.

Two Atu went into first one, then all the longhouses. "Empty," they reported. Finally, one of them noticed Taigu and scowled. "Boy, back to the boat!"

"But I'm a Zan!"

"Go back on your own, or one of us will tie you up and carry you back!"

From his expression, Taigu knew the man meant it. "I'll go."

He turned and walked back, slowly. He paused near the beach to take off his sandals and sling them over his shoulder, the sand in them made them rasp his heels. Then, heading down to the longboat, where the six oarsmen sat talking, he walked through loose sand, enjoying the way it felt hot on top, but cool underneath.

Something snagged his right ankle, and he stopped, thinking *Driftwood.*

It had caught him solidly. Using his staff for balance he knelt reached down, pushing his free hand through the fine sand, until he grasped it—it felt like a tree branch—and he pulled it up.

For a second he didn't know what it was, gnarled and the color of old leather. And then he recognized it.

Mummified, contorted, but unmistakable, it was a human hand. He gave an involuntary yelp and jumped up, staff instantly at the ready.

Immediately the jungle roared with in an excited cacophony. Birds exploded from the trees, insects and other creatures whose sounds he did not recognize added to the other-worldliness of it all. At that same moment, from somewhere toward the forest, he heard several men scream.

END OF PART ONE

Carl & Vincent
Denham
Sketchbook

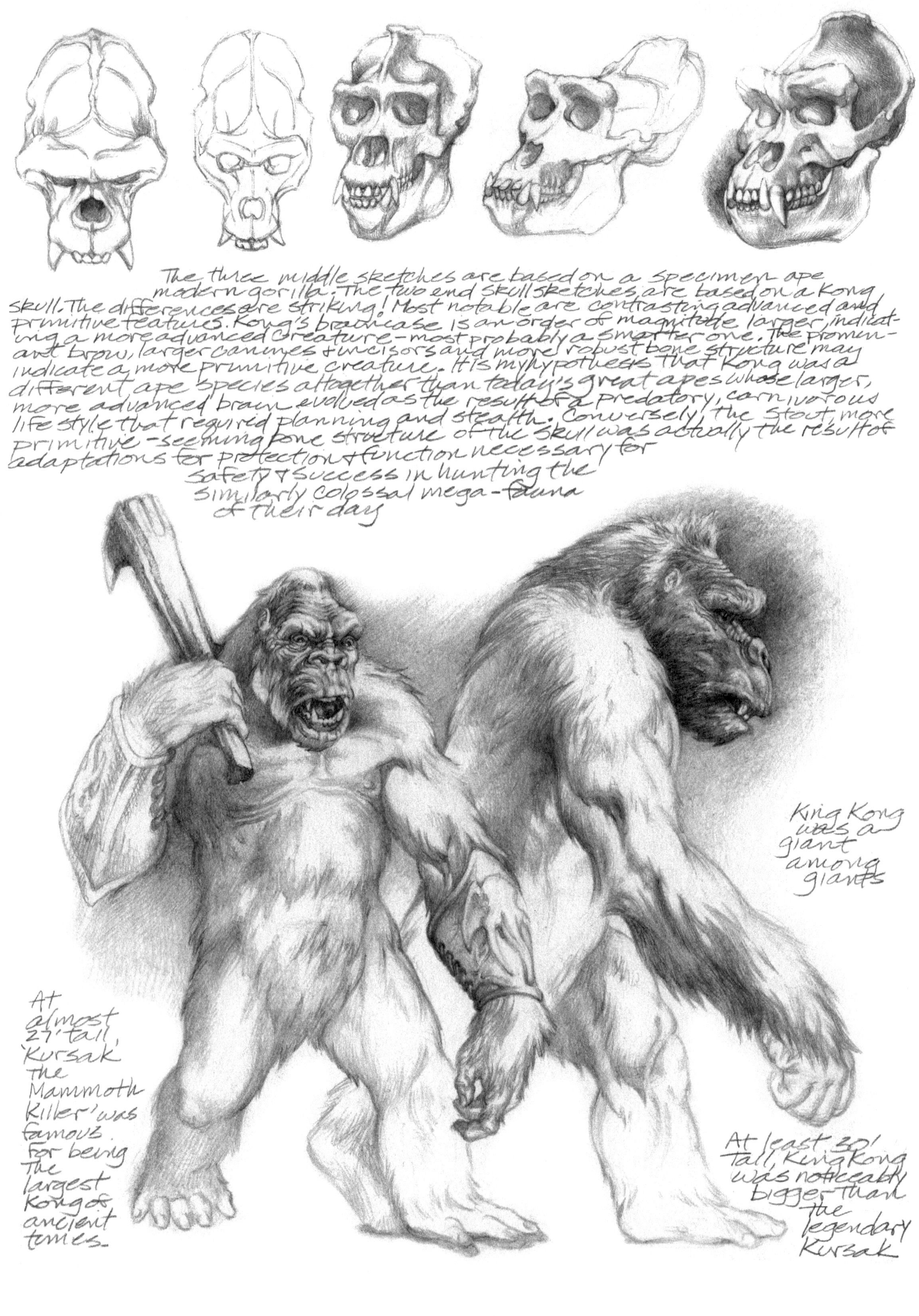

The three middle sketches are based on a specimen ape modern gorilla. The two end skull sketches are based on a Kong skull. The differences are striking! Most notable are contrasting advanced and primitive features. Kong's braincase is an order of magnitude larger, indicating a more advanced creature - most probably a smarter one. The prominent brow, larger canines + incisors and more robust bone structure may indicate a more primitive creature. It is my hypothesis that Kong was a different ape species altogether than today's great apes whose larger, more advanced brain evolved as the result of a predatory, carnivorous life style that required planning and stealth. Conversely, the stout, more primitive-seeming bone structure of the skull was actually the result of adaptations for protection + function necessary for safety + success in hunting the similarly colossal mega-fauna of their days

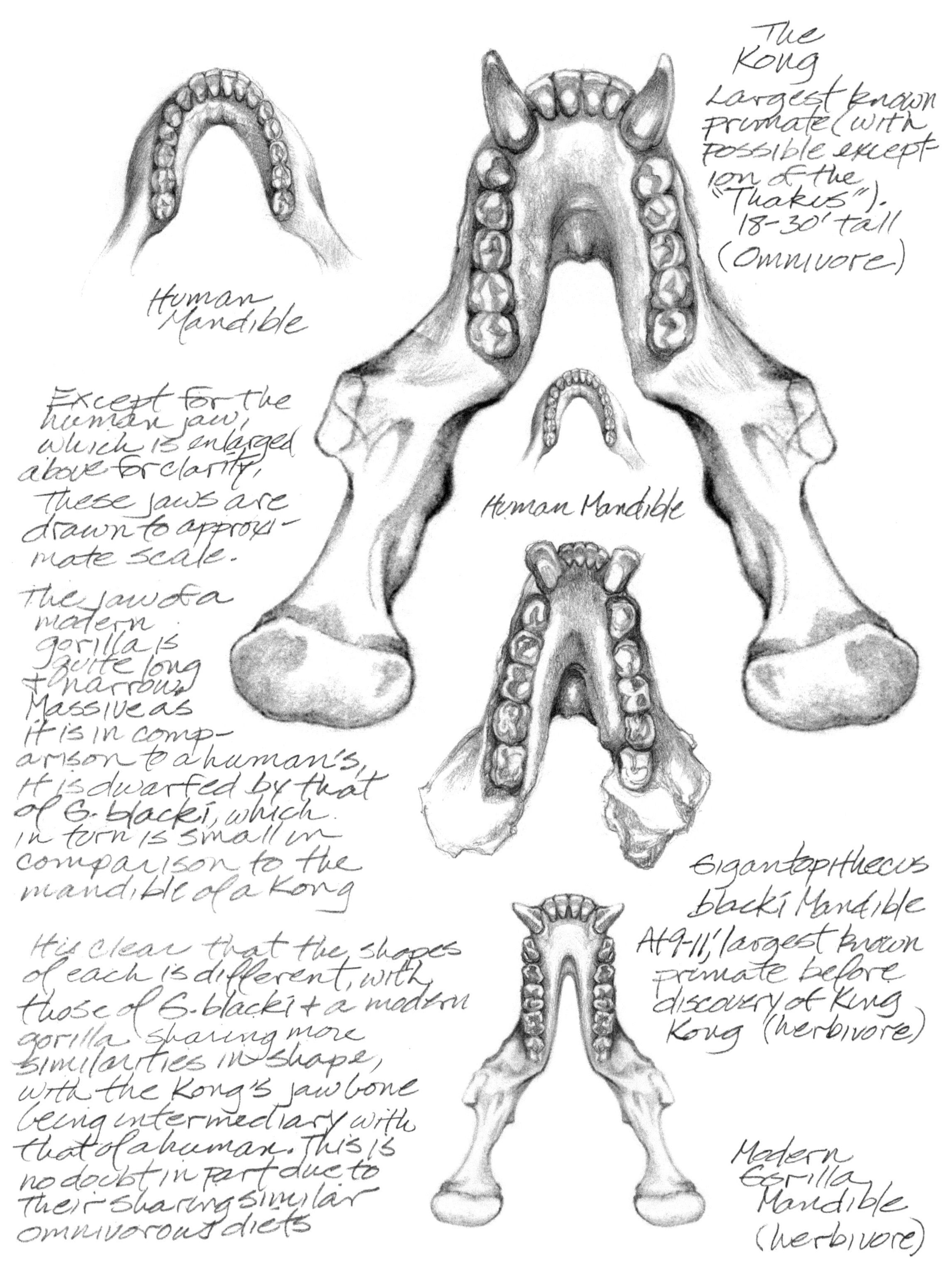

The Kong
Largest known Primate (with possible exception of the "Thakes"). 18-30' tall (Omnivore)
Human Mandible
Human Mandible
Except for the human jaw, which is enlarged above for clarity, these jaws are drawn to approximate scale.
The jaw of a modern gorilla is quite long + narrow. Massive as it is in comparison to a human's, it is dwarfed by that of G. blacki, which in turn is small in comparison to the mandible of a Kong
It is clear that the shapes of each is different, with those of G. blacki + a modern gorilla sharing more similarities in shape, with the Kong's jaw bone being intermediary with that of a human. This is no doubt in part due to their sharing similar omnivorous diets
Gigantopithecus blacki Mandible
At 9-11', largest known primate before discovery of King Kong (herbivore)
Modern Gorilla Mandible (herbivore)

These drawings of Kong skulls are based on specimens found in Kong's Skull Mountain lair. It is clear that one of the "eyes" of Skull Mountain was at one time a dwelling spot for some of the Kongs. It was safe from virtually all the larger carnivores that would have been a threat, and provided a perfect overview of the Wall. I believe this first happened during the Tagatu civilization's early expansion into the island when the Zantu & their Kongs first established outposts. Eventually, after the establishment of the Old City, the Zantu and their Kongs returned to their solitary existence with the Kongs eventually going completely feral. If any still exist, they are believed to occupy the far mountain.

This profile view of the skull of the mysterious super-anthropoid the Zantu referred to as a "Thakus," reflects a more primitive environmentally adapted relation to the Kongs. The spiky pre-protrusions and sharper canines are oddly saurian-looking. The armoured body & spiked keratin protrusions of the Thakus would have been well-suited for survival on Skull Island.

It is not known yet if the Kongs & the Thakus were able to interbreed, similar to the hypothesis that homo-sapiens & neandertals were able to do so. If yes, I wonder if King Kong's gargantuan size (even for a Kong) could be traced back to an ancestor having been a Thakus? It is known that offspring of lions & tigers are often abnormally large. Who knows what the gene pool of Kong and the Thakus contains — some day tests may be capable of determining such information.

Two major differences separate humans from the Great Apes:
The ability to stand erect, & the development of an opposable
Thumb,that enables the human hand to perform almost any
Task : 'Man stands alone because alone he stands' goes the Axiom

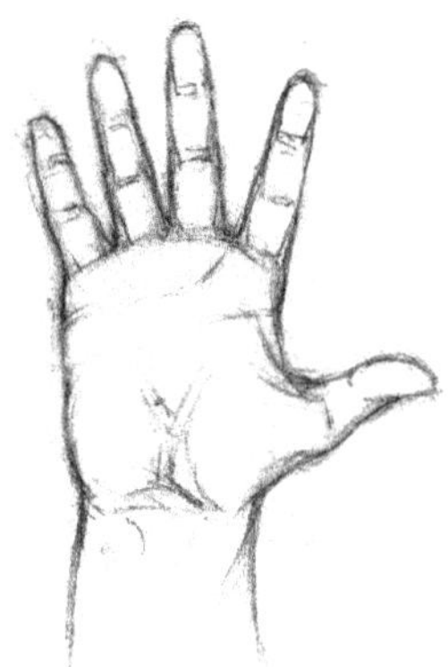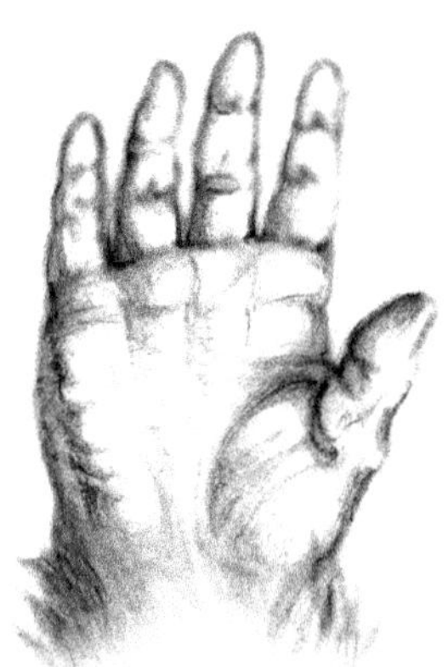

I believe the Kongs to have been well on their way to developing
the same physical advantages. Their hand structure is much
closer to that of a human than to a modern great ape

Modern
Gorilla
'Hand'

Modern
Apes are
still pri-
marily
quadrupeds.

Their hands
also serve
as feet.

Present day great apes
are incapable of this
hand gesture. Without
it they cannot
manipulate objects nearly
efficiently as is needed
to develop the necessary
eye-hand coordination
to stimulate similar brain
development

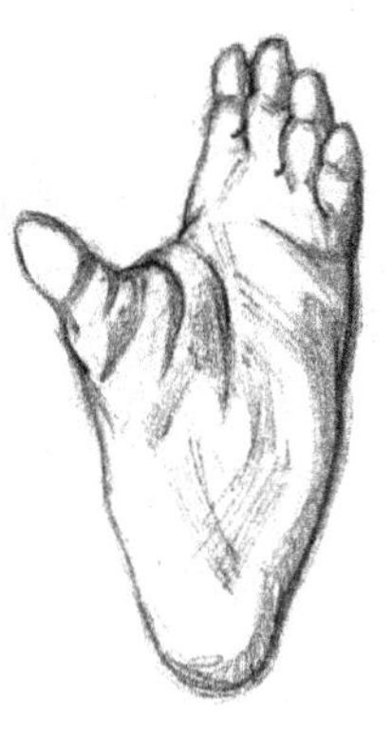

Modern
Gorilla
foot

human
foot

Kong
foot

Of note, Kong feet were of a structure all their own, dissimilar
to either the modern ape or human feet. While lacking the
full grasping ability of the gorilla, Kong feet lacked the structure of a modern human's, in particular the Kongs found adv-
antage retaining grasping ability over an optimum bipedal stance

Female Kongs differed considerably from those of all other great primates—with the (possible) exception of the mysterious race of Thakus—in that there was little noticible sexual dimorphism. A female Kong was nearly as large and ferocious as her male counterpart! When defending their young, their fury knew no bounds. No doubt these traits were a necessary adaptation to the tremendously dangerous environment in which the Kongs first evolved.

After seeing a female Kong in battle it might be difficult to imagine that when it came to their offspring, they were the most doting and caring of parents.

It was this parental care that enabled the race of Kongs to survive the initial, virtually impossible obstacles encountered during the Exodus and initial wars with the Death runners that so decimated the initial Kong population.

It is self-evident that the wounds inflicted by Gaw on
Kong's father in their penultimate battle were severe.
Somehow he survived & healed well enough to provide for
his family before ultimately sacrificing his life in a
futile attempt to save them from Gaw's next attack.
    Equally ferocious in defense of the
young Kong, the mother met a
similar fate.
    That Gaw could take
on two such power-
ful Kongs at once
underscores her
ferocity — and
King Kong's
rage in
defeating
her.

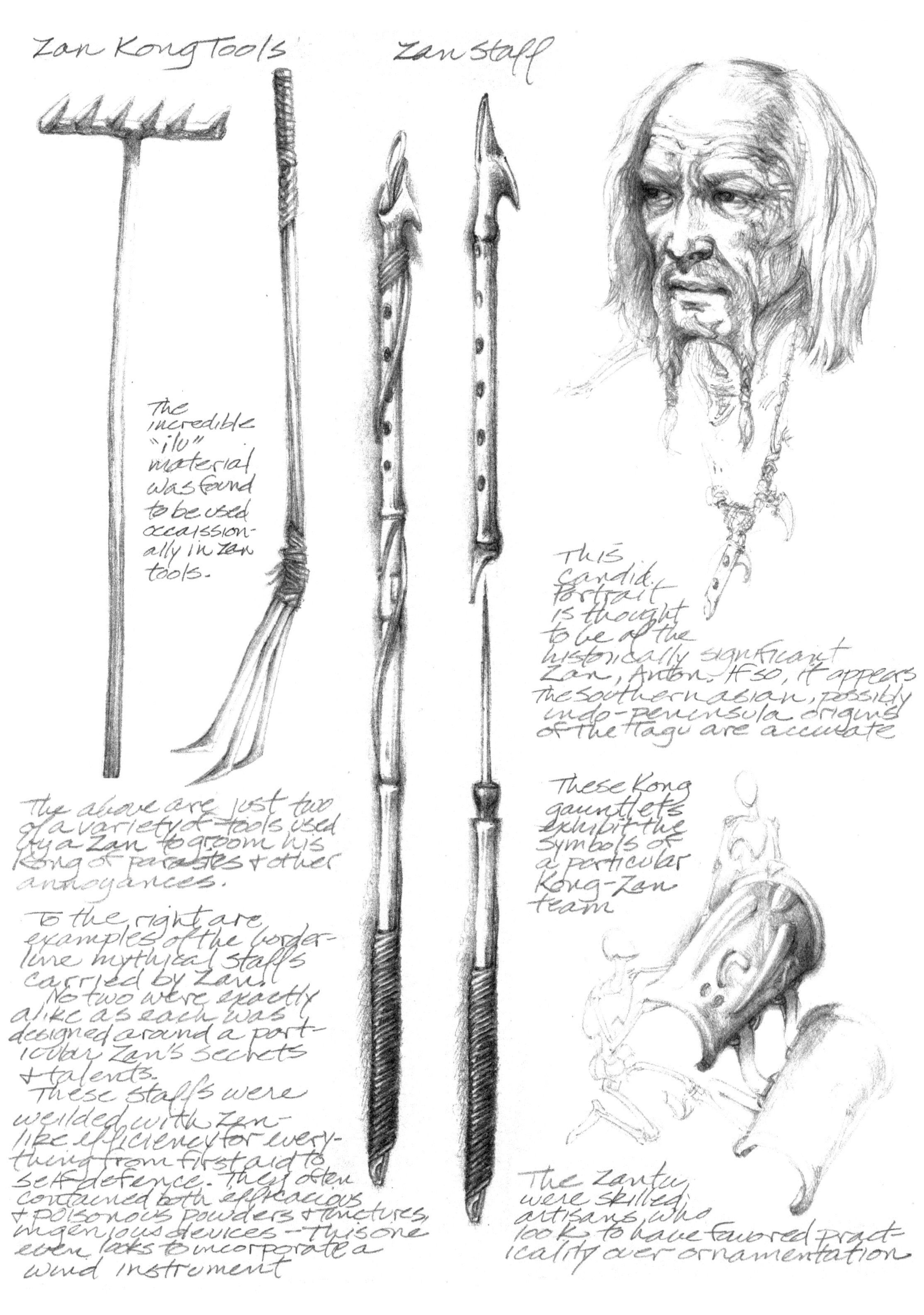
Zan Kong Tools

Zan Staff

The incredible "ilu" material was found to be used occaission- ally in zan tools.

The above are just two of a variety of tools used by a zan to groom his kong of parasites + other annoyances.

To the right are examples of the border- line mythical staffs carried by Zans. No two were exactly alike as each was designed around a part- icular Zan's secrets + talents. These staffs were weilded with Zen- like efficiency for every- thing from first aid to self defence. They often contained both efficacious + poisonous powders + tinctures, ingenious devices - this one even lacks to incorporate a wind instrument

This candid portrait is thought to be of the historically significant Zan, Anton. If so, it appears the southern asian, possibly indo-peninsula origins of the Ttagu are accurate

These Kong gauntlets exhibit the symbols of a particular Kong-Zan team

The Zantu were skilled artisans who look to have favored pract- icality over ornamentation

This chestplate is graphic evidence that even creatures as large + powerful as the Kongs were at risk when doing battle with the mega fauna of their day. Mammoths look to have been a major prey species of this Kong/Zan team
The material this Kong armour is made of looks to be thick, treated leather, perhaps in specially fused layers to create strength + add details.
It appears that the Kong-Zan partnership was so formidable that even the mighty 'Thakis' gave way when encountering them.
The relationship between a Zan + his Kong was such that their lives were utterly dependant one on the other. No one but a Zan who has known his Kong for life would attempt this

The defining feature of dino-saurs is in the hip structure, where the legs are oriented directly under the body

This overlay of hip bones shows the repositioning of the pelvic bones between a velociraptor and a Deathrunner

An early interpretation of a Deathrunner before discovery of actual bones

the ability of the Death-runners to use tools, + the possible existence of a culture of sorts, is still being debated.

The extraordinary increase in the braincase size of a Deathrunner is clear

Skulls drawn to scale

While young Deathrunners have functional wings, adults lose all ability to fly & gain full use of their hands

Both Deathrunners + the gigantic Eaw have a prognathus lower jaw, with varying amounts of chin feathers in common

Faces could be un-cannily expressive!

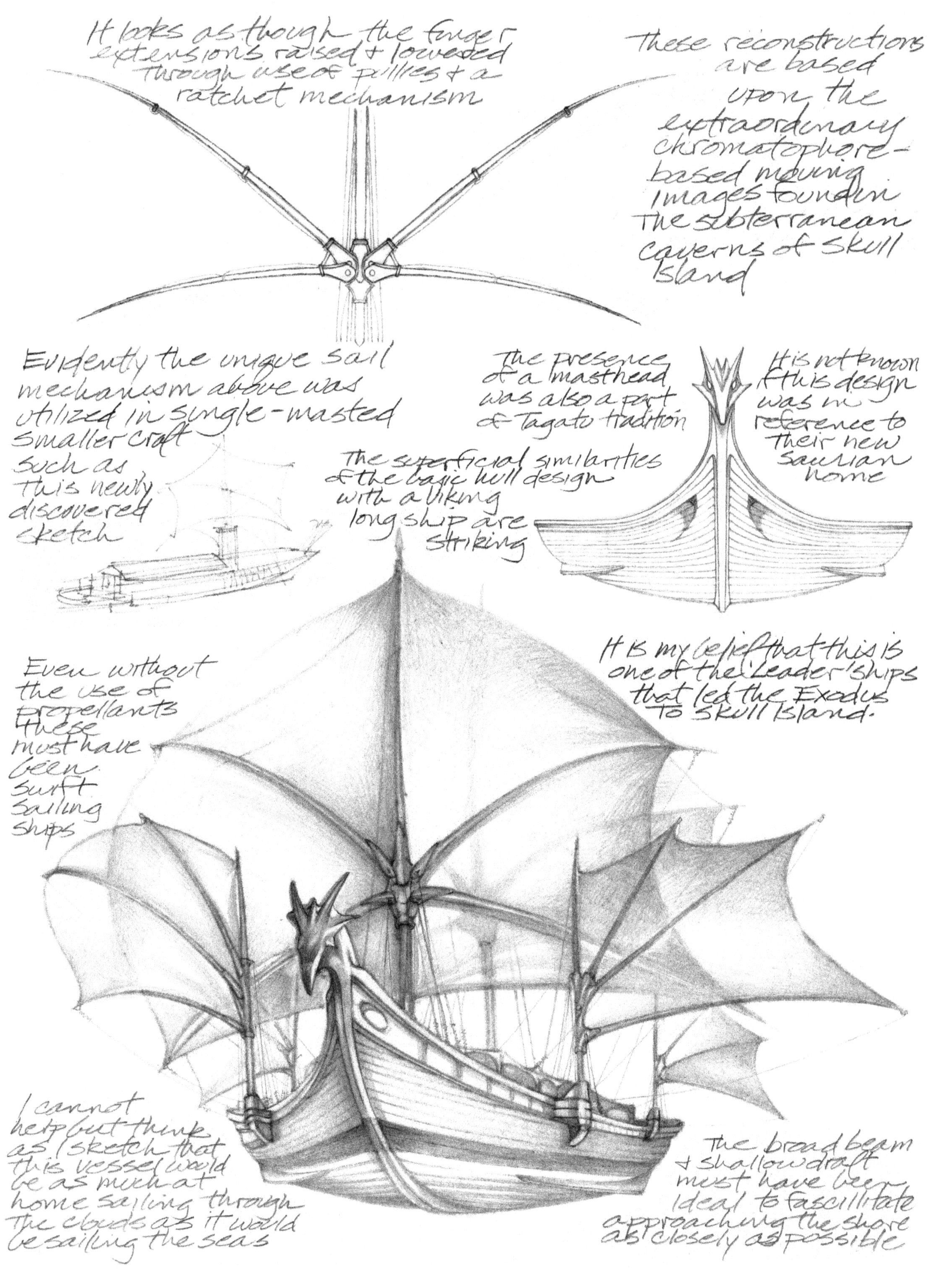

It looks as though the finger extensions raised & lowered through use of pullies & a ratchet mechanism

These reconstructions are based upon the extraordinary chromatophore-based moving images found in the subterranean caverns of Skull Island

Evidently the unique sail mechanism above was utilized in single-masted smaller craft such as this newly discovered sketch

The presence of a masthead was also a part of Tagato tradition

It is not known if this design was in reference to their new Saurian home

The superficial similarities of the basic hull design with a viking long ship are striking

Even without the use of propellants these must have been swift sailing ships

It is my belief that this is one of the 'Leader' ships that led the Exodus to Skull Island.

I cannot help but think as I sketch that this vessel would be as much at home sailing through the clouds as it would be sailing the seas

The broad beam & shallow draft must have been ideal to facillitate approaching the shore as closely as possible

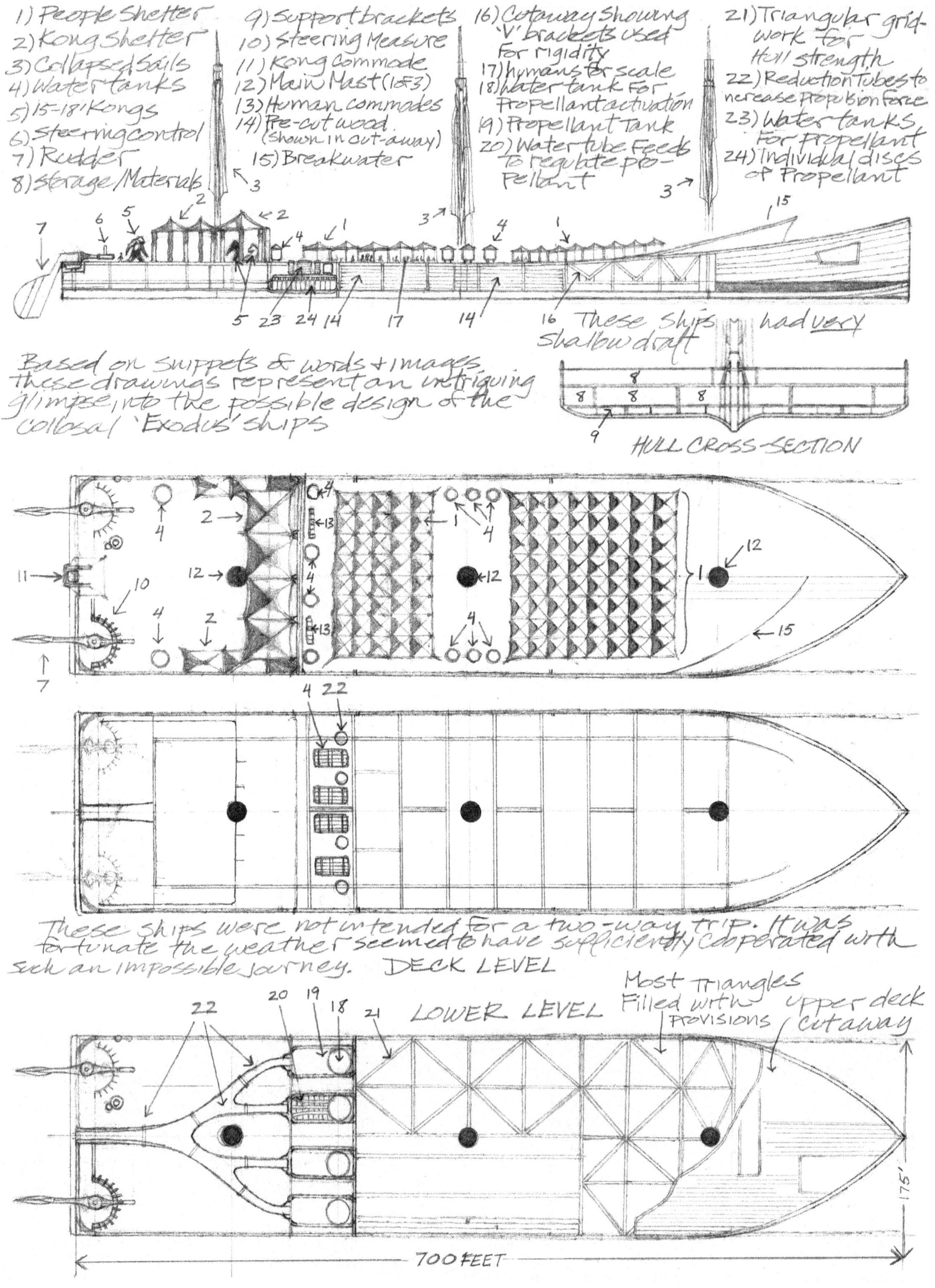

1) People Shelter
2) Kong Shelter
3) Collapsed Sails
4) Water tanks
5) 15-18' Kongs
6) Steering control
7) Rudder
8) Storage/Materials
9) Support brackets
10) Steering Measure
11) Kong Commode
12) Main Mast (18'3")
13) Human commodes
14) Pre-cut wood (shown in cut-away)
15) Breakwater
16) Cutaway showing 'V' brackets used for rigidity
17) humans for scale
18) water tank for propellant actuation
19) Propellant Tank
20) Water tube feeds to regulate propellant
21) Triangular grid-work for hull strength
22) Reduction Tubes to increase propulsion force
23) Water tanks for propellant
24) Individual discs of propellant
Based on snippets of words + images, these drawings represent an intriguing glimpse into the possible design of the colossal 'Exodus' ships
These ships had very shallow draft
HULL CROSS-SECTION
These ships were not intended for a two-way trip. It was fortunate the weather seemed to have sufficiently cooperated with such an impossible journey.
DECK LEVEL
LOWER LEVEL
Most triangles filled with provisions
upper deck cutaway
700 FEET
175'

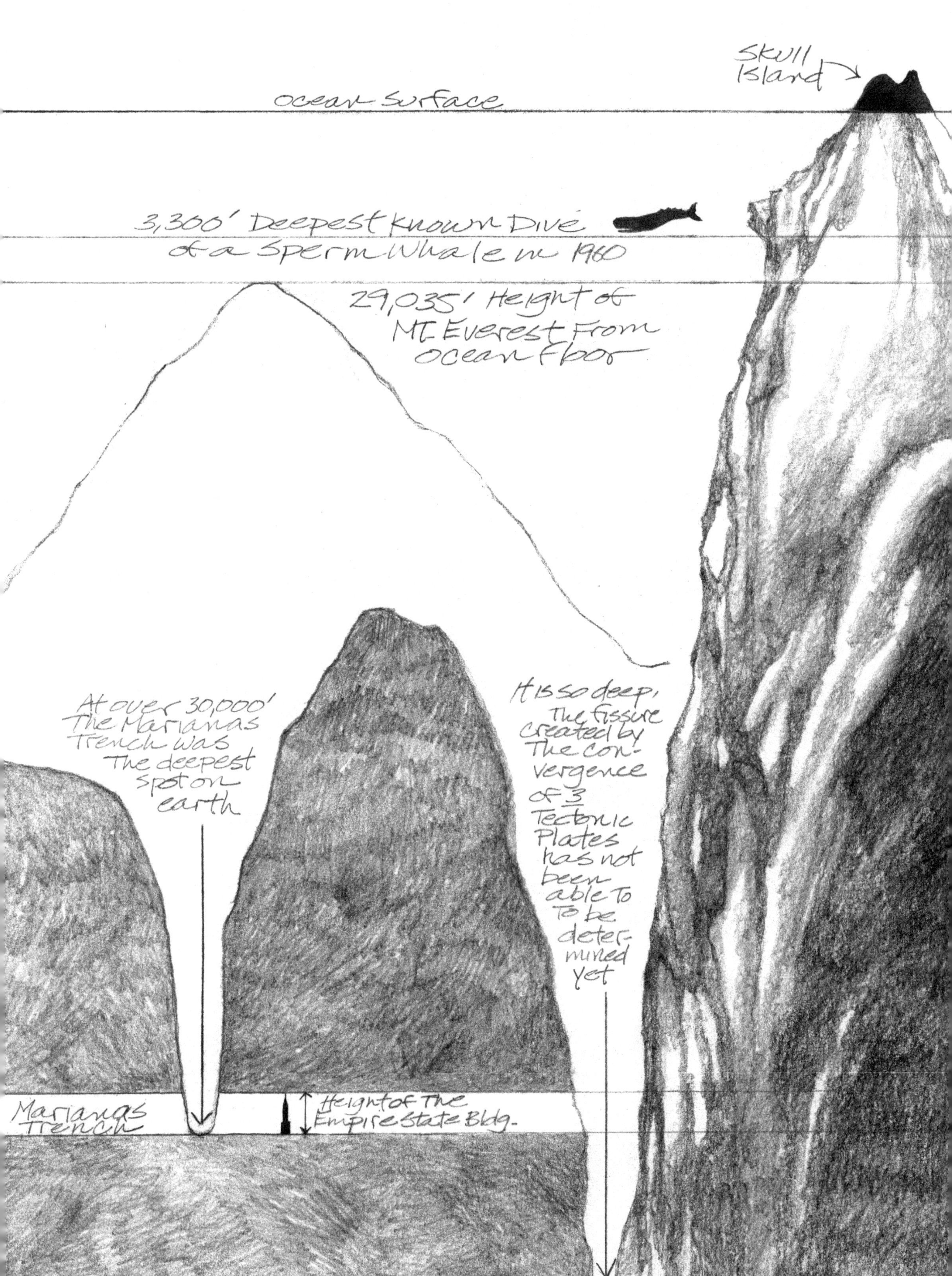

Skull Island
ocean Surface
3,300' Deepest Known Dive of a Sperm Whale in 1960
29,035' Height of Mt. Everest from Ocean Floor
At over 30,000' The Marianas Trench was the deepest spot on earth
It is so deep, the fissure created by the convergence of 3 Tectonic Plates has not been able to be determined yet
Marianas Trench
Height of the Empire State Bldg.

Of all the surprises found within the Wall, one of the most surprising was the existence on the Asian continent of a 2nd super simian along with the Kongs! Referred to as a "Thakus," this enormous creature was truly terrifying in its power & ferocity. A seemingly more primitive and brutish off-shoot of the Kong lineage, no remnant of a Thakus has yet been found outside of Tagatu records from within the Wall.

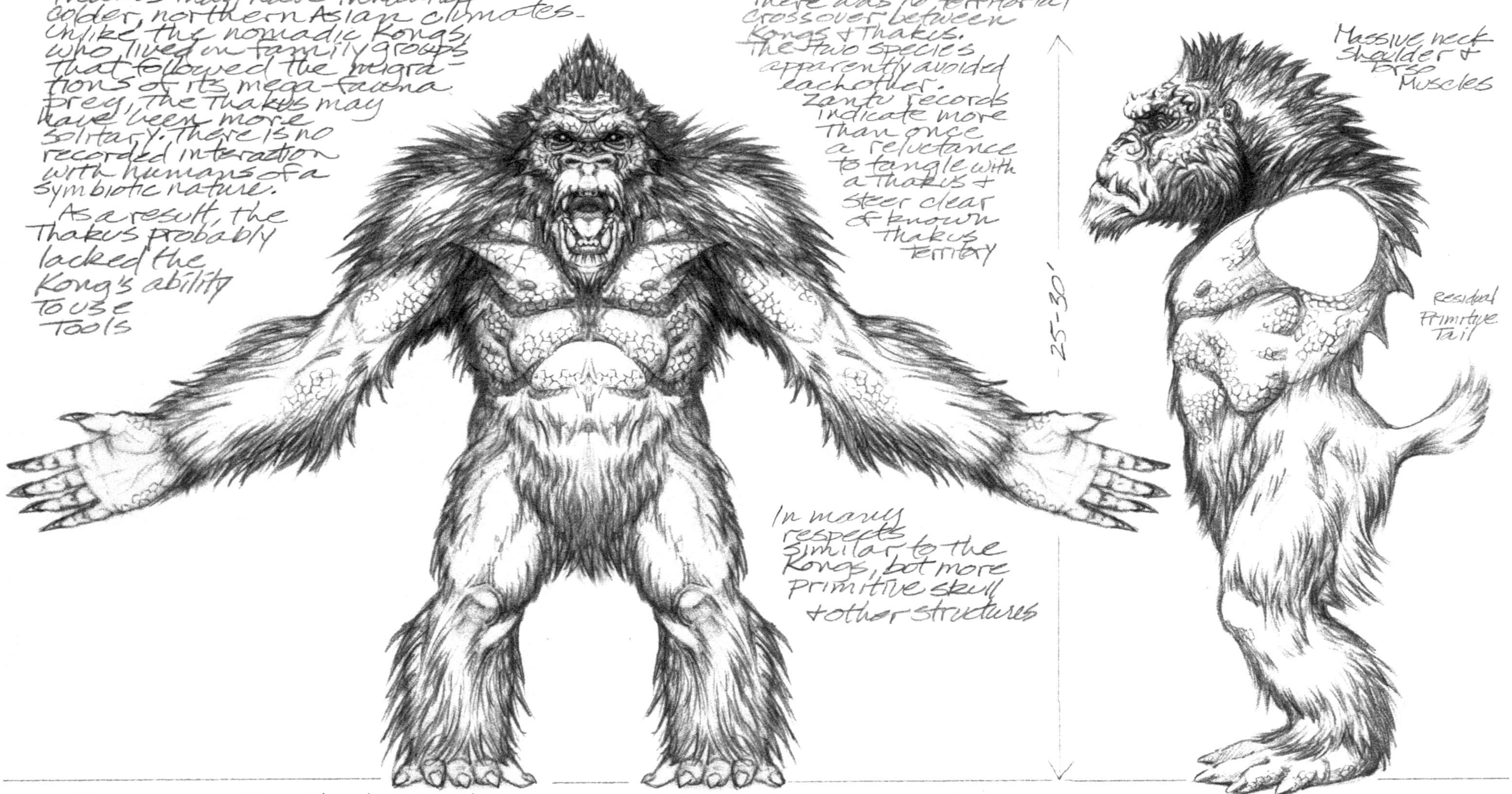

Thakus may have inhabited colder, northern Asian climates. Unlike the nomadic Kongs, who lived in family groups that followed the migrations of its mega-fauna prey, the Thakus may have been more solitary. There is no recorded interaction with humans of a symbiotic nature.
As a result, the Thakus probably lacked the Kong's ability to use tools

There was no territorial crossover between Kongs & Thakus. The two species apparently avoided each other. Zantu records indicate more than once a reluctance to tangle with a Thakus & steer clear of known Thakus territory

In many respects similar to the Kongs, but more primitive skull + other structures

25-30'

Massive neck shoulder & torso muscles

Residual Primitive Tail

It seems the Thakus lived in particularly harsh times. It was covered in coarse, boar-like hair on the head shoulders, forearms + even the back of the legs. This hair fused into virtual keratin spikes. The skin of the torso + other areas resembled thick, rhino-like plates + was fused w/ bony plates. This created a natural, incredibly tough armour.

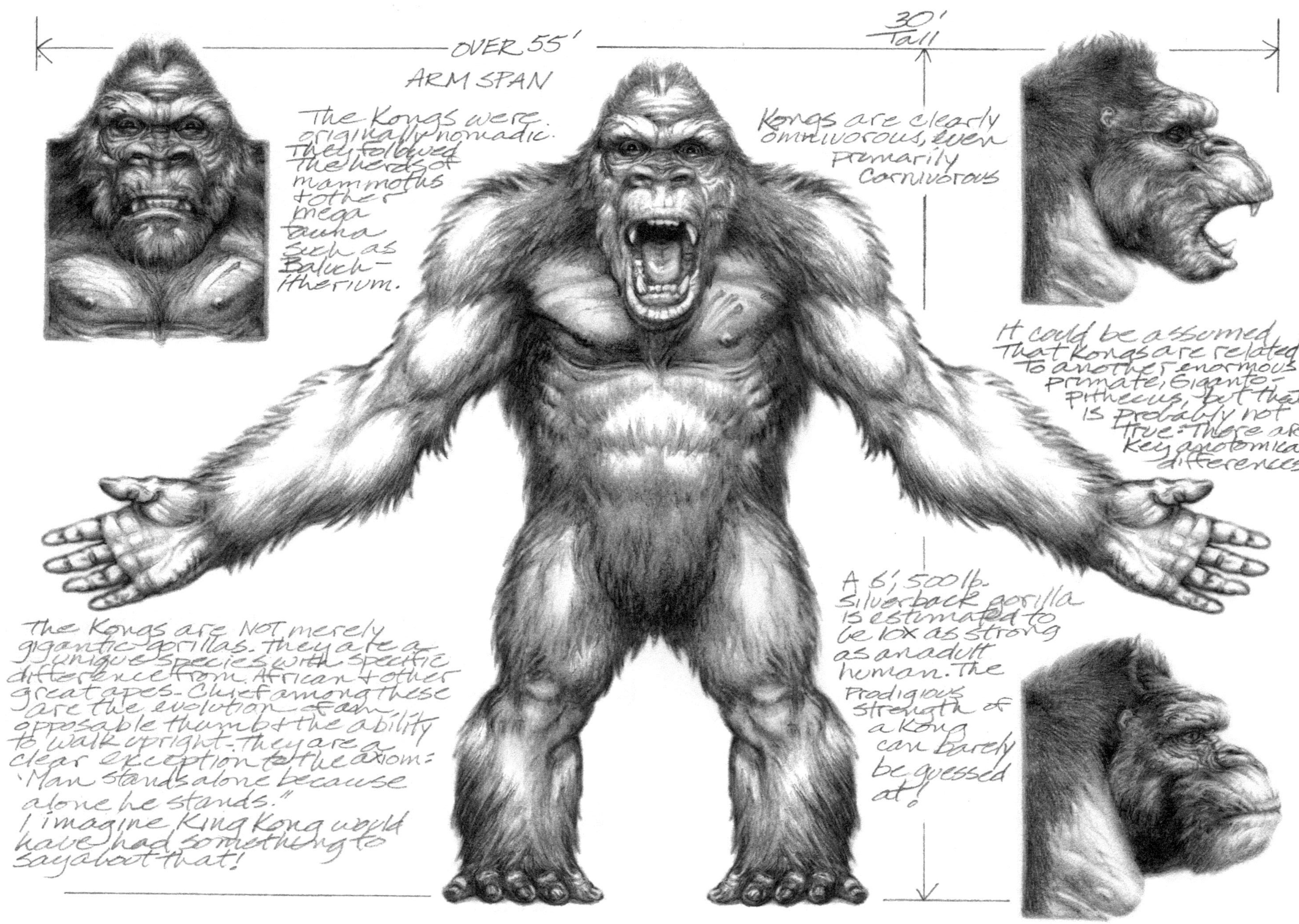

OVER 55' ARM SPAN
30' Tall
The Kongs were originally nomadic. They followed the herds of mammoths + other mega fauna such as Baluch-itherium.
Kongs are clearly omnivorous, even primarily carnivorous
It could be assumed that Kongs are related to another enormous primate, Giganto-pithecus, but that is probably not true. There are key anatomical differences
A 6', 500 lb. silverback gorilla is estimated to be 10x as strong as an adult human. The prodigious strength of a Kong can barely be guessed at!
The Kongs are not merely gigantic gorillas. They are a unique species with specific differences from African + other great apes. Chief among these are the evolution of an opposable thumb + the ability to walk upright. They are a clear exception to the axiom: "Man stands alone because alone he stands." I imagine King Kong would have had something to say about that!

I believe this best guesstimate
size comparison is accurate.
Gaw was an extremely large &
powerful saurian. she was made
all the more formidable by her
enhanced speed & intelligence
   The fully grown King Kong may
have been the only Kong who
truly stood a chance against
such a lethal adversary.
This Gaw is the one I believe

defeated by Kong to become King in his own right. There are indications of at least two other Gaws: A two-headed aberation, & the infamous Gaw-Uzi - the only Gaw believed to be a male.

Both the Deathrunner & The giant spider are large examples of their species.

I am still unsure if all Gaws had feathers & to what extent - or none of them did.

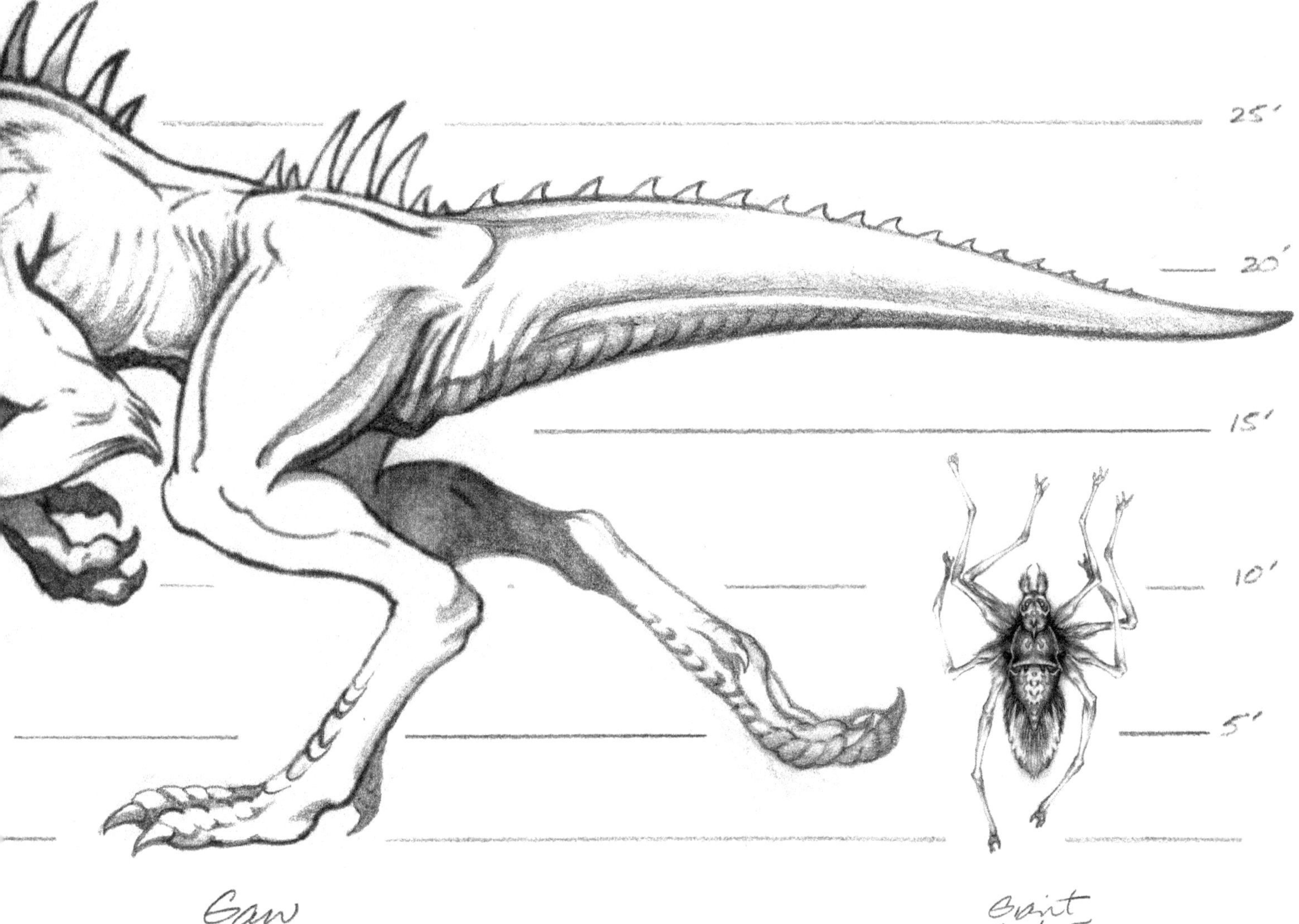

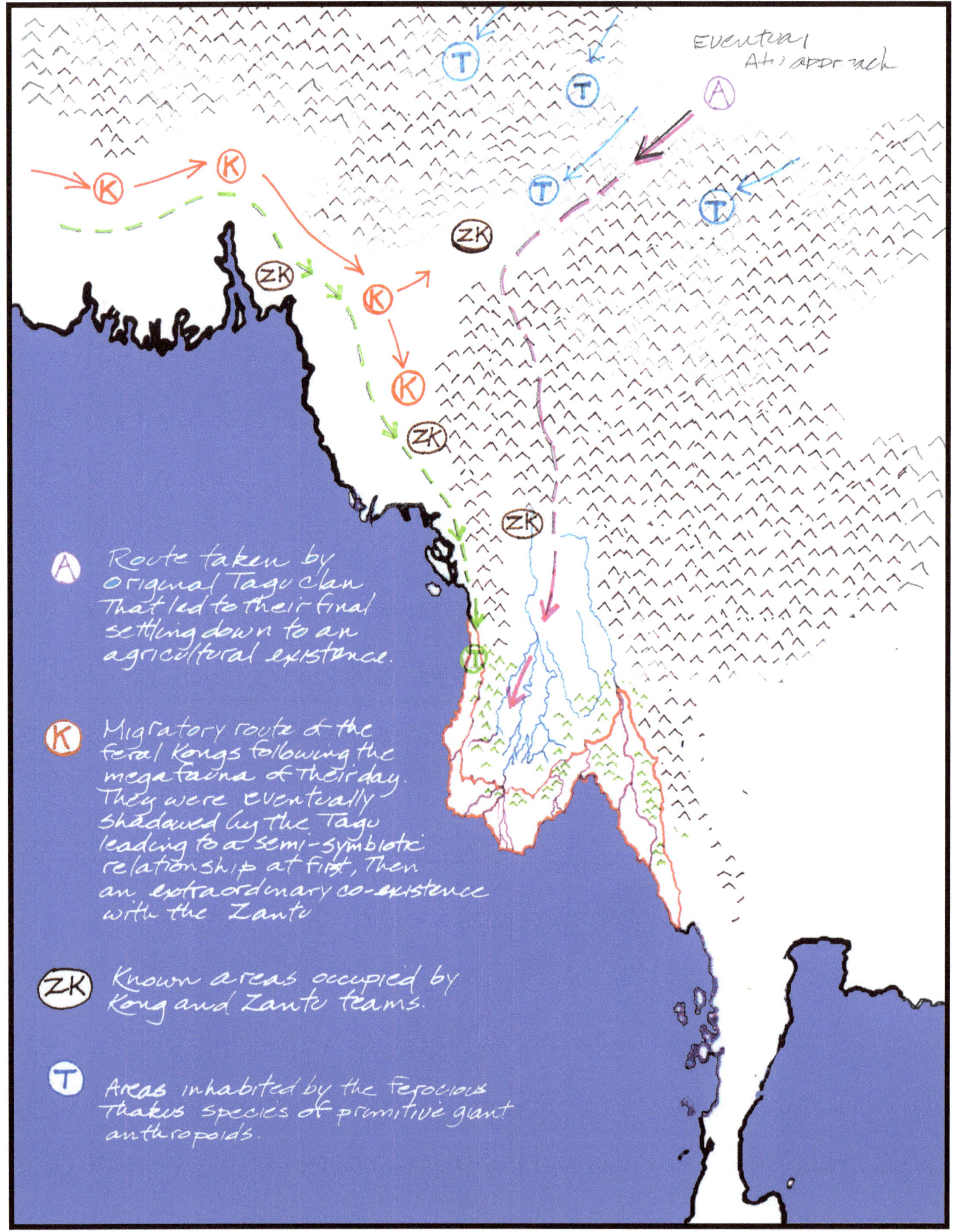
EVENTUAL
Atoi approach
A Route taken by
Original Tagu clan
That led to their final
settling down to an
agricultural existence.
K Migratory route of the
feral Kongs following the
megafauna of their day.
They were eventually
shadowed by the Tagu
leading to a semi-symbiotic
relationship at first, then
an extraordinary co-existence
with the Zantu
ZK Known areas occupied by
Kong and Zantu teams.
T Areas inhabited by the ferocious
Thakus species of primitive giant
anthropoids.

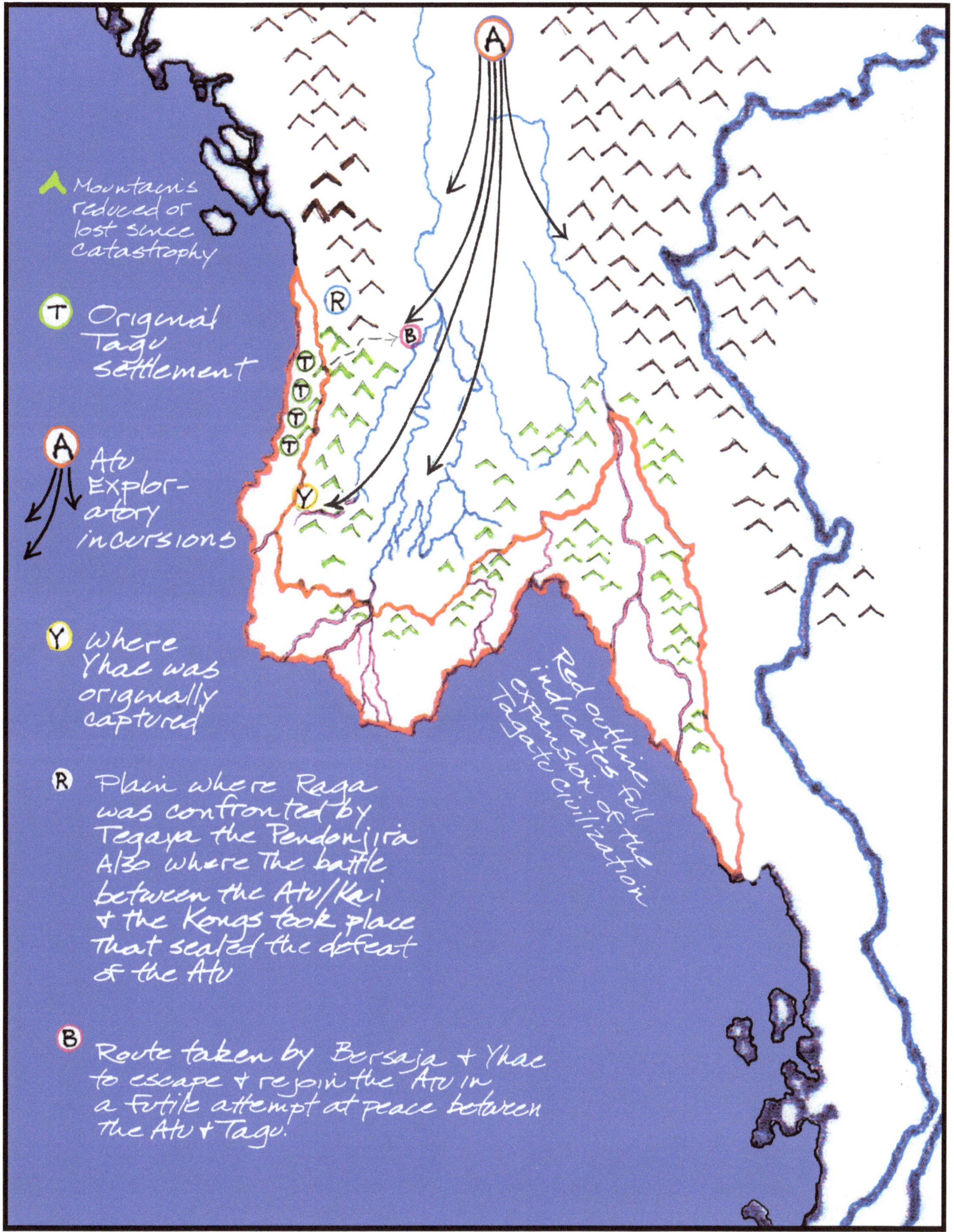
Mountains reduced or lost since catastrophy
Original Tagu settlement
Atu Exploratory incursions
Where Yhac was originally captured
Place where Raga was confronted by Tegaya the Pendonjira Also where the battle between the Atu/Kai & the Kongs took place that sealed the defeat of the Atu
Route taken by Bersaja & Yhac to escape & rejoin the Atu in a futile attempt at peace between the Atu & Tagu.
Red outline indicates full expansion of the Tagatu Civilization

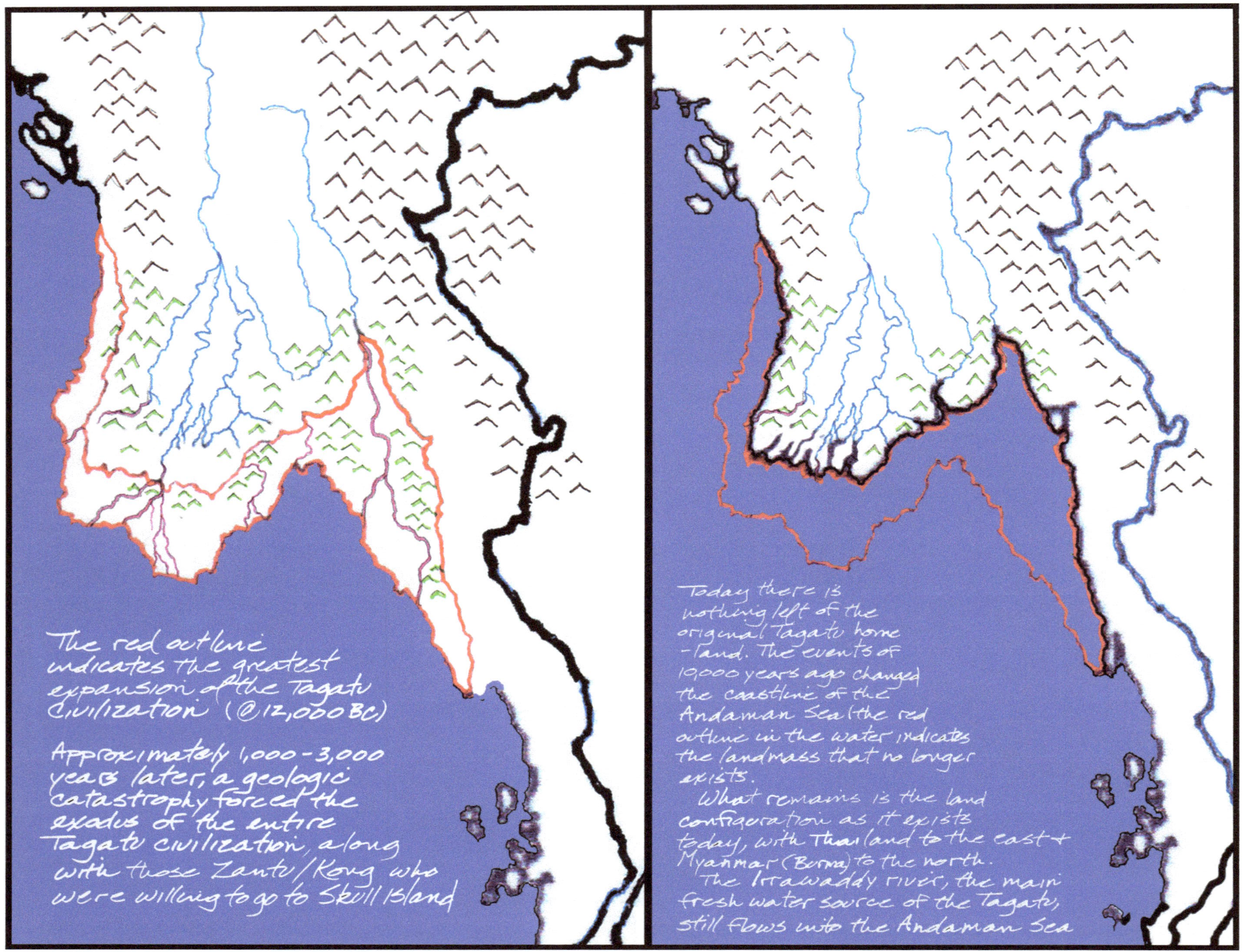
Today there is nothing left of the original Tagatu home-land. The events of 10,000 years ago changed the coastline of the Andaman Sea (the red outline in the water indicates the landmass that no longer exists.
What remains is the land configuration as it exists today, with Thailand to the east + Myanmar (Burma) to the north.
The Irrawaddy river, the main fresh water source of the Tagatu, still flows into the Andaman Sea
The red outline indicates the greatest expansion of the Tagatu civilization (@ 12,000 BC)

Approximately 1,000-3,000 years later, a geologic catastrophy forced the exodus of the entire Tagatu civilization, along with those Zantu/Kong who were willing to go to Skull Island

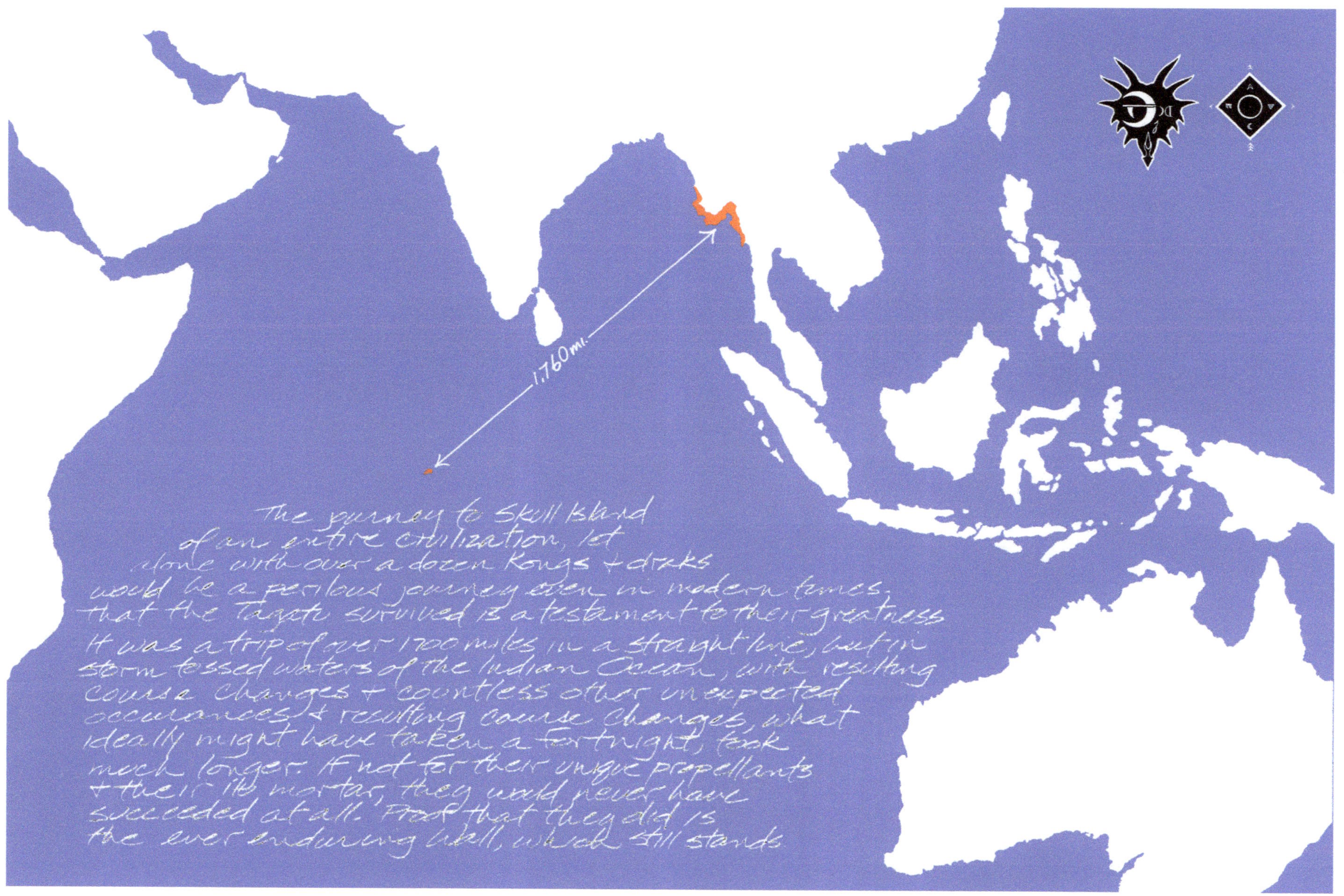

1,760 mi.
The journey to Skull Island
of an entire civilization, let
alone with over a dozen Kongs + dinks
would be a perilous journey even in modern times,
that the Tagatu survived is a testament to their greatness
It was a trip of over 1700 miles in a straight line, but in
storm-tossed waters of the Indian Ocean, with resulting
course changes + countless other unexpected
occurrences + resulting course changes, what
ideally might have taken a fortnight, took
much longer. If not for their unique propellants
+ their Ki mortar, they would never have
succeeded at all. Proof that they did is
the ever-enduring Wall, which still stands

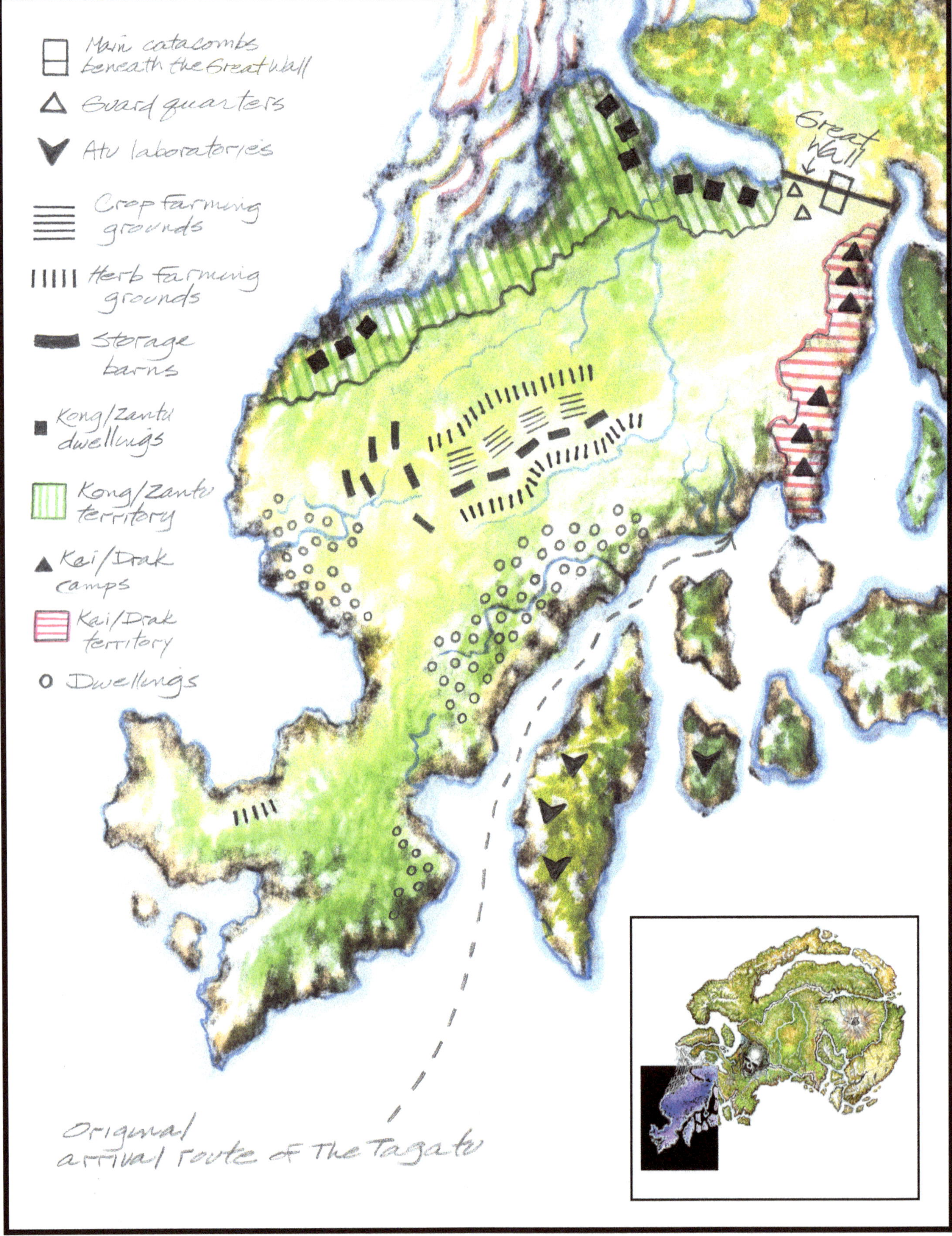

Main catacombs beneath the Great Wall
Guard quarters
Atu laboratories
Crop farming grounds
Herb farming grounds
Storage barns
Kong/Zantu dwellings
Kong/Zantu territory
Kai/Drak camps
Kai/Drak territory
Dwellings
Great Wall
Original arrival route of The Tagatu

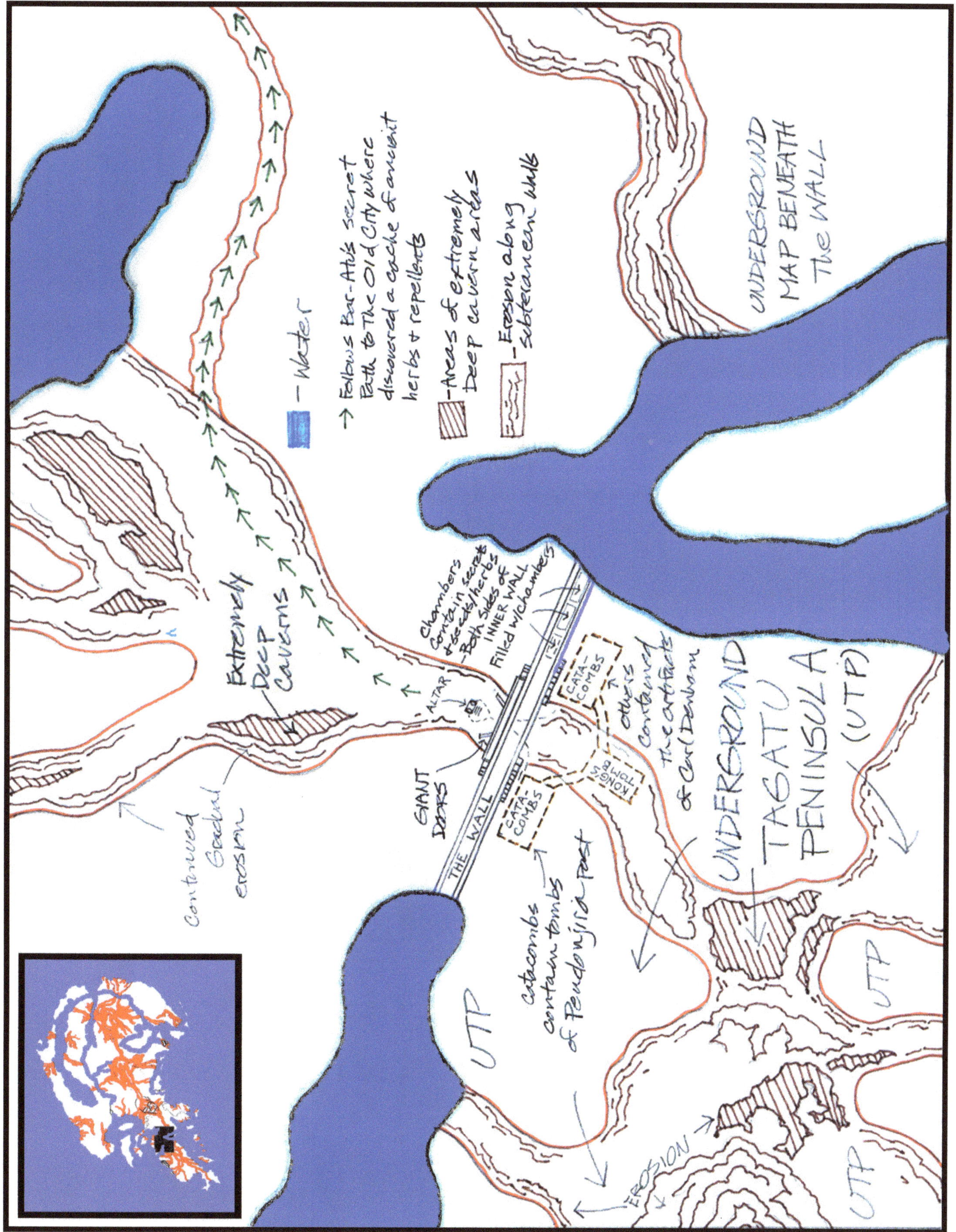
UNDERGROUND MAP BENEATH THE WALL
Water
Follows Bar-Atis secret Path to The Old City where discovered a cache of ancient herbs & repellents
Areas of extremely Deep cavern areas
Erosion along subterranean walls
Extremely Deep Caverns
Continued Gradual erosion
Chambers contain secret herbs/herbs
Both Sides of INNER WALL filled w/chambers
ALTAR
GIANT DOORS
THE WALL
CATA-COMBS
CATA-COMBS
KONG'S TOMB
others contain the artifacts of Carl Denham
Catacombs contain tombs of Pendonjira Past
UNDERGROUND TAGATU PENINSULA (UTP)
UTP
UTP
UTP
UTP
EROSION

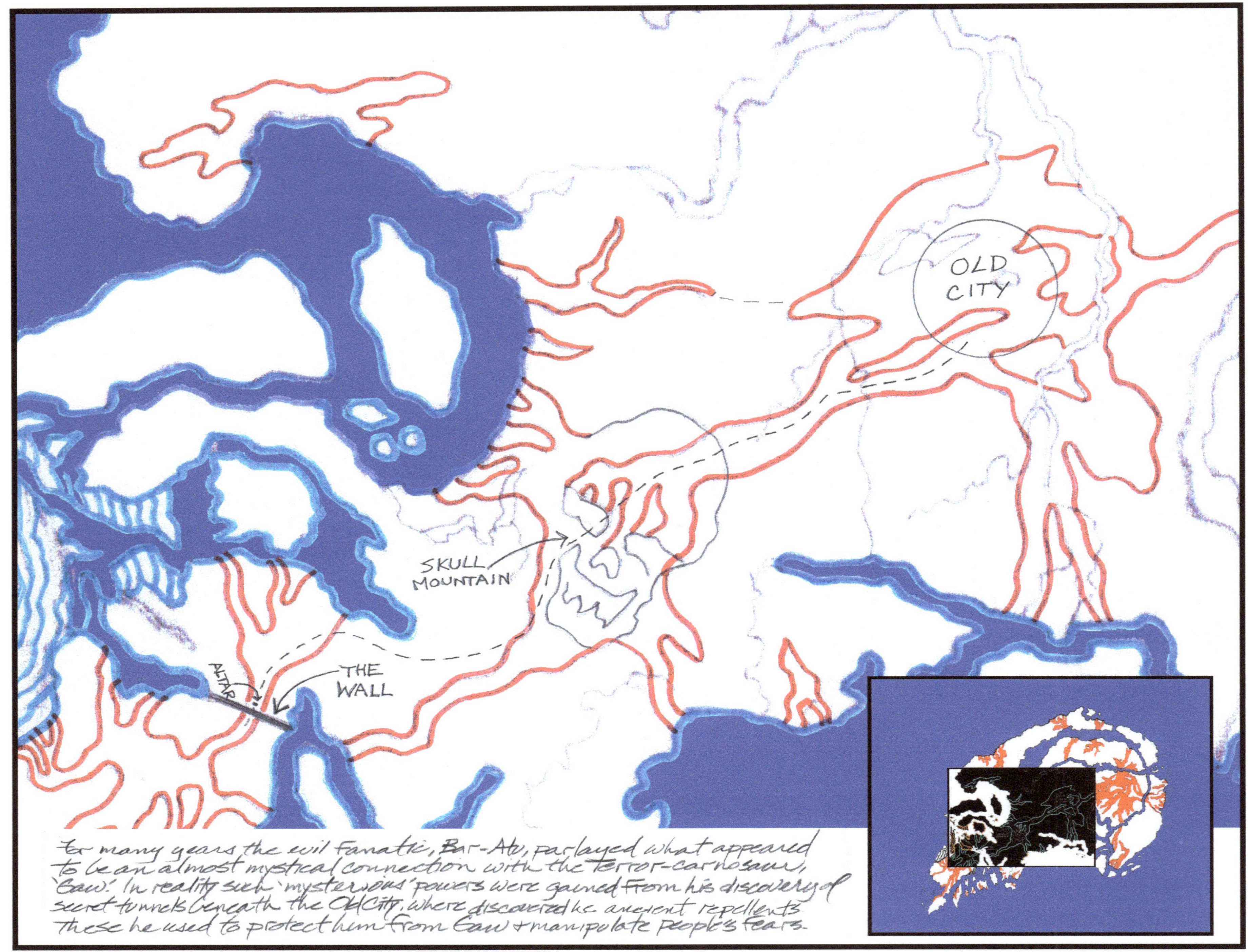

For many years the evil Fanatic, Bar-Atu, parlayed what appeared to be an almost mystical connection with the terror-carnosaur, 'Gaw'. In reality such 'mysterious' powers were gained from his discovery of secret tunnels beneath the Old City, where discovered he ancient repellents these he used to protect him from Gaw & manipulate people's fears.

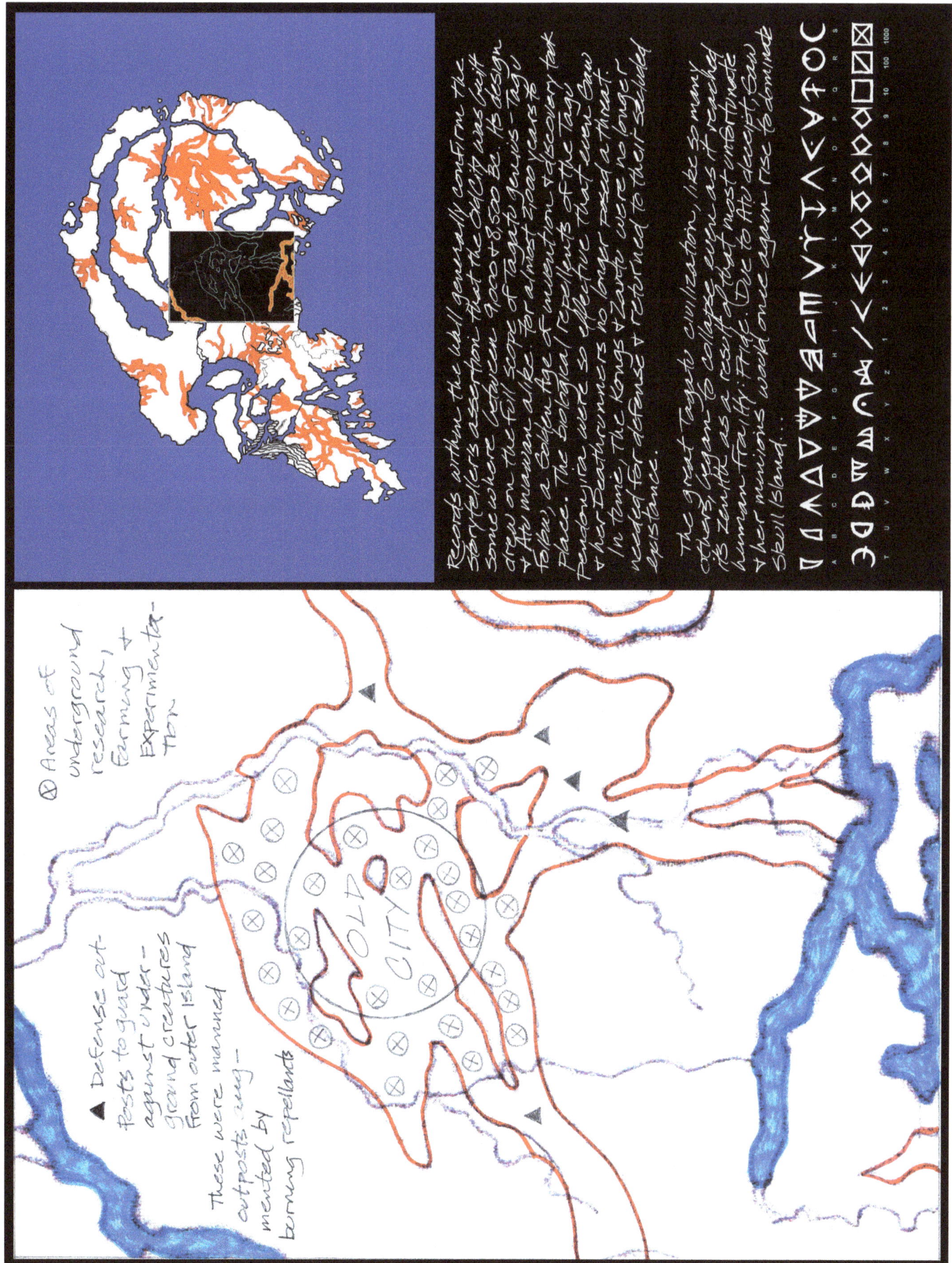
Records within the Wall generally confirm the Storyteller's assertion that the Old City was built some where between 9000 & 8500 BC. Its design drew on the full scope of Tagati genius - Tagu & Atu imanian alike. For almost 7000 years to follow, a Golden Age of invention & discovery took place. The Biological repellents of the Tagu Pendonyita were so effective that even Gaw & her Deathrunners no longer posed a threat. In time, the Kongs & Zann were no longer needed for defense & returned to their secluded existence.

The great Tagati civilization, like so many others, began to collapse even as it reached its Zenith as a result of that most inordinate human frailty: Pride. (Due to Atu deceipt, Gaw & her minions would once again rise to dominate Skull Island...
Areas of underground research, Farming & Experimenta- tion

Defense out- posts to guard against under- ground creatures from outer Island

These were manned outposts aug- mented by burning repellants

OLD CITY

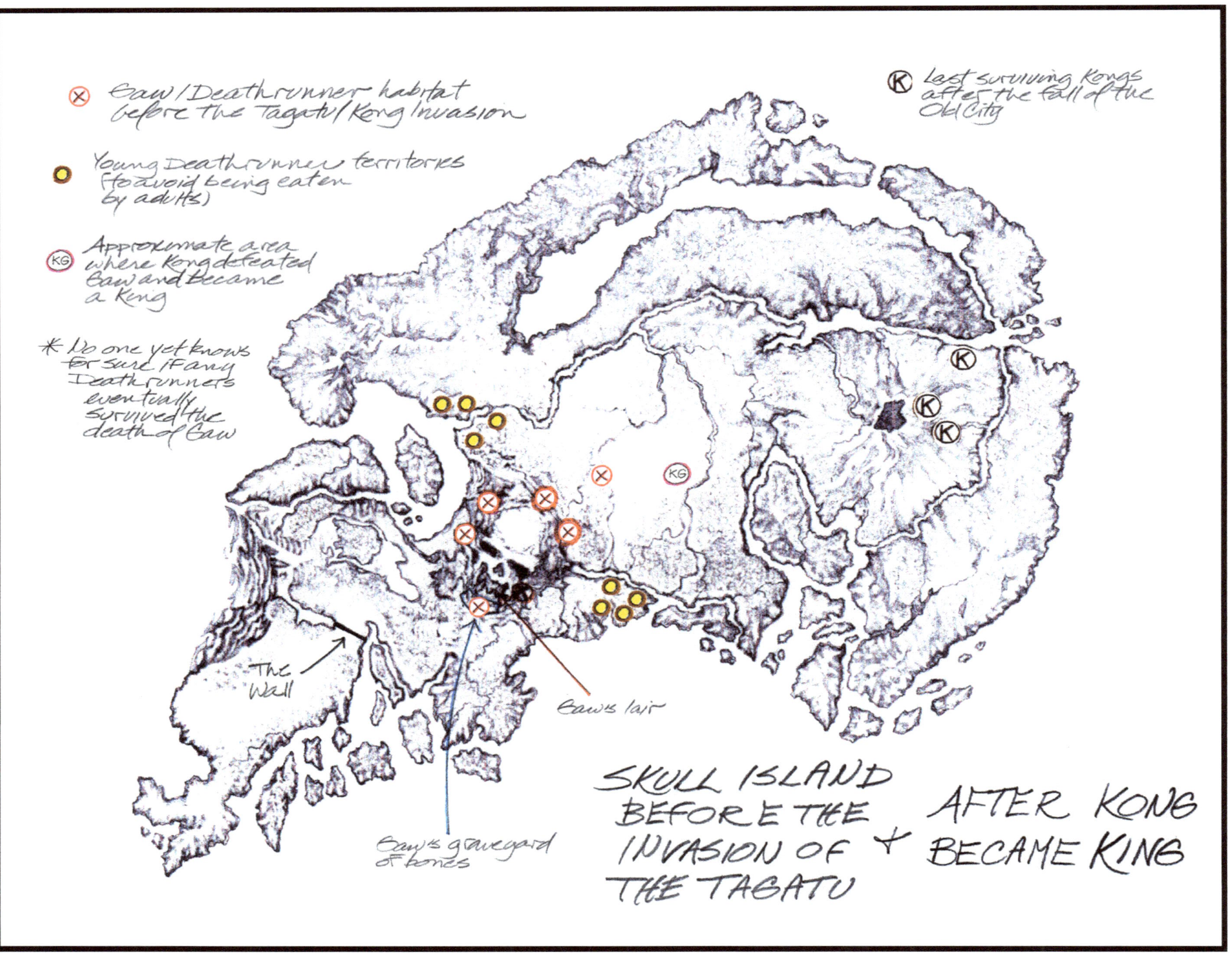
Gaw/Deathrunner habitat
(before the Tagatu/Kong Invasion

Young Deathrunner territories
(to avoid being eaten
by adults)

Approximate area
where Kong defeated
Gaw and Became
a King

* No one yet knows
for sure if any
Deathrunners
eventually
survived the
death of Gaw

Last surviving Kongs
after the fall of the
Old City

The
Wall

Gaw's graveyard
of bones

Gaw's lair

SKULL ISLAND
BEFORE THE
INVASION OF
THE TAGATU
&
AFTER KONG
BECAME KING

NEXT

SKULL ISLAND PART 2: THE GREAT WALL

The incredible conclusion to *Skull Island* tells how the forward-evolved saurian denizens of the island, the Deathrunners and their monstrous queen, Gaw, war to the death against the mammalian invaders. The inevitable battle for survival forces the Kongs and the Taigu settlers unite in creating their civilization's only hope: the iconic Wall. This ultimate achievement will span the millennia and play a crucial role in the rise and fall of the mythic beast-god of Skull Island–

King Kong!

About the Authors

Joe DeVito

Joe DeVito was born on March 16, 1957, in New York City. He graduated with honors from Parsons School of Design in 1981 and continued his studies at the Art Students League in New York City. Over the years DeVito has painted many of the most recognizable Pop Culture and Pulp icons, including King Kong, Tarzan, Doc Savage, Superman, Batman, Wonder Woman, Spider-man, MAD magazine's Alfred E. Newman and various characters in World of Warcraft, with a decided emphasis in his illustration on dinosaurs, Action Adventure, SF and Fantasy. He has illustrated hundreds of book and magazine covers, painted several notable posters and numerous trading cards for the major comic book and gaming houses, and created concept and character design for the film and television industries.

In 3D, DeVito sculpted the official 100th Anniversary statue of *Tarzan of the Apes* for the Edgar Rice Burroughs Estate, *The Cooper Kong* for the Merian C. Cooper Estate, Superman, Wonder Woman and Batman for Chronicle Book's Masterpiece Editions, and several other notable Pop and Pulp characters. Deeply rooted in the fine arts, Joe has sculpted two monumental statues of the Madonna and Child. One is placed in Domus Pacis at the Our Lady of Fatima Shrine, in Portugal. The second sculpture resides at the World Apostolate of Fatima (WAF) Shrine in Washington, NJ. Among his restorations is the historic Russian icon known as the Odessa Madonna for the WAF, which now resides in Kazan, Russia.

An avid writer, Joe with Brad Strickland co-author several novels, which Joe illustrated as well. These include *KONG: King of Skull Island* (DH Press), *Merian C. Cooper's KING KONG* (St. Martin's Griffin), *King Kong of Skull Island* and the upcoming books, *Skull Island: Exodus* and *Skull Island: The Wall*. He has also contributed many essays and articles to such collected works as *Kong Unbound: The Cultural Impact, Pop Mythos, and Scientific Plausibility of a Cinematic Legend* and *Do Androids Artists Paint In Oils When They Dream?* in *Pixel or Paint: The Digital Divide In Illustration Art*.

With the property in full development as a TV series and movie, DeVito's Kong IP spawned several multi-issue Kong tales, among them Boom! Studios' twelve-issue comic book and graphic novel series *Kong of Skull Island* written by James Asmus and penciled by Carlos Magno. An entire crossover series followed with the 20th Century FOX *Planet of the Apes* franchise titled *Kong on the Planet of the Apes*, written by Ryan Ferrier, penciled by Carlos Magno, and colored by Alex Guimaraes. While developing his newest creation, a faction world of truly epic proportions tentatively titled *The Primordials*, DeVito continues painting covers for *The All New Wild Adventures* series written by Will Murray, featuring Doc Savage, Tarzan, The Shadow, Pat Savage and King Kong – including *King Kong vs. Tarzan*, the first-ever authorized meeting of the two iconic jungle lords.

Joe is the founder of DeVito ArtWorks, LLC, an artist-driven transmedia studio dedicated to the creation and development of multi-faceted properties including Skull Island, War Eagles, and the Primordials. DeVito ArtWorks is exclusively represented by Festa Entertainment and Dimensional Branding Group.

www.kongskullisland.com
www.jdevito.com

Brad Strickland

Brad Strickland is the author or co-author of more than 100 books, including nonfiction, YA novels, mystery, science fiction, and fantasy works. A native of New Holland, Georgia, he is a retired Professor of English at the University of North Georgia. He and his wife Barbara live in Snellville, Georgia, with one cats and two dogs. The Stricklands also have two grown children, Jonathan and Amy, and two granddaughters, Elora and Stella.

Brad's books include many YA mysteries continuing the series begun by the late John Bellairs, historical mysteries featuring a young William Shakespeare and a teenaged Benjamin Franklin, a series of adult mysteries set in Florida and published under his pseudonym Ken McKea, and a good many TV tie-in novels, including fifteen for the *Wishbone* TV series. He has also written biographies, a nonfiction book about the Roanoke Colony's mysterious disappearance, and a guide to John Bellairs's fictional town of New Zebedee, Michigan.

The head writer for the Atlanta Radio Theatre Company, Brad has written and cowritten dozens of audio scripts and has also served as script supervisor, director, and actor. He usually specializes in character roles–such as an old New England farmer, a professor on the track of an alien monstrosity, or an enraged guard dog. For several years Brad has written for and acted in audio plays that pay homage to the Jack Benny Program, through the auspices of the International Jack Benny Fan Club.

With Joe DeVito, Brad has co-written several books about King Kong–like Joe, Brad is a huge fan of the original movie and the lore of Kong and Skull Island. A few years ago, when they visited San Diego for Comic Con, the high point of the trip for Brad and his wife was sharing meals with– among others–the great Ray Bradbury and Ray Harryhausen. It was almost–ALMOST–as good as an actual voyage to Skull Island!

SKULL ISLAND

1997

HISTORY
of
SKULL
ISLAND

1997

2004

2005

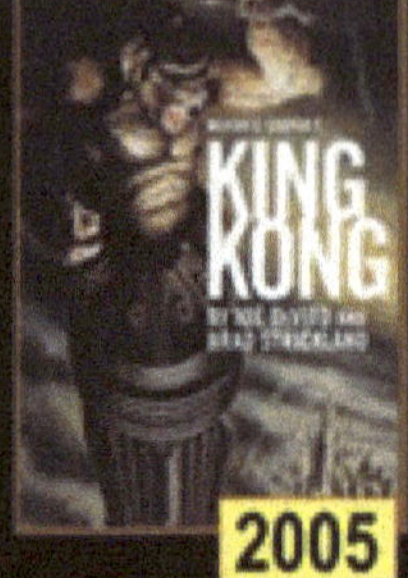

2005

Further details on the entire
KING KONG OF SKULL ISLAND
book chronology can be found here:
https://kingkongofskullisland.squarespace.com

2017

**2019
2025**

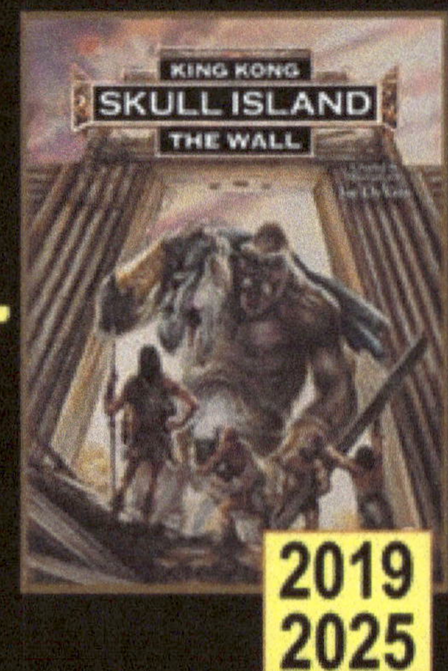

**2019
2025**

KING KONG OF SKULL ISLAND
BOOK CHRONOLOGY

KING KONG'S UNTOLD ADVENTURES!

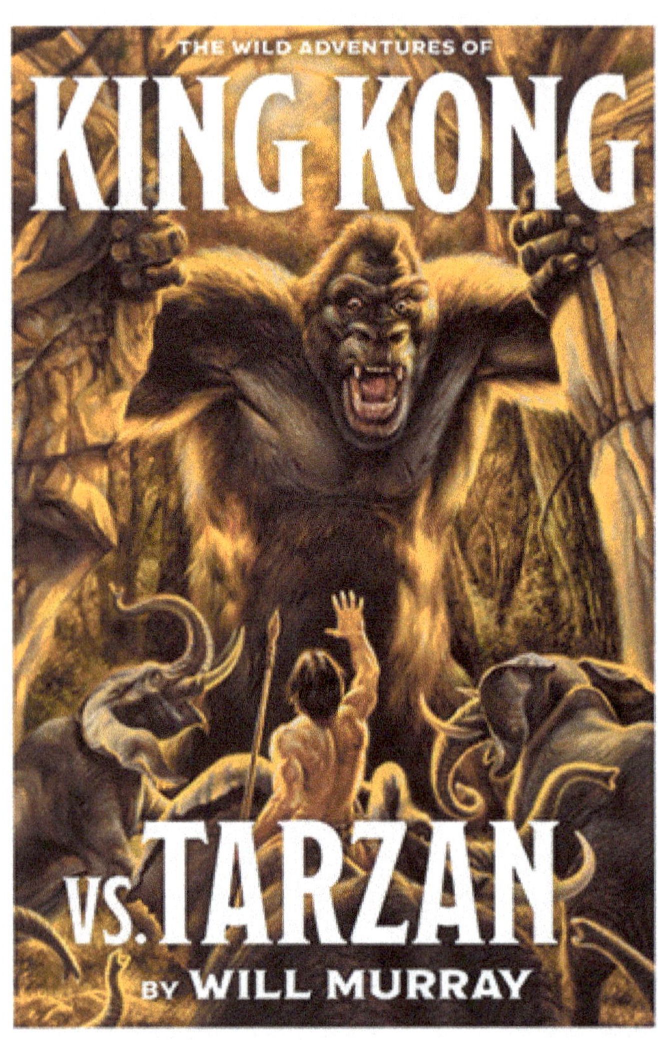

*King Kong exploded into the world's collective consciousness
when a fateful encounter with Carl Denham and Ann Darrow
led to an epic battle atop the Empire State Building.
But this was not the beast-god of Skull Island's first
confrontation with modern man!*

WWW.ADVENTURESINBRONZE.COM

OWN ICONIC
DOC SAVAGE ART

NOW AVAILABLE AS LIMITED EDITION FINE ART PRINTS!

FOR INFORMATION GO TO:

WWW.JDEVITO.COM

9 781966 434023